The Glory Road

The Glory Road

The Saga Lives On

Steven D. Ayres

Copyright © 2019 by Steven D. Ayres.

Library of Congress Control Number: 2019915601
ISBN: Hardcover 978-1-7960-6376-9
       Softcover 978-1-7960-6375-2
       eBook   978-1-7960-6374-5

All rights reserved. No part of this book may be reproduced or transmitted in any form or by any means, electronic or mechanical, including photocopying, recording, or by any information storage and retrieval system, without permission in writing from the copyright owner.

This is a work of fiction. Names, characters, places and incidents either are the product of the author's imagination or are used fictitiously, and any resemblance to any actual persons, living or dead, events, or locales is entirely coincidental.

Any people depicted in stock imagery provided by Getty Images are models, and such images are being used for illustrative purposes only. Certain stock imagery © Getty Images.

Print information available on the last page.

Rev. date: 10/07/2019

To order additional copies of this book, contact:
Xlibris
1-888-795-4274
www.Xlibris.com
Orders@Xlibris.com
802065

Welcome To

The

Glory Road

The Saga Lives On

The Complete Trilogy

Of

Fallow Are the Fields

We Danced Until Dawn

&

Under the Wedding Tree

And much more…

By

Steven D. Ayres

*The
Glory Road*

*A tell all tale
About life
& more…*

*By
Steven D. Ayres*

This Book is

Dedicated

To

All those readers out there

Who long for the Historical

Connection...

This is your age, embrace it!

The Author

Contents

Introduction xv
June 22, 1864 xxi

FALLOW ARE THE FIELDS

The Family 1
The Oncoming War 10
Signing Up 14
The Long Wait 17
A Day of Reckoning 21
Back Home 24
Spring Eternal 29
Too Close to Home 34
Loom and Gloom 37
Christmas at New Manchester 47
Off to War 51
The Front 59
The Long March Home 67
Augusta, the Wonderful 72
The Army Forever 81
The War Comes to North Georgia 84
The Bleeding South 95
The Road to Nashville 107
The Aftermath 114

WE DANCED UNTIL DAWN

New Beginnings 123
Let the Dance Begin 126
Baptizing in Sweetwater Creek 129
The Sweetwater Park Hotel and Piedmont Chautauqua 131
The Inglorious Fire 136

What Now?...138
Moving On..140
My Own Family..142
Glorious Times and Days...148
The Children Grow Up..150
The World Goes to War...152
Aviation and Puppy Feet...154
Adventures in the Sky..157
The Barnstormers and Barnstorming Willie 161
Austell Comes to Town 163
Bustling and Busted: The Depression Moves In.................................167
Prohibition, Pass the Bottle, Drink or Smell, and Groover's Lake 170
Flying the Loop for a Woman Golfer 173
The Lithia Springs Golf Course..176
Whatever Happened to Whom?...177
Exciting Developments 179
The Century Turned Fast and Furious..181
Hubert and Inez Get an Electric Stove 185
Sam Jones Is Preaching Today..187
New Orleans Comes to Mableton 189
Thelbert Grenoble, We'll Just Call You Bill...195
Remembering the Old Days..197
Final Words and Bless Be the Ties That Bind.....................................201

UNDER THE WEDDING TREE

All Hands on Deck...207
The Call to Duty...211
No Time like the Present...217
Cruising the Pacific with Uncle Sam...221
The Boys Come Home...225
Welcome to the Farm...228
Country Roads and Times..238
College Bound..242
The Law...246
Returning to My Roots..248
The Real Estate Business 250
Friends Near and Far...254
A Family of Entrepreneurs...258
Growing Up in Aviation, A Hobby Store, Farming, and Real Estate 263
Taking on a Family..271

Finding Myself and My Place in the Business World 275
How to Make and Lose a Few Million Dollars..280
Douglas County Makes a Wave–The Big Kahuna 288
The Secret of Arbor Place Mall...290
The Shock of September 11, 2001, and Other Times 293
The Flood of 2009...296
Old Barns and Weddings 298
The New Barn and More 303
Adventures on Motorcycles 309
Adventures with Airplanes..312
Let Freedom Ring: What a Day to Be Free!..322
The Benediction and Convocation 326

Epilogue 329
Appendix...333

Introduction

Once upon a time, as I was traveling along life's way, I happened upon an old shady and dusty road leading off into the immense forest before me.

There was an old man with his several goats apparently broke down on the side of the road with his beat up and shabby wagon full of all his worldly possessions. I ask the old man, "Where does this road go?"

To my surprise he just sorta ignored me at first, so I asked him again, "Sir, where does this road go?"

Well, he said, with a gentle grin, "That depends on where you are going. It goes many places depending on your desires and travel and how much time you have, and how much money you have, and how determined you are and even how much love you have in your heart! To some it just goes home and to others it will take you far, far away!"

"Ummm", I said, as I pondered his answer.

"You know, if you go on down yonder below the hallow and over the hill and across the next creek, if it ain't too high, you will come to a big old rock in the middle of the road that has been there for I guess a thousand years. Iffin' you go left, you go one way and iffin' you right, you go another way. I really can't remember which one is which, but iffin' you choose the bad way you will be sorely disappointed as you get on down the road, but there's always a good chance that you will pick the good one and on down the road you will fine one wonderful thing after another, for as long as you stay on that road. They call it the Glory Road. Now, that don't mean that you won't have any sad times or disappointments, but they will be few and far between, unlike the other road. The right way will bring you peace, love, understanding and wisdom even, if you are lucky enough to be one of the chosen ones."

I thanked the goat man for his words of instruction and wisdom and offered to help with his wagon and goats. He said, no thank you pilgrim, I've been here before, it won't be long and we'll be on our way again, but thank you kindly anyway.

With those few word, I parted and began moving forward once more along the shady and dusty lane that led off into the dark forest. Time and travel only, could eventually tell me where I was or where I was going, but time would tell.

Join me as we travel along through time and space along the "Glory Road" of life for the next 150 years and seven generations. You and your ancestors may have been here before and recognize some of the old landmarks, including the big old rock in the road…..

Travel light and keep your head up, stay alert and don't spit into the wind….

See'ya Pilgrim on the other side….

Enjoy your travels down the "The Glory Road!"

The Author

The

American

Civil War

Centennial

Had Began

1961 – 1965

100 Years

Ago

1861 – 1865

June 22, 1864

As I lay there, dying on the warm bloody ground of Kolb Farm, I realized that fate was a stranger bedfellow. The earth was inviting me to join it. To fold up my arms and give up the ghost, drawing to itself a desperate man caught up in an even more desperate time.

But, it was only a leg wound, was it not? Although the pain was tearing me apart inside as well. Eating me alive with more fear probably than anything else. Fear of the known and the unknown. Fear of the known and the unknown. Fear consuming me as much as the blood was leaving me, of being run over by the enemy and being the recipient of a sudden bayonet thrust to the chest or belly. To know that the distance between Heaven and Earth was growing ever shorter

Here on the battlefields of North Georgia only a few miles from my home, the tides of war would engulf me and forever flood the memories of my youth.

The story of my own trials in this war are not unlike those of thousands of other young boys and men drawn into the great conflict, sucked up by the rising pressure of upheaval and discordancy. Yet, nevertheless, it is my own story and so, like the willow that bends its humble head to the ground and shares its weeping with the wind. I would like to share with you the humble story of this Confederate soldier, as told to my memories some twenty odd years ago.

We had fought over this deadly ground once, now twice and the sweet smell of victory and the foul stench of defeat had both turned into the arrogant odor of death and dying. A smell that would not go away. Would not blow through the gentle wind because there was none. Just stillness and the heavy weighedness of silence. Silence now interrupted in the twilight of darkness by the moans and groans of broken brave boys, hurting and crying for relief. But, there was none, except for the dead and those about to die.

These were the anonymous words of a young lad only sixteen years old of the Confederate Army, too old to be with Mama, too young to be with Jesus.

The Author

FALLOW ARE THE FIELDS

The Family

I grew up in the low hills of northwest Georgia. It was a time when the world was much smaller than it is now. Days and weeks seemed to last forever, and the entire universe centered on the family farm. The year I was born was 1846, in the month of July, day of the sixth. Mama always said I was almost a firecracker since I just missed Independence Day by two days.

The family farm wasn't really big by most standards. It was just your ordinary one-horse farm. My dad always preferred a horse over a mule 'cause he said you didn't have to talk to a horse the same way you did a mule. A horse was, he said, almost as smart as a human being, but I didn't know where he got his information because some human beings I knew sure didn't have much sense.

Well, we had all the regular things little north Georgia farms had, I guess, like barns, chickens, a few cows, a couple of pigs, and of course the horse. We even had four hound dogs. Two were big old blueticks, one was a big yellow hound, and the other was an old, old white female hound, the mother of the other three. The daddy was, as my ma told it, the traveling-salesman kind of dog, and we'd never seen him but three times ever. Then there was the pet coon that my sister took up with, or should I say he took up with her.

Our house wasn't real fancy, but it kept most of the wind off you in the wintertime. It was an old clapboard-siding house covered with heart pine lumber. As a matter of fact, the entire house, I suppose, was built from heart pine, built to last a lifetime for several generations. We didn't build it, but a man named Mr. Duncan erected it about ten years or so ago. After a couple of years, his wife died with the pox; and since they never had any children, he just upped and decided to sell it to my pa. Made a real good trade my pa did from what I'd been told. We got the whole four-hundred-acre farm for the price of two horses, a two-horse wagon, and half the crops for the first two years, good or bad. The only thing we didn't know was how many rocks this old farm could grow. It seemed that every time we plowed an inch of ground, two rocks would grow out without you even havin' to plant 'em. We just couldn't eat rocks; that was the bad thing. After a while, though, we learned to do a lot of things with those rocks. They made good piles, real pretty like; and when we needed some, we always knew where to get them. Yeah, we used them for other things too, as foundations for buildings, walls, chimneys, and the like. We even built an entire springhouse out of 'em and a storm and root cellar too.

And we had a well, a good well too with one of those little house roofs built over the top so as to keep the rainwater out, I guess. At least you could draw water in the rain and not get wet, except for comin' and goin' to the well. On sunny, hot days, it was rather nice, and it was pretty good in the snowy weather too with what little snow we got.

Now I really didn't say too much about the house 'cause it actually wasn't much to talk about. It was your basic run-down old house of four rooms with a wood-burning fireplace on each end so as to keep the two ends of the house warm in the winter and the rest somewhere between chilly and barely above freezin'. I hardly ever remembered ice in the house during the wintertime, but it wasn't altogether uncommon if nobody tended the fires for a few days, like if we were all out huntin' or somethin'. My ma liked to keep a small fire goin' most of the time, even when it was hot, so she could make tea or coffee or biscuits. She cooked on the open hearth for most of my childhood until we finally built her a kitchen on the north side of the house with its own cooking fireplace. We couldn't afford a cookstove, like some people in the towns had, until I was fifteen years old.

The land around our farm was some of the most beautiful land on God's green earth. At least we thought it was. It had fields, trees, and streams running through big virgin hardwoods and more game than you could use almost– deer, rabbits, squirrels, and quail–and all the wild berries and fruits you can imagine. Between all that and the crops and domestic animals, there wasn't much we lacked for in the way of food. Of course, we did buy our sugar–what little we used–and we bought our coffee and tea. Our corn was ground down at the local mill, run by the Abernathy brothers, and made into cornmeal and our wheat made into flour. Two freshened cows kept us in all the milk, butter, and buttermilk we could use. Two dozen chickens usually produced about a dozen to a dozen and a half eggs nearly every day. So we ate pretty good.

Nothing like eatin' a hot sweet potato right out of the fire, with hot, meltin' butter drippin' all over it. Made your mouth water just thinkin' about it, didn't it?

Low mountains hung off in the distance to the north. Local folks called them the Allatoona Mountains, footstools to the bigger Blue Ridge Mountains, all part of the southern range of the great Appalachian Mountains. And we had a couple of smaller but very impressive hills just to the north of our farm. One of those hills was called Lost Mountain, and the other bigger hill was actually a real mountain, I guess, 'cause they called it Kennesaw Mountain. It was named after the little railroad settlement of Kennesaw, or maybe that was somebody's name. I wouldn't know. But what I did know was about Lost Mountain. The Indians named it that because when you looked at it from a distance, it really did look like a mountain; but when you got up to it, it was gone, like it was really lost, and you couldn't find it except you really could. It just wasn't no mountain anymore. It was more like a molehill. Now just off to the northeast of Lost Mountain was another little molehill called Pine Mountain, and then off to the northeast of Kennesaw Mountain was another good-sized hill called Brushy Mountain. Now all this didn't mean much right now, but as this story continued, you'd see that all these mountains and molehills had quite a significant impact on what finally happened around the family farm.

In 1846, when I was born, the world seemed to be a mighty peaceful place to live, provided you ignored the Mexican War and the War of 1812. Compared to what was coming, these were just uncivil pastimes—military exercises to prepare the powers that be for some real, downright dirty fighting. A civil war it was later to be called by some. To tell the truth, I never ever saw one thing that was "civil" about it. Most people referred to it as the War between the States or the "late great unpleasantness" as some old women called it. But I can tell you, for one, that it was definitely the most "uncivil" war that you can imagine, a sure 'nuff war between the Confederate States of America and the United States of America—the rebels, as we were called, and the Yankees or Federals, as they was called—down to the last man, I tell you. We were all Americans, and why we were fighting the way we were was a little bit beyond my country-boy comprehension. Well, some said it was for slavery, some said it was because of slavery, some said it was for states' rights, and some said it was because of states' rights. I wouldn't know. We didn't own no slaves, but now my grandpappy did up in South Carolina, my mother's father; and his father did too, up to about three hundred, I think. It took a lot of labor to run rice plantations, and at one time, I think they owned three different ones up on the Cooper River near Monck's Corner. My mother told me all about them losing the family fortune somehow and how her daddy had grown up there on the plantation and such. But I never knew him very good as I had only known him as a very young child.

Nevertheless, the fighting got started somehow. I guess when someone shoots at you, it's only natural to return the fire and shoot back; and before you know it, you get the whole darn country shooting backwards and forwards at each other. And you never knew who was who as far as being a foreigner was concerned or somethin' 'cause we was all brothers, fathers, sons, and such. The only difference you could tell was whether they was wearing blue or if they was wearing gray. Sometimes the shades changed, like butternut gray or light, shady blue, but you could pretty well tell, especially if they was already pourin' lead your way. Didn't matter too much what you looked like as long as you were still able to look at all.

Four years on the march away from home, back and forth all over the country, away from your loved ones and the comforts of home, was almost more than any one person could ever take. Camp life was mostly borin', and the biggest danger was gettin' sick. If you was to get sick, you had nearly four times the chance of dying as going into battle and getting the middle blown outa you with a miniball. No, sir, you sure didn't want to get sick in camp or while on the march. Hospitals were nonexistent for all practical purposes, and if you did ever see any, they was so full of the wounded and dying that they wouldn't have any room for you anyway, so you either got well or might as well go ahead and die. So many boys got sick, and it was so sad to know that there was so little you could do to help. One time I got sick with fever, just a-burnin' up, and there was hardly a kind hand to bring me a drink of water. For three days, I wished I had died; and finally, through some miracle, I just popped up and was fine.

Yes, the war was a terrible time. It was somethin' you wouldn't ever forget in a million years. And it affected everybody, not just the soldiers. It affected, at least here at home, all the civilian population all over the South and a good bit of the North too. It wasn't a pretty time, and it wasn't a wonderful experience like we all thought it was going to be. But it was exciting. *Terrifying* was really a more accurate description. I'd never been so scared in all my life as I was more than a dozen times during that war. There was just no describing what war was really like. One day you were one place, and the next day, you were somewhere else, always on the move when there was action and then in camp for weeks and months sometimes when nothing else was happening, a time when the generals were sorting out their battle maps and trying to match their wits with their backsides.

Now I didn't tell you about all my family back home in the early years. When I was born, I already had four older brothers. The oldest was named William Gordon, and we called him Will because he was so strong willed. He was big, strong, and very spiritual, being the oldest and all. I guess he had to have all the wisdom for the rest of us kids, and he looked out for us just like Ma and Pa would. He was a handsome fellow, and my ma and pa both thought that the sun rose and set on his shoulders. They was real proud of William.

Then there was Levi, the next eldest, who could plow a field in one day's time—I mean, a big field too. I'd never seen anybody who could get the work done like Levi, and he loved animals too. Had a certain way with them he did, not like most people who didn't understand what animals were about. Then there was Samuel, whom we just called Sam most of the time. Sam was a different kind of kid who never liked to work much, but he could do things that the rest of us couldn't, like work with words and pictures. He'd draw a picture and then write a little story to go with it like in a book or something. Ma taught us to read the Good Book, and that was where most of his stories and drawings would come from, although he often took somethin' from right out of his head and just came up with it. He'd get ideas from the farm too. He always did the milkin' 'cause he said it gave him time to think.

The brother just older than me was Benjamin; we called him Ben. He was just about a year or so older than me, and we were pretty close, much closer in some respects than the others, although we were all mighty close when it came to lookin' out for and protectin' one another. Ben, though, was special in his own way 'cause I and he were just like two fingers pointed in the same direction. He was smart, smarter than me I was sure, but he never acted like it. He could take apart and put back together anything that existed. He was specially good at taking care of the guns. Our huntin' rifles and pistols were always in tip-top shape 'cause Ben made it his job to see to that. If ever anything broke, no matter what it was, Ben would fix it better than new.

Then there was me; my name was Steven, but everybody in the family called me Stevie, at least when I was little. I guess it was 'cause I was the baby until my little sister came along. I was Mother's pet, I think. At least I liked to think I was. She was always doting on me and lookin' out for me, I suppose, as I was somewhat precocious and always gettin' into things. I just loved bein' curious about things and often got myself into trouble when I found out it was a lot easier to take things apart than it was to put them back together. Thank goodness for Ben, who could bail me out. You see, I just had a very exploratory mind and liked to look at things from inside out.

The real baby of the family was my kid sister, Anna, who was the most beautiful little blonde-headed girl on this side of the Mississippi River, probably the other side too. There was nothing that Anna wanted that Anna didn't get.

Talk about spoiled, bein' with five older brothers and all. Ma and Pa kinda spoiled her too, being the only girl in such an otherwise rough-and-tumble family. I guess every family ought to have at least one girl in it to sort of help balance things out some. But she was just like us, or at least she wanted to be. She was nothing but a tomboy all made up like a girl, and although we treated her like one of the guys, we knew she was only a girl. We loved her, though, and there wasn't anything or anyone ever causing her no harm. We made sure of that.

Life was hard back then, or so it seemed at times. But now looking back, I knew it was really easy 'cause everything was all planned out for you nearly all the time—I mean, what with the clearin' and plowin' and milkin' and feedin' and wood cuttin' and a million and one things that had to be done on the farm. Of course, with a family the size of mine, there were not only a lot of mouths to feed but also a lot of hands to help do the work. So it wasn't so bad. We were like our own little army of ants doing everything that had to be done, and we loved every minute of it. My Pa and Ma would see to that, anything to keep us busy 'cause idle hands made for idle minds, or so they said. I wouldn't know 'cause I never got that idle.

If we weren't working on some project or doing regular chores, we was a-fishing or hunting, spending time in the deep woods or down by the pond or on the creek bank. Summertime, we were all swimming whenever we got the chance to cool off in the hot afternoons, usually on Saturday or Sunday or both. Of course, every other Sunday was the meeting day at church. We couldn't get a full-time preacher, so we had a part-time one, but Ma always said we was still supposed to have a full-time religion all the time. On Sunday mornings when the preacher didn't come, Ma would gather us all around just like church anyway; and she would read to us from the Good Book and talk to us about being good, loving one another, forgiving one another, and things like that. If there was ever one thing my mother taught us, it was love, not just love-love but real, deep-seated love in your heart, the kind that she said God always had for you—you know, the kind of love that loved you even when you didn't deserve it for nothing. There was a particular lesson one Sunday that she shared with us that I never would forget. She said, "If you take God's loving grace and you spell the word *grace* out, each letter stands for a word." An acronym I think she called it. And that was that *G*od *r*eceives *a*ll his *c*hildren without *e*xception, and she did too. This just seemed powerful to me, and I never forgot it. That stood by for me too when it came my turn to go off to war. Regardless of what we do and who we are, God still loves us just like our parents, even when we don't deserve it. Not a bad thought to live by, I figured. If I too could live and love with God's grace in my life, I'd do all right, and I had.

I wanted to say a few things about my pa too. He, to start with, was a good man who looked after all of us mighty good. We never went hungry, and we never lacked really for anything we really needed. Sure, we thought we needed some things, but we didn't really; we just wanted them, like the time I wanted a new rifle when I was about twelve. He said I was still a mite young and needed to be a little older. But heck, I had been shootin' and a-huntin' since I was old enough to pull a trigger out there on the farm. Well, I pleaded and begged for I didn't know how long until, finally, he called me over by the fireside one morning. I'd never forget, and he said, "Stevie, I know you're young and still kinda little, but you've been a good boy, and you've been responsible about things, and I've got a surprise for you. I knew you've always wanted to have your own gun. So, son, I'm gonna give you Grandpa's old shotgun here." He took it down from the mantel over the old rock fireplace, and he placed it in my hands.

And he said, "Son, this, you know, was your grandpa's old shotgun, and it means a lot to me. When I was just a young boy, my daddy gave it to me to look after and take care of. And now, son, I'm passing it on to you." My face lit up like the Fourth of July, and my heart swelled with pride as I took it into my own hands, knowing that now it was mine–my own gun to take care of, to shoot and hunt with, and to protect. It was the nearest thing, I guess, I'd ever experienced to really feel like I was going into manhood. It was an awesome time and experience to know that my pa trusted me with one of the things that meant the most to him, and I would cherish it forever.

The Family Meal

The Oncoming War

The days were long in the hot summer months of June, July, and August. Everybody everywhere was talking about secession from the Union. Some couldn't wait to see us all get out of the Union and have our own state or country. Georgia was no exception to the cry for sovereignty. I never heard so many arguments and so much confusion over who was right and who was wrong. Slavery was talked about a lot, especially up in the North, mostly by people who didn't even have any slaves. Abolitionists they was called by most folks. I didn't really understand what all the fuss was about 'cause we sure didn't have no slaves on our farm. But nearly all the big plantations had slaves. Cotton was king, and the slaves were the labor for picking that cotton. Some masters had as many as a hundred or more, sometimes a lot more. Even though we didn't own any, I knew that my great-grandpa and my grandpa had owned as many as three hundred and somethin' up in Charleston, South Carolina.

Yeah, I guess we had been a part of all the ruckus too. On that rice plantation up at Monck's Corner–Lewisfield Plantation, named after the original owner, on the Cooper River–my grandpa on my mother's side had had a slew of slaves to help run it. As a matter of fact, they had owned three rice plantations all together along the Cooper River just up from Charleston because my great-grandpa had the good fortune to marry the daughter of an owner of two plantations. So I guess in our family, rice was–if not king–at least a queen. As a matter of fact, there was hardly a day went by that we didn't have rice for at least one meal. But I never saw any of these slaves 'cause we never went up to Charleston when

I was growing up; something had happened a few years earlier that caused the family to lose all the plantations and everything that went with them. My great-grandma had died, leaving all three plantations with my grandpa, who later remarried unfortunately, so my new great-grandma–no blood relation–became a stepmother to my grandpa and his brother. Soon afterward, their father died, leaving them to be raised under the eye of the stepmother, who really didn't give a pea turkey what happened to them. She had a child by a former marriage whom she doted on and gave all her attention to. Now my great-grandpa, in his will, had left Lewisfield Plantation to my grandpa and his brother, who were both minors at the time. A shrewd, smart, and I might say crooked Charleston lawyer was the executor of his estate. He did see that the boys were cared for and got everything they needed, but in the meantime, all the wealth of the estate was used up, and the plantation fell into disuse and was actually abandoned for some time. As the taxes piled up, it just didn't seem practical, I guess, to pay on something that wasn't producing at the time, and the old lawyer just milked it for all it was worth and then let it go. First thing you knew, the plantation was sold to satisfy taxes, and some old codger from Maryland bought it on the courthouse steps for next to nothin'. And that my friend was the end to the great rice dynasty of my early family. So you see, slavery sure was not an issue to me and my family now.

Now states' rights were another thing. Nearly everybody I knew said that we had a right to do what we goldanged pleased and that no stuffed shirt in a monkey suit from Washington was going to tell us what we could and couldn't do. No, sirree. Iffen we wanted to have slaves, that was our own goldarn business, and we could own them just like we owned that mule over there. After all, we bought them, paid for 'em with our own hard-earned money, fed 'em, cared for 'em, gave 'em a place to sleep and somethin' to do all day so as to ease their savage minds.

Now I wanted you to know I didn't take to that kind of thinkin', but a lot of people did back then. If you asked me, a black man had just as much right to be free as I did–to have a family and maybe a little farm so he could feed his family and not have his wife and children sold away from him whenever some master wanted to. Yes, it seems to me that freedom is somethin' that belongs to every human being. But you know, blacks in those days weren't exactly considered "human beings" unfortunately. They was just considered chattel or personal property. Why, the word *chattel* might just as well have meant "cattle" for all the proprietary of the word. At any rate, these things were a fact back then, not just some made-up thoughts of the imagination. I heard tell of an uncle even over in Alabama who was a slave trader who made a lot of money in the slave market before the war. Didn't matter to us none, though, 'cause we'd never seen any of the money; and besides, we did think it was wrong.

Well, talk of secession and possible war went on for some time. That summer, especially, was hotter in more ways than one. It was actually kinda exciting, like thinking that, hey, maybe we might have an actual war or something. It was hard to imagine that it could happen, but times were uncertain, and nobody really knew what would be the final outcome of it all. If the Northerners would just let us alone, everything would be fine and dandy, but that probably was not going to happen.

Georgia seemed to be caught up in the middle of it all, I think, what with Virginia and South Carolina a-whoopin' and a-hollerin' all about states' rights all the time. And then there was Alabama on the other side and Mississippi and Texas, which were all gettin' pretty vocal about it all. Then there was the sovereign state of Tennessee, which said they would do whatever they wanted to, no matter who said what. The only thing was, a lot of people in Tennessee didn't seem to know what they wanted. They didn't have all the rich cotton land that the lower states had, and things just looked a little different to them up in all those hills they had all over the place. But one thing for sure was they did identify with the South, and whatever all the other Southern states did, they probably would too. It was kinda the same with Kentucky.

Missouri never could make up its mind, and all they could ever do was fuss and fight eventually all over the state. You talked about a state of confusion, Missouri was it.

Then there was Florida; the state of flowers Ma called it. I wouldn't know 'cause I never had been there, but they said it was real pretty at the ocean specially, and there was all the sand in the world in Florida, so much sand that you didn't even have to look for it. It was all over the place like snow in the winter in north Georgia. Well, Florida, we all thought, was a sort of sissy state, being where it was and all and being almost surrounded by water. We knew that from our geography in school. The only real importance it would have in the event of any war would be all that water around it. Shipping would be bound to be affected, and this could be important to the South. Also, it was the back door to the South, and it would be a fine way to stab the South in the back if ever the North could be past our front door. Fat chance they'd ever have of doin' that. Anyway, Florida was obliged to do whatever the other Southern states did because it really had no choice anyway.

North Carolina was bound to the South like a button on a boot. There wasn't anywhere the rest of the South was goin' without North Carolina being right there too, right beside its little sister, South Carolina. The coastal areas of the Carolinas and the naval stores of pine, pitch, and tar up in the inlands were going to be mighty important to the South in any future contest between sides.

The talk around town, out the little town of Salt Springs, Georgia, was pretty brash about the possibility of secession and even war, if that was what it was all to come to. Most folks didn't want war, but if that was what it took, then most were anxious to get on with it. After all, everybody knew it would be no contest between us and them, whoever them was, Yankees mostly. You know, it was like two kids on the street arguing about marbles; and the first thing you knew, ever'body was a-takin' sides, getting ready for the biggest brawl you ever did see.

We didn't get to town too much, but when we did, everybody would stand around the post office at the Bowden house, where Judge Bowden and his family lived, and talk about how we were gonna show them Yankees what we was made of. If we did go to war, it wouldn't last long before we wiped the daylights out of them bastards and gave them really what for. And it seemed that everybody wanted in on the action, like it was all going to be over before they got their own chance to kill them a few Yankees so they could brag about it. I'd never seen anything like it, the way people talked. Didn't make much sense to me, but what did I know? I was just a simple country boy on the edge of a great event. Somewhere and sometime we would all get our own chance to contribute to this great adventure before it was all over. We never knew just how much we'd get to see and do over the next four years or so. There was even talk about gettin' up a regiment of soldiers right here in Salt Springs. They was going to be called "the Salt Springs Regulars." Groups were already forming up all over the area, like down at Campbellton, the county seat of our Campbell County, and companies beginning to form at Dark Corner, Winston, Sandtown, and Sweetwater Town and maybe down at New Manchester Mill, where a small town had grown up around New Manchester Manufacturing Co.–Factory Shoals it was called–where they had built a five-story yarn mill, the biggest in the whole state at the time. Only time would tell when all these boys would gather round from all over the country and when this great conflict would begin in earnest.

Signing Up

Nowhere were things more exciting than around the family farm three miles west of Salt Springs. With a family the size of mine, there was bound to be a lot of talk and figuring on who was going to do what. All my brothers wanted to jump right in the fray before they missed out on this once-in-a-lifetime adventure. They all just figured we'd all get in there together to whip the Yankees in a few weeks, and we'd be back on the farm before spring planting.

William, being the eldest, decided that he would lead the way; and without telling Ma or Pa or anyone else, he went down to Salt Springs and signed up with the Salt Springs Regulars. By now, a small camp was beginning to form down on the banks of Sweetwater Creek just south of town. My pa was real proud that William was the first to take a positive step toward doing something. My ma was, of course, pretty shaken up about it 'cause she knew our family had a lot to lose if this thing didn't turn out like we thought. And it was just so difficult for a mother to think of her boys going off to fight in some ruckus war as this. Actually, Will wouldn't have to report for another week so as to give him time to get his loose ends together and get whatever gear up he might have, including guns and knives, and time to say his rightful goodbyes to his family and friends. I think this also gave one the opportunity to brag a little about how he was going off to war and all.

Part of the reason that Will signed up was that, on Sunday meeting day at the church, the preacher preached so hard about our homes and families and how it was our "divine right" and responsibility to fight for and protect what was ours and our way of life. The preacher said that hell itself could be right here on this earth iffen we didn't stand up and do what was right. Little did he know then that we'd have hell to pay for what was to come anyway. Well, that preacher was probably responsible for some dozen or more good boys going down to the camp on Monday morning to get signed up in the Confederate army.

Some people up north were calling us rebels and said this was nothing more than an out-and-out rebellion by the Southern states that, by now, had formed a confederation as they called it, an agreement to stand together come what may, fighting or not. And the new confederation was to be called the Confederate States of America, just like a brand-new country. After all, the United States of America was the same thing when we broke off from England and all those English dandies. Great Britain, the greatest power on the face of the earth at that time, couldn't stop us then, even with all their power and armies and navies, so who was to say that now we just couldn't do the same? Everybody thought it was a mighty fine idea to have our own country. After all, we really were different from the Northerners. There were lots of differences when you came right down to it, like how we were brought up and the way we lived and how we looked at life in general. Most of us boys grew up on farms, and we ran in the woods a-huntin' and playin' all the time. The woods and fields were our first and second homes. We knew how to shoot, hunt, fish, and do all the things you had to know to survive in the wild.

Why, most of them Northern boys all grew up in cities and towns—well, maybe not every single one of them, but most of them did. I mean, listen, some of 'em boys were from New York City. Now what would you think they knew about being in the woods and living off the land and such? Nothing. Nothing, I tell you. They was a bunch of sissies, if ever I did see one. Why, everybody said right off it would take ten of them to make one of us when it came to wits and guts. Later, we'd find out they had plenty of wits and guts, although we never let on that we knew that. There would be some hard-fightin' men to come up and out of that army, and that was for sure.

There was some things that the North really did have in favor of them though. And that was almost everything except willpower. They had more men; they had more guns, more industry, more cannons, more food, more ships, more everything. The resources they had far outnumbered all that we had except maybe our slave labor, but what good was that going to do us now? Blackies wouldn't be fightin' for the South, no way. I guess we'd just have to take care of 'em somehow. They would come in handy in digging trenches and other defense fortifications, some thought. But who was going to need all that?

Over the next week, much talk went on in the family about who was going to do what. Samuel and Levi, especially, were set on signing up too. So finally, my pa and ma called for a family meeting on Friday night so we all could discuss our plans. It was agreed that some of us needed to stay and keep the farm and all going and to take care of Ma and Anna. It was further agreed that Samuel and Levi would go and sign up together since they were the next two eldest boys, and the rest of us–me, Ben, Pa, and of course Anna–would stay with Ma on the farm, at least for now. So this was the plan. In a few weeks or certainly within a few months, Will, Samuel, and Levi would all be back on the farm again. Or so we thought.

So on Saturday morning, Pa, Ben, and I went with Sam and Levi over to the sign-up camp on Sweetwater Creek. We wanted to see them off and get in on part of the excitement and all. Boy, were we all excited about all this! The camp was growing, with more and more boys coming in from all over the area. Captain Maxwell signed them up and turned them over to a Sergeant Gunn, who we all knew to be a pretty rough-and-tumble sort of man who used to run the mill down at Mitchell Creek. Sgt. Jerome Gunn was a fine and stout man of good character. As a matter of fact, he was the sergeant for Company C of the Salt Springs Regulars, the same outfit that William was in. We didn't know right then, but this regiment was to become a part of the First Georgia Volunteers. Their lieutenant was a fine gentleman named Buford H. Fordham. It was to be a fine regiment, and we were all so proud of them.

The Long Wait

It wasn't but a short time that we got word that the camp had moved out somewheres toward Atlanta, not all that far but sure far enough when you were talking about your family being gone.

Atlanta was a real city now by most standards. About ten thousand people lived there, and to me, that seemed like all the people in the world. I guess about half of them would be off to fight in the war, maybe not that many, but then I wasn't quite sure about numbers. Maybe a fourth of them would go. Anyway, Atlanta had really grown into quite a city because of the railroads.

Originally, the railroad out of Augusta had terminated or just plain stopped there because of the Chattahoochee River, so they just called the point Terminus. A small settlement soon grew up with a trading post called Whitehall's and a little tavern run by Mr. Mitchell. First thing you knew, everything around there was Whitehall Street, Mitchell Street, and Peachtree Street, after Mr. Mitchell's young peach orchard, which seemed to go out in all directions. The road to Decatur came in about the same point where all the other roads did, and soon it just became the dead center of town. Some people even called it Five Points. It was a wonder the town didn't take up that name. It was also surprising it wasn't called Peachtree City. A few years later, the mayor had a little darling baby girl, and he and the town council decided to rename the town Marthasville after his daughter. Well, either the little girl turned out not to be so wonderful or something else happened 'cause, a few years later, the name was changed to Atlanta, and that stuck. Now where the name Atlanta came from I was not exactly sure. It was a real mystery, but I always thought it had something to do with Atlantis, the lost city. But who knew? Atlanta certainly was lost; if ever there was an unlikely place to have a city, this was it–no port on the sea, no port on the river. The Chattahoochee River was not navigable this far up by any big boats. The only thing that Atlanta originally had going for it was that the railroad ended there, and it was like the far-western frontier. Of course, this was all just before I was born, so what would I know? When the railroads kept building, connecting up with Chattanooga on the Tennessee River and southwesterly down to West Point on the Chattahoochee River, then Atlanta took on a whole new significance as a sort of railroad hub. Maybe some of the founding fathers or at least the railroad people were pretty farsighted way back then 'cause they sure did hit on a good idea that seemed awfully stupid at first. "Typical of government," my pa would say except, most of the time, the idea stayed stupid.

Out of Atlanta to the west ran a road that most people just called the Alabama Road 'cause that was where it went to Alabama. Made sense to me. It went through a settlement called Lick Skillet, where a road split off to the south to go to Sandtown and a little farther to the town of Campbellton, our county seat when Campbell County was formed.

After going through Lick Skillet, the road came on through to the Chattahoochee River, where there was a ferry called *Gordon's Ferry*, and then on westward to the next little settlement that would come to be known as Mableton, after the Mable family farm, and then on out to Sweetwater Town on the banks of the Sweetwater Creek and then just a ways across and down the creek to what I called my little town of Salt Springs. The next big stop off on the way to Alabama was a place called Dark Corner and Villa Rica and then Tallapoosa, and then you was in Alabama about halfway to a little place called Birmingham. We never went past Tallapoosa, so I can't tell you about what it was like beyond there.

Just north of Salt Springs was the town of Powder Springs and Marietta, where Kennesaw Mountain was near, and just south of Marietta back toward Atlanta was the little settlement of Smyrna. South of Salt Springs was a new little settlement called New Manchester, which had grown quite a bit since they built a big, five-story textile mill there on the shoals of Sweetwater Creek. Later, this would have an important bearing on the war 'cause they were soon making Confederate uniforms there.

Many of these places I'd mentioned would take on a whole new meaning in the upcoming war here at home. Little did we know that we didn't have to go off to fight, that we could've stayed right here and done plenty of fighting. And some of us would.

Weeks passed, and we heard no word from the brothers until finally, one day, we got a letter from William. He was over in Atlanta somewhere near

Decatur, and he said that he, Samuel, and Levi were all doing fine. They were getting ready to move out soon and would be headed north somewheres. He didn't know where, but they thought it would be up north somewhere, maybe Virginia, to meet up with some more troops and go for a march on Washington. They were all pretty excited about the prospects of that. There was nothing more boring for a soldier, they said, than to be all ready to go and fight and to not be able to. Frustration was a daily enemy too, and you had to fight it off every day. It wouldn't be too long now before they got a chance to show their stuff.

Around home, things were still somewhat normal. We sure did miss having Will, Samuel, and Levi at home on the farm, however, and it took a lot more effort now to get all the things done. After all, we were all so used to being together all the time that being apart was very difficult at first. We waited every day for some new word from the front and to hear what was happening. We would get some news each week from the *Campbell County Bugle*, which was circulated throughout the area. They got news from Atlanta and other places and were able to put together a smattering of news regarding troop movements and what everybody speculated was going to happen. I guess a lot of it was kept secret. How secret could you keep something like an army on the move though? I mean, there must be thousands of soldiers by now on both sides, all just a-itchin' for a fight.

The best we could tell was that the Confederate army was about to make a move on Washington DC and that, very soon, there was bound to be an engagement with the enemy. We waited and waited as patiently as we could, but we heard nothing from the boys gone off to war. Finally, a letter came in at Salt Springs from William. He, being the eldest son, had taken on the responsibility for him, Samuel, and Levi to do the writing and tell us back home just what was happening to them and how they were doing.

> The letter read,
> June 30, 1861
>
> Dear Ma and Pa,
>
> Hope everyone at home is doing fine as we are all doing real good here in the army. We have traveled a great distance already and are getting very near to Washington itself. Probably in another week or so, we expect to be there. Don't know exactly what will happen then, but we expect to meet up with the Yankees sooner or later. Every soldier is pretty anxious to get on with it all. This camp life is for the birds. Gets awful boring sometimes.

Samuel and Levi are doing fine too and wanted me to ask you, Ma, if you might be able to send us some of them sugar cookies you always make up. They sure would be good and would help remind us of home.

Levi stepped on a snake the other day down by the creek when he was filling up some canteens. It turned around and bit him on the leg. Some of the boys said it was a moccasin, but I don't think it was. We couldn't find no fang marks on him, just a sort of bruise. Anyway, we're watching it real close, and he hadn't come down with any fever or anything, so I guess he's going to be okay.

Samuel said to tell you that he's getting a lot of ideas for some stories and picture drawings, but time to draw has been limited 'cause they keep us a-working and drilling nearly all the day. He did want me to tell you how good he can shoot. As a matter of fact, there was some talk about him maybe getting into some sharpshooter outfit; he is so good. Must be those baby blue eyes he has.

Well, they're about to call for lights-out, and we got to rise with the sun every morning, so I reckon I'll close for now.

Be sure to tell Ben and Stevie and Anna hello and that we miss them all, and we love you all very much.

> Your Loving and Devoted Son,
>
> William

A Day of Reckoning

Every few days now, we would pick up some gossip of news about the armies. It seemed like it would be just a matter of days before there was a real battle.

We didn't really count Fort Sumter, back in April, 'cause it was a limited engagement, although it was against a United States garrison in Charleston Harbor. It was actually the first real fighting that went on, but it wasn't between two armies really, at least not like what was about to happen now. Fort Sumter finally just surrendered, and that was the end of that. It was good for Charleston, though, 'cause of the harbor and the ships and all. But it had been a long time on this continent since two major armies clashed, not counting the Mexican War, of course, or the War of 1812.

This was going to be a different sort of war, one fought between Americans on American soil. It was bound to be considerably different. We were confident it would end in our favor and not last very long. After all, it was more like a big family brawl. We had even heard about some families splitting up over the idea of secession and slavery and the whole business. Some Southerners, I heard, even went up north to join the Northern army, but I didn't think we actually knew of any personally.

Well, there was one real strong abolitionist from Macon who, we had heard, went north to Chicago to help raise a regiment. Didn't know his name right off, but everyone considered him a traitor to the South, and if he ever got caught, I was sure that he would be hanged.

Late in July, the word finally came that the Southern boys had met the Yankees at a little place just south of Washington called Manassas Junction. A pleasant little creek ran through the countryside called Bull Run.

According to the reports, it seemed that all Washington had come out to witness the great spectacle. Even dandies with their ladies came out on the hillsides in carriages and such and–would you believe?–with picnic baskets. Some picnic this was to be. According to all the reports, the two armies went at it, and fighting broke out all over the place. After a few hours, the Yankees decided that they had had enough and started skedaddling back to Washington in total disarray, sometimes even getting ahead of the spectators and carriages. It must have been one of the most unsightly scenes ever imagined.

We all knew that, when it came time for a showdown, the Yankees would turn tail and run. They just didn't have it in 'em to really fight. After all, what were they fighting for? They didn't have no darkies to save. The only thing they had to save was their hides.

If the rest of the war went like this, it would be a short war indeed. Washington itself lay right before the Confederate army. Now there was nothing to stop the advancement of this great assemblage of fighting men from all over the South. Three months tops, and this war would be over.

We thought we were unorganized but no way compared with the Yankee or Federal army. When they started to run, they were all over the place. There wasn't anything organized about their retreat at all. Officers were just as bad as the enlisted men. All they could do was run for their lives.

There was one thing that came out of all this confusion that seemed to help some of our boys, and that was about the flag. You see, the official Confederate flag–the Stars and Bars–looked so much like the United States flag–the Stars and Stripes–that, half the time, some of the boys didn't know which was which. So General Beauregard decided to use a battle banner that would be easily recognizable by our boys. It was a cross of blue with thirteen white stars on it for the Southern states, bordered by white, all on a beautiful field of red. And it was almost square. "It was a wonderful-looking flag," all the men said, and there was no confusion about whose flag it was. The men really seemed to like it, and it had since become known as Beauregard's battle banner. I expected that more units would begin to use it also.

The next day or so after the Battle of Bull Run, as most people began to call it, time was spent mostly removing the wounded and the dead. "It was an awful sight," said those who were eyewitnesses to the event. But the morale was so high, by now, in the Southern army that it seemed it would be an invincible force.

By the time the armies got themselves ready to fight again, it was already too late to make a direct move on Washington. In just a matter of days, the defenses around Washington had been strengthened so that it would have taken Napoleon's army itself to have broken the lines. No, for now, the Confederates would back off and regroup themselves. There would be another time for aggression. Right now, the South wanted to enjoy and bask in its great victory. Maybe after this, the North would give up and just say, "Okay, we'll let you alone. Go home." But this didn't happen either.

Back Home

Meanwhile, back home, things rocked along as they'd say. There got to be a considerable amount of unrest, though, among most people because they didn't understand why everything was a-taking so long. If you were going to fight, then do it and do it now. This dragging things out was not the Southern way. But most folks just didn't understand what it took to run a great army. I mean, you didn't just up and go at the drop of a hat. And when you did go, you gotta know where to go and when. It took a lot of everything to sustain an army of forty to fifty thousand men.

Well, in my family, things were going pretty good so far. Pa was working on a new field down by the lower spring. Ben and I were trying to help him as much as we could. It had been a hot summer working out there in the blazing, hot sun, but at least the spring was close by, and the old gourd dipper we kept hanging on the tree above it made many a dip in the cool, clear spring water. When we'd take a break, we'd be a-standing around the spring; and I, Ben, and Pa would all get to talking about the war and all. We were missing out on this once-in-a-lifetime, greatest adventure. But Pa said that war wasn't all that glorious at all, that it was really a sad and awful thing to have to take a man's life so you could save your own and live by your own ideas instead of his. It was no small consideration to do that, he said. "But there does come a time in a man's life when he has to stand up for what he thinks is right, and if war is what it means, then that is what it takes."

He said he sure was proud of Will, Samuel, and Levi and what they were doing, but he sure did miss them around the farm. "I guess we all feel that way," said Ben. "But you know, Pa, we want to do something too. Me and Stevie been talking about all this, and you know the war is going to be over so soon, and we won't even be able to say we had a part in it all. And, Pa, we're ready. We're ready to go and fight too, Pa."

Pa just took another slow sip of the cool spring water as he thought real hard. You could always tell when Pa was a-thinking real hard 'cause he didn't say a thing; he just looked like he was so calm or something. Pa kinda reminded me of our horse when he was getting shod. He just stood there at attention with all his power and all his purpose, and he didn't even flinch a muscle while the blacksmith went to work on all four hooves. Pa was powerful and calm at the same time just like that. And you never knew just exactly what he was a-thinking.

Pa wanted to join the army too. We knew he did 'cause you could see it in his eyes. But we couldn't tell just exactly what he was planning to do about it all. We thought that maybe he would go off and join the army and have Ben and me stay home to look after Ma, Anna, and the farm. We were old enough to take care of things. Ben was sixteen already, just barely, and I was almost fifteen, shy by just a few days.

There are just some things a man has to do at the right time and in the right place. There was more than opportunity here; there was most certainly responsibility to fight for one's homeland. It would be a difficult decision for Pa, for he was torn between two worlds, that was for sure. Ma would accept his decision because she understood too deep down in her heart. Pa was a man's man, and he was too proud not to do his part, whatever that was to be.

One late morning, sometime after all the chores had been done, Pa came round the old barn with Chester, our horse, all saddled up and packed with what looked like camping gear. He called Ma out and asked for Anna, Ben, me to all gather round. He said it was time now, his time, and he was going to find Gen. Joseph Wheeler's cavalry and sign up for one year. Maybe it wouldn't be all that long even.

Pa took each one of us individually, and as he knelt down, he hugged and kissed Anna first and then stood and hugged me and then Ben. Then he walked over to Ma and embraced her like he might never see her again; he kissed her ever so gently, and then he turned around and got up on Chester. Chester was a big bay about sixteen hands high, which was a pretty big horse. He looked mighty good that morning, with Pa sitting up there so proud. With a quick throw of the reins, he and Chester turned and began to canter down the path to the gate. When they got to the gate, Pa and Chester turned, looked back for one last time, waved, turned again, and cantered on down the road till they were out of sight.

We would really miss Pa around the farm and sitting around the family fireplace, but this was how it must be, and everyone knew it and understood it except for Anna, who cried a lot at first. She was only twelve years old at the time, and she didn't quite make sense of it all. She didn't know that Pa had no choice but to take off for the war too.

Things around home got mighty quiet for a while, with Pa being gone as well as Will, Sam, and Levi. We kept waiting for some word, a letter or something; but for a good while, we never heard from any of them.

Then one Saturday we had to go up to Salt Springs. Ma wanted to get some yarn so she could make some sweaters for Pa and the boys; when we found out where they were, she could send them to 'em. While we were there, we checked down at the post office, and Judge Bowden said there were two letters for Ma that had just come in the other day, and he knew we'd be anxious to get them. As a matter of fact, he was about to have them run out to the farm if we didn't show up real soon.

Ma couldn't wait till we got home, so out on the front porch of the post office, she sat down on the steps with all of us gathered round her to see what the news was. She opened Pa's letter first.

Dearest Ginny, April 10, 1862

I wanted to write to you and let you know that I finally located General Wheeler's cavalry and got joined up over in Alabama. We were only in camp there for a few days when we got the orders to move out. And it seems we have been doing nothing but riding ever since then. My immediate commander, Major Harding, is a good man who has since been wounded.

Just a few days ago, we were in a major engagement at a place called Shiloh's Church. Some of the boys were calling it Pittsburg Landing, being there on the Tennessee River. There was some fierce fighting that went on, especially in a place some of the boys called the Hornet's Nest. I think the whole place turned to a hornet's nest before it was over. I don't know for sure if I killed anyone, but I'm pretty sure I must have. There was so much shooting going on all over the place it was really scary. Our main mission was to protect the railroad supply lines around Corinth, Mississippi, and to keep them free from the Federals. We were constantly in and out of skirmish fights all up and down the lines. But I think we held them off like we were supposed to. It seemed like we whipped them good on the first day, but by the second day, the Federals seemed to get the upper hand, and we withdrew from the area. A lot of good boys on both sides went down in that awful fighting. This fellow right next to me took a miniball right in the head. I sure feel sorry for his family and all.

Tell the boys and Anna that Chester is still doing fine and hasn't taken any bullets or anything. He's okay and still riding strong.

I've got to go now as we are fixin' to move out soon. Tell all the children I love them and miss them very much. I think you can write to me, care of Nashville, Tennessee, as I think we are headed that way. Love to all.

Your Loving and Devoted Husband,

R. B. Jett

Ma looked up and off into space for a moment like she was lost to this world. Then all of a sudden, she quickly began to open the other letter she was holding in her trembling hands. And she began to read out loud.

March 15, 1862

Dear Ma and Pa and Family,

Hope everything at home is okay and that all are doing fine. We are all okay and doin' pretty good today. We are still in Virginia under the command of Gen. Joseph Johnston, and we have made camp near the Rappahannock River. It appears that we may encounter the enemy again soon, but we don't know when or where exactly, maybe down near Manassas Junction again, but we don't know.

Samuel and Levi send their love and ask that you all remember us in this terrible war. Fortunately, we are still in the same unit, being the First Georgia Volunteers Regiment. We're a strong regiment, and we have done good on the battlefield with only minor losses. We have been very lucky so far. Please pray for us that we will be safe and be able to come home soon. We are all looking forward to spring and some warmer weather as it has been a very cold winter in the camps and on the move all the time. I'll write again as soon as I can. Love to all.

> Your Loving and Devoted Sons,
>
> William, Samuel, and Levi

Ma looked up again with that starry look in her eyes. She had drifted off to that far-off place again and had to bring herself back to reality.

"Well," she said, "we'd best be off. We've got a lot to do. Let's get going." Ma was always like that; she wanted to be busy when things began to get on her mind. It was the only way she could handle it. She loved all of us kids and Pa, and she longed to have us all back together again. A mother's love has got to be the strongest love on this earth, I think.

Ma said that good news called for a celebration, so we could all have some peppermint from the Cowan's General Store. We did, and boy, did it taste good. We loved candy and didn't get it except on special occasions, and Ma thought that this was one of those times. As we all made our way back to the farm, we thought about the letters and talked about how it must be for Pa and the boys way off somewhere, where everything was new and exciting, and how awfully afraid they must be sometimes about the fighting but also how very brave they all were. We wished we were there to sort of just see them all and be with them. Perhaps they would be able to come home later in the summer, and we hoped and prayed that they would. That night at the supper table, we all said a special prayer of thanks to the good Lord for watching out for them and taking care of our family.

Spring Eternal

Soon the daffodils were blooming all around the farm, and there was the sweet smell of jasmine and dogwood. Even the forever reaching and clutching honeysuckle was blossoming, with its rich aroma cascading through the clear, clean spring air. The world was at peace once more for as far as we could see and smell.

Ma loved the springtime, and she said it was the time for renewal of all things. She would begin to plant seeds of flowers everywhere she could because she loved the flowers so. She said they were like little children except you got to see them grow up all at one time in a matter of days. Anna helped Ma with the flower planting mostly. She said it was fun playing in the dirt, digging and piling, fertilizing and burying little secrets of seeds all over the place. Nobody knew where they were except her, Ma, and the good Lord, who would look after them and bring them the angel water to quench their thirst.

Anna was a good child, a good little sister. "Somewhat precocious," Ma said, "always getting into things, but that's the way girls are." You would have thought that Anna would still have been a tomboy, growing up around all boys, but she wasn't much now. She was quite a little lady. Took more after Ma than any of us would have ever imagined. She almost always wore a plain and simple little dress that sometimes was made from sackcloth, like the flour sacks because they were the best, and Ma could sew anything she put her mind to. Made all of Anna's dresses and most of our clothes too. By age thirteen, just on April 28, Anna was turning into more than just a young girl. Something mysteriously strange was going on all over her body, and her long golden hair was looking unusually radiant in the morning sun as it glistened over her shoulder. When she went to the well to draw water, she no longer walked the same way, nor did she look just the same. Like the springtime, it seemed that she too was a pretty young flower soaking up the spring sunshine and sipping on the angel water. Her beautiful green eyes reflected the lush green countryside of north Georgia.

Anna had a beau from over a little pea patch farm near Powder Springs. She had met him at church sometime back. His name was Luther Gates. Luther was tall and lanky and a real good size for his age, which wasn't much more than Anna's. He had curly dark, almost black hair and was clean shaven 'cause I didn't think he could have grown a beard yet iffen he wanted to, not enough whiskers yet, or the cat kept licking them off. Luther was a handsome enough young man, pretty spit and polished when he called on Anna, even shined his shoes once. They'd mostly just sit around on the porch swing at night and talk about nothin'. But one thing he could do, though, and that was play banjo, and he would often bring it over in the evenings. Ma, Ben, and I loved to hear the banjo playing 'cause it was real different from the guitar that I played and Ben's harmonica. When we'd all get together, we could really make the dogs howl. We'd always start off by playing "Camptown Races," and we nearly always finished up with a rip-roaring rendition of "Dixie." Then we'd play "Dixie" real slow and reverent at the very end like it was some kind of musical prayer for the boys off in the war. It'd give you goose bumps every time, especially when Ben would come in with his moaning and whining harmonica. Then we'd just sit around real quiet until somebody jumped up and said something.

It was too early for watermelon yet, but Ma liked to make what we all called "dancing custard," a kind of milky, starchy, sweet stuff she'd cook down from white rice with fresh eggs and finally bake in the oven skillet. After that, it would have to cool down for a long time down in the spring cellar house. When it was real cool, it would be cut up like pie and served with coffee or lemonade, depending on whether it was daytime or nighttime. We called it "dancing custard" 'cause it was so good that it always made you want to dance. Ma was a great cook and could do almost something with anything. She could make a possum dinner look like it was fit for a Tahitian king, just like in our schoolbook. One time she fixed this possum up and brought it out to the table all on fire, but when the fire went out, the possum wasn't burnt at all. It was as good as it ever was, which was pretty good considering that it was possum, not exactly our favorite critter for dinner. But in those days, you got by on whatever you could.

The best thing that Ma ever fixed, of course, was her Sunday go-to meeting day, young Springer, Southern fried chicken. It'd pretty near melt in your mouth before you could eat it. It was so good. Next Sunday, Luther Gates was supposed to come over to eat dinner with Anna, so we'd be bound to have fried chicken then.

Well, Luther Gates did come over that next Sunday, and we did have that delicious fried chicken. I got a leg and two thighs 'cause those are my favorite pieces, as well as mashed potatoes and gravy, green beans fresh out of the garden, and Ma's hot butter biscuits covered with sweet golden honey. Not bad eating for a poor country boy.

At dinner, Luther made a startling announcement. He said that he was going with his uncle John Henry on Monday to join up with the Confederate army. We all just kinda dropped our mouths open for a minute. When the silence broke, Anna jumped up from the table a-crying and ran outside on the porch. I guess she just couldn't take someone else she loved taking off to war and leaving her here all alone. Took her a good while to settle down actually. It interrupted our dinner some but didn't stop Ben and me from getting another biscuit and some more honey. After all, we wished we were going too. This whole war was going to be over, and we weren't even going to get to see any of it.

Luther loved Anna, and Anna loved Luther. He said that, when he came back, he wanted to ask her hand in marriage and that they would settle down on a little piece of land his father had set aside for him over on Noses Creek. "This is a tough time," he said. "And a man has to do what a man has to do." Just what did a man have to do, I wondered, to show that he was a man and not a "scared chicken shit" as some of the boys called some of the fellows? It was a man's world, and soon we'd all have to show what we was made of, tough iron like two-edged steel or just saltwater taffy.

I reckon, on Monday morning, Luther and his uncle John Henry went on over to Powder Springs and got signed up with some of the Powder Springs boys. There were several outfits that had been formed from that area. I was not sure if they were able to join up with some of them or in some other regiment. By now, you never knew 'cause a lot of the regiments were already looking for replacements.

Luther would do well, though, for he was an easygoing sort of guy who could get along with just about anybody. Now his uncle John Henry was sort of rough and tough and didn't make friends real easy, but he was a nice enough fellow. John Henry was big and burly, weighed about 225 pounds, and had a nice full beard and mustache. I knew him from holidays mostly, when some of the townspeople would get together for celebrations. Also, he was a pretty good friend of Pa and helped out around the farm once in a great while, like when we were doing some stump blowing with black powder down on the bottom land near Gothards Creek. John Henry would make a fine-looking soldier in uniform if they could find one big enough for him. Old Luther would look okay too, but they could probably put the whole of him down one pant leg; he was so skinny and lean.

That Monday morning was a hard time as we thought about Luther and his uncle John Henry going off to war. Lots of boys had gone from around home already, and more and more were leaving every day. Wasn't no end to it, it seemed. We heard that some of the armies were already way up into the thousands of men. That was hard to imagine when you never saw more than a handful of people at a time anyway. One time I saw about 350 people at a Fourth of July parade in Carrollton, Georgia, and I thought that was all the people in the world. In terms of fighting side by side along with a thousand men and going up against another thousand men on the other side, now that was awesome. Somehow I envied Luther and John Henry.

The days went on by slowly for a while. With little word from the front and not seeing too many folks anyway kept us a bit isolated down on the farm. Every day we'd be hoping for a letter or some word about Pa, Will, Samuel, and Levi. And now we were listening out for Luther and John Henry.

Summer came on, and the roads began to get dusty from the lack of spring rains. June was always such a hot month anyway, but this year, it seemed a little hotter a mite earlier. The crops really needed more rain. Everything in the garden was a-starting to wilt down a little. Unless we got some rain soon, the garden and crops weren't going to do very well. But like Ma said, "Some things you just can't do anything about, so you have to go on and accept them." Lack of rain, I guess, fell into that category.

Tomorrow would be boring again, I was afraid, and I didn't really expect anything out of the usual to happen. Just another quiet, dry, hot day on the farm. Maybe Ben and I would go swimming down at the pond or on Sweetwater Creek at our old swimming hole. Yeah, that was what we'd do—go down to the old swimming hole and cool off.

The next day, that was exactly what we did. Anna stayed near the house with Ma 'cause she wasn't as crazy about swimming as we were. It was Saturday anyway, and we always took most of Saturday off from work when we could, at least half a day in the afternoon, but this day, we took off early for the creek, about midmorning. You'd got to give the sun time to get up over the trees so as to dry you off when you got out of the water. I never did like to swim in the shade. Just wasn't right. Didn't feel right.

We had an old rope swing tied way up in a tree on the bank and had even fixed a sort of platform up on the big limb. We would climb up there and jump, swinging way out over the creek, and then drop loose. We thought this was the most exciting thing in the world to do. Most of the time, the younger kids wouldn't climb up in the tree because it was too high. You had to be pretty brave to take such a big chance as that.

Splashing and jumping and diving, we played nearly all morning and into the early afternoon. There was half a dozen or more of us who had gathered at the creek that day from the surrounding farms. Some of the kids, like Ben and me, had brought some biscuits, sausages, and the like from home. Everybody got kinda dried off, and we found us a cool, dry place up under the trees to have our lunch. Ben and I were the oldest boys there, and then there was Ty and Lonnie, about twelve and thirteen, from the Fraiser farm. And there were their two kid sisters, Joyce and Marilyn, who were identical twins, about ten years old. No skinny-dipping today, not with girls. So we left on our britches. And then there was Scott and Jeff Perryrnan, two brothers from the Perryman farm who were about nine and ten, respectively. We had all become good friends over the years and had been swimming in this old swimming hole together for a long time. While we were eating our lunches and resting on the bank under the cool shade trees, we began to talk about the war up north in Virginia and up in Tennessee. It all seemed like a long ways off for us all on that warm summer day. Nearly all of us had elder brothers, fathers, and uncles who had gone off to fight in the Confederate army. Scott and Jeff's father had somehow got caught up in the Confederate navy and had gotten assigned to some ship they called the *Alabama*. They said from the few letters they had received that their pa was doing real good and that they had already fought and sunk a number of other ships up and down the coast. The Fraiser kids said their pa was in the artillery and had command of four big cannons in the Twelfth Georgia Light Artillery. He said in a letter that, when the war was over, he was going to bring home each one of them their very own cannonball as a keepsake.

Ben and I told them about our pa and how he was in the cavalry with our horse, Chester, and how they had fought at Shiloh Church and all. And we told them about our brothers, Will, Samuel, and Levi, who had been at the Battle of Bull Run near Washington, and how later they had been in some other battles up in Maryland and Virginia. They said they had even been as far up as West Virginia with the First Georgia Volunteers Regiment.

We were all bragging, of course, about who was the best and who had done the most. Then too we were awfully proud of our families and the contributions they were making to this war. To us, it was all like a game of checkers.

Too Close to Home

That summer, we did learn of some very exciting news that had taken place practically right under our noses. Why, we had been invaded. The great state of Georgia had been invaded by Yankees–Yankee spies actually who had come down from up north to steal a railroad locomotive by the name of the *General*.

It had all taken place just about twenty-five miles north of our farm over at Big Shanty, Georgia. The train had been coming out of Marietta early that morning, and they had stopped over at the Lacy Hotel for their usual breakfast stop there at Big Shanty, just near Kennesaw Mountain. As a matter of fact, it was the next stop after Kennesaw Station.

While the engineer, fireman, conductor, and other passengers had gone in to eat breakfast, a guy by the name of Andrews and about twenty-one other men–spies––somehow took over the train and took off with it right up the tracks toward Chattanooga. "Unbelievable," everyone said. Their objective, it was said, was to destroy the key railroad bridges along the Northern rail line and to disrupt and cut off the Southern supply lines to the Confederates in Nashville. Also, such a raid was supposed to strike terror in the deep Southern heartland of Georgia as no enemy army had ventured into the South this deep. It was to show us just how vulnerable we were to the Yankee critters.

Their plan was carried out with great precision, at first, and things looked pretty good for the Yankee invaders. But they didn't count on a Mr. Fuller, the train conductor, who was determined to see that the general was caught up with. He and another man took off after them on foot until they found a pump car that they then took to chasing down the general. Steam locomotives were fast, but they still had to take on wood and water, and Mr. Fuller knew that, sooner or later, he'd be able to buy some time in the chase.

Somewhere on up the line, Mr. Fuller intercepted another locomotive named the *Texas*. It was heading south and had been pulled over on a sidetrack for the general to pass going north. Mr. Fuller commandeered the *Texas* and, going backward as fast as he could, pursued the general. It must have been one of the most exciting chases that ever took place, what with all the smoke billowing from the grinding and chugging locomotives a-chasing each other up the long grade to Kingston and Dalton.

Those Andrews's raiders, as they was later called, must have tried every trick in the book to stop Mr. Fuller and the *Texas* from catching up with them. The chase was so close that Andrews didn't have time to tear up nothin' along the way. In the meantime, Mr. Fuller had been able to get off a telegram to Dalton before the lines up there were cut, telling them that the *General* had been stolen and to intercept them at all cost.

It wasn't too long until the Confederate cavalry was closing in on the general. They had already tried setting some of the cars on fire, blocking the *Texas*, and trying to wreck it. Didn't work, though, and by the time the Confederate cavalry caught them, there was a shootout, and all the Yankee spies took off in different directions, trying to get away.

Nearly every one of them was captured eventually, along with Mr. Andrews, who was actually a civilian. They were all tried in a military court over in Atlanta and found guilty of treason and being spies. Except for some who later escaped, they were all hanged, including Andrews, down at the old jailhouse in Atlanta, and they were buried in Oakland Cemetery.

This was big news happening right here at home, practically within just a few miles of our home. It really made you stop and think about how close things were beginning to get, and it made you wonder if this would be about the end of it or if this would just be the beginning of a larger Yankee invasion.

Most people said the South would never be invaded by the Yankees, that they would never get this far down. There were a lot of ground and a lot of rebel soldiers between here and up north. But the Yankees did seem to be inching down the map a good bit. As long as they didn't come any farther, maybe we'd be all right. Nothing can be as unsettling as a fox in the henhouse. Out in the open and on ground of our choosing, that was the way you wanted to fight a war. Gen. Stonewall Jackson, 1 think, had once said something like that up in Virginia or somewhere.

Now there were a soldier and a general of men. They said at the Battle of Bull Run, "There stands Jackson and his men like a stone wall." Ever since then, the nickname just stuck like honey to a biscuit. They said he was a very religious man who often called on the Almighty and that he sorta kept to himself a lot. All the men didn't necessarily like him that much except they had a profound respect for him as a military leader, and they would follow him anywhere and anytime. We needed more leaders like old Stonewall.

The Confederate army, about this time, was headed up by a general by the name of Albert Sidney Johnston, whom Pres. Jefferson Davis had a great deal of confidence in. He was an aggressive leader and fighter and was making good progress with the war when he was wounded at the Battle of Shiloh Church. Quite a way to end a long and illustrious military career, which had begun back in the Indian wars and the war for the then republic of Texas before it became a state. The loss of General Johnston was a serious loss for the Confederacy and would be felt for some time.

Johnston's replacement was a man by the name of Robert E. Lee. Lee was a simple man from Virginia, an educator, a West Point graduate, and an officer in the United States Army at the outbreak of the war. As a matter of fact, before he resigned his position, he was personally offered the job of being commander of the United States Army, but he declined when his beloved state of Virginia seceded from the Union. Fortunately, we got him on our side. Gen. Robert E. Lee would prove to be a real godsend to all our boys in gray.

The war was getting weary now. A good while had passed since Will, Samuel, and Levi had first joined up and then Pa. The glory was fleeting very fast as news of the dead and wounded continued to come in from points all over the South and North. God must be watching over Pa and the boys and protecting them from harm.

Almost two years had passed now, and it all seemed like an eternity. Word from Pa and the boys had been sparse, and most of the news we got was from the newspapers and word of mouth. What would become of it all? Indeed, what would become of all of us?

Loom and Gloom

Nowhere was the war more devastating than on the people staying back home, left back home to survive on whatever remained available and with whoever was still there–the young, the old, the feeble, the disabled, women, and girls of every age and description. Ma and Anna were no exceptions. They were certainly caught up in between things, between family. Some had gone off to war, some still here to look after. Luther Gates, Anna's sweetheart, had gone to war, and she longed for him and worried for his safety. Ma worried continuously about Pa and the boys and prayed for them every morning and every night.

One evening after supper, Ma gathered us all around the table and cut us an extra piece of apple pie each, poured some more coffee, and said that she wanted to talk to us.

Ma said, "Boys, I have an announcement to make concerning our future here and what I think our contribution should be to help end this terrible war. Anna and I have been talking. We've been talking seriously about the possibility of Anna and me putting in an application down at the New Manchester Mill. For almost two years now, the mill has been making Confederate uniforms for our armies, and we know we can't shoot a gun, but we can sew and do something for our men here at home. Now I don't know if they can use us right now, but I heard that they were a little short on help because of the war and all and that they could probably use some extra hands. My plans would be for me and Anna to walk back and forth to the mill at first, and if it got to be too much, we'd see if we could get a room or something down at New Manchester. It's about six miles here from the farm, and it wouldn't be too far, but we'll just have to see. It would be you boys' responsibility to keep and maintain the farm and home here as best you can. You're old enough now, and I think I can depend on you for that much. Now what do you think, boys?"

For the longest time, there was nothing but silence. Neither Ben nor I was able to say a word. We were really dumbfounded. Could this be our ma and younger sister saying all this and planning to do what we thought unthinkable? And here we were, almost two grown men, doing nothing ourselves to perpetuate this national adventure, while the women of our family were fixin' to take off like they was soldiers themselves or something–and leave us here? I didn't think so.

Ben spoke up first and said, "Ma, I guess you have to do what you think is the right thing to do. That's the way you have always taught us, and I know you have to follow your heart. And it's probably better that Anna go with you and you two stick together. Stevie and me will take care of the farm for right now until we can get signed up in the army."

"No," Ma said emphatically. "I can't have more of my boys and family committed to this war. Somebody has got to stay here and take care of our home. I just can't risk you and Stevie a-taking off to join the army too. I won't have it, and you'll not do it except over my dead body, and that's final."

"But, Ma," Ben said, "I'm seventeen years old. In another year, I can be conscripted anyway, and Stevie's sixteen almost."

"Yeah, Ma," I interjected, "we want to fight too. We want to be soldiers."

"I'll not hear of it, not another word," Ma said. "Your job, for now, is to stay here and take care of this farm. Is that clearly understood by both of you?"

We didn't say nothin'. We just sat there like two bumps on a log–a log that had just been whacked upside the head with a mighty blow from a sharp ax. We respected our ma a lot. No, we reverenced our ma almost with the holiness that only the good Lord Himself was really due. If Ma said we would stay put, then we guessed we would stay put, at least for a little while. We would just have to see. Yeah, we would just have to wait and see. It was only a matter of time, and we all knew it. Things would never be like they was before. Our family would never be back all together again. Things would be different, very different. They had to be. They would be.

Two days later, Ben and I walked Ma and Anna down to the New Manchester Manufacturing Mill, taking with them a few things so that they could stay if somewhere was available.

The day was fair and clear when we started out. But by the time we traversed the six miles or so, it had clouded up pretty bad. As a matter of fact, some thunderheads were rolling in, and the sky was turning an ominous gray like the uniforms our brothers and Pa were wearing, like the gray yarn and wool and cotton cloth that Ma and Anna would soon be making into Confederate uniforms. The trees hung low over the winding road down and over Beaver Run Creek as we neared the destination.

It wasn't long before we came on the upper waters of Sweetwater Creek, the delivery system for tons of power captured by the fall of what everybody called the factory shoals. Nearly a fifty-foot drop in three hundred yards made for a wonderful setup for a moderately long mill run. It emptied through the water gate archway onto a massive fifty-thousand-pound undershot waterwheel. It was most impressive, as was the mass of the five stories above, reaching up out of the ground and climbing almost up to heaven itself. It was truly an awesome sight to see, something so massive and industrial buried away in the woodland on a creek side fifteen miles from Atlanta. People said it was the tallest building in the whole state of Georgia. I knew that I had never seen any buildings this high in Atlanta before or anywhere else. It was truly magnificent, with its copper shield roof gleaming like a gold ring even under the overcast sky.

As we neared the great factory, we began to pass several people coming and going on various errands and such. One kind lady who was walking by herself stopped for a minute and introduced herself as Mary Ferguson, wife of Angus Ferguson, who had the gristmill just up the stream a ways. She was very nice and said she had been down to the big mill to visit her sister, Martha, who helped in the company store. Mrs. Ferguson invited us all down to her husband's mill for dinner that evening if we could as they had built them a little house up near the mill, and she longed for some women company to talk with. Ma told her how much we appreciated the invitation and that we would be more than happy to oblige. She passed on down the little winding road along the creek until she was out of sight in the bend of trees. The water rushed down the mill race as we raced along with it, ever closer to the industrial behemoth that sucked up the water like a giant sloth and spat it out just as fast. The roar of the turning waterwheel and the massive cranking and creaking of leather belts, drives, and textile machinery brought new life to the otherwise barren sounds of the forest. And people too, not quite as noisy, were muttering around like ants clambering in and out of the massive man-made anthill of brick and mortar.

It was not only a factory but also a true factory town, with houses of various types scattered over the surrounding hillsides and a store or two thrown in to round out its mysterious ambiance. You couldn't see it all at one time because of the density of the forest. Massive trees hung low over the entire specter of the town, like they was trying to hide it all in a green foliage camouflage from the Yankee army and, indeed, from all prying eyes. As we approached this land of mystery and intrigue, we made our way up to what was obviously the company store. Once inside, our eyes adjusted to the dim light, and we could see an older, middle-aged woman behind the counter putting something into a round tin.

"Hello," she said rather briskly as we stood there, trying to take it all in and letting our eyes further adjust to the darkness of the interior.

New Manchester

"Can I help you?" she said.

"Yes," said Ma. "My daughter and I are looking to make application to the mill for work."

"Aha," said the lady. "Well, what you'll have to do is go over to Mr. Cranbell's office over at the mill itself. It's on the second floor, just up the stairs over there, and he will be able to help you. I hear they are looking for a few replacement workers, especially since the war has taken a number of our able-bodied men."

"By the way," she said, "I'm Martha Jenkins, and you are?"

"Virginia Jett," my ma said. "But my friends call me Ginny, and this is my daughter, Anna, and my sons Ben and Steve." Ma almost never introduced me as Stevie out in public anymore because she knew it sort of embarrassed me. She saved that for a sort of personal endearment now.

"Pleased to meet you," said Mrs. Jenkins.

"Yes, I think we met your sister, Mary Ferguson, on the road down to the mill here. She has been so kind as to invite us to dinner this evening."

"That's wonderful," Mrs. Jenkins said. "Maybe I'll see you at dinner. I nearly always eat with my sister now as my husband, Mr. Jenkins, is off fighting in the war–you know, like nearly every other man around here."

"Well, that would certainly be nice to see you this evening, Mrs. Jenkins. We shall look forward to it."

"Oh, call me Martha, please. All my friends do, lady friends, that is," she said with a sort of smirk and tickle.

"Okay, Martha," Ma said. "Well, we'll see you this evening, and thank you very much for your kind assistance." And with that, Mrs. Jenkins nodded to the side and smiled as we turned and walked out the door, back into daylight once more.

Just across the road and up the way a bit was the large factory with its staircase built onto the side. We'd have to enter there through this rather heavy door and ascend to the second floor to get to Mr. Cranbell's office.

The heavy door swung almost effortlessly as though it was used a hundred times a day, and probably, it was. The stairway was well lit from the natural light outside because of the windows all around it on three sides. As we began to climb the stairs, the old boards of the stair–worn smooth with use and oiled for preservation–creaked softly and vainly as we marched upward. Sunlight, now breaking through the clouds, broke also through the windows of the thick walls and cast a beautiful warm glow across the wooden floor of the first landing as we turned to the next flight of steps. Upon reaching the second floor, we entered the closed door to the main part of the factory; and like a sudden rush of water, the noise from the working machinery suddenly gushed over us and inundated us with the magical sounds of massive machinery operating at full force and speed. It was a sound and sight like none we had ever seen or heard before in any of our lives. We were truly amazed and excited.

A few steps, and we saw the sign for the superintendent's office, and Ma proceeded to knock on the door. "Come in. The door is open," an older male voice hurled from the other side.

"What can I do for you?" said the short robust figure of a man in his middle fifties.

"Are you Mr. Cranbell?" said Ma.

"Why, yes, I am, ma'am. Can I help you?"

"Mr. Cranbell, my name is Virginia Jett, and this is my daughter, Anna, and these are my two sons Ben and Steve." Everyone nodded and greeted one another with a polite smile but without words. Ma was the spokesperson here, and she would do all the talking.

"Mr. Cranbell, we have come to make application here at the factory, that is, for me and my daughter, Anna. My sons are going to return to our farm and care for it during our absence and in the absence of their pa and three brothers, who are all off fighting for the Confederacy."

"Ooooh, good, Mrs. Jett, that's wonderful, very commendable. We need every God-fearing man who can bear a weapon right now." He took a big sigh, like he just released an anxiety-laden thought of tension, like maybe we were going to win the war 'cause our family was making such a monumental contribution to the war effort.

"We want to help make uniforms here at the mill for our boys. We're not exactly skilled in textile manufacturing, but we can both sew really good, and we know how to use a loom. And we're willing to learn anything we need to learn to do the job."

"Well, you know, we don't pay much, can't. Just isn't in the budget, but we do pay almost a fair wage, a dollar a day for you and the missus each, and you'll have to find your own room and board. Yes, I could use two good women in the loom room and the button room. Can you start right away, say, like, day after tomorrow? That'll be on Wednesday morning at eight o'clock."

"Yes, sir," said Ma. "We'll be here."

"You can fill out your paperwork then, Mrs. Jett, for you and your daughter, Anna," said Mr. Cranbell.

"Thank you very much, Mr. Cranbell. We look forward to seeing you then, sir," said Ma.

Anna sort of curtsied, and Ben and I shook Mr. Cranbell's hand to show our gratitude as well.

As we left the factory and embarked back into the sunlight, which was now shining brightly in the midafternoon, we decided to look around the town a little and see what was all there.

It was a peaceful town of about three hundred people or thereabouts, with a good number of homes of all sizes and descriptions scattered over the surrounding hillsides. But mostly, the structures were built up on a big hill just above the factory. The streets were little more than wide enough for the passage of two wagons abreast and were relatively unimproved, all dirt and all meandering, like here and there, up and down and around the hills and hollows around the mill. All were somewhat like a bunch of Indians hunkered down around a massive stone pot from which brewed a mysterious life-sustaining concoction of porridge.

That evening, we did have our supper with Mr. and Mrs. Ferguson. Mary and her husband, Angus, were two of the nicest people you would ever want to meet. And as she had said, Mary's sister—Martha Jenkins from the company store—was there as well.

We had a wonderful supper of beans and ham, sweet potatoes, grits, and crisp corn bread from freshly ground cornmeal, all dripping in hot, melting butter with all the fresh milk we could drink. It was out of this world. For dessert, Mrs. Ferguson served little tea cakes called funnels or something, with white sugar sprinkled all over the top and strawberry preserves on top. Mmm, mmm. We were in high cotton as they'd say.

During the meal, there was a lot of talk going on about nearly everything you can imagine, from the war to new buttons they got in down at the mill, bright, shiny brass buttons with the Georgia State seal on them. Ma and Anna would probably be the ones to start sewing them onto the Confederate uniforms as they had to be sewn on by hand and not by machine.

Everyone was concerned about the progress of the war. Mr. and Mrs. Ferguson had two sons who were off fighting in the war, who last time they wrote were somewheres up in Maryland, according to their letters, a place called Antietam Creek in Sharpsburg, Maryland. Her boys were under the command of a General Longstreet. Mr. Ferguson said that they had been defending some kind of stone bridge over the creek and held the Yankees off forever almost, when finally the lines broke, and they lost the bridge. Eventually, General Lee was forced to retreat over the Potomac River into Virginia. According to Mr. Ferguson and the information he had picked up, this movement into Maryland had been a real effort by General Lee to gain Maryland recruits, pick up the European recognition, and force the North to sue for some kind of peace settlement. But it just didn't quite work out that way. The newspapers said, a few days after the Battle of Sharpsburg, that President Lincoln had issued an emancipation of the slaves in all the slaveholding states.

According to the Fergusons, this was not going to go over well with our boys, and it would just make them more determined to fight. But then on the other hand, it might make the Northern soldiers more determined as now they had more to fight for. Wouldn't hurt them anyway.

Tom and Harry, the two Ferguson boys, had also fought in some other battles called Gaines's Mill and again at Manassas Junction.

Ma said that Will, Samuel, and Levi had mentioned some of those names in one or two of their letters. As far as we all knew, all the boys were all right and had not been wounded or killed in any of the action.

Mr. and Mrs. Ferguson said they heard a lot of news, being there around the gristmill they operated on the upper banks of the Sweetwater Creek, just about a mile above the factory at New Manchester. They got the news from just about all the surrounding farms as the families came in from time to time to get corn and wheat ground into flour and cornmeal. Nearly everybody in the county had at least one or more family members off fighting in the war. And they knew and saw some of the other miller families from time to time from Maroney's, Alexander's, and Perkinson's. News traveled faster by mouth than it did in the newspapers. By the time something got reported and the papers got out into circulation and reached us, folks had already heard about most things, which were now in print.

At the supper table, Anna had told Martha Jenkins and Mr. and Mrs. Ferguson how her beau, Luther Gates, was joined up too and that she had received two letters from him. He too was somewhere up there in the Maryland and Virginia area, and he said that he had gotten himself wounded in the leg from a well-placed bullet, but it wasn't real bad, and he was going to be able to save his leg. Thank god. She told them how she worried about Luther day and night.

After supper, Mrs. Ferguson said we could all stay over at their place that night if we didn't mind, with some of us sleeping in the loft, in the barn, or on the floor, but we'd do something. So we all figured how and where we were going to bed down for the night.

Martha Jenkins, during supper, had already invited Ma and Anna to stay with her at her nearly empty house down at New Manchester since they would be working at the factory and had to have somewhere to live. She said she would really enjoy having the extra company, and it would be good for all of 'em. So that was settled, and all would be taken care of.

The next morning after a hearty breakfast, Ma and Anna left with Mrs. Jenkins to go on back down to New Manchester, and Ben and I headed out for home. We had some chores to catch up on and a lot of thinking to do as we pondered our part in this great undertaking. Somewhere sometime, there must be a special place for us in all this adventure. We weren't about to live out our lives on the sidelines while the rest of the world just went a-flying by like great flocks of Canadian geese. This time of year, they were heading south, but we knew for us we'd be a heading north. We would bide our time for a few months on the farm and get everything in the best order we could, and then around Christmastime, we would tell Ma and Anna. We would have to be as strong willed as Ma, or she wouldn't let us get away with it. It wasn't going to be so easy, not with nearly all the family already gone. On the other hand, maybe she would understand and give us her blessing, and we really did need that to take with us. It would be a hard long road ahead.

Christmas at New Manchester

December 25, 1862, was a very special time in my life down in Georgia. It would be the last time, for a long while, that I would see my mother and sister, Anna.

Ben and I had been talking a lot, and we had decided to join up in the army ourselves right after Christmas. This would be our last family reunion for some time to come.

We had all been invited to come down to Mrs. Jenkins's house at New Manchester for Christmas so we could all be together, and Martha, as we called her, had invited Mary and Angus down to have Christmas dinner. It would be good to see them again and to share news, conversation, and the joyous celebration of the birth of Jesus, our Lord and Savior. We didn't have much to give, but Ben and I had been doing some special wood carvings to give as gifts, and we were anxious to share these with our family and new friends.

As we made our way east down toward New Manchester, a light snow began to fall early that Christmas morning. Maybe we'd have a white Christmas this year, almost never did 'cause the snow just didn't usually come until later in the winter. But who knew? Maybe it would come early this year. As we approached the large factory mill, we could see the warm gray smoke of celebration from around fire hearths softly rising into the layered sky blanketing the cozy woodland.

From nearly every home, Christmas smoke billowed like pipe smoke, heralding the beginning of something good and wonderful. Although the factory was operating on a half shift this day, the air of activity was everywhere. People were bustling up and down the small streets, going here and there, and there was definitely the excitement of a holiday permeating the cool north Georgia countryside.

The company store, where Martha worked, was shut and locked up for the day as we passed by and noticed the big green wreath made from pine and cedar boughs gracing its door. On it was a big red ribbon and bow decorating the fresh evergreen. It was our first real sign of Christmas.

Making our way on up the hill and around the curve toward the summit, we noticed a fair amount of commotion going on. The mill factory itself hummed away with the bumping, grinding, muffled sound of big machinery, which ran now day and night except for very rare occasions when there would be a break in the supply of materials coming out of Atlanta or from Alabama.

The house that Martha lived in was an unpretentious two-story boxed dwelling built like a square with a little front porch and a ridged, gabled roof with a chimney in the middle. It too was pushing out gray smoke interrupted with burning cinders, a sure sign that someone had just poked up the fire. The house was a clapboard siding and had never been painted. As a matter of fact, most all the houses and buildings had not been painted but had conditioned themselves under the natural weathering of the elements to soft gray and earth tones of color. The chimneys were made from bricks, a rich red color from the natural red Georgia clay, fired only a few miles away at the brickyard at Salt Springs, which had supplied most of the building brick for the factory itself. Between the colors of it all, the surrounding evergreen trees, good old Georgia pines and cedars, and the freshly fallen snow created a sort of surreal appearance, like one might see in some storybook. The white stuff continued for quite a while, but it would never accumulate enough for this Christmas to be considered really white.

Ben knocked on the door with his free hand, and in just a minute, the gate to heaven swung open. Inside, we were warmly greeted by Angus first and then Mary, his wife; and as we took off our overcoats and hats, Anna and Ma came bursting in from the kitchen into the cozy warm receiving room, where a blazing, warm, hot yellow fire created an ambiance of warmth and safety. After warm hugs and kisses and all that good stuff, Angus came back in with a glass of wine for each of us. Now we didn't drink per se, but Pa always said, and Ma did too, that a glass or two of libation was acceptable at special times like holidays and such. So we accepted with profound gratitude. After everyone was served with their own glasses, Angus said that he wanted to make a toast.

"To the boys in gray, may they weather the storms and survive the fray, come home in victory, and be safe today!"

"Hear, hear!" Everyone joined in the sentiment. We had a fine meal, a real king's treat, that day. We were indeed fortunate to have so many good cooks to spoil us men. We especially enjoyed the rich company and conversation, the fellowship of being with others who cared about you and who you cared about with all your heart. It was a happy, wonderful, and joyous occasion that day at New Manchester in the home of Martha Jenkins.

The afternoon lingered on until dong-dong-dong-dong went the large bell from the factory belfry, signaling the four o'clock hour and the changing of shifts, one shift off and another one on. The war effort had to go on except, this day, Ma and Anna wouldn't have to go to work as they were on the half shift that was off for Christmas. Normally, they would go on at four and work till midnight, when the graveyard shift came on. It wasn't uncommon at all for many of the workers to have to work double shifts. This day, this hour, we would have the rare leisure of family being together, and we would cherish the opportunity to bask in the love of family and friends.

After a while, it was time–time we knew to tell Ma and Anna, Angus and Mary, and Martha what our big decision was. Ben, being the oldest, delivered the foreboding news, and I reiterated nearly every word soas to give greater confirmation and affirmation of our decision. I guess I sounded like some Little Sir Echo as we carefully made out our case for such an important decision.

At first, there was nothing but silence and then some crying by Anna and Martha. Angus just looked up and across at Ma for some sign of acceptance, and Mary looked too with some kind of face like, *Well, what can we all do?*

Ma didn't say anything. She just stood up, turned and left the room, and went back into the kitchen, raising her hand as she went, as she often did, as a sign not to bother her for a moment till she could regain her composure. The rest of us just sat there in the parlor for what seemed like an eternity, until Angus said in his characteristic Irish drawl, "Well, boys, I, for one, am proud of you. You'll both make fine soldiers. Look out for Tom and Harry, will ya?"

About that time, Ma reentered the room; and with her arms crossed, she stood before us and said, "Ben and Stevie, as hard as it is for a mother to let go of her babies, you have my blessings." And she threw open her arms as a signal for us to draw near to her loving arms so she could grasp hold of the things she loved just one more time to let us know just how very, very much we meant to her. And as we hugged our mother, Anna came up and joined in on the hugging and kissing, and then Mary and Martha had to join in as well. All the while, Angus stood close by but maintained a manly distance until he too broke down and had to give us a proper Uncle Angus hug himself.

"For the luck of the Irish," he said. By this time, we were all shedding a few tears. We all understood the gravity of the situation, but we each knew in our hearts that there was no other way.

Ben and I left Martha's house that day knowing that we had made a man's decision, and now it was up to us to be the man we each thought we were. We knew that we were young, but we could hunt and shoot with the best of them, and in our hearts and minds, we knew we'd be good soldiers for the Confederate army.

Off to War

Ben and I secured the farm the best we could. No one would be around to take care of the animals, so we turned the cows and hogs out to forage as well as the chickens. The cats and dogs would be on their own too, but they had long ago learned how to forage off the land and around the farm. They would be all right. At least they would survive somehow.

In getting our things together, we figured we'd better travel light but take whatever we could to be as self-sufficient as possible. So we gathered up some blankets and various gear, like the old wooden canteens and our cartridge boxes we had made ourselves in anticipation of becoming soldiers. Ben had a revolver he had acquired through trading and an old squirrel flintlock, and we both had a few knives of various descriptions. Then it was time to take down Grandpa's old shotgun, which was now mine. Since giving it to me, my pa had been sure to leave it at home for some home protection and to get wild game with. Now it would become my main line of defense or offense with some blue-bellied Yankee. Maybe the army would have some standard-issue rifles and equipment, but we didn't know, and it might be some time before we met up with the regular army.

Leaving the confines of our peaceful farm was a traumatic experience. Neither Ben nor I had ever left for such an extended purpose or indefinite time. As we looked back at the gate for one last look, we fought back the tears of sadness that we might never see our home again, but the excitement of adventure overcame our emotional farewell, and we moved on down the road toward a new world and a new beginning. Two days later, we were in Atlanta, Georgia, the big city. The day was New Year's Eve, December 31, 1862. It was an exciting time in an exciting place. The city was alive with activity, with wagons and horses and people going up and down every street in every direction. The air was clear and crisp with an overcast sky and just a hint of snow hangin' in the cool breeze.

Ben and I had a little money with us that we had brought from home, and we decided that today we would have a fine dinner in a fine Atlanta restaurant and that we would celebrate the eve of the New Year in style with the big-city folks.

That evening was pretty special as we sat down to dinner at about six o'clock in Herron's Restaurant, one of the finest in the city. We had a big order of special pot roast with candied yams, mashed potatoes, greens, corn, and cranberry sauce and all the hot butter biscuits we could eat. The young lady who waited on us was named Stephanie as she had introduced herself when we sat down. She was a tall, slender, and beautiful young girl of just about our age with long blond hair put up in a bun. She was wearing a calico dress of burgundy and white with some frilly lace, ribbons, and bows. She was a real pretty girl, and her manners were perfectly matched in every way. We told her we were off to join the Confederate army and that this was our going-away dinner, so we really wanted to do it up right. She was so excited about our adventure that she could hardly contain herself and said she would do everything she could to see that we had a good time and enjoyed ourselves every minute, and she did.

She kept our coffee hot and full and made sure we had anything and everything that we could possibly want. And for dessert, she even served us seconds on apple pie.

During the meal, Stephanie said that, later that evening, there was to be a New Year's Eve party at her father's home, and she wanted us to be invited if we could come.

We told her we'd love to come, and she gave us the address at 286 Peachtree Street. She said it was a big, two-story Victorian house at the corner of Marshall and Peachtree, and we couldn't miss it. There would be lots of people there from all over, and we should have a very good time.

We were thrilled to have somewhere to go for New Year's Eve, and to have met such a nice girl as Stephanie was a real bonus. Who could know what new doors this evening's adventure would open for two country boys like us?

That night, we arrived cautiously, not knowing really what to expect or how we might be received by almost total strangers, except for Stephanie, that is.

The house was easy to find. It was probably the largest house anywhere around the area, although there was a number of fine large homes, the likes of which Ben and I had only seen from time to time. We had certainly never been in one like this before.

We made our way up the laid brick walkway under the cover of a light snow flurry. The wind was blowing now and rather cold, but the lights in the house made it look warm and inviting. And we could hear the merriment of people's voices and music emanating from within.

We ascended a few steps, walked across the wide veranda porch, and boldly knocked on the front door. Within seconds, the door was opened by a black man servant, a butler slave I was sure, who said ever so graciously, "Yesss, sirrr. Won't you come in please, sirs."

"Yes, thank you. We are here to call on Miss Stephanie by her invitation."

"Yesss, sirrrs. I will fetch her for you, gentlemen. Please be seated here in the hallway."

In just a few moments, the Negro man returned, followed by the most beautiful young lady in all Atlanta, indeed Georgia itself.

"Hellooo, hellooo, how are you?" Stephanie said. "Did you have any trouble at all finding our home? I'm so happy you could make it. Do come in."

And before we could do very much more than just gasp, she was leading us away into the inner sanctum of the festivities.

"Thank you, John," she said to the butler as she took Ben by the right arm with her left and lifting her skirt with her right hand; we made our way down the grand hallway to the ballroom.

You could have put our whole house in that ballroom; it was so big. The people were gathered all around in fine suits and dresses–real Southern ladies and fine, well-groomed Southern gentlemen. We felt more like rag muffins ourselves, but what we had on was the best we had, and it would have to do. At least we were clean and presentable.

As we entered the large doorway of the ballroom, Stephanie called out loud for everyone to hear. "Ladies and gentlemen," she said as she grabbed me with her right arm, "I'd like to introduce you all to two new friends of the Confederate army, Privates Benjamin and Steven Jett, off to the war effort. Everybody, make them feel welcome."

And with that, she turned and giggled with a girlish excitement like, *Wasn't it just all so grand?*

Ben said, "Well, Stephanie, we really haven't gotten signed up yet."

"But we're going to first thing tomorrow," I chirped in real quick.

"I know you will, boys, and I wanted to let everyone know what a fine thing you are doing, going off and fighting in the Confederate army and all. It's a fine and noble thing."

"Well, thank you, Stephanie. We think we'll make good soldiers," I said to give reassurance to the idea.

"Come, come. Have some punch and cake and cookies and meet some of my friends." And we followed Stephanie, halfway dragging us across the large ballroom toward the punch table as the festive patrons all applauded us like they were sending us off to the war right then. It was certainly a memorable occasion for both of us, one thing we would long remember in the days to come.

At the party that evening, we met nearly half the population of the city of Atlanta, I think. Never had either Ben or I met so many new people in one place. And they were all very nice to us, just as cordial as ice cream to apple pie. And we fairly melted in the warmth of their enfoldment.

Stephanie, we found, had three sisters, Heather, Holly, and Heidi. Heather was older by a few years and was married to a nice young man named Matt, whose family owned a local wholesale food brokerage business. It was from his family that Stephanie and Heather's father and mother bought most of the food for the fine restaurant they owned, Herron's. Holly and Heidi were actually half sisters by a former marriage. Their mother had died some years ago due to some freak carriage accident with a train. They were even older than Heather, and both of them were married and had several children of their own. Their husbands were both off in the army, fighting for the South.

Stephanie's parents, Mr. and Mrs. Lucius D. Herron, were both very pleasant to meet and seemed to take an instant liking to both Ben and me. Mr. Herron was a bold, brash man with whiskers and mustache, slightly balding, and more than slightly potbellied. You could tell he was in the food business and loved it. He was jovial and had the greatest sense of humor. He insisted we stay through the fireworks and that we come again to visit his home and family.

Mrs. Herron was just as nice and cordial. She had the most Southern elegance about her I had ever seen. She made sure that we had plenty to eat and that we had plenty of pink punch. Her countenance was most becoming to a lady of wealth and standing, and her fine jewelry spoke wonders about the family fortune. They were indeed a wealthy family, but their mannerism only showed a kind of gracious Southern hospitality.

Just a while before midnight, I had the good fortune to meet another wonderful person, Stephanie's cousin Debbie from Augusta, whose family was up in Atlanta visiting for the holidays. She was a very special girl who had long brown hair and beautiful big brown eyes and a figure to match. She was gentle and unassuming but had a streak of vivaciousness in her that made her come alive with excitement at the littlest thing. She would be the first love of my life, the first girl–yeah, woman–to take my breath away in one fell swoop. My heart went pitter-patter-flutter-flutter, and I thought that I would not be able to contain myself for all the excitement I felt for this wonderful girl.

Debbie Langford and I watched the fireworks together that night over the snowy Atlanta skyline. Our hearts were joined as we held hands and marveled at the unfamiliar sights of blues, reds, and greens exploding and bursting overhead like giant epithets of love.

The party had been a godsend to us in the midst of all this turmoil of war and strife. We would long remember the kindness we felt there and the warm personal relationships and friendships that were born that cold December evening.

That night, the temperature fell even more, and the snow crept in like on silent cat feet until, by morning, the whole country lay like a white virgin wool blanket across the Georgia landscape, its beauty unsurpassed and its whiteness unblemished by tracks or ruts. It indeed was a winter wonderland, one to be full of surprises and excitement for sure.

After a good, hearty, and late breakfast at the little hotel we were staying at located on Whitehall Street, Ben and I figured we'd best be going on down to the local recruitment office, which was down on Alabama Street. So we did.

Upon entering the recruitment office, we were greeted by a Sergeant Lawson, who introduced himself and said he was looking for a few good men this morning to start off the New Year right. It was New Year's Day, January 1, 1863.

We told Sergeant Lawson we were there to sign up with the First Georgia Volunteers as our brothers were already in that outfit, and we wanted to fight with them. He said that would be just fine and dandy, but the First Georgia was already up in Virginia somewhere, he thought, in the Shenandoah Valley. What he needed were men for a new regiment being formed up called the Ninth Georgia Light Artillery. We told him we didn't know nothin' about cannons and such and that we'd really like to be in the regular infantry along with our brothers up in Virginia. Well, he sort of scratched his head and said, "Well, look here, boys, I can't really do much about putting you fellas up there with your brothers, but I'll tell you what, let's compromise. Say, I'll sign you up with the Ninth Georgia Light Artillery, and iffen and when you run up on your brothers and the First Georgia, you can put in for a transfer. Fair enough?"

I looked at Ben, who looked at me, and we sort of nodded in agreement. After all, what else could we do? We couldn't stand around talking about joining the army and never do nothing. It was now or never.

"Where do we sign, Sergeant Lawson?" said Ben as we both moved closer to the table where the paperwork was.

"Right here, gentlemen. Just make or sign your name iffen you can write."

"Oh, we can write, sir, and read too, and we're both pretty good in math," I said.

"Gooood men. We need soldiers who are educated, in the artillery especially. It's sort of higher branch of the service, you know," he said reassuringly. "See the supply corporal over there, and he'll fix you up with uniforms and such, and you'll need to report immediately out to Fort Walker on the edge of town to a Sergeant Masterson who is with the Ninth. Can you remember that? Just in case, here are your orders you are to deliver to Sergeant Masterson. And good luck, boys. God be with you both." And he turned to some other paperwork like he was real busy.

We were in the army now, and we both looked pretty sharp in our new Confederate uniforms and kepi caps. We would be issued our weapons and some more gear out at Fort Walker, we were told. So with a great deal of pride and our chests a-bulging out, we made our way out on the edge of the city to Fort Walker, which had been built as part of the defense system for the city of Atlanta. As a matter of fact, work was always going on around the city, building various defense works of all kinds, even though nobody thought that Atlanta would ever need them; it was just in case, just basic military precaution, we were told.

Fort Walker was, without a doubt, the most military of anything that Ben and I had ever seen. Uniformed soldiers were all over the place doing various tasks from walking guard duty to engineering to cooking. Some were working with cannons and cannon placements, and we figured that would be what we would be doing pretty soon. We asked the duty guard at the entrance which way we'd find the Ninth Georgia Artillery and Sergeant Masterson. He gave us some general directions and set us on our way. Shortly, we arrived at a special camp just on the other side of Fort Walker where the new regiment was forming up.

We found Sergeant Masterson drilling some soldiers around a piece of field artillery. He was barking out orders right and left and fairly near hollering every word that came out of his mouth. Ben looked at me, and I looked at him with that kind of look that said, *Do you think it's too late to get out of this?* But we both knew better, and we moved on down the hill.

A light snow blanketed the ground from the night before, and all around, the men resembled rabbits jumping here and there. The whiteness of the snow only gave greater emphasis to the intense exercises going on with the cannons.

"So, cannoneers you want to be, eh?" said Sergeant Masterson. "Well, this is the place to be, I'd say. Where you two from anyway?"

"Salt Springs, Georgia, just west of Atlanta" was Ben's reply.

"We're farm boys," I said. "But we're here to fight."

"And fight you will, lads. Fight you will eventually," said the sergeant. "We're being moved out in a few days up toward the Carolinas. You'll probably see plenty of fighting before we're through. Our destination is up in Virginia to meet up with General Lee."

He leaned over, looked around to see if anybody was close by, and half-whispered, "We're getting ready for a major invasion of the North. Yep, going to make another move right on Washington itself or something."

Ben and I both made faces at each other and then smiled like, *Well, all right.*

"Get your gear settled and tent assignment from the quartermaster and report back here when you're finished. We'll be here awhile. Now get movin'!"

We shuffled off through the snow and finally found the quartermaster's headquarters. A Major Johnson signed us up and turned us over to a Corporal Delaney, who gave us the standard issue of one tent for two men, two blankets, two canteens, two mess kits, and two Remington Zouave rifles, .58 caliber, along with the appropriate cartridge boxes, one hundred rounds of ammunition, and a tin box of percussion caps with a cap box to go on our belt. We were also issued two haversacks, sort of cloth sacks for carrying our personal belongings.

"Sign here," said the corporal. "You don't always get the rifles like this, being in the artillery and all, but we just got this new shipment in, and the major said, 'Go ahead and issue them out before some other outfit confiscates them all.' After all, the artillery can't fire the cannons all the time. Oh yeah, I almost forgot. Here, take these bayonets and sheaths also. You might need them one day too. Also, here are some red arm and neck cuffs and red pant strips to indicate you are in the artillery. Sew them on as soon as you can, and here's a couple of nine pins to indicate the Ninth Georgia Light Artillery."

"Well, thank you very much," we both said. It was better than Christmas morning getting all this stuff. Ben and I were pretty excited as we made our way to the camp area and began to sort out our priorities about camp. First, we'd get our tent set up and sort of organize our personal equipment, examine our new weapons, and so forth. We could hardly contain ourselves; we were so excited about everything.

We got back to the field and reported to the sergeant at about noontime, and the Company P we were in was just breaking up for the midday mess call.

"Just fall in with the rest of the company!" barked the sergeant. "You'll get your hands on the piece soon enough!"

We joined the other soldiers and enjoyed a good mess of beans and pork with some biscuits, not like Ma's but still pretty good. While eating, we began to meet some of the other fellas in the company, and it was good to make some new friends, fellow soldiers in arms. Boy, what more could you ask for! We were real proud of ourselves and felt like we were on the greatest adventure of our lives.

The afternoon was spent learning and drilling all about the "piece" as it was called. We would be working and firing a twelve-pounder cannon that was capable of spitting out a twelve-pound solid shot ball to a total distance of about one mile. We could also fire canister, a mixture of grapeshot and shrapnel, or we could fire an exploding shell that carried a timed fuse, depending on our objective.

Ben was given the job of rammer, while I was given the job of loader. The procedure went something like this: One man would swab the barrel with a wet swab on the end of a rammer pole to be sure that there was no live fire in the breach. Then while another man held his thumb, wearing a leather thumb stall, over the breach hole to prevent the sucking in of air, another would place the one-pounder charge in the barrel mouth, another would ram it home to the breach, another–me–would set the projectile ball in the barrel mouth, and another–the rammer, Ben–would drive it into the breach. Then the artilleryman would prime the breach hole either with powder or sometimes with a friction primer called a lanyard placed in the hole, and the piece was ready to fire. At that point, the corporal in charge–the aimer–would be responsible for setting the sights and elevation and would then give the artilleryman the command to fire. He would then either light the breach primer powder with a match line, on the end of a sword usually, or pull the lanyard-type friction primer, and–boom!–the cannon would fire. This was the general procedure, and it took five men to do all these various tasks at speed and the piece commander to sight it for elevation and direction. With everyone doing just their special jobs, a battery could get off about three rounds per minute at maximum performance after a lot of practice. And practice we did over and over and over. Of course, most of our drill was just dry firing, but we did a right smart amount of actual firing so as to get used to the piece and practice accuracy of fire and procedure. During a battle, there would be no time to learn or to practice as the sergeant said. Our very lives and those of our men would be depending on how well we each knew and did our jobs, and of course, we had to know how to interchange jobs as well in case the need was to arise. In short, by the time we were through with our training, we would know everything there was to know about that cannon, and we would know how to use it with deadly accuracy and precision. We were the Confederate artillery corps, and we were proud.

We were under the command of a Colonel Meyers, who was a tall lean man with a full, bushy red beard and mustache, a rather jovial commander who had a dry sense of humor and who loved his men. He also loved the military and seemed to have great respect for every soldier. We were, indeed, fortunate to have such a commander, and we would do good on the field of battle. We each knew it in our hearts.

In about two weeks, we got our orders to move out. It was somewhere in the middle of January 1863. Ben and I had both written to Ma and Anna and had told them what a fine unit we were in and that we were headed out for the front, wherever that was.

The Front

Two more weeks passed as we traveled north through the snow, rain, sleet, hail, and even some beautiful sunshine. We had already made our way past Augusta, Georgia, and Camden, South Carolina. Soon we would be passing over into North Carolina, the Tar Heel State. We were pretty excited about seeing all this new country and places we had never been before.

We kept moving north over mostly flatland until, within a few more weeks, we were joining up with some other and larger forces. We were at a sort of staging point for meeting up with the others somewhere in North Carolina, and we would soon begin to move in great force up through Virginia and across the Potomac River.

Some of the boys had been engaged in some light skirmishes along the way but nothing major, mostly sharpshooters and occasionally some outlying picket lines but no major forces. Ben and I had not been shot at, at all, thank goodness; and by the same token, we had not fired on the enemy up till this time.

Our first encounter with the enemy was in the wilderness of northern Virginia at a place called Chancellorsville and Fredericksburg, Maryland. It was there that we got our feet wet, so to speak, as we–under the joint command of Gen. Stonewall Jackson and Gen. Robert E. Lee–pounded the enemy with long-range artillery fire from a place known as Hazel Grove. Our collective actions there brought Southern victory but at some considerable costs. At places like Marye's Heights and the Sunken Road, there was a great loss of life, and it became known as the Second Battle of Fredericksburg, somewhat like the first back in December of 1862. But this time, we lost another great commander when Gen. Stonewall Jackson was mistaken for the enemy upon returning to the Southern lines, and he was shot by one of his own men, it was said. He lost an arm as a result of his wound and, ten days later, contracted pneumonia and died. He was a great leader, and it was said that General Lee himself grieved deeply over his unfortunate demise. He even said, if it could have been him, he would have traded places.

Now we had fired on the enemy, and we had taken our place in battle from a distance as good artillery always liked to do, if possible. But we hadn't seen the elephant as they'd say. We hadn't exactly looked death in the face yet. Perhaps our time would come. Colonel Meyers and Sergeant Masterson were proud of our actions thus far and said we had done a commendable job and to keep up the good work. That made us feel better, and we were anxious to contribute even more to the war effort as soon as we could.

In Virginia, we had become a part of the army under the direct command of Gen. Robert E. Lee and would become a small segment of the large invasion force to invade and assault the Northern states of Maryland, Pennsylvania, and New York perhaps. We had even heard that we might even take Washington DC, either going or coming back. Generally, we would stay toward the inland and away from major population areas like Boston, Baltimore, New York City, and others along the Atlantic coastline.

There was even talk that if we did go on with our invasion in the North, many Southern sympathizers, like in Maryland, would probably turn to the South and secede, giving the Confederacy a great, big boost toward victory with all the additional soldiers we might gain. The Lord knew we needed every available man we can get to fight the Yankees. We were still badly outnumbered, but for some reason, the Federal army didn't really take advantage of their superior numbers in force. I guess they really did agree that it took ten Yankees to equal one good Johnny Reb. And nearly all the statistics backed up this premise. There was a certain conservatism about the Federal army, like they weren't going to fight unless they absolutely had to, and everything and every advantage was on their side. Maybe it wasn't such a bad strategy.

For months now, we had been gathering up and moving northerly into the enemy territory. We had encountered little or no resistance from the local population, although they were mighty surprised to see an invading army of so many on their own home soil. Resistance was only token as nobody really knew where the main force of the Federal army was. It probably was somewhere around the area, but we just didn't know. And apparently, they didn't know where we were, or they would have been on our tail like a duck on a June bug, at least I thought.

Gen. Jeb Stuart's cavalry was the eyes of this great army, and he and his men were busy running circles around the Federal army, apparently trying to embarrass it into surrender by mere intimidation. Word had it that if he could just go around them a few more times, the Yankees would fall over dead in the deep ruts made by General Stuart's cavalry.

But it seemed that General Lee hadn't heard from General Stuart in several days, and everybody was somewhat in the dark about general maneuvers and positions.

Seminary Ridge, Gettysburg

In the meantime, we kept working our way down the roads of Pennsylvania, heading north. The countryside was beautiful and green and reminded me a lot of how my own homeland looked this time of year. Right at the end of June, it was beginning to get a little warm during the heat of the days, and the days were long with a lot of daylight from dawn to dusk. We were making good time, and the weather was fairly good and dry.

I'd never forget that morning of July 1, 1863; we were making our way down the pike toward some little Pennsylvania town called Gettysburg when we began to hear the fire of muskets and, a little later, the undisputable sound of field artillery. North or South, we weren't sure yet, but we knew it wasn't us 'cause we were still moving forward in the column.

It wasn't long, probably an hour later, when we got our orders to advance rapidly so as to deploy our artillery on a relatively high ridge just westerly and south of the hamlet of Gettysburg, called Seminary Ridge. It was called so because of the old theological school that was located on it. It offered a supreme view of the underlying countryside to the east and would be a good place to position our artillery. Within a short time, the Ninth Georgia Light Artillery was in position and ready to fire when commanded. The enemy had been intercepted on the right somehow, and it was our orders to place a long-range barrage toward the opposite ridge and valley as soon as the enemy could be sufficiently located and identified. Somewhere around midmorning, we began to let them fly at maximum range about a mile over. We were firing on a line of dismounted cavalry that had been formed so as to fire on a column of Confederate infantry that had soon broken ranks and was engaging the enemy. It didn't appear to be a very strong force of Federals, maybe just one regiment or two; but still, that constituted probably a thousand soldiers or more. Unless they received reinforcements, they wouldn't be able to hold that line for very long. What we didn't know was that this was just the tip of the iceberg and only represented the long, extended arm of the Federal army.

For several hours, we bombarded the Federal position until it became obvious that reinforcements were beginning to arrive. The line was strengthened and extended, and eventually, the Federals even brought up a Federal battery and placed it in the wheat field opposite our lines. It appeared that they would try to blast us out of our position among other things.

Pretty soon, here it came right over our heads, solid shot and exploding shells. We would soon be taking some direct hits if we didn't knock out that battery. It was pretty different now, being the ones shot at by artillery, and we weren't exactly happy about it. Colonel Meyers redirected our fire to the immediately assaulting Federal battery before us and said we would have to take it out before it took us out. Within minutes, we were redirecting our fire, laying into that battery everything we had but using mostly exploding shells.

We must have taken and delivered perhaps a hundred rounds each way, doing only minor damage to each other's positions, when darkness began to fall; and suddenly, everything just stopped on both sides. The dead and wounded were scattered over the area, and it was customary to use the twilight time to care for the wounded.

As for us, we had lost one man in Company A and four wounded. One artillery piece out of four in our battery had been disabled, and we would have to work into the night to restore its utility if we could. By nightfall, campfires began to be seen all over the area, and it became obvious that this would more than likely really turn into a major engagement before it was all over.

As Ben and I got something to eat from the mess tent, we took our plates, sat down under the stars, and looked up at the great heavens above. We talked and wondered out loud about the world and how God must be looking down on all of us and wondering what in the world we were all doing down here, fighting and killing one another. We had even heard by rumor that some of the Federal batteries on the opposite side were commanded by a General Ayres from New York State who, we were sure, was related to us back on our mother's side of the family. We had heard of him being a military career man, but we had never met him, and we really didn't know him, just the fact that he was probably kinfolk, and that sort of gave you a funny feeling. I guess if we never saw him in person, we couldn't be too related. But that was the way this war was. There were actually brothers fighting against their own brothers in this war and probably right here in this battle, sometimes fathers against sons and certainly uncles against nephews and such. It was a crazy, mixed-up war, I'd have to say, the likes of which we had never seen.

The next morning, we were up bright and early, and the cracking of gunfire soon commenced with the early sun. This would really be a day to remember as lines on both sides began to form up, and new positions were taken. From where we could see, the Federal line extended far to the right, including a little molehill of a mountain that was called Little Round Top. It was the end of the line for the Federals, but why they didn't occupy the higher and bigger hill to their left was beyond my understanding. It would have most definitely given them a superior position over our assaulting lines; however, the implications of such strategy would only be known later.

While we began to blast the Federal lines to the east, an assault of Confederates under the command of McLaws began to advance on the valley below. They made their way through a wheat field and a peach orchard in some of the fiercest fighting we had ever witnessed. Along the way, they captured a Federal battery. They then moved forward, and the extreme right flank moved through a real rocky knoll area at the base of the Little Round Top. This rocky knoll area would later be known as the Devil's Den because the fighting there was so ugly and bad. Thank god that Ben and I were not down there and didn't have to go through that awful, hellish sight just before our eyes.

As we kept our bombardment up, the ground fighting kept going on throughout the day until our boys began to make frontal assaults up the slope of the Little Round Top. It was some real fighting going on, and it appeared that it was only a matter of time before we took that hill. But the Yankees were as stubborn as hornets and just wouldn't give an inch. So finally, in one big flanking movement, the Confederate line swept up the far right of the slope in an effort to outflank the Federal line; but just as our boys reached the upper part of the slope, they were met by a down-sweeping Federal bayonet charge, which effectively disrupted the assault and saved their line. It was some god-awful fighting, and both sides lost a lot of men. While all this was going on, there was more fighting down the line, extending all the way down to Gettysburg and around a place called Culp's Hill, where the fighting had been equally dramatic and deadly this day. It also included, appropriately, a place called Cemetery Hill, there on the outskirts of town. By nightfall, both Federal flanks had been thoroughly assaulted as commanded by General Lee, who wasn't about to let the enemy get away without being engaged.

By the next day, a plan was on for an even more dramatic assault on the center of the Federal line, to be centered or focused on a small clump of trees along a stone wall. The ground to be covered would be almost a mile of open terrain and would constitute one of the most dramatic military charges of infantry in the history of the world, with about fifteen thousand men participating in the singular assault.

By this time, our batteries had been repositioned, and it would be our duty to lay a heavy barrage of long-range fire on the enemy line toward the center to cause as much damage as possible. Then at the appropriate time, we would be directed to give support and cover to our assaulting infantry as they made their way across the great gulf of space between us. Well, we did just that, and we fired practically every ball and exploding shell we had in our caisson's supply wagons. There was insufficient time to bring up our reserve supply wagons, so the assault would have to begin immediately to support the momentum of the effort. During that time, the Federal line was being constantly reinforced and resupplied with both men and munitions. The Federal batteries were beginning to be a dreadful thing to deal with also as they seemed to be constantly replaced even when knocked out.

The time came, and under the direct command of General Lee, General Longstreet had placed Gen. George Pickett in command of three divisions, two of which were A. P. Hill's corps. And the assault began, which would forever henceforth be known as the famous Pickett's Charge. It was undoubtedly one of the most awe-inspiring military undertaking in history.

We kept up the long-range cover for our boys for as long as we safely could, and then basically, our job was done. It was all we could do for the gray line as it made its way, wave after wave after wave, into the conflagration of battle before them, facing head on exploding shells, thousands of musketry fire, and cannon canister at point-blank range. As we watched in wonder and disbelief, we finally saw our battle banner briefly cross the stone wall precipice and rise triumphantly into the smoky sky. Then almost as suddenly as it ascended, it came down; and within a few minutes, the Stars and Stripes was up again, waving at us in angry defiance, and our boys began to fall back, at least what was left of them. They were falling back in a slow line of receding gray, much like the giant wave that crashed on the beach, spraying its foam in the air and then reluctantly drawing away from the extremity achieved by the surging effort.

It appeared that there would be no battle tomorrow or the next day as we had depleted and exhausted our resources in both men and firepower over these past three days—three days that would go down in history as being especially awesome and deadly in the loss of human life and spirit. Some fifty-three thousand brave men were wounded and dead. How unbelievable, yet how true. Almost immediately, we began our preparations for a withdrawal to the South; and over the next few days and weeks, we moved south without ceasing until we had once again crossed the Potomac River and entered Virginia. We were getting tired and somewhat ragged, but we kept our spirits up. We were still ready, willing, and able to fight, and we would fight again another time.

The Long March Home

It rained for the next two weeks as we made our way south toward home and familiar ground. The cannons, caissons, and supply wagons bogged down deep in the soft black-and-gray mud of Virginia, a rich and handsome soil unlike the red clay of my native north Georgia. But mud was mud no matter how you looked at it, no matter how much you admired its richness, no matter how much you despised its stubborn uselessness. Mud was mud, and we had plenty of it. Every so often, we'd have to take poles we had cut and just knocked the caked mud out from between the spokes so we could keep moving. It was a toilsome retreat, especially under the extreme circumstances of defeat and loss.

Finally, the rains let up, and the sunshine broke through, bringing warmth and refreshment to our rain-soaked bodies, clothes, and equipment. Somewhere along the way, we also regained our composure and complete self-confidence as we knew this war was far from over. Our big opportunity to defeat the North on their own ground had failed, and we would have to accomplish victory another way, probably on our own home soil.

A few days' rest came as we made camp temporarily and attempted to put back together all the pieces of our broken regiments. New plans were being made, and new strategies for war were smoking in the air along with the crisp smell of a side of bacon cooking for breakfast. It would be the first time in weeks we had eaten cooked food, and it sure was good.

After breakfast, mail call arrived with the usual whooping and hollering that went along with a rare rejoicement of renewing old contacts and relationships with home and loved ones.

"Steven Jett!" the quartermaster called as he flung a flying piece of paper toward where I was perched up on this log, listening to the long litany of names, never expecting to hear mine at all. I was there mostly for entertainment, just something different to do. Nobody had been writing to me or Ben, except two letters we did get from Ma and Anna back in the spring.

Who could this letter be from? I wondered as I swooped down like a chicken hawk to fetch it almost before it hit the ground.

The address was just "Steven Jett, Ninth Georgia Light Artillery, Army of Northern Virginia." I examined every word as it looked so official and was written in the most beautiful Spenserian* handwriting I had ever seen.

Carefully, I opened the envelope to reveal its contents, and it read as follows:

May 15, 1863

My Dearest Steven,

I just had to write to you because I have been so worried about you and your brother Ben. So many boys have been killed or wounded since I first met you at my cousins' house in Atlanta. By the way, Stephanie is doing fine, and her family is all in good health, except her father has been considerably overworked keeping adequate food and supplies for the restaurant, what with the war going on and all. Everything is beginning to get a little scarce with the war demanding so much, but we understand. Even here in Augusta, things are a mite tight.

Steven, I hope you are doing well and have not had any trouble with so many of the things of war. I know there are so many hardships and circumstances over which you have so little control. But I also know that you'll always be brave and face whatever you have to, like the fine soldier I know you have become.

---

*An artistic handwriting of the period widely taught in the schools, characterized by flowing lines and beautiful curves.

I have really missed you, and never did I realize that I could miss someone so much as you. I never believed in love at first sight, but in your case, I might be able to make an exception. I hope you don't think I am being too forward, but I have enclosed a lock of my hair for you to carry with you in hope that you will remember me and know that someone is thinking about you. If you come by Augusta, maybe you can get a furlough to come and visit me and my family.

Well, goodbye for now, and be sure to tell Ben hello for me and that he can come too.

Love,

Debbie Langford
118 Savannah Street
Augusta, Georgia

As I pulled out the shiny lock of beautiful brown hair, it glistened in the morning sunlight and beckoned my heart from some far-off place to draw near and be comforted. Nobody had ever sent me a lock of their hair before, much less a beautiful girl who seemed to really like me, maybe even love me. She did sign her letter with "Love." Maybe all girls wrote like that to fellas off in the war just to make them feel good. Oh well, it didn't matter because it worked. I did feel better. As a matter of fact, I felt great, and I couldn't wait to tell Ben and to show him the beautiful and mysterious lock of brown hair she had sent to me.

Occasionally, along the way, we heard at various times by letter from Ma and Anna back at New Manchester. They were doing fine and working in the mill every day, making mostly Confederate uniforms and some shirts and trousers. Sometimes they would make socks; it just depended on their particular stock orders. Ma did say that Mr. and Mrs. Ferguson and her sister, Martha Jenkins, were doing fine and that Martha was still running the company store. A few more people had moved into the settlement as the mill had put on some extra shifts to meet the war demands. Mr. Cranbell ran a tight ship there at the mill and was a good superintendent as Mother said in her letter. Also, a Mr. Henry Lovern—who was her immediate supervisor and Anna's—was a good man with a good sense of humor, and it made the life and work there more bearable under the hardships they were experiencing.

Mother had heard from Pa only twice by letter since he had left for the war, but he was doing fine at last count and was still riding with General Wheeler's cavalry. Chester, Pa's horse, had been shot out from under him and killed in a skirmish in Mississippi, called Brice's Cross Roads. Pa got a bad saber cut on his left arm, but it had been healing real good and was almost as good as new by now. Of course, he had to be issued another horse, and it never was as good as Chester, but it was better than walking all over the country.

Ma also had heard from William, Samuel, and Levi, who had been all over the place with the Salt Springs Regulars and the First Georgia Volunteers. She thought they might have even been up in Virginia, maybe even in West Virginia in the Shenandoah Valley with Gen. Stonewall Jackson's army. According to their letters, they had all seen plenty of action, and Will had been promoted to captain and was working in the medical corps in some capacity. He had told her how much pain and suffering he had seen in the field and how arms and legs were amputated with regularity among the wounded. Ben and I knew this was true because we had seen a good bit ourselves. Everybody knew if you got wounded, it could easily cost you an arm or a leg; but if you got a gutshot, there was a better than good chance that you wouldn't survive.

Samuel and Levi had been in some pretty thick action, and Levi had a miniball graze the top of his head during one battle. It blew his slouch hat right off his head and liked to have killed him, but it didn't. Samuel had burned his hands pretty bad on some hot rifle barrels during one engagement, and some artillery blasts had given him a concussion and knocked him out for a while, but he was okay after a few hours. They thought he was dead, but he hadn't even been touched, just knocked unconscious for a while. Ma and Anna prayed for us all as they figured all they could do was to pray and trust in the good Lord to take care of us boys and Pa.

Anna had heard some distressing news concerning her beau, Luther Gates, and his uncle John Henry. Seemed that they were both crossing some creek up in Tennessee when their regiment was ambushed by the Yankees. Before they could get across to the other side, a good number of soldiers were shot and killed, including Luther and John Henry. They never had a fighting chance under the circumstances. Anna, of course, was grief stricken, and all she could do was go on, knowing that she would never hear Luther's kind voice again or his beautiful banjo music. They had planned to marry sometime after the war. Now all that was changed, and she'd never see Luther again. These were some sad times, and nearly every family was affected in some way. I felt sorry for Anna, and my heart grieved for her, but that was all I could do.

News had finally reached the Army of Northern Virginia that Vicksburg had fallen sometime around the third of July, just about the same time as Gettysburg. Vicksburg had been under siege for a long time by the Yankees under the command of a Gen. Ulysses S. Grant and a General Sherman. The fall of Vicksburg was a mighty blow to the Confederacy as it was a real key to the Mississippi River. But everyone suspected that, after the fall of Fort Henry and Fort Donelson, it was only a matter of time before Vicksburg would be surrendered. After all, it had been under siege for over six months, and the civilian population was living on roots, rats, and whatever could be scrounged up for food. They were living in holes in the ground like gophers and mostly coming out only at night to get some fresh air from the constant bombardment of siege artillery. Maybe it was a blessing to them that now it was all over except for the Federal occupation, which couldn't have been any worse than what they had already experienced. But you know, it was humiliating for them. After all, the South was a proud people, and Southerners would endure hell itself if that was what it took to defeat the Yankee army. And oftentimes it was.

It was now midfall, and we arrived in Augusta, Georgia, in anticipation of making a winter camp, if possible. Perhaps while here, I would be able to get a furlough and visit Debbie Langford and her family. I sure did hope so. Ben and I both needed some time off and some sort of refreshment from the drudgeries of war and being constantly on the move.

Augusta, the Wonderful

Ben and I both obtained a three-day furlough while we were in Augusta, Georgia. The weather was better now, and we were experiencing a few days of relatively warm temperatures. It was a welcome relief from having so much foul weather for so long. We just hoped it would last during our furlough so we could enjoy ourselves.

Augusta was a fair-sized city, being on the Savannah River just up a ways from the port city of Savannah, Georgia, where many goods and war supplies were always coming and going. Even as far up as Augusta, shipping was pretty heavy. It was a well-founded city of about the size of Atlanta, and we felt fairly comfortable in finding our way around. We decided that we would stick together as much as possible and that we would go look up Debbie Langford and her family first thing.

We asked some directions and soon found our way to 118 Savannah Street. The house that bore that address was rather large and somewhat pretentious looking, and we were not sure that we looked presentable enough to announce our arrival. Nevertheless, we made up our minds to go on, and we walked up to the large polished door and rapped the brass knocker, sending a sharp metallic sound resonating to the inside. There was no response for some time, so we tried again. Still, no response. We waited, anxious that either we might be turned away or no one was home. The time was midmorning, and we finally determined no one was coming to the front door, so we went around to the back of the house, where we soon discovered a Negro woman of middle age who was just commencing to pluck a chicken. She had obviously just rung its neck.

Augusta Fire Wagon

"What y'all want thar?" she said, startled at our sudden appearance.

"Well, ma'am, we're here to pay our respects to Miss Debbie Langford and her family."

"She ain't here, ain't been here for two weeks now, her folks neither. Gone up to Atlanta to visit kinfolks. Who are you boys anyhows?"

We told her who we were, how we had come to know Miss Debbie and all, and how I had got a letter from her while up in Virginia.

"Oh, I sees," said the woman. "Well, that's most likely where's they are right now, up in Atlanta. I's just gettin' this here chicken ready to boil up for dinner tonight. Don't know whens they'll be back really, maybe this week, maybe next."

"Would ya tell Miss Debbie we came by to see her, and would ya give her this here whistle I carved out of a stick for her?" It was all I had, but I wanted to leave something for her to let her know we had really been there to see her.

"Yes, sire. I sho' would be glad to, sir." And with that, she took the whistle in her hand and drew it up to her face to examine it more closely. I sure hoped she wasn't going to blow on it to see if it worked or not. When she saw my apprehension at her more than casual interest, she quickly lowered it back down and slowly put it in her apron pocket.

"Yes, sir, I's be glad to give it to her. I sure will," she said even more reassuringly.

We told her we would be around town for a few days and that maybe we'd get a chance to check back with her, and then we told her goodbye.

Now we had three days to do nothing, it seemed. So we made our way down Main Street to see the sights and sounds of the big city, and there were many. Just as we began to relax a little, here came this racing team of fire wagon horses, followed by the craziest-looking fire wagon you ever did see. It was ringing its bell to beat the band, with four razzle-dazzle old men barely hanging on for dear life as they rounded a corner onto the Main Street and headed down the street right toward us as fast as they could go, throwing up dust in a great billowing cloud the size of Texas. All we could do was scramble out of the street and onto the wooden sidewalk, barely escaping with our lives. Turning and watching in disbelief, we watched the horses and wagon with the clinging men make a sliding turn again into the next street to the right. The bell was still clanging as fast as the fire wagon was going, and the dust continued to rise like it was caught up in a great whirlwind. By now, we could see smoke coming up into the pure blue sky maybe two or three blocks away.

We decided, *Hey, why not?* We had that kind of look that only brothers can have without really saying anything out loud, and with that, we took off after the storming fire quencher as fast as we could go. After all, maybe we could be of some help in putting the fire out.

When we got there, we could see that it was a two-story building already totally engulfed in flames. The men with the pumper began to douse the flames with water, but it was more like throwing grease on a pan fire. It only sizzled and looked like it made the flames spread out more and higher.

We helped form a bucket brigade from one of the watering troughs and threw all the water we could on that fire, mainly in an effort, I think, to try to save the adjoining buildings 'cause we sure wasn't going to be able to save this one.

After everybody worked with the fire for about two hours, we all stopped and let the last part of the fire take the rest of its toll while we began to really survey the damage that had been inflicted. Even our artillery couldn't have destroyed a building like this fire did, so completely and so effortlessly, just "poof" almost, and it was nothing but ashes when it finished.

After the fire, we found out that the building that had just burned was an apothecary that had long served the west side of town. That had probably explained some of what seemed like chemical explosions occurring during the fire.

We hadn't counted on the extra excitement with the fire and all, but it was right down our alley literally, and we took advantage of all the–well, I almost said "fun," but I meant the excitement of the terrible fire. Yeah, you know what I mean.

The afternoon moved on quickly because of the fire, and we soon found ourselves getting somewhat hungry. It was already late afternoon, and we figured we'd just have an early supper. We had just a little money, not much but probably enough to eat on a few times, so we found this tiny, little café that served up hot meals, and we proceeded to make real pigs out of ourselves until we were so full that we could hardly move.

Friday night it was, and there was bound to be some entertainment in this tinhorn town, and we were going to find it. As it worked out, we discovered a theater and found out that some kind of Shakespearean play was about to begin just that evening. *Romeo and Juliet* it was billed.

We paid our two cents per head and took the best seats in the house we could find next to the piano. For two hours, we watched and listened, watched and listened some more, and watched and listened some more. Finally, the final curtain came down, and we were able to get up and leave. It had been pretty good, especially for us country boys who had never seen such a play, even though we were familiar with the story. The lady who played Juliet was magnificent, if not a little old for a fourteen-year-old girl. Nevertheless, she brought off her part with perfect credibility until she was supposed to be lying there dead, and she kept coughing, once even rising to an upright position and then lying back down to be dead again. All in all, it was high-class entertainment.

After a good night's sleep in a real bed in the local hotel, we were in no hurry to vacate the fine feather bed we had collapsed into, so we slept until about nine o'clock. The whole day of Saturday was before us, and we were anxious to make new discoveries in our newfound town of Augusta.

After breakfast, we walked around the town for a while here and there and, by late afternoon, happened on a little bar saloon where we were tempted to sit down and have a couple of drinks. We were very tempted. In fact, we were so tempted that we actually did sit down; and before I knew what had happened, Ben said, "We'll have two whiskeys, please." When they came, I wasn't sure if I should sip on it, swallow it whole, or get up and run out the door before I did something I was sure to regret. Following Ben's lead, I decided to sip it at first. After a few sips and a few twisted expressions, we both decided there was only one way to handle a shot of whiskey, and that was to wolf it down all at once in one smooth swallow, like a man was supposed to. After three more, we were getting pretty good. And we were getting pretty mellowed out as the afternoon moved on into the twilight.

It was about that time when the women came down the stairs and made their way into, across, and through the saloon, each finding their own particular roosting spots among the patrons at the tables and at the bar.

One of the girls was especially beautiful. In fact, I knew she wasn't a girl at all but rather a very sophisticated woman of the world who took a position on a stool at the bar, alone for the moment, apparently buying her last few moments of freedom for the evening. You could tell she was a woman tormented by her own beauty, torn between the lust of men and the sanctity of her own inner soul. As she turned slightly and surveyed the room with her wandering eyes, she stopped momentarily when she spied me and Ben sitting at our table halfway across the room. For a moment, our eyes met, and we both smiled as people did sometimes, like when you passed each other on the street and you didn't really know each other, but you sort of wished you did. But there wasn't time for that, or was there?

The piano player had moved to the instrument and was beginning to plank out soft love tunes of some kind that Ben and I had never heard before. After a few numbers, the lady in the pale blue dress at the bar turned and left the counter; and carrying her drink, she strolled with all the ease of a gliding lark over to our table, where she said in the sweetest, softest voice I had ever heard, "Hello, boys, where y'all from?"

We introduced ourselves and told her where we were from and so forth.

"My name is Gwendolyn. May I sit down?" she said.

"Why, yes, yes, you can, Gwendolyn," we both said, half-falling all over ourselves as we both jumped up to help her with her chair.

"You know this is a mighty big town, fellas."

"Yeah, we know. We've been exploring around town some while we are off on our furlough," I said in a very matter-of-fact sort of fashion.

"Found anything interesting?" she said in her sultry voice.

"Well, yes, as a matter of fact, we have," said Ben.

"Just yesterday we helped put out a fire down on Farley Street at the apothecary."

"Do you think you might want to put out a fire tonight?" came her reply.

"Well . . . I don't know," Ben said as he looked over at me with eyes as big as saucers.

"Do we want to put out any fires tonight, brother?" he asked while trying to reach for the bottle and get another drink.

"Can we offer you a drink, Gwendolyn?" I said.

"Just call me Gwen. All my friends do, Steve," she said as she touched my right arm with her left hand, which she left resting there for me to feel the pulse of rushing red blood coursing through her hand–a hand of exquisite beauty, graced with rather lavish rings of gold, silver, and diamonds. I had never been touched this way before, and it made me queasy with excitement and apprehension. This lady was making advances toward me, and there was no doubt about her intentions. What would I do now? What would I do?

I lifted my left hand to reach for my drink because it was as if my right arm was paralyzed by her soothing warm touch, and besides, I didn't want to draw away. I was just scared a little.

"Why don't you come on upstairs with me for a little while?" she said in her sexiest voice. "We'll just rest a little and maybe have another drink. What do you say?"

"I say okay, I guess, but what about Ben?"

"Oh, I've got a friend who can take care of Ben, all right." And with a pert and cute turn, she called over to a girl at the next table. "Carol, would you be a darling dear and come here, please? I've got a friend I want you to meet." And with that, Carol excused herself and strolled ever so graciously over to our table and stood next to Gwen with her hand on the back of her chair.

"What can I do you for, darling?" she said as she surveyed the situation.

"My friend's brother here, Ben, needs a companion for the evening, and I thought you might oblige. What do you say, sweetheart?"

"Oh yes, I think I would be up to taking care of some little old soldier boy off from the war, don't you?" she said sheepishly and with a little wry sort of humor.

"Then we're off to never-never land, you all. How about we see y'all after a while?" And with that, Gwen rose, took me by the hand, and led me away and up the stairs, and all I could do was just look back at Ben and Carol with a look like, *Well, if you don't rescue me, it's going to be too late 'cause I just don't have the strength or will to resist.*

For some reason, money was never discussed that evening as we entered room 18, the number an omen of legality, I thought. The things that happened behind that closed door I could never discuss with anyone, but I can tell you this much. In the nocturnal mystery of that momentous event, I underwent my own sort of "baptismal of fire" in the comforting arms of the most beautiful woman I had ever known. It was a time I shall never forget.

That night, I slept like a baby until dawn when I jumped up out of bed, put on my clothes, washed my face, and combed my hair. I went over to kiss Gwen, who was still sleeping and lying there like a goddess. She was dreamingly drawing her right hand through her tousled blond hair as her eyes half-opened and saw me kneeling down to her side as she smiled.

I said, "Gwen, I don't have much money. I know I'm supposed to pay you or something. Here's a dollar. It's all I have."

She didn't say a thing at first; she only shook her head no and smiled at me, and then she said, "Let's just say it was for the war effort, okay?" And with that, she touched her lips with her two fingers and then reached out and touched mine. "Take care of yourself, soldier."

"I will, and I'll always remember you, Gwendolyn, always and forever." Those were the last words we ever said to each other, and I never saw Gwendolyn again after that, but I would always cherish her sweet memory over all the years to come.

As I made my way out the door of the saloon and onto the porch sidewalk, I found Ben sitting on the steps, leaning against the wooden post. He looked pretty contented, if you asked me.

I said, "Well, how did it go last night, brother? Was she all you could ask for? Did you really do it?"

"Well, she was all I could ever ask for, all right, and it was sure some fancy time. But you know, I think I must have passed out somewhere between getting upstairs and finally getting into bed. I mean, Carol was a handful, if you know what I mean. But somewheres along the way, things got mighty fuzzy. Guess I did it, though, 'cause I sure don't feel lacking for anything this morning."

I just listened and raised my eyebrows a little as I looked at Ben and shook my head in agreement. "Yeah, I know just what you mean, big brother. Same thing must have happened to me." And with that said and out of the way, we never discussed the incident again.

It was Sunday now and the last day of our furlough. Ben and I both thought that, since we had been so sinful on Saturday and Saturday night, at least we owed equal time to the betterment of ourselves. After all, we certainly weren't heathens, not by a long shot. At least we didn't think so, but we figured we could do some good by going to a real, bona fide church for Sunday morning preaching. It had been so long since we had heard a real live preacher that we probably wouldn't recognize one if he hit us right in the head with the Good Book itself. Nevertheless, after asking a few directions and looking for the corresponding steeple, we located the First Methodist Church of Augusta, Georgia. There were lots of people going in, and it appeared that we were just right on time for the Sunday morning worship service. We entered through the great wooden double doors and found a partially filled pew toward the back. There were other soldiers there too scattered throughout the congregation, so we didn't feel quite so conspicuous in our gray uniforms. Folks spoke to us from all around until the singing started. We must have sung a dozen hymns before they called for the offering to be collected. The offering plate was approaching me only two or three pews up, and I realized that all I had was that one dollar in my pocket that I tried to give to Gwen. Maybe I should just give it, but a whole dollar was an awful lot to give to a church you didn't really know, and besides, it was my last dollar. If I didn't, I would be shot dead in the next battle I was in and my soul go straight to hell because I kept it for myself? Hell no, I wasn't going to keep that dollar for me, no way. I wouldn't have had it anyway iffen it hadn't been for Gwen. No, this dollar had to go in that plate, and that was the end of self-discussion about that; and with a quickened reflex, I reached in my pocket, grabbed the dollar just in time, and practically threw it into the collection plate as it went by me and onto Ben. Ben just passed it onto the next fellow without barely a thought or mind. *Well*, I thought, *he would just have to live with his own self about that.* Maybe he had to spend his last dollar, or maybe he didn't. We didn't ever talk about it.

Finally, the preacher commenced to preaching, and he preached and preached and preached. "The Bible," he said, "was the living Word of God, and everything that proceedeth out of the mouth of man was to be inspired by God and judged by Him in every way. No man could take it upon himself to be his own counsel when it came to the security and spirituality of the soul. God would be the judgment, and God would provide the punishment or the reward. Amen and amen." That, I believe, was the essence of the service that morning; and by a quarter till one o'clock, everyone was a mite ready to go eat, I think, 'cause after the altar call, which lasted another twenty minutes, the benediction was said, the doors flung open, and everybody flooded out the doors like the torrent of a great river current that had been released from a dam. Thank goodness sometimes that Sunday was only once a week.

Boy, we were starved and ready to get some grub of some kind. It didn't much matter what, but first, we had to see if Ben had any money because I had put that last dollar in the collection plate. Fortunately, somehow Ben still had about two dollars and some odd coins, so it looked like dinner would be on him. We found a little place and chowed down for our last civilian meal for a while. We had to report back to camp by sundown, so that afternoon, we just drifted along Main Street and back toward camp. We discussed whether or not we should call on the Langford family again, and we both decided not this time. They surely wouldn't be back anyway just since Friday morning. We'd try them another time. After all, we both had a lot on our minds by now.

The Army Forever

Believe it or not, the camp actually looked good as we arrived "home" and found our familiar old friends and surroundings. It seemed like we had a great adventure in town, and we really did, but now it was time to get back to the war.

We got a pretty good night's sleep that evening, even after we had told our friends about all our adventures—well, not necessarily about everything. "Discretion is the better part of valor," I had always heard, and it seemed to apply in this case. The night was cool, peaceful, and restful.

Morning came bright and early, and old Sergeant Masterson was already kicking his heels up in the morning air.

"Get up, you sorry rascals, you pitiful excuses for soldiers!" he yelled at the top of his voice as he made his rounds from tent to tent. Reveille was blowing on the bugle, but there was usually no big hurry.

"We're moving out!" came his next words. "We're hitting the road by noon! Breaking camp! Orders!" This time, the sound of the bugle took on a new meaning.

Just where we were going was never said. South? North? East? Or west? Who knew? Just movin' again. Part of the strategy of running an army, I presumed, was to never let the enemy know where you were or how many of you were there. It was all a big guessing game. Worked too, I guess, 'cause old McClellan of the Army of the Potomac had grossly overestimated our forces a number of times, we had heard. It was a good thing for us too 'cause, in reality, his numbers were vastly superior to ours. It would have been a hard lickin' to have beat them on several occasions. This time, we didn't have to worry too much about that because all the armies seemed like they was so scattered here and there all over the place. But then too you never knew when you'd meet up with some blue-bellied Yankees and have to yank their teeth out.

For days and days, we marched, and it began to be obvious that we were headed either for Atlanta or maybe up by Marietta way. We were going west, and that would be a logical place to pick up additional supplies and munitions, although we were pretty well supplied from Augusta, and we were ready for action if it was encountered.

The pace of the march picked up, and by early September, we had already been by Atlanta and Marietta and on our way to meet the Federal army somewheres up toward Chattanooga, but we didn't know exactly when or where. It appeared that Chattanooga had fallen prey to the Federal army and that it was making a move south and possibly would try to drive its way all the way to Atlanta before we could stop them. But by about the middle of September, we caught up with their little prank at a place that would henceforth always be called Chickamauga, after the Indian name of the little creek that ironically meant "river of death." At first, the fighting was just a skirmish, kinda like at Gettysburg; but within hours, it too had escalated into a full-fledged battle.

The Ninth Georgia Light Artillery was now joined up with Gen. Braxton Bragg's army, and it was the Confederate strategy to catch the advancing Federals off guard and lure them into the folds of the Confederate army. It all seemed pretty good except that the engagement was made a little premature, according to later estimates. This battle turned out to be one of the fiercest and bloodiest battles of the war as men on both sides were spread out over almost a forty-mile front, and by the time the forces consolidated, all hell had broken loose.

Our artillery was directed along the centerline of the Federals up on a slightly higher ridge to the west of our position. We let them have everything we had in the initial bombardment till our boys began to make their advancement. Finally, the advance was so concentrated that the Federal line collapsed under the heavy assault and actually withdrew from their position, leaving somewhat of a gaping hole in the now divided Federal line. It would seem that the Yank was now in a really difficult position, and he was. There must have been something like fifty thousand men on each side of this engagement, and all havoc was breaking loose as the Federals began a withdrawal toward the little town called Lafayette–except that the left flank of the Federal line stood firm on a little hill called Snodgrass, where General Thomas defended his position till the withdrawal could be completed and till nightfall, when he too withdrew. For his famous stand that he made under heavy and enduring fire, he would become known later as "the Rock of Chickamauga" among Yankee circles.

One brave Confederate hero would emerge from the assaults on Thomas's position, a Maj. John Herbert Kelley, who 'cause of his determination and persistence would later become a brigadier general. This gentleman I had great reverence for and respect as I had the opportunity to meet him on one occasion after the battle during an encampment. He was from Pickens County, Alabama, and had been raised as an orphan by his aunt and uncle. He was a self-made man and a good soldier whom I admired greatly. His personage and countenance would become somewhat of a mentor for me as the war moved on from battlefront to battlefront.

By now, we had intelligence reports that had trickled down through the ranks that the Federal army was once again occupying Chattanooga. Confederate forces soon occupied the crest of Lookout Mountain and Missionary Ridge, overlooking Chattanooga down in the basin, sort of. By the latter part of November 1863, the Federals had mounted major assaults against Lookout Mountain and Missionary Ridge. The Federals defeated our forces at Lookout Mountain; some had called it "the Battle above the Clouds" 'cause it was so high up that sometimes the Confederates couldn't even see the blue Yankee lines as they charged up that mountain. They had done almost the same thing over on Missionary Ridge on the east side of Chattanooga and had finally driven our boys back into a retreat and off the ridge by the following day. Now the Yankees seemed to be entrenched in Chattanooga, and it appeared they would spend the coldest part of the winter there since they now controlled the supply routes on the Tennessee River and had good rail service from up north. It would seem that the Yankees were getting ready for something even bigger, and it would have to be pretty soon.

For the winter, we would camp in the vicinity of Dalton, Georgia, creating a temporary stalemate for the two armies. Before long, a new objective would be determined, and we'd be at it again.

During all this time, we had heard good reports on damage inflicted by General Wheeler's cavalry, which our pa was riding with. They had wreaked havoc all around the enemy in Chattanooga and, at one point, had destroyed three hundred supply wagons with teams of six mules each, making over 1,800 mules destroyed also. "Break the back of the supply line and starve them out" was the philosophy of those actions, and it almost worked. Probably caused the Federal army to make its move earlier than actually anticipated.

The War Comes to North Georgia

Nowhere was the South more vulnerable now than in the tender heart of north Georgia. In the peaceful green hills of our homeland, the ravages of war would take a mighty toll, in quiet places with obscure names that most of the world had never heard of before, places like Resaca, New Hope, Pickett's Mill, Allatoona Pass, Pine Mountain, Lost Mountain and Kennesaw Mountain, Kolb's Farm, Ruff's Mill, Nickajack Creek, Peachtree Creek, Decatur, Ezra Church, and Jonesboro. All were preludes to the ultimate fall and surrender of Atlanta, Georgia, itself. Few corners of the world, either before or since, had seen and been the object of more destruction and devastation due to the ravages of war that my own homeland had.

Charred by the fires of death and christened by the rains of spring, the death angel came with all his fury to lay waste and havoc. Some called him Sherman, others just called him "fate," and still others refused to believe that the sanctity of this great land had actually been invaded by the blue devils from hell.

The struggle went on for a long time. The major force of the invasion was met with resistance around Dalton, Georgia, and later Resaca, where a major engagement took place. Unable to defeat the Confederate army head on, the Federals ultimately attempted a flanking movement around to the side of the Confederate lines. It worked, and the blue line advanced south. The whole tenor of this campaign would be mostly a long series of flanking movements to the south, movements and engagements around some of the most formidable earthworks and entrenchments ever built by the Confederate army or any other. This was guerilla warfare fought in a wilderness of heavy forests, few roads, and not too much open country as most of north Georgia was farmed in smaller parcels because of the terrain. It was, most of the time, very hilly, if not downright mountainous.

The Confederate victory at Resaca would soon be of little consequence as the gray line retreated to New Hope Church, near Dallas, and made another frightful stand against the advancing blue bellies. For two days, we fought tooth and toenail with the Yanks over hilly terrain and fallen and broken trees, laid into the advancing enemy to impede their progress. Our batteries did considerable damage against the enemy, but the general topography of terrain would not allow for the proper and more expedient use of artillery. It was as if we were firing giant pistols at close range, and we were constantly in danger of being run over by the enemy ourselves.

Soon the Federals were trying another flanking movement around the Confederate right at a little place called Picket's Mill. It was there that our batteries were directed across a rather steep ravine to enfilade the enemy with cross fire in front of the Confederate line if such an advance should take place, and it did. It was an awful site as the Yankees moved forward and across that wooded ravine. They were not only met with a very stiff resistance from the gray Confederate line but were also blasted with canister fire from our batteries on the side in one great blur of confusion and destruction. There must have been over eighteen hundred men of the enemy decimated by our fire. The flanking movement against our line had failed this time, and on the next move, we would have to be sidestepped again.

Later, I would discover that my mother's great-uncle John Henry Gordon was shot in the left leg at New Hope Church and would be discharged among the wounded to return home as best he could. At the time, we didn't even know we were in the same battle. But that was sort of the way this war was, with almost a hundred thousand men fighting in total on the two sides. We had probably forty to fifty thousand soldiers, and it was like a large city of military personnel being constantly moved and shuffled around wherever the need called for.

Cassville had fallen hard to the Federals also before New Hope Church, and the little town had taken a terrible beating from Federal artillery. Mr. Cass, the namesake of Cassville, being a Northern sympathizer, had taken off for the Northern territory; and later, the town and county of Cass would be renamed something more appropriate for a Southern community. The ladies' academy there, being on the hills along the Federal battery placements, was saved from burning; but the rest of the town, almost in its entirety, was destroyed by fire.

The route of advancement would force the Federal army to move along the rail supply lines as this was part of the idea in being able to support the trailing Federal army from the rear for as long as possible, although this would become increasingly more difficult as the army moved farther and farther into enemy territory, our territory.

By the time the Federal army had advanced across Cass County and down to Dallas in Paulding County, we were getting closer and closer to home as our farm was just below Powder Springs, which was just south of Dallas. How far would we go? And where would we end up? Would we be fighting right on our own farm homestead in a few days? It looked like that was exactly what was going to happen.

As things would have it, we entrenched again around the hills just south and southeast of Dallas, Georgia. We, as mostly always, had very good defensive positions but rather poor positions for an offense against the enemy.

At Dallas, however, there was a rather rare Confederate offensive tactic in the charge of what most called the Orphan Brigade, a regiment from Tennessee and Kentucky made up mostly of orphans from those states. They made a vicious and valiant charge against the Federal line just south of Dallas across some considerably bad terrain, including a big hollow with a ravine in the center. Their advancement was noble and to be admired by all, but it added little to the solvency of the Confederate position, and the losses were very great.

Twin Peaks of Kennesaw Mt.
Looking from the Family Farm.

By the early part of June 1864, the two opposing armies were already in the vicinity of Lost Mountain and Pine Mountain. On a clear day, you could see Lost Mountain from the top of the hill near our farm. The armies were spread out across a wide front in this tag match of touch-and-go fighting, shoot and flank, and re-entrench tactics. This defensive strategy was working, sort of, for the Confederate army, but we were losing ground almost every day. There was almost constant skirmishing all around the area as the two lines sort of moved back and forth along, maybe a twenty-mile front, give or take.

Over on Pine Mountain, I heard we lost one of our best and ablest generals, Gen. Leonidas Polk, who took a cannonball right through the belly. It happened while he was standing on the hill, surveying the countryside. Old Uncle Billy, as the Yanks sometimes called Sherman, observed Polk and some other high officers on that hill and, just for the heck of it, directed that a few artillery rounds be dropped their way. And boy, did they hit the mark.

Signals were sent to Gen. Joseph E. Johnston, now atop Kennesaw Mountain, and it was said that he was mightily distressed at hearing the news about General Polk.

Now with Johnston on Kennesaw, the Confederate line swept around like a great snake from Marietta, up and across Big Kennesaw, down and back up Little Kennesaw, up over Pigeon Hill and southward over Cheatham Hill, and over to Kolb's Farm. This was now a twelve-mile consolidated front, less than twenty miles from home. As a matter of fact, we could always see Kennesaw Mountain on a clear day from our upper fields on the farm. Sometimes I would remember just stopping to look at her and admire her, like she was some mysterious and majestic lady way off in the distance. I had never suspected in a million years that, one day, I would be a part of a major battle over the possession of her twin peaks.

It had fallen our lot to position the cannons on top of the mountain and across the ridges to the south as far as possible. Because the enemy was to our front, the cannons had to be pulled by ropes and man power up the steep southern slope of the mountain to get them into the proper positions. This was a difficult and arduous task that took us over rocky terrain and sometimes a slope exceeding forty-five degrees or more. I sure never thought that we'd be dragging cannons up this rocky mountain by hand. This was the pits, if you asked me, but the only question was, would we get them in position in enough time to do some good? Well, yes, we did; and if you talked about a defensive position, we had one. Also, we were in a good position to be very aggressive with the artillery pieces, what with four pieces on top of Big Kennesaw and four more pieces atop Little Kennesaw; we were in an excellent position to overlook the Federal activities, and we began a careful and methodical bombardment on key elements of the enemy below. We had other artillery spaced out along the twelve-mile front all the way to Cheatham Hill. And with our men in gray snugly entrenched just below our artillery, we were truly ready for the enemy. It would only be a matter of time before the Federal line would make its move against us.

We figured that Sherman would definitely make a move on our position as we commanded the entire area and held the key to Marietta, a major stronghold before Atlanta. Although the conditions were most unfavorable for the Yankees, they had historically been rather successful in similar situations, like at Lookout Mountain and Missionary Ridge especially. They were not going to be overintimidated by this little mountain as precipitous as it was over the surrounding terrain. One disgusting soldier, undeserving to wear the gray uniform, said that them Yankees weren't going to pay no more attention to this little hill than if it were Gov. Joe Brown himself. I thought that was mighty irreverent talking about the governor of the great state of Georgia, even if he had been something of a hardhead about certain things, like being selfish with the state defense arsenal. Ben and I were doing our duty with the artillery, but sometimes we hankered to be down there with the infantry where it seemed the real fighting was going on. But every day old Sergeant Masterson would remind us of how important our jobs were, how the infantry couldn't make it without the artillery, and how proud we should be of the fine job we were doing. And I guess we were; it was just all so formalized and organized, it seemed. We ran those batteries like machines—machines of death and destruction. And we did a good job.

When we first arrived at the top of the mountain, it was during the night, and all was darkness as we began to make the final preparations on the gun pits, which had already been dug and built pretty much during the hours before. By daylight, we were able to look out across the great expanse of the countryside below, and we could see how very beautiful the north Georgia land really was. For all the times we had looked at and admired the mountain, we had never ascended her slopes and seen what real visionary treasures lay exposed at the summit. To see them for the very first time under these circumstances and conditions was most unusual, we thought.

Within a couple of days, the blue forces were swelling below us, and it was rather obvious by now that the Yankees just couldn't stand to not take a stab at us. It would be a foolhardy attempt by Sherman to make a frontal assault on such a defensive position, but then it never had stopped them before. *So what would be different about this time?* they, no doubt, thought. They would make the assault, and they would make it soon. It was hot by now around the last of June 1864. The war had been stubbornly going on for more than three years.

On June 22, General Hood—under the command of Gen. Joseph E. Johnston—was directed to pull his forces from the Marietta side, around the southern side of Kennesaw, to the south at Zion Church, where he was to prepare to engage the Yankee line, or near Kolb's Farm. This precipitous assault on the right Federal lines would culminate in two unsuccessful attacks with heavy losses to the Confederates. As we found out later, the unsuspecting Confederates were going up against a well-entrenched Yankee line, and over fifty-two artillery batteries were bearing down in both a direct fire and an extended line of enfilade fire designed to catch the Confederates in a heavy cross fire, which they did.

Although the assault at Kolb's Farm was costly to our side, it did tend to stem the flanking of the left Confederate line at that time and evidently caused the Federals to have more confidence in making a frontal assault themselves.

By June 27, all hell broke loose, and the Federals began to mount an assault like you wouldn't believe. From where we stood, we could see blue lines moving in great force across the fields below toward the base of the mountain.

We were directed to place as much fire as possible on these moving lines, which were constantly being followed by more and more forces. We were getting off about three rounds per minute, which was right at our maximum rate of fire. The barrel was getting extremely hot, as it always did at this pace of firing, and you had to be careful that you didn't accidentally place your bare hand on the almost gleaming hot iron. The constant barrage of roaring explosions, as the cannons fired, took a heavy toll on your ears, which sometimes would bleed from the repeated concussions. And what was worse was that there was hardly any break in this infernal pounding of artillery and musketry fire.

We could see the blue regiments moving forward on our lines across the fields and up the base of the slope. Somewhere along the base of the mountain, we began to lose sight of the blue bellies because of the remaining trees; but at that point, our rifle pits were well covered all the way over the slope, and we began to cut them down like rats in the woodpile. But there was so many that they just kept a-comin' wave after wave after wave, it seemed, until the whole area was saturated with musket fire coming and going. It was like Gettysburg but in reverse as, this time, we were the well-protected and well-entrenched defensive line on a steep mountain.

The Federals, no doubt, thought that, like Missionary Ridge, they would just overrun us with numbers, but it wasn't working here at Kennesaw Mountain. The Federals would advance so far, and then they would fall back for a while. In a little bit, here, they would come again with new vitality and renewed determination.

The bullets were passing in the trees and overhead like a tremendous swarm of hornets all around. And the sting from one of those hornets could, and often was, very deadly.

"Zing, zing, zing, whiz, pow, pow, pow!" went the barrage and counterbarrage of heavy rifle fire.

Our artillery fire was still being directed above our own line and onto the enemy in the open field above, designed to inflict as much additional damage as possible. And I believe we were doing a pretty fine job. Sherman had made a bad judgment call this time, and the Federal losses multiplied.

We were also picking up some Federal artillery fire with exploding shells toward the top of the mountain for a while when they were trying to cut down our positions and knock out some of our batteries, but because of the steep elevation, the Federal artillery was mostly ineffective.

Down the line, we heard that a major assault–or rather the bulk of the assault–was taking place against the lower slopes at Little Kennesaw, Pigeon Hill, which was much lower and full of great boulders and even farther over at a place that was to become known as Cheatham Hill. The assaults in these places, especially at Cheatham Hill, were massive and unbelievable as we were told. The attack on Big Kennesaw, where we were with our battery, was really a feigned attack while the real business was being conducted on the lesser slopes. But in all this time, the gray line never broke.

After a long-drawn-out effort of almost two weeks of this kind of stalemate, Sherman decided to turn his attentions elsewhere. He began to withdraw into a great flanking movement once again, and he moved his army south and southwest toward Powder Springs and toward the Chattahoochee River. He would just do the old dancing side step one more time.

From then on, we too had to take a new posture and retreat to protect our territory. Although we had been successful, even victorious, at Kennesaw Mountain, still, it mattered little in the overall consideration of stopping the advance of the enemy.

Of course, Atlanta–the heart of the great South–lay behind us and across the Chattahoochee River. Our movements and activities now would carry the two armies, parts or whole, to new places with new names like Smyrna, Ruff's Mill, Nickajack Creek, and the Chattahoochee line just on the northern side of the great Chattahoochee River, last stopping point before approaching Atlanta.

There would definitely be fighting and various levels of skirmishing in all these places as the massive Federal army moved around like a great sloth, destroying and absorbing all in its path of resistance.

Federal cavalry raids were sent out all throughout the area to gather foodstuffs; foraging they called it. There probably wasn't a house, farm, village, or whiskey still untouched within fifty miles on either side of the great blue monster.

I knew our own farm must have been raided for anything useful they could find, although it wouldn't be much at our place, and they probably burned the house and barns just to spite. We hadn't heard any word from the family, what with all the goings-on and being constantly under attack or pursuit, entrenching a new position, or being on the move.

We hardly had time to spit in between minor engagements. We had heard that Salt Springs had been invaded as well as Sweetwater Town and even New Manchester, where Ma and Anna were working in the factory mill, and that the Federals had captured and burned the mill and most of the town. We could only hope and pray that Ma, Anna, and the others had somehow safely escaped to Campbellton or maybe to Columbus or West Point. We prayed for their safety every day.

It had been some time now since we had heard any word from Pa, who was still riding with General Wheeler's cavalry, which was doing much damage to the perimeters of the Federal army and causing great havoc on their supply lines. But we didn't know exactly where they were or how Pa was doing. We could only hope and pray.

Also, Will, Samuel, and Levi were out there somewhere. Who knew where? How they were doing was only a guess by now. This war had really torn our family apart, and it might be years, it seemed, before we might all be together again, if ever.

But we didn't have much time to be depressed or think about it all as we too, every day, were fighting for our lives, our army, and our beloved Southland. Where would it all end? What would be the final outcome of this great travesty that had divided this nation and had pitted brother against brother and father against son within many families? Thank goodness our family was all Southerners, and we were sticking together in this fight. If we died on the battlefield or elsewhere, it would not be by the hand of our own family.

The days passed, and as they did, the armies jockeyed for positions of defense and offense. Within a few weeks, the Confederate army had moved across the Chattahoochee River and set up new defensive positions along the eastern outskirts of Atlanta along a little creek called Peachtree.

By now, it seemed that Pres. Jefferson Davis had become disenchanted with the maneuvering tactics of Gen. Joseph E. Johnston and had replaced him in command with fighting Gen. John Bell Hood, whom he knew would engage the enemy as he had at Kolb's Farm and other admirable attacks. He was definitely a fighting soldier, and now more than ever before, President Davis was wanting a fighting offensive to ward off the ever-advancing Federal army. After all, he reasoned that if Atlanta fell, the South might well be doomed, and he was probably right in that thought. Much debate ensued over General Johnston's replacement, but perhaps it was time to make a change. Something had to be done. But it seemed that circumstances were not to favor our great Southern army.

After the Federals also advanced across the Chattahoochee River and set up for a line of attack, Hood ordered a Confederate assault from Peachtree Creek, and all hell broke loose again. The fighting was fierce and conducted through and under the cover of much undergrowth of vines, trees, and scrub often so thick that the enemy was laying into each other without notice or forewarning. There was a lot of hand-to-hand fighting and musketry fire at extremely close range. It was like fighting in a briar patch. After several unsuccessful assaults at considerable loss, Hood ordered a general withdrawal back to the more established Confederate lines.

By now, the Federal army was swinging around the Atlanta fortifications to the northeast side toward the settlement of Decatur, where another major offensive by the Federal army was taking place. The fighting was awesome and centered on partly a stately new home that was ironically under construction by the Hurt family. It would be devastated in the conflagration that ensued as the two armies moved back and forth, attempting, among other things, to gain or keep control of the Western and Atlantic Railroad, which ran through Decatur from Augusta on its way to Atlanta. This too would cut off a major artery to the nerve center in Atlanta. And having accomplished this, the Federal army moved around farther to the east where the battle continued in what was to become known as the Battle of Atlanta, where the living, dead, and wounded were all immortalized in the fighting around and for Leggett's Hill, one of the last bastions of defensive positions held by the Confederates. Thousands died, thousands more were wounded, and thousands of others would live to fight again another day at Ezra Church on the west side of Atlanta and at the Battle of Jonesboro on the south side. There at Jonesboro, General Hood attacked the Federal army, resulting in heavy losses, and the Federals gained control of the Macon Railroad and the Rough and Ready West Point Railroad. The seal of fate was finally placed on the city of Atlanta, Georgia.

On the night of September 1, 1864, the Confederate army evacuated the city of Atlanta, blowing up valuable and badly needed ammunition stores and supplies so that they would not fall into the hands of the enemy.

On the morning of September 2, 1864, Federal troops moved into the city and began formal occupation. On September 5, President Lincoln declared a national day of celebration of the fall of Atlanta and several other Union victories, such as Admiral Farragut's victory at Mobile Bay.

Though the South had been severely wounded, the war would rage on for some time.

The Bleeding South

Atlanta had fallen, and all hope of saving the great city from the devastation of the Yankees had fallen with her. One of the last great bastions of Confederate resistance was now in the hands of the enemy. But the Confederate armies were still intact, if somewhat diminished in numbers.

General Lee and the Army of Northern Virginia were still fighting up north somewhere, and other armies and regiments were scattered all over the country. We happened to be here in an evacuation from Jonesboro, Georgia.

It was our understanding that we would make our way out of the supposed path of the Federal army and somewheres toward the north. We had done all we can do right now under these circumstances. We had fought hard and long with all that we had. We did the very best that each man could do against overwhelming odds and a well-supplied enemy.

As we made our way northerly and around the western side of Atlanta, up toward West Georgia, we saw many signs of death and devastation as a result of the Federal raiding parties over the countryside. Hardly had a significant farm been untouched in some way. Many houses and barns had been burned in retribution for the so-called uncivil acts by the civilian population against the occupation and presence of the enemy.

As we arrived at Campbellton, Georgia, along the south banks of the Chattahoochee River, we witnessed the ravages of war that had been indirectly visited on that little town, the county seat of our own Campbell County. Only the churches and the Masonic lodge remained standing along with a few homes. All the other public buildings and places of mercantile had been burned and destroyed. A policy of scorched earth Sherman called it. Take the war to the civilian population and make them pay for it. After all, Sherman said, "War is hell."

Ben and I decided, since we were so close to home and in particular to New Manchester, that perhaps we could get a short furlough to visit Ma and Anna, check on them, and be sure they were all right. Fortunately, we secured a three-day pass, and it would be our responsibility to catch up with the regiment wherever it was as it headed northward.

So after taking a ferry across the river, we headed up a ways toward New Manchester. Now just up the river was the confluence of the Sweetwater Creek with the Chattahoochee River. From there, all we had to do was go upstream several miles to get to New Manchester.

But first, we would arrive at the site of the old Alexander's mill, which had been burned to the ground along with the miller's house and the few outbuildings. All was destroyed. Ben and I were anxious for the safety of Ma and Anna, and we wondered what had happened at New Manchester.

There was some evidence here and there of some rather significant fighting that had gone on evidently in defense of the mills. Ben and I didn't even know that there had been any fighting around these parts, but later, we were to find out that there had been a fair amount, nothing major like we had seen but still a good bit of skirmishing and such.

Arriving at New Manchester, we found a ghostly and ghastly sight. The formerly magnificent five-story mill factory of New Manchester was nothing but a somber blackened ruin of standing bricks with no insides, no floors, no wood, and no roof. Every inch of flammable wood had been burned and charred out. The remains of the walls stood as a silent testimony to what must have taken place. There was no one around to tell the story. Everybody was gone, even the dogs.

The company store and all the houses had been burned to the ground also. There was not one single standing structure left. Foundations lay like dead comrades in arms, slain by the oppressors. Silent and smokeless chimneys stood as deaf-mutes shocked by the horror of what must have happened. The only sound on this otherwise bright, sunny morning was the roar of the river as it rushed ever onward over the shoals and the gentle breeze blowing carelessly through the great trees, many now also killed and dead from the apparent great heat of the fires.

We finally found the remains of the house that Ma and Anna were living in with Martha Jenkins. There was nothing. We could only conjecture what had happened, and we figured that all the occupants of the town must have fled south to Columbus, West Point, or perhaps Macon. Surely, Ma and Anna and the others were safe.

After surveying the general grounds and rubble, we decided to go on up the creek to Mr. and Mrs. Ferguson's home and mill and see if perhaps we could find Mary and Angus.

About a mile up the creek, we found a similar sight, only in a smaller scene. The mill and their home had been burned and destroyed also. No sign of life existed except for the birds singing in the trees and the rush of the river. It was all so eerie. What had happened to everyone? It was truly a mystery.

Ben and I decided to camp there for the night, and the next day, we would go into Salt Springs and find out just what had taken place. Surely, someone would be in Salt Springs.

That night as the whip-poor-wills began their almost mournful laments, Ben and I sat close to the campfire and talked about the war, all the circumstances and situations we had been in, and the close calls we had had ourselves. I didn't really want to, but I couldn't help crying over all the tumultuous circumstances. It was just too much. Finally, I too fell asleep in the deep of the night there on the bank of Sweetwater Creek, and my thoughts faded into the obscurity of the darkness.

The sun rose lazily the next morning as it nosed its way through the tree limbs and scrub brush on the opposite ridge across the creek. There was no hurry, no early morning bugle call, no shouting to get moving, nothing except the sweet songbirds of morning heralding the creation of another day. Ben and I both awakened as though we had been in some drunken stupor the whole night before. It would take a few minutes before the solitude of tranquility could be shaken off and before we could get our wits about us. Today we would travel up to Salt Springs to investigate just what all had really happened around there.

About three miles up the road, we came into Salt Springs, the sleepy little town we had known in our childhood before the war. The little town, what it was, was surprisingly intact and appeared to be relatively unscathed from the ravages of war. There were a few scattered homes here and there, and the livery was open, as well as the blacksmith shop, but that was about it. The old brick factory had obviously been burned and was only charred remains. The Bowden house and post office were still standing as they were, one and the same.

Everything looked fairly normal to us as far as we could see. We had seen a few folks here and there, but nearly all the fields we had seen everywhere were lying fallow with almost no one to work them. Normally, we would have seen local farmers and even city folks working their fields, for now we were in late harvest time, but there was little or nothing to harvest after the Yankees had been through. It was most eerie to see in our imagination the ghosts of so many dead soldiers working their fields as over 90 percent of all soldiers in the Confederate army were farmers just like us.

The big trees surrounding the Bowden house post office were a welcome sight, and the shady grove they created was a comforting sanctuary for the lingering citizenry as everybody picked up their mail and whatever news they could from long-seen loved ones. Actually, we too were more anxious to see if any mail had arrived for us or any of the family than we were to talk immediately to any of the folks standing around the grounds, of which there were only a few scattered about.

We walked in the door of the two-story piedmont-plantation-style house, and taking off our caps and carrying them in our hands, we rather slowly and reservedly made our way over to the grilled box that served as the official post office. No one was there, so we rang the little bell that was provided.

Ding! No one came.

Ding! Ding! Ding!

"Ooookayyyy, okayyy, hold your horses. Be there in a minute" came a gruffly old voice.

About that time, from the back of the wall came old man Bowden himself, looking just like he did a hundred years ago, only older and a little more frayed around the edges.

He leaned back his head to lift the lower part of his bifocals so he could see just who we were and what we wanted.

He squinted a little and made a little expression of surprise on his face, which was followed by the most delighted smile and countenance. "Why you're R. B. Jett's boys, aren't you, sons?"

"Yes, sir, we are."

"Let's see, you're the youngest boys, aren't you? Ah, Ben and Steven, I think."

"Yes, sir, Judge." You know, he really was a judge too, and we wanted to be mighty respectful.

"Do you have any letters for our family, Judge?" we asked with great anxiety.

"Well, boys, I don't know. A lot has been going on around here lately. There might be, yes. It seems that there have been several letters to come in over the last few months, and no one has picked them up since, let's see, since I guess the Yankees came through back in June and July. Matter of fact, boys, this isn't really a safe place for two Confederate soldiers to be, even if you are on a furlough or something. I'd be a mite careful around these parts 'cause Yankee patrols have been all over the area, not as bad now as it was but still the same. You need to be careful.

"Yeaaaah, here they are. I'd just set them aside for you, figured somebody'd be here sooner or later to claim them for the family. You can just take them all. There's four letters here. Good luck and Godspeed, boys. Blessings on you and your family. Let me know how everybody's doing."

We thanked the judge, and taking the letters, we turned and walked slowly out the door and back into the outside light, where we could see good to read the outside of the envelopes.

Four letters. "One, two, three, four," we counted together. They were addressed as follows: "Mrs. R. B. Jett" on one, "Mrs. R. B. Jett and Family," on another, "Mr. William Jett" on the third, and "Mr. Steven Jett and Mr. Ben Jett" on the last one. Who could that one be from?

We too, like the others around, found us a good shade tree, and we settled down to read the news, thinking that it was our family duty to open and read all the letters, even the ones addressed to Ma since we didn't know where anyone was or just when we might see any of the family again, if ever.

We figured that we'd save the more personal letter to us for last and that we'd start out reading the letter to Ma. Ben would read the first one, and then I'd read the next. The letter read as follows:

May 10, 1864

Dearest Wife,

Please know that I am well and in good health. I hope you and the children are also. I worry a lot about the boys off in the war, and I worry a lot about little Anna, although I expect she is quite the young lady by now.

We have moved since I wrote you the last time. We are now camped on the south bank of Holston River at a Methodist camp ground. I wonder why it is I haven't heard from you lately. Let me know if them seed I sowed before I left home is likely to grow. When I get in reach of home, I will come home some morning before day and wake you up with sweet kisses.

Give my love to all.

Your Loving Husband,
R. B. Jett

"Okay, Ben, I'll read the next one. I'm gonna read this one from Will."

August 30, 1864,
Fort Gilmer

Dearest Mother and Family,

We have been on the move here lately from the beautiful valley of Virginia to our present position southeast of Richmond, where our Company B is in charge of the artillery. We are in sight of the Yankees, and though several shells have been thrown into the fort, there has been no attack since I have arrived.

There is fighting nearly every day. Sometime in sight of our lines of breastworks and that of the enemy is close to each other and extend a distance of thirty miles along the countryside. Heavy cannonading is going on all the time.

I am so sorry that you all have had some of the problems you have had. It is grief to me to know that the enemy destroyed all you had to live on. God knows I would be so glad to see this cruel war come to a close so I could return home to my family. Don't be uneasy about me as I haven't taken up with bad habits so commonly practiced in the army.

I will write again as soon as I can.

My Love to All,

Will

"So William has ended up in the artillery too. How about that Ben?" I said.
"Yeah, I hope he likes it better than we do," Ben said.
"Let's see this one now."
And Ben began to read aloud.

August 15, 1864

My Dearest William,

"Oh boy, this is going to be good," said Ben.

Yesterday was a day I'll never forget in a million years. The Yankees have been bombing us here in the city for several weeks now. The first person killed by an exploding shell was a little twelve-year-old girl down on Mitchell Street. I don't know who she was, but they said she was one of Mr. Hardy's nieces and that she was working in the general store for him part time during the summer to earn money to go to art school. What a pity!

But yesterday, William, I went down to Mama Leana's house to get some butter; and when I got there, the whole house had been destroyed from bombshells. I looked around as best I could until, under some big boards, I found a foot sticking out, and I just knew it was Mama Leana's, and it was. She wasn't dead yet, but she was all bloody and had a great big gash in the top of her head, and her arm and both legs were broken. I tried not to panic but ran to get help. We got her out and over to a makeshift hospital at the Christian church so the doctors could see her as they were so busy already with the wounded and all.

The doctor dressed her wounds and put splints on her arm and her two legs and said it would have to be up to us to take care of her from there on and to watch for fever settin' in 'cause it probably would.

After three days if she has survived, she'll need to see the doctor again, but only God can know if she will live through all this, especially at her age of seventy-four.

William, I miss you so much. My heart nearly breaks with hurt and not knowing where you are or that you are well. I wish we had gone ahead and gotten married before the war 'cause we may never have a chance to consummate our love for each other.

I am so sick and tired of Atlanta and all this so-called siege. Some days we get almost five thousand shells a day, and we have to live in holes in the ground like they did in Vicksburg. A lot of folks evacuated the city, but most felt that our army will be able to defeat the enemy and save our splendid city. We can only pray to God for its salvation.

I have to go. Please write me and tell me you are still alive and how much you love me as I must have some comforting words from you.

All My Love Now and Always,

Sharon

"Well, well, ummmmm," I said.

"Yeah, that's old Sharon Hamilton, isn't it?" said Ben.

"I remember her. Don't you? She came out to Salt Springs one time with her uncle to look at some mules, and that's when she and Will met down by the creek when their wagon broke down. Remember?"

"Yeah, I remember, all right. She's all Will could talk about for two weeks, and then he started to court her over in Atlanta, didn't he?"

"Yeah, sounds pretty nice though. We'd better save this for Will. I just hope he doesn't get pissed off for us reading his mail."

"Nawww," said Ben. "He'll be all right. After all, we are his brothers, you know. We got to look out for each other." He had a grin and then a big smile.

"Okay, let's see, we got one more to us," said Ben. "Let's flip to see who reads it."

"No, go ahead, you can read it," I said. "I'd rather listen anyway."

Grave Robbing at the Bowden House

July 4, 1864

My Dear Steven and Ben,

Hope this letter finds you two in good spirits and in good health. I was so sorry to have missed you boys last fall down here in Augusta. When I got home, Lucy told me that you had come by, and she even gave me the whistle you made for me. Works pretty good. Thank you very much.

I was going to write sooner, but I really didn't want to get caught up by two soldier boys like you, even if you were real cute. I figured, like all the other young men, you'd just go and get yourselves killed or something. So I didn't really want to experience the pain. Selfish of me I know, but that is the truth. But tonight was the Fourth of July, and I couldn't help but remember the exciting time we had at cousin Stephanie's up in Atlanta and how we watched the colorful explosions and held hands.

Ben, I adore you. But, Steven, I love you with all my heart. I miss you so much and would like to see you again as soon as this stupid war is all over. Stephanie plans to have another big party soon as it will be her birthday November 4, and we plan to go up to Atlanta to celebrate her eighteenth birthday. Please write to me and try to come to Stephanie's birthday party if you can. I will not rest one minute until I see you again and know that you are all well. Until then, I will carry your whistle with me every day. And when I blow it, I'll be calling you home.

Love to All,

Debbie Langford
Augusta, Georgia

"Boy! Hey, how do you rate so high up there?" Ben exclaimed.

"I don't know," I said. "Just lucky, I guess, very lucky indeed."

"I can't get over that," said Ben. "She was supposed to be in love with me. Really, though, I like Stephanie. She's more my type."

"Boy, my butt's about worn out," I said as I got to my feet. The late morning sun was moving across the sky, and the early morning shade had shifted to the east.

We'd have to be going soon because we had to be back to our unit by sundown the next day.

We were getting our things together when, out of the blue and with no warning whatsoever, a Yankee cavalry patrol came riding into the yard of the Bowden house. Must have been about fifty riders, it seemed, just all of a sudden. Ben and I decided to sit back down under the darkness of the shade tree and try to look as unobtrusive and as inconspicuous as possible. We'd probably stand out like a sore thumb. It was too late to run or try to hide.

The captain, I supposed, rode up to the steps of the house, got off his horse, and handing his reins off to an adjutant walked inside. They were carrying the colors of the Fifth Kentucky Calvary.

In the meantime, the men sort of spread out, and some rode over into the small family cemetery just across the way. A few men got down and began removing the top slab of a sarcophagus so as to expose the inside. They were being rather rambunctious and carrying on considerably. Suddenly, one of the soldiers took a rifle butt and began hitting it against something inside. We heard the crashing of glass breaking. Then he reached down and pulled out this gold watch and chain and held it up like it was some kind of treasure he had just captured.

"Ain't no dead rebel gonna need this no more!" he shouted.

About that same time, some old-timer walked over, sat down by me and Ben, and watching the action began to tell us that old man Bowden's son-in-law, Captain Summerlin, had been shot and killed at the Battle of Kennesaw Mountain and that he had a young baby son. His mother wanted him to be able to see his father when he got older, so they had buried him aboveground in a casket with a glass window on top. Evidently, the Yanks had heard about it from somewhere and had figured on robbing the grave.

Ben and I did have our muskets down at our sides, and we did have a couple of sidearms, but we knew we'd be no match for a whole cavalry detachment. All we could do was watch the indignity perpetuated on the fallen comrade. It had been a common practice for the enemy of both sides to rob the dead of any treasures found, and this was not too different, although it really stuck in our craw to see this happen not more than two hundred feet away.

While all the commotion was going on, we figured we'd use the opportunity to try to slip away, and we sort of excused ourselves and told the old man to watch our cover as we tried to escape.

Just as we were moving back and down the way behind us toward the privy hedge, some blue-bellied Yankee saw us and headed our way. We made it to the privy hedge and quickly hid in the bushes.

About the same time, the captain had come back out of the house, put on his gloves, and remounted. Upon remounting, he quickly turned his horse around and bounded off in the opposite direction away from the house. The other soldiers followed except for the one who was trying to find us. We laid low and did our best to not make any noise that would give us away. By that time, Ben and I both had our handguns out and ready for whatever might be required. The privy hedge was so thick that the horse couldn't maneuver through it, so the Yank dismounted and began to flail through the hedge, trying to flush us out. By now, maybe five or ten minutes had passed, and we figured that the rest of the raiders were on down the road already. This raucous-looking Yankee was cursing up a storm at us and demanding that we come out and surrender ourselves.

We stood fast, and just as the Yankee finally opened up the last bushes with his saber, hacking away as he came in, "Bang! Kapow!" went the unmistakable screaming roar of a single round from Ben's Colt Army .44-caliber revolver. The bullet entered the middle forehead of the Yankee, and blood rushed out in a great burbling spurt as his eyes opened wide and white in unbelief, and he slowly slumped to the ground.

Boy, we've done it now, I thought.

"They're going to be back on us like ducks on a June bug," I said "Let's get out of here."

By that time, the old man who had been talking to us caught up and told us to go on and get out of here and that he would take care of the dead Yank. He'd get a shovel and bury him right there under the outhouse, a very appropriate spot, and nobody would ever be the wiser.

So we thanked the old man and decided the best and only thing we could do was to get out of there as fast as we could. We grabbed up the Yank's horse, and Ben jumped on first and then me behind, and we rode off double, carrying our muskets and gear as best we could, heading for home, which was in the opposite direction of where the raiders had gone anyway.

Three miles west, we came to our gate at our fence line. The old house was about another thousand feet down the white sandy road. The fields were all grown up from neglect, and the vines and grass were out of control everywhere, but it was home. The main house, smokehouse, well house, and corncrib were all okay, but the large old barn had been burned to the ground. The house door was open, and the house had obviously been ransacked and looted. All the livestock was gone; the chickens and even the dogs were gone. Probably been shot for target practice. We'd heard that the Yankees did that just for fun and sport.

We were both tired and depressed to see our farm in this sort of condition, but it really was good to be home for the first time now in almost two years.

We decided not to hang around too long as the raiders might be on our trail, and we needed to get on back to our unit, so we soon rode out, leaving the farm and our memories behind us.

The Road to Nashville

The pain of defeat lingered in our minds and bodies for weeks after the fall of Atlanta. Ben and I were no different from other soldiers, and we too felt our pain at seeing our homeland taken and destroyed so mercilessly. As we made our way back to our Army of Tennessee, we saw destruction everywhere–homes and barns burned and fields destroyed. But things were not over yet.

The fourth day's morning at about four thirty, we finally found our unit as it had been moving around quite a bit. It had last made camp just west of Salt Springs at a place generally called Skint Chestnut. The army was fairly spread out, but we were able to finally locate our unit, the Ninth Georgia Light Artillery. First thing we did was report in, to Sergeant Masterson, who reprimanded us at first for being late and then congratulated us on finding them at all that soon.

"Get some shut-eye for a few hours if you can. We'll be on the move again soon, I expect," he said in a fatherly sort of way.

By the next evening, we had made our way to a place called Dark Corner, where we set in for camp for a day or two. We didn't know for how long, but we had heard that we would be making a move on Allatoona Pass, where a Union supply depot was now stationed along the northern railroad and Federal supply line. General Hood, who still commanded the Confederate army of about thirty thousand men or so, hoped to draw Sherman out from Atlanta and to have the opportunity to reengage him in the rolling hills of north Georgia once again, affording him the opportunity of defeating the Federal army. This could be possible as it seemed that Sherman's objective all along was to engage and destroy us, the enemy, which he had only partially done up to this point and time. Soon the enemy was to be engaged at Allatoona Pass, and Sherman had already sent part of his army northerly from Atlanta under the command of a General Schofield, in pursuit of General Hood.

The garrison at Allatoona Pass was under a greatly fortified defensive position, although they could not match the numbers of the impending Confederates. An opportunity was extended for them to surrender and avoid a bloodbath, but the commander declined as he had already been signaled from Sherman, atop Kennesaw Mountain, to "hold the fort." And hold the fort he did after a very heavy and costly assault by our boys, who were ultimately unable to break their lines of defense because of the restrictive topography of the pass itself; and finally, the assault failed. We must have put a hundred rounds of fire from our cannon alone into the mouth of that pass, and it did no good.

During the melee, Sergeant Masterson caught a random shot miniball in his right shoulder, and he began to bleed profusely. I grabbed him up, yelling, "The sarge has taken a ball! Get me a compress or something!" I grabbed up a piece of jacket that had been thrown down and immediately began to press it onto the wound to suppress the bleeding. Evidently, an artery had been severed from the way it was bleeding. He'd probably lose his arm at least if he didn't downright bleed to death. We got him over to the side and up against a tree and made him as comfortable as we could until the fighting was over.

After the battle, we were gathering up the wounded, and Ben went over with a friend of his, George Scott, to check on Sergeant Masterson.

He was so still.

"Hey!" George yelled. "The sarge is dead, I think! He won't move!"

Apparently, he had gone into shock after losing so much blood; and unable to suppress his own wound, he had just slowly bled to death. We all felt so bad, like it had been our fault; maybe had we been able to do more, we could have saved him. We had, by now, known a lot of men who died in battle or from wounds, but the sarge had truly been like a father to us all. George, in particular, just broke down and wept.

"He was a good man," said Ben.

"Yes, he was a very good man indeed," I agreed as we proceeded to carry him to the back lines. He was from Oconee County, Alabama, and we knew he would want his family to know the circumstances of his death. It would be up to our commander to make the full report and to notify the family.

Things were not the same now that Sergeant Masterson had been killed. George Scott was promoted to sergeant to take his place, but he really didn't want to be no sergeant. By now, we were just all doing our jobs like some kinds of animals. All we did was fight and march, eating when we could and when we had the food. If we didn't have it, we just skipped eating, but we never skipped fighting or marching.

By now, we were well on our way to Nashville, Tennessee, to attack the Federal army there, and Sherman's men had already turned tail and went the other way back to Atlanta. He obviously had other plans of some kind.

By mid-November 1864, we knew that Sherman had forced the civilian evacuation of Atlanta and had set it afire, destroying nearly the whole city or what was left of it. He then set out for the Georgia coast across the great state of Georgia with nothing between him and the Atlantic Ocean but the "fat of the land" to live on and feed an army of sixty thousand men. They would cut a swath about sixty miles wide and lay total waste to everything in their path. With no opposition, Sherman would arrive at the Atlantic Ocean and capture Savannah, Georgia, right at Christmastime, when he would present the city as a Christmas present on December 24, 1864, to President Lincoln.

We, under the command of General Hood, would press on toward Nashville by way of Spring Hill and Franklin. The Army of Tennessee still had a lot of fight even now, and we were ready once again to engage the enemy. Hood was just looking for the right opportunity, and he finally got it at Spring Hill. But before the lines could be put in place for the attack, the Federal army–under General Schofield–made a nighttime escape less than six hundred yards away from our advance pickets, away from Spring Hill, and into the town of Franklin. By the next day, November 15, 1864, all the Federal supply wagons had crossed over the Harpeth River, and the troops were well entrenched on the south and west sides of town with very good defenses. General Hood was so mad that he ordered eighteen thousand men to attack as soon as possible. By three o'clock in the afternoon, the Battle of Franklin had begun. It would rage on for six hours until around nine that night.

The fighting was fierce and covered a fairly long line. Our job, as usual, was to pound the tar out of the enemy positions as best we could. We took some fire ourselves but were a moderate distance from the heavy fighting.

Five great Southern generals would die in this one battle alone. They were O. F. Strahl, States Rights Gist, John Adams, H. B. Granbury, and Patrick Cleburne. The latter two generals had led, among other things, a brilliant defense in the Kennesaw line at Cheatham Hill against five brigades of assaulting Federals. But Franklin would be no match for fortitude or fame, and the battle would claim its own day of infamy. At the conclusion of this battle, the five generals would all share the same makeshift morgue, being the front porch of the Carnton home, just on the outskirts of town, along with fifteen hundred fellow comrades to be buried in the family graveyard. Over eighty-five hundred casualties would be suffered from both sides, about three Confederates for every one Federal. It was a devastating blow to the Confederacy, and what was worse was that, during the night, Schofield pulled right out of Franklin, abandoning his positions, and moved right into Nashville, where he joined up his twenty-five thousand men with General Thomas's thirty thousand men, who were already entrenched and vastly fortified.

Supposedly, Grant had ordered Thomas to attack us; but for some reason, he was taking his own sweet time. And sure enough, it was working for, instead of against, him. Now with Schofield's troops, he had amassed a sizable fighting force against our own dwindling strength of about twenty-three thousand.

Hood was caught in a classical sort of stalemate. He was overwhelmingly outnumbered, so a frontal assault on Nashville would be really, strategically unwise, yet he had nowhere else to go. It was doubtful that he could muster an orderly retreat of his army because of the circumstances. So, we waited for almost two weeks when finally, on December 15, 1864, Thomas ordered his own attack against our positions just south of Nashville. Starting out in a dense fog at around six in the morning, our lines were first attacked by Negro troops of James B. Steedman against Cheatham's division on the right–yes, the one and the same Cheatham of Cheatham Hill fame at Kennesaw. This would be a secondary action while the main force of the Federal attack would fall against our weaker left line and then a hard attack at the center. Somehow–and I didn't know how we did it–our artillery unit of one hundred forty-eight men held off a four-thousand-man Union infantry division for two hours before the left line began to fall apart. Cheatham was brought into the center to reinforce the position, but when Schofield's Federal reserve was brought in, the odds were too great, and Hood ordered a retreat.

By nightfall, Thomas was sure he had defeated us, but he hadn't. By the next day, we had moved two miles to the south and were ready again.

The Federals once again moved on us in great force, although we had formed a shorter and much stronger perimeter. The progress of the battle this day was slow and delayed. One Federal assault on the right had been thrown back by our boys, who were doing just fine until, almost at the same time, two impatient Yankee generals decided to storm the steep hills on our left line with two brigades at about four in the afternoon. We can't believe it, but spectators were over on the far hill, yelling and cheering on the Federal troops as they made their way up the steep slopes. Within a very short time, they were at the top and waving the Stars and Stripes in mortal defiance of our now estranged line. About the same time, the right line gave; and flags, not ours, were waving over there.

It appeared that the Union flag was all over and that our lines had fallen indeed. Before losing our entire army, Hood ordered a retreat, and a heavy rain began to fall. Our spirits were dampened both inside and out during that gloomy and deadly afternoon.

This would be the last real battle of the war that I and Ben would fight in. For us, the war was essentially over. This final battle ultimately left the whole of the Army of Tennessee routed and in final disarray as we retreated to the south. It would be the end officially of our army as we knew it. Hood would soon resign his command, and every soldier was on his own.

It was almost Christmastime, and nearly everyone headed for home or for other parts unknown. Some units stayed together as best they could. Many were captured by the enemy.

In our own case, we had to abandon our cannons and left the batteries to the discretion of the Federal army. We skedaddled as fast as we could to the south. Stragglers would be picked up by the Yankees over the next several days for those who hung around. We sure didn't want to see the inside of no Yankee Northern prison.

We crossed hills and dales, creeks and dense underbrush as we escaped toward the south. About twenty miles away, we met up with other soldiers who had reconvened into smaller separate units, totally unorganized and with little purpose or direction at this point. There were three of us—me, Ben and George Scott—who had stayed together, and we decided to camp for a few days with this group we met up with on the bank of a fair-sized creek. It was a beautiful site to camp and would make a good place to rest up for a few days.

Most of the fellas were from the infantry of a number of different units. It wasn't long before we were making new friends and all discussing the battles and the whole goldarn war and what we were going to do now.

We all set around large group campfires with lots of talk way into the night. Several men had volunteered to serve as pickets around our perimeter for whatever good it would do. I never heard so much mouth at one gathering of men ever in my life. We heard about everything, from what I would consider stupidity to downright treason. Some wanted to surrender; some wanted to fight. Some just didn't "give a damn" anymore what happened.

Mostly, Ben, George, and I just listened; and, every once in a while, we might interject a word or two but nothing profound. By the following day, everyone pretty much decided that we'd all head toward home; and then if we wanted to rejoin with some other outfit, we would. Most of the men had fought some long and hard campaigns. They were tired and worn out. There were no supplies, no food, and no munitions. Many were barefoot. We were no army now. We were just a bunch of evacuees. So, either one by one or in small groups, they began to leave the camp over the next few days. After the third day, we decided we too would head for home.

All I can say was it was a long walk home. We kept mostly to the back roads and camped in the woods at night. We had to be careful not to expose ourselves too much, for Yankee cavalry patrols were all throughout the area, and we had to avoid certain parts entirely.

The news of the rest of the war that we picked up here and there wasn't too good either. General Lee was having a terrible time, and everybody said it was only a matter of days before it was all over. The South would not win this war. The odds now were too great. There was not enough left of us or our supplies to last much longer. Georgia itself had been invaded and cut completely in half by Sherman's army, who was now fighting in the Carolinas. Richmond, Virginia, the capital of the Confederacy, was barely holding on, and Lincoln had been reelected. It seemed we were doomed.

As we moved south, Ben, George, and I got to talking; and we decided, for us, that it wasn't over until it was over. We would move toward Virginia and try to meet up with some of the other boys up there. After all, somewhere out there was Will, Samuel, Levi, and Pa. As long as they were fighting, we would fight with them if we could find them.

Over the next several weeks, we moved toward Virginia ragged and torn and tired but still willing. Our progress was slow, and the only food we had was what we could find or kill along the way. It began to seem like a futile effort. We were making such slow progress that we figured maybe we should just try to catch up with some of our boys in the Carolinas, if possible. By the middle of February, we met up with the army of Joseph E. Johnston in South Carolina. We joined up with a regiment of irregulars made up of mostly Georgia boys from past scattered regiments like ours. We were issued weapons from fallen comrades, ammunition, and food; that was about it. Our commander was an older white-haired man named Col. Reginald Davis, whom we understood had seen a lot of action throughout the war. He was a good man with an even temperament and good disposition. We would do good under his leadership. We were ready to do whatever had to be done.

Sherman was moving out of the now captured Charleston, South Carolina, where all rail lines had been cut, and the city had succumbed to the Federal occupation. Now even Fort Sumter flew the Federal flag once again.

As Sherman cut his way across South Carolina, he pushed Johnston and our army into North Carolina, where in the latter part of March 1865 we would once again meet the enemy face-to-face at Bentonville. The only hope was for Johnson to be able to move far enough north and Lee far enough south to join forces. Then we might have a chance—a real chance, a last hope sort of chance. But that, it seemed, was not to happen.

At Bentonville, our army of gray was faced with overwhelming odds, and the so-called battle ended up being a series of defensive maneuvers as we were forced to fall back into retreat even further, much like the tactics of the old days in North Georgia only a year earlier.

By mid-April, word had come that General Lee had surrendered his Army of Northern Virginia at Appomattox Court House, Virginia, on April 12, 1865. Our fate was sealed, and a few days later, General Johnston surrendered our army to General Sherman, and the war was over, really over!

The Aftermath

These had been difficult years for everyone. There was hardly a family in the South or North who had not been touched in some way by this terrible war. Aside from the physical brutality of the war itself, there was the mental anguish of dealing with the physical loss of health, family, homes, and nearly all personal possessions of any kind.

We still didn't know what had happened to Ma, Anna, Pa, Will, Samuel, or Levi. Somehow you just went on without thinking too much, in the hope that they were all right. During the war itself, we didn't have much time to think anyway. We stayed pretty busy looking after our own hides, but now the war was over. A general armistice had been proclaimed, and it was time for all soldiers of the South and all but the regular army of the North to go home.

On the twenty-fifth day of April 1865, we mustered out of the Confederate army. We were permitted to take with us all our personal gear; weapons, if any; and any food available. Those with horses were permitted to keep their horse, so as to return to farming as soon as possible. The day we left camp was a dark, gloomy day, with rain threatening almost all day. It was a time of both sadness and joy inside. Sad, of course, because, finally, our cause was lost; on the other hand, there was joy because now maybe things could get back to normal. Or could they? Could things ever be normal again after something like this? I doubted it seriously. This was only wishful thinking.

The road back home was long and difficult. There was no longer the army to look for to direct our purpose or needs. Many of the boys couldn't accept the fact that the war was over and that we had lost or been defeated or given up, whatever had happened. The truth was almost impossible to believe.

For the next several weeks, we–like thousands and thousands of others–made our slow and painful way across the forlorn Southern landscape. Some would have homes and family to return to, others would have only parts of families and pieces of homes to return to, and still others would have nothing at all.

We bypassed Augusta, Georgia, on the way home as it just wasn't in our hearts to go there this time. We made our way as quickly as we could back toward Atlanta or what was left of it, our last big stop before home.

When we got to Atlanta, we found the city–much as we had heard–in a state of depression and misery. Most of the city was destroyed and burned with charred remains everywhere. Hulls of once formidable buildings were standing empty and hollow, with only silent brick and stone walls remaining as testimony to the devastation of Sherman's army. Many homes, in fact, the fair majority of homes, had been burned to the ground. People were living in huts and shacks of makeshift debris and in small camps around and throughout the city. There was a sort of vitality and urgency to the activity that permeated the city, something like a three-legged dog trying to keep up with the day-to-day demands of survival. By now, people had returned to the monumental tasks of cleaning up and rebuilding, but it would be a long and slow progress for quite a while.

While we were there, we decided to look up Herron's Restaurant– Stephanie's family business–down on Luckie Street, but it too was not to be found. As a matter of fact, the entire area had been totally destroyed. It was so unbelievable. How could almost an entire city just be wiped off the face of the earth? We tried to find their home up on Peachtree Street, but it too became painfully obvious that their home no longer existed either. The splendor and beauty of all the fine homes was gone. Only charred remains and an occasional tall standing chimney were all there was to be found. We asked some questions regarding the Herron family, but nobody knew where they were or anything about them. Most people, we were told, had just left the city for other safer places. Now that the war was over, perhaps they would return, but maybe they wouldn't. What did they have to come back to anyway?

"I bet they all went down to Augusta," I said to Ben.

"Yeah, probably did," he agreed.

"But you know, I don't know if I'd ever come back to something like this," Ben said.

"Well, we did, and this is what we found. I wonder what we'll find when we go home ourselves to Salt Springs and the farm."

"Couldn't be any worse than this," Ben blurted.

So, with additional fear and trepidation, we advanced on Salt Springs and home. Within a short distance of the sleepy little town, we could begin to tell that everything looked just about normal as far as we could tell. It was all pretty much like the day we had last been there back in the fall, of last year, the day we killed the Yankee grave robber. Well, it wasn't actually the grave robber himself, but it was one of his cohorts who, we knew, must have been just as bad.

We had barely escaped with our lives that day and at best could have spent the rest of the war in a Yankee prison somewhere. Ben and I made a vow not to talk about the incident to anyone at all because there still could be possible repercussions, although we considered it an act of war and not murder. Some things were just best left alone, and this was one of them.

We checked for mail at the Bowden house, but Mrs. Bowden said that there hadn't been any mail coming in for months now as she guessed all the service had been suspended. She was mighty glad to see us, though, and was so thankful that we had survived the war and all. She also said that we'd be pleased to know that our pa was home and had come by there about a week earlier and to please give the message to any of the family. She also told us, as she had told Pa, that Mrs. Jett and our sister, Anna, had been taken by the army, along with most all the folks from New Manchester, to somewheres in Marietta or Roswell and that they hadn't been heard of since. Rumors were that the army sent them all up north somewheres so as they couldn't work in no more mills down here in the South. She hoped that they were all okay, but she just didn't know anymore. Can you imagine herding people up like they were cattle or something and just shipping them off somewheres else to a strange place or something like they weren't even human? I mean, these people were civilians; they weren't soldiers. They weren't any threat to the Federal army, all forced against their will. This just didn't happen. We'd never heard of anything like this happening anywhere else during the war. Why here? We would find them somehow, and we would vindicate their wrong. You could count on that.

The final walk home was the most difficult three miles we had covered, I believe, in all our journeys up to this time. Our minds were so full of anticipation and anxiety that it was all we could do to contain ourselves. Each mile seemed longer than the last until, finally, we arrived at our front gate. From there, we made our long walk down the white sandy road that led to the house.

No dogs were barking to welcome our arrival, only the silence of the soft breeze blowing gently through the large old oak trees surrounding the house with the occasional sound of a spring songbird filtering through.

As we approached the front porch, we saw the familiar old door swing open, and a man we had never seen before moved slowly forward, walking on one leg and a crutch. It was a man ravaged by the terrible cruelty and weariness of almost four years of war. It was like we had never seen him before, but it was our pa.

As we hurried up the steps, he—as best he could—moved to us, and we all three embraced with tearful eyes and heartfelt thanks at our reunion. We began to laugh almost hysterically for just a moment, laughing, I guess, at the impossibility of it all and how amazing it was that we were back on the farm, where only a short time ago we were only young boys with a young pa—farmers of the land gone off to war and to return again all as changed men, men who had seen the "elephant" and lived to tell the tale and a thousand and one other stories to share with our grandchildren in the years to come.

Yes, Pa had lost a leg, but he had come home to his family, at least to where his family used to be. Now it was an incomplete family like a torn, ragged, and precious cloth that used to protect us all with surety and safety. Now we were broken pieces, and we must each determine our future. As soon as we could catch our breath and talk again, Pa, Ben, and I began to talk about Ma and Anna and what supposedly had happened down at New Manchester and then about Will, Samuel, and Levi, what had happened and where they all were. We had heard so little in the time we had been gone. We each had bits and pieces of information, and we began to share what we did know.

Pa had received several letters from Ma and Anna from up in Indiana, where they were living in a little town called New Albany. They were okay and doing fine, but they sure did have a story to tell.

Pa said, "As soon as I got home, provided I did get home alive, I was to write to her and Anna and let them know so that they could make preparations to come home. I have written them and expect to hear back from them soon. God, in His providence, has protected them otherwise from many of the terrible things of this war. We can thank God for that much."

Then with tears streaming down his iron-hard face and with pain in his gruffly voice, Pa said, "We lost Will, boys, up at Petersburg just at the end of the war almost. He was working his cannon when a shell exploded overhead, and he took home a mass of shrapnel. His commander said he was one of his best officers. He had made captain."

We were all silent at hearing the unsettling news about Will. There was nothing we could say, hardly. We knew firsthand what it was all about, and we always suspected that some of us would not return because of statistical impossibility, almost. We too shed our tears as we fought back the emotional trauma.

"Samuel and Levi, were captured by the Yankees in some action up north. I don't know exactly where or what the circumstances were," said Pa. "I haven't heard from them yet or any other news about them. I just hope they're coming home all in one piece. May God watch over them is my only prayer."

"Let's go get some grub," Pa said with as much enthusiasm as he could muster up. So together, we fixed up the best meal we could with the meager provisions we had. It was a fine thing to be home on the farm once again. We would talk for long hours and share many stories over the next few days while we were getting reacquainted with our pa. He was a little different now as were both Ben and myself. We had all been through too much.

As we worked to put the farm back into some kind of order, the days drifted lazily by. It was time for spring planting, even though late, and we'd have to work hard to get some kind of crops planted in. We borrowed some seed from some of our neighbors and put in just enough for a good garden as we didn't have any horse or mule to work the fields. We would be busy for a good while, for there was a lot to do to put the farm back into shape. And every day we waited and watched down the long sandy white road for our brothers, Samuel and Levi, and for Ma and Anna. One day they would be back, and we anxiously awaited their return.

Finally, one day we were chopping wood up by the long sandy road when a noise was heard like someone shouting and a-hollering. We looked up and saw the limping figure of a tall man coming down the way with as much speed as he could get himself going. It was Samuel, good old Samuel. But where was Levi? We threw down our tools and ran to meet him like the long-lost brother he was. When we got to him, he was a-sobbing and laughing at the same time; he was so happy to be home. He was a wretched mess with tattered clothes and barefoot and looked almost like a skeleton.

"Levi didn't make it, y'all," he said through his tears. "He caught pneumonia while in prison this past year, and he just couldn't shake it. I done everything I could to save him, Pa," he pleaded.

"It's okay, Samuel," Pa said. "We know you done your best to take care of Levi. It weren't your fault." And he put his arms around Samuel and hugged him tight, and we helped him walk onto the house. We filled Samuel in on all the news about the rest of the family. He couldn't believe it about Will, and he was really upset too about Ma and Anna and what had happened to them. It took days and days for the truth to settle in as we all tried to get on with the new work to be done, but our hearts weren't altogether in our work as we strived to rebuild our home and our attitudes.

It wasn't long before we got a letter from Ma and Anna informing us that they would be home around the first of June. The days were getting a lot warmer now, and it was almost summer. The first of June had come and gone, and we were still waiting. On occasion, I would walk up to the high ground and look out across the fallow field and see the beautiful mountain. She was almost waving back on the distant horizon, and she seemed to be talking to me and reminding me that she was still there and that the world was a good place to live. She said to me that life was good and precious and that there was a place and purpose for all of us. She said that life would be good again and that I too would find my own destiny among the stars and hills of this great land.

With tears in my eyes and with sweat on my brow, I looked the other way across the field and saw my beloved mother and sister coming down the dusty road. Both heavenly and earthly, we were all home.

THE END

WE DANCED UNTIL DAWN

New Beginnings

Steven Jett, now aged twenty-one, went to the well to draw water for his mother, who was preparing Sunday breakfast for the family. The year was 1867, and it was Easter Sunday in the month of April. He dropped the bucket quickly until it splashed in the deep cool water below, fell to the side, and began to fill up and sink until the old rope went slightly taut with the added weight. With the grace of a conductor, he rhythmically wound up the windlass as the wet resource rose to the surface of the earth.

This day, Anna–his little sister, now almost a grown woman herself–would be baptized at Salt Springs Baptist Church, not actually at the church but down in Sweetwater Creek behind and near the church. She, like many others, had found Jesus and salvation back during the winter, and everyone was looking forward to the spring baptizing on Easter Sunday during the first warm weather. Any other time would have been too cold and would have subjected everyone saved to catching pneumonia and an early departure for heaven for sure. This would be a fine day for such a ceremony.

Ben, two years older, was walking on the wild side these days as he had moved to the big city of Atlanta. While walking was not his favorite thing, he had–two months before–set out on foot, heading for the new life of a city dweller. They had not heard from him yet but expected a letter just any day now. He would do well in the city, they hoped, and much opportunity awaited him there.

Their ma and pa had settled back down on the family farm again with the idea of making a new start after the war. But things would not be the same anymore. Too many circumstances had transpired, and life on the old farm could never be the same again. They missed their brothers William and Levi, who had died during the cruel long war. Every day their memory was etched in their minds as they went about the regular and mundane chores of the old farm. Only Samuel and Steve were around now to help their pa with the plowing and clearing and other heavy chores.

Of course, Anna was a godsend to her ma as she always was. Not only was she all grown up and beautiful now but she also was a very learned young lady as she had had the privilege of some very good tutoring while in New Albany, Indiana. The civilian deportation, of which she and her ma had been a part when they were removed from New Manchester, Georgia, during the war in July 1864, had had a profound effect on both of them. It was like their eyes were opened, and they now saw the entire world in a whole new way. And a whole new world it was.

It was a bit difficult for Samuel to get settled back in too. He had seen the "elephant" and the "world" just like them, and when you had looked death in the face and had lived to tell about it, nothing was ever the same again. He was back at his artwork again in fair earnest and hoped to get a job as a traveling journalist and artist. He admired the work of Waud, the great war artist and correspondent. And he had seen many of the new photographs of Mr. Mathew Brady, who was his real hero. Samuel was a good artist, and he would excel with this talent in the coming years.

The memory of William and Levi would live on through their lives as they each struggled to get in the harness of their choosing. Steve would carry a daguerreotype tin picture of both William and Levi in his pocket for the next several years as a reminder of how fleeting life could be. The war had taught him many things and had given him many experiences, not the least of which was that life had no guarantees, not for you and not for me. We live life on the edge of a great abyss, and we never know what life-changing events tomorrow will bring.

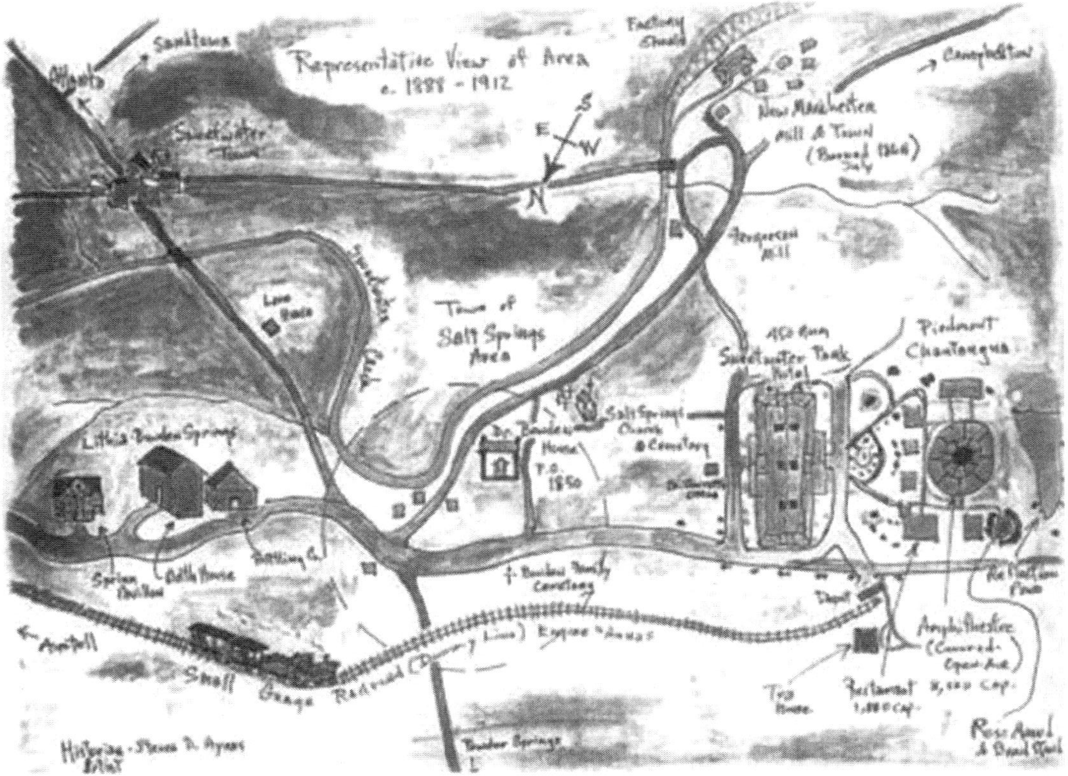
Representative View of Area
c. 1888 – 1912
Atlanta
Sandtown
Sweetwater Town
Factory Shoals
New Manchester
Mill & Town
(Burned 1864)
Campbellton
N
S
E
W
Ferguson Mill
Town of
Salt Springs
Area
Sweetwater Creek
Lithia Bowden Springs
Salt Springs Church & Cemetery
Dr. Bowden House
P.O.
1850
450 Room
Sweetwater Park
Hotel
Piedmont
Chautauqua
Bottling Co.
Spring Pavilion
Bath House
Bowden Family Cemetery
Depot
Amphitheater
(Covered-
Open Air
8,000 Cap.
Restaurant
1,000 Cap.
Tap House
Rose Arbor
& Board Walk
Austell
Small Gauge Railroad (Dummy Line)
Bowden Springs
Historian - Steven D. Ayers
Artist

Let the Dance Begin

It might be said, "You have not really danced until you have danced all night long in Douglas County, Georgia." Certainly, this would be the sentiment of many a well-wisher of long ago. For dancing in this area and in this era was a favorite entertainment of the rich and famous and the not so rich and the not so famous.

When they celebrated, they danced, and they said, "A good time was had by all." They really meant it, and more times than not, they meant all night long until dawn. Only in the wee hours of the early morning, when the sun first would peek into the day, would things slow down and the music go home. These were, for the most part, happy times.

In the near years after the War between the States, there were both a great settling and a great unrest. Some called it defeat. Some called it reconstruction, and others called it a new opportunity to start over.

The Jett family was one of the latter. "Let's start over" was the general attitude of Steven Jett and, indeed, most of the members of his family.

His father, Richard B. Jett, was now only half a man physically, having lost a leg at the Battle of Knoxville, but he was still twice the man of any man I had ever known. My grandfather had always been like that for as long as I could remember. The stories he told of the great war were awesome and kept me on the edge of my seat from one sentence to the next. Sometimes he would leave me hanging and just let me wonder what happened, forcing me to conjure up my own idea of the ending. Then he would hit me up with some line like, "The bear killed me."

"No, he didn't, Grandpa. He didn't kill you."

By that time, he was off onto something else, and he always knew he had gotten your goat.

My name was Charlie Callihan Ayres. My mother's name was Anna Jett before she married James Callihan in New Albany, Indiana. He was my daddy, a fine enough gentleman, I am told, but I never knew him as he was killed even before I was born. He died in a mill accident in the factory just at the time when the war was almost over. They were loading some heavy machinery off a big wagon when the rope line broke, and it fell on my daddy, killing him two days later. They tried to do all they could, but nothing could be done. At age seventeen, he went to an early grave way before his time. I knew he was a good person, a good man, but still a boy in the eyes of many folk. My mother named me Charlie after him. Little did my grandpa know that, that day, when my mother and grandma came home, that part of that bundle they carried was me, less than a year old but ready to whip the world. If only I knew what the world had in store for me. No easy rides for me anymore. It would be nip and tuck from there on.

When I was only two, my mother married another man named David Ayres, but everybody just called him Bud. By the time I was five, he had adopted me and given me his own name. Over the next fifteen years, he and my mother would have ten more children.

We lived in Villa Rica, Georgia, the first home of a little drink called Coca-Cola. And that was another story.

There were gold mines in Villa Rica, and by the time I was thirteen, I had me a job working in the mines. The year was already 1877. I was only a gofer, you might say, but I was a good one. There was nothing I didn't, wouldn't, or couldn't do—except go down in the mines. They were strictly off limits. Well, it was dangerous work—I knew it was—but it was exciting, and I wanted to do it. Some of the shafts were vertical drops of one hundred, two hundred, and three hundred feet or more. One, I believe, was four hundred feet deep, and off these would be horizontal shafts going out for hundreds more feet in all directions. Well, basically, whatever direction the gold was leading them, that was the way they would go. It was dangerous but glorious working in a "glory hole" as they were called. Sometimes the glory hole would peter out, and then it became just a big, long deep dark hole in the ground.

My glory days were coming. Soon I was schooled on how, with the careful skills of real miners, we would chase the golden ore to get more and more. It wasn't exactly pure gold, but you could see it there in the rock, and sometimes you could see a great concentration of it. This was what you worked for, and this was what you followed. Miners were little more than gopher rats; in fact, that was our nicknames. We dug like gophers, and we would send up bucket after bucket of the glittering rock. When it got to the top, up on the surface, they would run the ore through a big crusher called a hammer mill, which would crush it up in little pieces and then even smaller pieces until it became a fine dust almost. Then you could really begin to see the gold glittering in the north Georgia sunlight. We called it "sunshine from the ground."

There were various ways of collecting the dust, but one of the main ways was by using mercury and cyanide. Sometime later, large concrete vats would be built to process the stuff through a series of huge tanks about thirty, forty, or fifty feet across. In the end, they would end up with pure, twenty-four-karat gold that would be cast into little bars worth hundreds and thousands of dollars.

This was a great job for me, and I would continue in this line of work for some time into the future until I got hired up at the livery at the brand-new Sweetwater Park Hotel. That too would change my life forever.

Baptizing in Sweetwater Creek

Today would be a marvelous day, what with baptizing going on and the singing and the general fanfare of it all, not to mention the food and eating that were to follow. No respecting woman in the area would not want to flaunt her talents when it came to a culinary event like "dinner on the grounds."

In the year of our Lord 1867, it was not uncommon for hundreds of people to gather round the church grounds on such an occasion.

Salt Springs Baptist was typical of the small Southern Baptist churches growing up all around the country. And unlike our brethren the Methodists, we were not beholden to "sprinkling" our saved like an April shower. We were more inclined, even mandated by our name, to enjoy complete submersion–buried in sin, risen to walk in the newest of life in Christ Jesus, our Lord, in the name of the Father, the Son and the Holy Ghost. Amen.

I, Steven Jett, often wondered what God was going to say to the poor Methodists, who only had a token dunking and barely got wet. After all, how could you wash away all your sins that way? Would God be pleased with Baptists, who really went all out? The only thing was some of the Baptists would baptize by laying you down in the water on your back, which more times than not resulted in almost drowning the poor victim. They would often come up a-coughing and choking because they forgot to hold their breath or their nose or both. Some more refined preachers got the notion to "bury" people facedown in the water, which was, of course, contrary to usual burial techniques. It did save the patient from the danger of drowning, but did it still give them the same saving grace as being buried or baptized facing up? Only God would know, I suppose, but He must be favorable to it because I understood the Episcopalians and Catholics and many others did it by just dripping water on you, again like the Methodists. So, who really knew?

Anyway, it was not just baptizing that sometimes concerned me but it was also the whole idea of religion. I mean, how can everybody be right and everybody be wrong all at the same time? I knew that there were other people in the world who believed in other things, like the Calvinists, the Shakers, the Quakers, the Mennonites, and the Mormons, not to mention the Jews, the Muslims, the Hindu, and those of other Asian and Middle Eastern religions.

Just one thing I figured was that God had some way of sifting them and us all out. And He must take a special forbearance for "trying" whatever that effort might be. So, we didn't really know, but that was why our religion was based on faith as the preacher would say.

This afternoon at high twelve, fourteen new souls will be saved in Sweetwater Creek according to plan. And Anna, my little sister, who was nineteen this month, would be one of them. What a glorious day!

My ma, who already cared for him like her own, would take care of her baby Charles. My little nephew, about one year old now, was just beginning to toddle around. When Anna came home with a baby, we couldn't believe it–and married too and already widowed on top of it. My goodness, what was the world coming to?

The Sweetwater Park Hotel and Piedmont Chautauqua

The world was coming to its senses but very slowly. We were in the throes of reconstruction in the South, and things were about as mixed up as mincemeat pie, which I never liked anyway.

By 1870, our farm had left the political boundaries of Cobb County and had taken on the political mantle of Douglas County, newly formed from a portion of old Campbell County, which was basically split into several new counties named Carroll, Douglas, Coweta, and Paulding, I think. It was sort of confusing. The land didn't change, but the boundaries did. For a while there, I didn't think we knew where we lived. But by 1870, Douglasville was named the new county seat, beating out a couple of other less desirable locations in the county. Or maybe it was just because the Vansant family had "given" the land of forty acres to the new government for the purpose of establishing the county seat at the location of the old Skint Chestnut high on the ridge, having been an old Indian trail marker for the past several decades, maybe even a hundred years.

Well, there was good reason to take the high ground, and one day there would be a fine new red brick courthouse built on that very spot to replace the small log cabin courthouse first erected. The new red brick courthouse would be built and open for use around 1888 and would serve the surrounding community for a long time.

There was an interesting story about our county name and how it happened to come about. During the period immediately after the War between the States, the entire South was experiencing reconstruction in every way. Part of that circumstance was involved with the state legislature that, because of the befuddlement of politics, was dominated by blacks. Among many things that were done in the name of "change" was to give honorary names and titles wherever and whenever the opportunity arose. When our county was first chartered by the state legislature, it was therefore given the name of Douglass with two *s*'s on the end, supposedly after Frederick Douglass, the great black abolitionist of the North. But somehow later, when the more credent influences of home and heart won over, the name was officially changed to the name of Douglas with only one *s*, after the great orator, politician, and opponent of Abraham Lincoln–Stephen A. Douglas. And this stuck and has ever since!

Now that the name of our county was official, we could, I believe, concern ourselves with some other things–things like the building of the Sweetwater Park Hotel in Salt Springs and the building of the Lithia Springs Hotel in Tallapoosa, Georgia. Boy, this was confusing then, and I knew that future generations were bound to have trouble with this bit of history.

In the year 1884 or thereabouts, a Mr. E. W. Marsh made one of his regular trips from Atlanta to Douglasville to visit and spend time with his sister, one of the Mozley family, I believe. On his return home back across the county, he became ill. The driver of his horse and carriage or buggy persuaded him to stop and rest at the home of John C. Bowden in Salt Springs–yes, the very one and the same who had been our postmaster all the time during the war down at the Bowden house. Recovering, Mr. Marsh stayed there for several days.

While he was there, he was provided with all the "salt mineral water" he could drink from the springs; and soon to his astonishment, he was again in formidable, good health.

Upon his leaving, he insisted on taking a good quantity of the mineral water with him back to Atlanta to continue in his treatments and to also have the water analyzed, which he did.

After the test results were all in, the chemists had found that this particular water was very rich in bromide salts and, in particular, a bicarbonate of lithium, the lightest known metal. It was a "miracle water," and by 1888 and 1889, the World Congress of Physicians was meeting right here in Salt Springs, which would soon be known as Lithia Springs, Georgia.

In short, this miracle water was good for what ailed you, be it gout, dissolving uric acid at will; insomnia, making you sleep like a baby; stomach upset; clear thinking; constipation; or consternation–you name it, it would cure it. It was a panacea of medicine, if there ever was one.

By now, 1888, the land for the great Sweetwater Park Hotel had been purchased, about eight hundred acres, and the fanciful hotel was having its open house. It was the Fourth of July, and Henry Grady was to be the guest speaker. He was to give what was henceforth to be known as his "New South speech."

I remembered it well, for we had long looked forward to this great event. Ma, Pa, Samuel, Anna, Charles, and I all went to see, hear, and marvel at this great event.

Charles was already thirteen years old and had already gotten a job down at the livery near the hotel where all the horses, buggies, and fine carriages were coming and going every day by the hundreds. It was not your typical sleepy little town anymore.

Ma was working in the dining room and kitchen, and Pa, now about sixty-three, was working down at the depot, loading and unloading carboys and demijohns of lithia water for the hotel mostly. Sometimes too he would work down at the spring itself, supervising the bottling operations of the fine lithia water, which was now being shipped all over the world. It was a grand undertaking.

Lithia Springs was being compared to Carlsbad, France, after its famous mineral springs. We were known as the Carlsbad of the South. Also, we were compared to Saratoga Springs, New York. Some referred to us as the "Saratoga of the South." A rich and envious history to inherit to be sure.

About this time, a small gauge railroad had been placed and established between the actual springs and the Sweetwater Park Hotel, which was located about a mile to the west. This little railroad was not connected to the main line, it just ran to and from the Springs and became known as the Dummy Line because it really did not go anywhere except back and forth, but it carried joyous, happy people and precious life-giving mineral water up and down the track every thirty minutes of every day. It did further connect with the Bowden-Lithia Springs and/or Ben Scott Hotel in Austell, once known as Cincinatti Junction.

We had a wonderful little steam engine named *Anna*, not after my sister Anna but after sweet Mrs. Anna Watson, the proprietor's wife of the Sweetwater Park Hotel. And the lucky fellow who got to drive the train every day was me, Steven Jett, now forty-two years old, still a young man by my standards but a strong, mature age by most social standards of the time.

Farming was still necessary, but business had given way to the excitement of changing times and changing ways. And while Samuel had taken on the general responsibility of the farm, he too was busy with his new photography business at the Sweetwater Park Hotel.

People who came there were rich, richer beyond your wildest dreams, richer than most folks, I'd say. And they wanted to have a permanent memory or two of the great resort and their presence here.

After all, the Sweetwater Park Hotel had at least 250 rooms and was said to be fifty years ahead of its time. It was the first establishment in the South to have electric lights only because it made its own electricity with a steam-powered generator in the basement–a true marvel of its time. All you had to do at night to have light was to flick a switch, and presto, there it was.

And because the hotel had a very deep artesian well, it had all the water it would ever need, enough for private bathrooms, the kitchen, and even fountains in the beautiful landscaped yards. It was a paradise created out of the backwoods of America, a thing of beauty, of culture, of social aplomb, and of unspeakable splendor.

By the following year or so, a great movement was afoot to expand the resort development and to build what would become known as the Piedmont Chautauqua.

It would be lavish in design and sumptuous in its undertaking. One thousand workers were brought in from Atlanta and over the South for the massive undertaking of building an open-air amphitheater that would seat eight thousand patrons and protect them from the rain and hot sun. A restaurant would be built to seat one thousand diners at a single seating, and other fine and elaborate buildings would be built to house various possibilities such as a lyceum for lectures and speeches, language arts, music, and religion as well as science and philosophy–a summer holiday paradise for education, entertainment, and betterment of the mind, spirit, and body. There would be plays and concerts from Shakespeare to John Philip Sousa on the Rose Mound, covered in roses surrounding the band gazebo. What a beauty it was!

This would become the periodic holiday home of famous people and patrons from all over the world–the Vanderbilts, the Astors, Presidents McKinley and Teddy Roosevelt giving speeches and tantalizing the crowds with stories of bold game hunting and charges up San Juan Hill in Cuba. Walt Whitman, no doubt, must have been inspired, at least in part, to have written *Leaves of Grass* on the spacious and wandering veranda of the magnificent hotel and bucolic lawns graced with giant oak shade trees, flowing fountains, and the beautiful reflection pond below the gigantic theater–the pond that lovers reveled in, riding their boats on lazy afternoons and evenings.

At night, the grounds were ever so romantically illuminated by the burning of pine and pitch knots cradled in iron lamp holders, creating an ambiance of heaven.

All this was served again by another special train called the *Piedmont Chautauqua Special*, which ran from Atlanta to the Sweetwater Park Hotel twice a day, once in the morning and once in the afternoon. The train to glory, I called it, along with my little engine *Anna*, and we burned the tracks up every day, going back and forth.

"The Piedmont Chautauqua at Lithia Springs, Georgia" c. 1890 ← Oh! What Fun!

The Inglorious Fire

Never have I had so much fun and seen so many wonderful people come and go at the Sweetwater Park Hotel as during these wonderful, or should I say "wonder-filled," years up until January 12, 1912.

It was midnight now, and the great fire had been burning the glorious structure since midafternoon. It was awful, absolutely awful. No words can describe the absolute agony that my heart and everybody else's was experiencing that fateful day and night.

It was all I could do to keep from totally breaking down. I did weep heavily. Our lives were so intertwined with this great hotel and grounds.

No one knew what had actually caused the fire. But once it was started, there was no turning it back. All the water in Georgia could not have stopped that inferno. By nightfall, it was like looking into the firepits of hell itself and seeing only red-hot coals of past glory, beauty, and lives clinging to their last hope of consciousness before moving on from this world into the next.

I wept with a silent fever burning in my soul. For it was such a loss that not even the great war had affected me so. For times here had been so good, so wholesome, so beneficial, so progressive, so exciting, so wonder filled. But that was to be no more, not now, not ever again.

No one whom I knew of perished in the terrible fire, and that was fortunate. But a mystery persisted, for there had been some forewarning of an impending disaster by several people in the last year or two of its existence.

Business was down, and the tremendous throngs of days gone by had dissipated from a torrential river to a smaller river and then a smaller stream to a steady flow of a creek to more like a trickle. Ends were getting more difficult to meet, and finances continued to diminish. Some speculated that the fire was purposely set to recover insurance money, but it could never be proved. For the next five years, the courts were covered up with its entangled aftermath of lawsuits and countersuits.

There was an ongoing mystery—and still is to this day—regarding a great fortune lost in the fire that was never recovered—a fortune of gold, silver, jewelry, and precious stones that supposedly had been put up for security purposes in the fireproof safe of the main purser of the hotel. It was never found and never accounted for in all the years later and would remain a total mystery to this day.

Needless to say, we all sort of lost our livelihood about the time of the Sweetwater Park Hotel fire. And although much remained of the Moorish Chautauqua grounds, there was a great waning interest in all that remained; and like the ruins of New Manchester, the grounds fell into disuse and disrepair. Finally, they were so bad that most things were torn down one at a time and salvaged where possible into other things of more pressing necessity. It was a slow but certain death of all that had been beautiful and elegant.

Somewhere along the way, the little engine *Anna*—my dear little engine and train—was no longer necessary and sold to a mining and logging company far away up north. I did not know exactly where. It was a sad time. The rails were eventually pulled and used in other endeavors and purposes. The main line of the Western and Atlantic Railroad, put in around 1888, remained open and now went all the way to Birmingham, Alabama, and on to New Orleans, Louisiana. The main line near the Lithia Spring itself switched off northerly and went all the way to Cincinnati, Ohio. That junction became known as Cincinnati Junction and would later be known as Austell, Georgia.

The world was changing again, and I didn't much like it, I didn't think.

What Now?

By now, I, Steven Jett, was sixty-seven years old, too old to do too much but too young to stop living. Only a year had passed since the great fire and my father, R. B. Jett, was approaching eighty-eight. He was getting a mite feeble but still got around good for a man with one leg. He was surrounded with new grandchildren from Samuel's family and me and great-grandchildren from Anna and Charlie's family.

Ma, my precious and loving mother, had died in 1910 on a dark and rainy February day of the twenty-fourth. It was on a Tuesday, and the kitchen and dining staff had been given an extended holiday due to the slackening crowds. It had rained considerably the last two weeks, and the streams and creeks had flooded, with the swelling banks now overflowing with the torrential rain. Gothards Creek was one of those streams, and while it was not so totally threatening, it was out of control somewhat. The cows had wandered away and had gotten themselves caught up on a small island surrounded by water. It seemed only a matter of time until they would be doomed. No one was at the farm at the time, and the only reason Ma knew about the cows was that Mr. McKenny, on his way home to his farm, had made the discovery and stopped by to alert the Jetts.

Ma put on what rain gear she had and set out to rescue those cows. She was on foot and making her way down toward the creek when lightning struck a big poplar tree just near her, glanced off, and hit her directly, killing her instantly. The only evidence, of course, that we found was the severe burns she had and the burnt, split poplar tree just off to her side. It was fast and sudden, and I was sure that she never knew what hit her, bless her soul. God has a strange way sometimes of calling us home.

We grieved for days and days and never got over it and still haven't. But we went on as we had to as she would have had us to do, for she was a strongly driven, God-fearing woman who knew her Lord and her duty in life. We were taught by her to be the same. There would never be another like Mother, for she was our world, our rock, and our connection to all things. Now we would have to live without her. Somehow the poor cows survived.

Moving On

Samuel had excelled with his photography. In fact, he had captured several wonderful photographs of the Sweetwater Park Hotel, the grounds, and even the great fire. It was making him wealthy as he traveled the South taking photographs at beautiful places like Indian Springs in Jackson, Georgia; Jekyll Island; Chattanooga; Atlanta; New Orleans; Washington DC; and even New York City. And before he died, he would capture the parklike beauty of a place called Chautauqua, New York, the namesake of our own Chautauqua right here in Lithia Springs, Georgia. His pictures were beautiful and meaningful, each one telling a story about life and living. He would leave behind a chronicle of timeless beauty in his art.

Samuel would marry three times and have a total of fourteen children—whom he knew of. There may have been others.

I don't believe I could relate to you all the details of his families, and it is probably a good thing, knowing what he really thought of marriage—mainly, that you didn't need it, and it didn't need you. So much for the light side of life.

* * *

Anna was a different story. She, as I have told you—did I not?—was married first in New Albany, Indiana, to a young man named James Callihan, who was soon lost. But she carried his child, whom she named Charles. And she carried, of course, his name, and so did Charles, until she remarried and they became Ayres. He would grow into a fine young man and would ultimately become a telegrapher at Powder Springs station with the railroad. He would marry and father seven children, three of whom would die at or near birth unfortunately. The four girls surviving would grow to be fine women and establish wonderful homes for their families around the Powder Springs area.

My Own Family

My own family would be unique and caring, mixed with the graciousness of love and the love of adventure!

My wife, Lucinda, was my love and my joy. We were married only a short year when the Lord took her away from me. Scarlet fever was to blame. I thought my world had ended. My heart was torn from me, and I had no direction for my life. I went into a deep state of depression. I even considered ending this depressing and despairing life, but then I met a new friend one day. His name was Robert Akers from Owl Rock Church. He wasn't the pastor but a deacon, I guess, from old Campbellton, Georgia—what was left of Campbellton after the county seat was changed to Carrollton and after almost all the fine old houses and buildings were moved out and away to other places. It was a sort of ghost town, but Robert lived there still among the ruined, rotten, and forgotten. Robert and his wife, Beverly, invited me to their home, and Robert was responsible for getting me the job as the engineer on *Anna*, the little engine that could change anybody's life in one short run! In short, he saved my life! I will be forever indebted to him and his lovely wife and their three boys—Bryan, Zachary, and Jake—and one girl, Denise. Robert became a great friend, and now they all lived in the Lithia Springs area.

Robert's sister-in-law, Aunt Betty, we called her, also became a great friend of the family and would always come over with her mother, Mrs. Jones, when we all got together for good food and some good hollerin'—some of us called it singing. And some of us called it music makin' like, we said, in church. We were making a joyful noise anyway. We sure had some good times!

* * *

After I got my life back together, I was operating the train one day when the most beautiful lady climbed aboard wearing a full-bodied blue silk dress with white lace, a matching blue-plumed hat, white gloves, and a matching parasol. She was with her mother and father, Mr. and Mrs. McKenzie, from Mansfield, Georgia, which I would later discover from down near Covington. Her name was Carol.

When we got to the station, I slowed the train, got it stopped, and hopped back quickly to help the guests of my choice off the open riding car. I helped her mother first, of course, to show my good manners and then her to show my good taste.

Carol was formal and elegant. She was definitely aristocratic with a large dose of vivaciousness. She was cute, beautiful, and courtly all at the same time. So, I wasn't exactly sure how to treat her except nicely, with courtesy and respect.

I would soon discover that she was here to accompany her parents, who were signed up on the summer program of the Chautauqua to lecture on no less than the social and cultural mores of the native tribes of New Guinea, South America, as seen and observed through the eyes of itinerant missionaries of the Gospel of Jesus Christ of the fellowship of John Wesley of the Holy Methodist Church of America. Wow, that sounds like a mouthfull!

As a young girl, she had gone with them into this godforsaken land–a land of savages, headhunters, and worse; a country of cannibals; a place where it was nothing to have your neighbors over for dinner quite literally. And you consumed your ancestors as part of the sacred rite of passage and honor.

Yes, I thought, *this girl is for me.*

At first, though, she paid me little attention, no doubt thinking, *Aha, he is just after my body*. But she was wrong, for I was after her body, her mind, and her heart.

* * *

Several weeks passed, and we occasionally ran into each other here and there, especially in the large dining hall restaurant of the Americas at the Chautauqua or sometimes in the Sweetwater Park Hotel dining room. On several occasions, her family invited me to join them, and I did, relishing every moment of their very cordial and exciting company.

As we got to know each other better, we gained her parents' permission to walk or stroll through the lavish park by ourselves, taking in every flower, every tree, and every songbird of the sky.

We listened to John Philip Sousa on the Rose Mound, and we sat on the romantic park benches liberally placed throughout the landscape.

In the evenings, we strolled along the curved pathways in the soft moonlight, guided by the regular torch fires of the trails.

The "Dummy Line"

And in the grand ballroom of the hotel, we danced and danced and danced until dawn. Then we would have a sumptuous and lavish breakfast fit for royalty in the dining room before separately retiring for a few hours' rest to meet the requirements of the next day. Hopefully, they would be small and few.

The Piedmont Chautauqua
Lithia Springs, Georgia

Glorious Times and Days

These were glorious times and days. Often on days available, we would row in the boats in the reflection lake, soaking up lazy sunshine and blue sky while playing the ukulele. I was pretty good.

We would read the morning newspapers together on the wide veranda of the hotel and rock ourselves crazy while discussing the cares, problems, and opportunities of the world. The world was our oyster, and the pearl was right here.

On special days, we would take a one-horse buggy and drive down to the old Manchester ruins on Sweetwater Creek at Factory Shoals and take in the sights of rushing water, wildlife, and sometimes the stars.

It was a wonderful world, and we were in love.

In time, Carolyn–as I often called her–would become my wife, and we would have four wonderful children–three boys named William Duncan, Napoleon Bonaparte, and John Thomas and a sweet little girl named Carolyn Elizabeth.

After my father, Richard B. Jett, had passed away from old age at ninety-four, the farm was left to me, Samuel, and Anna, one-third each per Pa's will, for he was a just and God-fearing man who felt like he should make a New Testament division of the farm instead of leaving it all to the eldest male child as in the Old Testament. It was a good plan and a good will. Samuel, Anna, and I and all the family missed Pa something terrible and always would. We loved him as he loved us with all our hearts. The only thing we could do now was to live the remainder of our lives as a testament to his good name and reputation.

Carolyn was a good wife and the love of my life. She nourished me in so many ways, both physically and intellectually, with her love and understanding of life.

She so impressed me in so many ways. I'd never forget one occasion when we were courting. We had been riding horses on her parents' large plantation in Mansfield, and we stopped in the edge of a wood by a small stream. We dismounted the horses, sat down in the thick grass by the little bubbling rocky stream, and began to play frolicly and wistfully with the passing water. About that time, Carolyn looked up; and pointing across the open field, she directed my attention to a small hill across the way.

"When I die," she said, "that is where I want to be buried." She was only eighteen years old. I knew I was about forty-two at that time, but it was common for older men to take a younger wife back then, and many did, including me. But the thing that amazed me was how a young person like her, of her youth and vitality, could even imagine her death, much less be planning ahead in such a way. She was very mature for her age, very smart and very wise! It was, however, a little unsettling, this "vision" for the future!

The years we lived on the farm raising our family were rich times indeed and very good and happy years!

The Children Grow Up

The children eventually grew up to be young adults. They got as good an education as we could give them.

All three boys attended and graduated from Emory College at Oxford, Georgia, over the course of several years. Their time there prepared them for the various life experiences that they would later confront in business, religion, politics, and society in general.

Carolyn Elizabeth would go on to become a newly minted graduate of Agnes Scott College in Atlanta, preparing her for a life course in astronomy. She would later find her specialized work at the Lowell Observatory on Mars Hill in Flagstaff, Arizona, where in 1913 it would be discovered that the universe was in a "red movement"; in other words, we were all moving apart–something, I believe, we already knew, but you couldn't put your finger on it. Now you could!

When we looked at the stars and the beautiful night over the farm, we would always think of Beth, as we called her, and how maybe she was looking back at us somehow from far, far away and signaling us with her love!

* * *

Later, William Duncan became a merchant and had a mercantile in Powder Springs. He was very successful and married and eventually had eight children and took up flying aeroplanes when he was thirty years old in 1930. He flew until 1936, carrying the U.S. mail between Atlanta and Birmingham and sometimes to Chattanooga and Macon. He was a great pilot who had a lot of close calls but never "bought the farm" as they said in those days. He didn't die in other words!

In 1936, he hit the barnstorming circuit full time and went all over the South, mainly with his aerial stunts and the flying circus of Kalamazoo. By 1939, he had joined the U.S. Army Air Corps.

Will, as we called him, used to tell us about flying at night between cities like Atlanta and Birmingham. What you would do was fly from one beacon light to another about every thirty miles until you got there and then pray that the weather was good enough to land, provided they could get enough car headlights out on the field to see it. Wow, these were some new and crazy times!

* * *

NB or Napoleon Bonaparte worked for a while in his elder brother's mercantile in Powder Springs and gained valuable business experience.

It wasn't long when he and his brothers, John Thomas and William Duncan, opened up a new and bigger mercantile of their own in Douglasville, Georgia, the county seat. This enterprise, over time, was to become immensely successful.

They would soon build a larger building just west of the red brick courthouse and call it Duncan's Mercantile, after William's name as he had funded most of the capital. It sounded better than just Jett's, they thought; and besides, Duncan's wife insisted that it not have the Jett name as she had been adamantly opposed to my father's service in the Confederate army and having participated in so many Veterans Day affairs in years hence. She said it was like reliving the war over and over every single year, and she was tired of it and did not want the stigma attached with the notoriety of the family name. I was surprised he stood for it, but he did. Women can be fretfully difficult sometimes.

At any rate, their business–the Duncan Mercantile–was very successful, selling everything from square nails to coffins to flour sacks to silk scarves to the latest in men's and women's fashions.

John Thomas Jett would make an annual trip to New York City to visit the warehouses and make the latest selections of fashion and merchandise. He was a masterful buyer, and NB was a marketing genius. Together, they all made a fortune.

In the early 1900s, they opened a bank in Douglasville, the first one there–the First National Bank of Douglasville, Georgia. It had an opening value of $10,000. John Thomas was, of course, its first president.

The World Goes to War

Everything was happening. The economy was going gangbusters. The Wright brothers were giving up their bicycle business for the sky. The aeroplane business was started on December 17, 1903, when the first aeroplane–invented by the Wright brothers, from Dayton, Ohio–carried Orville on man's first ride through the sky. Since that day, the world had not been the same!

By 1914, the Great War to end all wars had visited on this earth, and the aeroplane had made its mark among other things over the skies of Europe.

William had little hope of flying just yet but just did get into the excitement by joining the army and being assigned as a medic. He would soon be serving in the mud and misery of trench warfare in the middle of France, which would give the family a new legacy.

In honor of the beautiful country of France and his sacrifices there, he would name two of his children after his two favorite French cities, Noble and Grenoble. This legacy would extend way down to future generations yet unborn and unknown.

Survival in the war was often dependent on building snow caves during the harsh, bitter cold, whitewashed winters of Europe. The Kaiser Wilhelm of Germany was not an easy monarch to deal with, but eventually, he was defeated, and the world gained order once again.

William came home in due time but not before he had witnessed the wonder of the Lafayette Escadrille and the flying circus. The air war over Europe set new standards for machines, war, and eventually travel.

William was bitten by the "air bug," and upon arriving home back in the States, still in one piece, he would pursue his own air adventures in airmail and barnstorming.

* * *

By now, Steven Jett was seventy-two years old and holding on pretty good, but time was getting away from him.

Father was using a walking cane now most of the time, and even though he had been active many, many years in all his Confederate Veterans reunions, especially since the 1880s, he just wasn't quite the same. Father was a proud man. He and his brother Ben had fought at Gettysburg with General Lee, at Chickamauga with General Longstreet, and at the Battle of Kennesaw Mountain, the Battles of Atlanta and Franklin, and the Battle of Nashville. His father and brothers had fought all over the country during the Civil War. And two of them had died. His daddy lost a leg at Knoxville, Tennessee.

The war had ended, but we still heard about it all the time, even more so than the Spanish-American War in 1898 caused by the explosion of the USS *Maine* in Havana Harbor, Cuba.

Even the recent world war had not overshadowed the War between the States mostly because it had been Americans against Americans. Over 650,000 were lost in casualties, no wonder, but then the war in Europe was no picnic either.

Aviation and Puppy Feet

By 1936, at the age of ninety, Steven Jett–my father–had passed away from old age, joining my dear mother in heaven. Mother had passed some years earlier during the great influenza epidemic that swept the world, killing millions worldwide. It was difficult to say the least, for Mother and Father both had been such a stabilizing influence in my life and in the lives of my brothers and sister.

Airplanes was my relief and life adventure. You could forget almost everything when you were up in the sky and punching clouds.

Nowhere was aviation more advanced and growing yearly but in Atlanta, Georgia. In a letter to my uncle, I penned the following words:

April 18, 1929

Dear Uncle Charlie, Chicago, Illinois

It is with great pleasure that I write to you concerning my current intention to begin an air service business at Candler Field here in Atlanta, Georgia.

It is mainly a dirt racetrack now, but we have been able to procure nearly permanent rights to a goodly portion of the center field, which we are currently using for a crisscross set of runways.

If the wind is too much out of the south or north, we have the ability to land either way and have long runways to the east and west. It is much like the old aerodromes that I saw in Europe during the war. Mostly, they were just big circular fields, so you could land or take off in any direction, depending on the wind.

Please be advised that I have been flying airmail between Atlanta and Birmingham and have built up a good bit of flying experience.

It is tough and dangerous sometimes, especially at night and in bad weather, but you learn here and there. Enough to stay alive.

Some guy named Jeppesen is even flying around the country, measuring mountains and towers and such, so we can get a record of elevations and adjust our altitudes in bad weather to avoid dangerous obstacles and terrain. It will be a big help. Already, because of his efforts, many a young flyer has been saved.

Just the other day, he measured Kennesaw Mountain at 1,864 feet above mean sea level. You know, that is where my father fought in the Civil War, on top of that mountain. Never thought I'd be flying over it nearly every day. Boy, what would old General Sherman or General Johnston have given to have had just one good airplane and pilot like me! The armies only had balloons, but they worked pretty good. Didn't use them too much though.

My idea, Uncle Charlie, is to start some kind of passenger service out of Atlanta.

I want to use a Travel Air 4000, like what we carry the mail in. At least I can carry two passengers up front like we do the mail. Two passengers is not much, but people pay good money to get somewhere in a hurry.

All I need is $2,000 to buy me a new plane, and I will be in business. I have saved $500 from my flying work so far to keep me going.

If you are able to help, I will make you a full 50/50 partner, and we will share the profits.

We could call it the Chicago/Atlanta Airline. I could make the nine-hundred-mile trip in only four stops for gasoline.

What do you say? Write me back as soon as you can and let me know. We want to get a jump on these other boys. Times' a-wastin'.

Respectfully,
Your Nephew and Admirer,
William Jett

* * *

Maybe, just maybe, by some miracle, we would be able to get into the air business.

My uncle Charlie Seignious in Chicago had done well. He had made an early fortune in the real estate business, and he was very favorable to airplanes and airplane travel. He even owned his own airplane named *Puppy Feet*, a nice Standard Aircraft biplane. Of course, almost all the aircraft of that day were biplanes.

One day when he was flying *Puppy Feet* on his way to Atlanta, he flew over a cemetery up near Chattanooga; and in a frivolous and contemptuous attitude, he stuck out his tongue at the cemetery. Immediately, within seconds, his engine quit, and he started coming down back to Mother Earth. Well, he was finally able to get the propeller windmilling enough to get the engine restarted and running again. That was one good thing about magnetos. He was so thankful, and never again did he show righteous indignation or contempt for the justly departed!

Adventures in the Sky

While I waited to hear back on my quest for fortune and fame, I continued in my flying adventures. I would do something every day to make me a better pilot and a few extra dollars.

One odd job I did land on was carrying dead people. It wasn't exactly rocket science (hey, what was that?), but it did pay some money, and the flying services were not too risky when your passengers were already dead.

At any rate, it was a living for a while, and I got to know the southeastern United States pretty good.

One night when I was coming back from Savannah with my dead cargo, I had an interesting experience when I discovered that he wasn't so dead after all.

I had just leveled off at about 3,500 feet, and the lights of the countryside were popping on over the landscape. It was a full moon night, and I could see pretty good actually. At first, the moon was a deep orange and red as it peaked up over the horizon. It was huge!

Just about that time, I looked up to the front cockpit; and to my astonishment, someone or something was looking over the side!

Before I knew it, I went into a right roll and spiraling dive. Guess I had let my airspeed drop too low when I had gotten distracted by the dead man that was now alive!

Down, down, down we went in that infamous graveyard spiral, the kind nobody lived to tell about or how to get out of it. Round, round, round we went. Somehow I could only say I instinctively threw the rudder into the direction of the turn and held it. *Left rudder, left rudder, left rudder! Step into the turn, step into the turn, step into the turn!* All my training kicked in, with reflexes working automatically in a consciousness dulled and blurred by the dizziness. *Lower the nose, lower the nose, lower the nose! Hands off the controls, hold left rudder, hold left rudder!*

Finally, once again, we were straight and level. We had lost 2,000 feet. Wow, what a ride! We were lucky. We? Who were we? It was supposed to be just me and this dead person on the way to Atlanta.

If that body wasn't already dead, I bet he was by now. But I looked up to the front cockpit, and lo and behold, both arms were stretched up into the air like we had achieved some great victory. And indeed, we had. It was a victory dance in the air!

The person looked around and gave me a big thumbs-up!

Okay, I thought, *whoever you are, we'll get to the bottom of this when we get to Atlanta.*

So we continued on the otherwise uneventful trip until we began to see the lights of Atlanta in our horizon.

I couldn't have missed it this night, even if I had been blind!

We dropped our altitude and headed for the field. Our only lighting system was some smudge pots that were lit at about dark and usually burned for three to four hours until they went out–a pretty good lighting system, I think. It would be years before we got real lights.

The landing was smooth and easy. We taxied up to the old Blevins Hangar for the night, and I shut her down.

By that time, I was getting pretty curious about my unscheduled passenger and was really ready to really give them what for.

Suddenly, the passenger popped up, sprang out of the front hole, and jumped to the ground.

This person was about five feet four inches or so, I'd guess, and didn't really look like a full-grown man.

Next thing you knew, off came the leather helmet and goggles, and the hair fell out–long curly brown hair. It was a girl or a woman or something. It wasn't a man anyway.

"Boo! Boo! Boo!" she said in an excited high-pitched voice. "Happy Halloween!" She laughed so hard that she bent over and almost fell to the ground. I about fell over myself. I had forgotten all about it being October 30, and when I realized what had happened, I about rolled away with laughter and consternation.

"My buddies put you up to this, didn't they?"

"What buddies?" she said girlishly.

"All my flying buddies–they thought this would be really funny, didn't they?" I said.

"Well, they thought it would be a pretty good gag. And I think it was, but you like to have killed us with that spin over Dublin," she said.

"Moonlight Surprise!"

"I ought to kill you anyway, you rascal stowaway. You like to have scared me to death up there."

"Didn't though," she said. "And glad I didn't. Come on, let's get some coffee. My name is Linda."

"I don't know if I want to drink coffee with a dead person or not. I guess so."

So we went in the little cramped flight office and said hello to Gramps, who was dispatching that night.

"Where did you two vagabonds come from?" he asked.

"Savannah by way of Dublin and Macon," I answered, "with dead cargo or supposedly dead cargo." And we went through the whole thing again for Gramps.

"Would have busted me up if I had been there," he said. "Get you some coffee over there, and I think there might be a couple of doughnuts left in that box."

"Linda Winkles," she said as she held out her arm to shake hands. "I'm a friend of Bud's, Bud Johnson."

"Bud, aha! So he's the one behind all this?"

"Yeah, he thought it would be a pretty good joke, being it was Halloween and all–and a beautiful full moon too. Sorry, it shook you up so much. It was pretty scary when we went into that spin. I thought we were goners. I really did. Hey, you're a pretty good pilot. Where did you learn to fly like that?"

"Souter Field in Americus, Georgia," I said.

"Souter Field?"

"Yeah, that's where Charlie Lindberg traded his motorcycle for an old army surplus Jenny. He got a couple of hours of instruction from Smitty, the same guy who taught me. Pretty good instructor."

"Yeah, I hear Lindberg is getting ready to fly the Atlantic solo to win that big prize, New York to Paris nonstop, solo."

"Yeah, now that is going to be some flight if he makes it alive. That's a lot of water to fly over, even if you do have a specially built Ryan aircraft. I hear that he can't even see out of the cockpit without a periscope, at least forward anyway."

"A periscope?" said Linda.

"Yeah, you have to look into it to see up through some mirrors to see what's in front of you. You can only see out the little side windows. I bet he doesn't even get off the ground. Nobody can fly with eighty gallons of gasoline."

"Well, I wish him luck," Linda said.

"Yep, he will sure need it."

"Maybe they will call him Lucky Lindy!"

The Barnstormers and Barnstorming Willie

"Where are you from anyway?" I asked Linda.

"Savannah actually, but I met Bud Johnson a couple of years ago up here in Atlanta. Said he was thinking about going barnstorming across the country and needed a girl to throw in the act–you know, wing walking or something."

"Well, you do handle it pretty good, I'd have to say. But wing walking, hey, that's something else."

"All you gotta do is hold on," she said.

"Yeah, all you gotta do is hold on–and don't fall off."

"What about using a parachute?" she said.

"Too careful. Not scary enough for the crowds. Besides, no parachute is going to do you any good at five hundred feet."

"You got a point there," she said.

"Give me another doughnut, will ya?" I said.

"Hey, you heard about the new diet doughnut they're coming out with, haven't you?"

"No," I said very emphatically.

"Yeah, it's gonna have two holes in it instead of one," she said as she giggled all over.

"Real funny," I said.

"Well, they are."

"Get outta here. What are you going to do now that you are stranded in Atlanta?" I said.

"Oh, I don't know. I'll probably hang out here on the couch until morning. Tomorrow I'll give Bud a holler and see if I can get a meal and a lift."

"I gotta go home," I said. "The wife will be looking for me sooner or later."

"Married, huh?"

"Yeah, kinda."

"Kinda?"

"Yeah, sometimes it feels like I'm married. Sometimes it don't."

"Well, if you're married, you're married."

"Is that right? What makes you such an expert on marriage?"

"Two years of being married to the wrong person, not now though. Got a divorce. My folks didn't like it, but I wasn't going to keep living a lie with someone who treated me like a doormat. I would have killed him in another year. Now I'm fancy free again, and I love it. No husband, no ties, no lies."

"It's a two-way street, you know."

"Yeah, but now this street just goes one way, baby," she said as she slid her two hands quickly together and apart. "And that's the way I like it!!!"

* * *

Later, me, Linda, and Bud went into barnstorming in 1936. We had all become great friends, and flying and dangerous adventure was our forte!

Bud and I would fly two airplanes, and Linda would wing walk from one to the other. We scared and thrilled a lot of people. Linda never did fall off, thank goodness, and the Kalamazoo flying circus was a real success!

Austell Comes to Town

Meanwhile, Samuel–my uncle had been doing some adventuring himself. Uncle Sam, as we called him, had been doing a lot of artwork and perfecting his skill at photography.

My father's brother was a real ladies' man, and during his lifetime, he had pursued the fairer sex with great enthusiasm.

I'd have to go back a ways to tell you some of his story, way back to 1914 and before.

Alfred Austell Jr. had just graduated from Yale University with a degree in business. He was the son of Alfred Austell Sr., the Confederate Civil War general, the financier of the Western and Atlantic Railroad to Cincinnati Junction, now known as Austell, Georgia.

Alfred Jr. was Samuel's very good friend, especially during the heyday of the Sweetwater Park Hotel in Salt Springs, now often referred to as Lithia Springs.

Before college, Samuel and Alfred Jr. had met one day, playing croquet of all things on the grounds of the grand hotel. It was a great way to meet and entertain the ladies. They would be all decked out in their off-white suits, and the ladies would be dressed to kill. What a sight!

You might say that Alfred Jr. represented the old money of the time, and Samuel, having made a respectable small fortune for himself, was a good example of what you might call the nouveau riche!

Together, they made a fine pair, a tag team that was unbeatable when it came to charismatic behavior, the likes of which were exemplified daily around the Sweetwater Park Hotel and the Piedmont Chautauqua.

For several years now, young Alfred had been away a good bit up in New Haven, Connecticut, priming up for life at Yale. Now that he was out finally, the world was his oyster. Maybe, you might say, it was a whole platter of oysters!

To reward himself for the hard work of four years' study and sacrifice, upon matriculation, Alfred Jr. bought himself a brand-new automobile, a red Locomobile built by the Stanley Steamer Company. The *Red Devil* he called it. It was a beauty!

Automobiles were pretty much a brand-new thing at that time, and people lined up along the streets in all the little towns as he blasted through at ten miles an hour!

Showing off was not the point; it was only the by-product of pride and excitement that everyone felt for the newfangled devices. The first person whom he ran into when he brought it home was Samuel, his best friend.

Samuel had seen a few automobiles in Atlanta and other places but nothing like the *Red Devil*. Up and down the roads they went, going here and going there, leaving a boiling cloud of dust the size of Texas everywhere they went. When they got tired of riding the wind, as they called it, they would go home to Alfred's plantation down on the Chattahoochee River in southeastern Douglas County, where his father had, years before, purchased the old Gorman Plantation and *Gorman's Ferry*. Now it was known as *Austell's Ferry*.

Alfred's father was getting older now, and he began to turn much of his holdings over to the young new general with the Yale pedigree!

The Austell Plantation, there on the Chattahoochee River, had been widely known for some time as a party place—a place to dance the night away until the early morning light came streaming across the river water.

It was a fairly big house as the old general had added onto the old Gorman house and expanded it more to his own choosing. Now it was quite lavish in an old-fashioned sort of way, and dancing was the thing to do.

Especially, every full moon night was one to celebrate. So at least once a month, there was a party going on.

On one of these occasions, a girl by the name of Mimi Stoker attended at the party and dance. She was the niece of an industrialist business magnate from Atlanta, a friend of Mr. Austell's, who was now an Atlanta banker and financier.

At 10:18 p.m. on June 25, 1914, the sky blue eyes of Alfred Jr. met the deep-sea green eyes of Miss Mimi Stoker. And the world would never be the same again!

They would never marry, but she would become the lifelong companion of Alfred Jr. and over time would be the inheritor of all the world had ever given to young Alfred.

For years, they would drive the *Red Devil* all over Douglas County and back and forth to Atlanta, taking care of "Daddy's business" as Mimi called it and their own.

Mimi loved to drive the *Red Devil* and let her long blond hair blow in the fast wind, wild and free like her, while Alfred and Samuel and perhaps another girlfriend would be a-hootin' and a-hollering and laughing all the way to the bank and back.

Miss Mimi, as she was always called, drove the first car ever onto *Austell's Ferry*, and the *Red Devil* crossed the Chattahoochee River in a record time of eleven minutes, only to blast away in another giant cloud of red Georgia dust. It was a grand and exciting life!

They would gather at dusk down by the river on Saturday by the carload, by the buggy load, by the wagonload, on horseback, or just on foot, and they would cook a whole pig on the spit with a big fire in the ground. They would then eat until they could eat no more; the band would play all the great tunes of the day, songs like "Down by the Old Mill Stream"; the libation would flow; and they would all dance until dawn.

After many years of this good life, young Alfred—now an older and more mature man—took on a mysterious illness. We never knew exactly, but I think he really died from pneumonia. Probably those late-night dances got the best of him finally. It was a great loss, and all who had loved him mourned his passing with considerable grief.

Miss Mimi was the only one left now, and for years already, she had been acting as hostess and mistress at the Austell Plantation and acting as manager for the *Austell's Ferry*. She did a good job and always prided herself on running superior flats on the river.

Being no others, all was left to Miss Mimi. She continued and stayed on in her matriarchal capacity, even with no children, for many years until she finally went to heaven herself, having died a quiet death in old age there on her beloved banks of the singing Chattahoochee River, having now been immortalized by Georgia's poet laureate Sydney Lanier.

Out of the hills of Habersham, down through the valleys of Hall, I run down to Douglas County on my way to the oyster-laden reprise of Apalachicola Bay and the beautiful Gulf of Mexico.

You see, we are all really related with one another and all things. As we move through life, we become one with one another in thought, in actions, in spirit, and in our loving memory. So, when you look at nature, pause, think, and remember those who tread this way before, for it one day will be you.

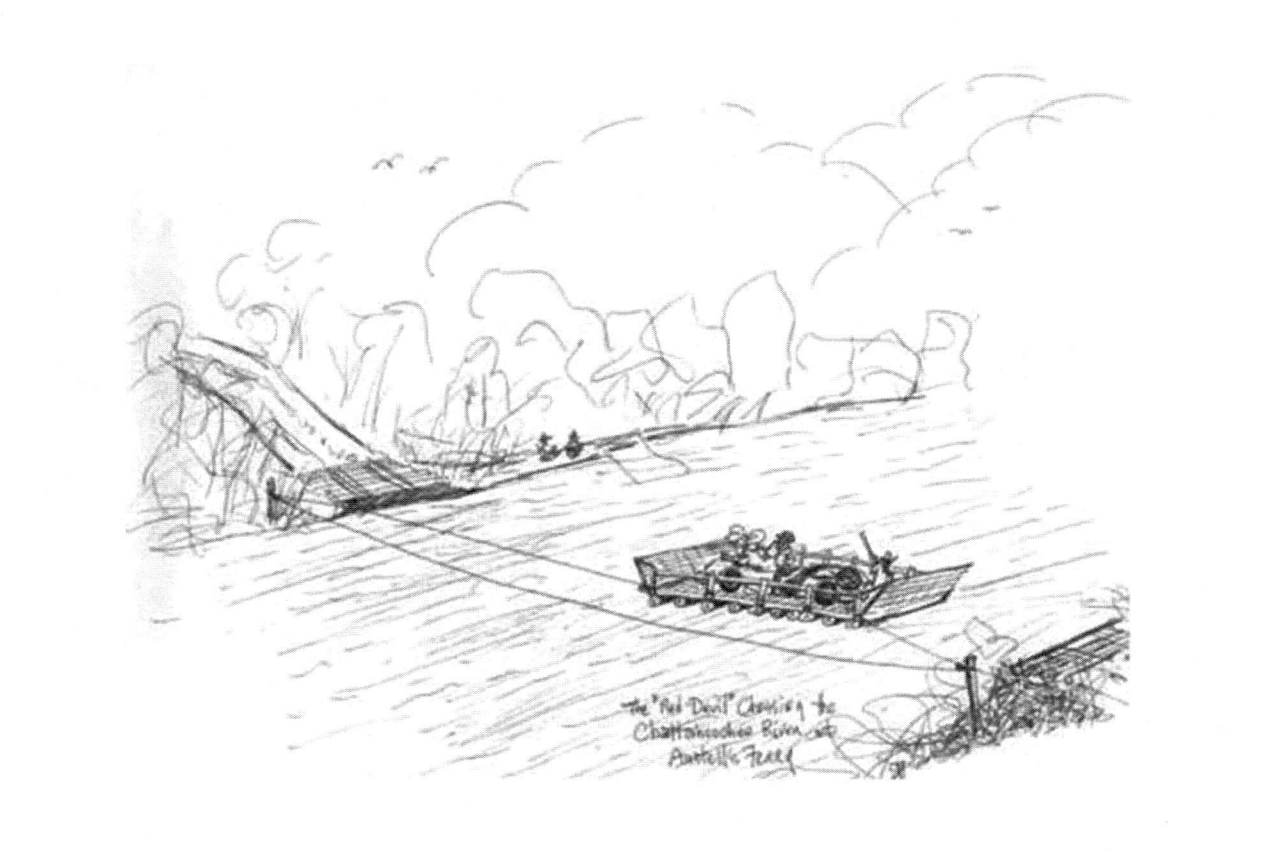

The "Nel Dewitt" Clearing the Chattahoochee River Like Pamela Field

Bustling and Busted: The Depression Moves In

Sixteen years passed since that fateful day when the great fire swept away the glory that was Lithia Springs on January 12, 1912. The charred remains and vacant land had lain idle for all these years, a testimony to the profundity of life-changing events.

The year 1928 was strange in many ways. Things had been quite good up until now, at least in Douglasville and the economy in general in Douglas County and elsewhere.

Napoleon Bonaparte Jett, NB as he was called, had loved every day he ran the Duncan Mercantile business in Douglasville, Georgia. He just loved selling things. And his brother John Thomas Jett, often just called JT, loved buying things. So they had the perfect combination of relationship.

JT would travel far and wide to find a bargain or something unusual or different, something they did not already carry in their wide-flung inventory from nail to top hats.

New York was his favorite place to go, and he went there about once a year to stay abreast of changes in the latest fashions and technology.

On one of his trips to New York, JT met a man named Justin Hanover of the Hanover Furniture Company. They bought wholesale all the finest furniture built from all over New England. Mr. Hanover and JT became fast friends as well as close business associates.

Mr. Hanover, educated in Georgia, had even married a young lady from Atlanta, a vivacious, cute-as-a-button petite redheaded charmer named Tara Hill. She too would soon befriend the Jett family over the next few years and become a great liaison for North and South cultural relations.

The Hanover family, as it turned out, was quite wealthy and had acquired its own small fleet of merchant ships to ply the waters of the Atlantic between New York and the London markets of Europe.

Justin himself had spent his college years in the Deep South and graduated from Emory College at Oxford, Georgia. While there, he had made connections with the Candler boys, sons of Asa Candler.

Oxford, for that reason, was one of the first little towns around Atlanta, and indeed in America, to carry the new cola syrup, which was mixed with carbonated water to give you a sparkling new drink that everybody just loved. Because of this early connection, Justin was able to get the syrup introduced to the New York market and later began shipping the syrup by the ship full to London and hence all over Europe. It wasn't long before things were going very well for the Hanover family.

JT and Justin shared many ideas and good times over the next several years of their acquaintance and friendship. Not only did all the boys share a common alma mater, Emory College, but also shared a love for business, money, and all the finer things in life. A good education can carry you far!

* * *

Rather suddenly in 1929, things just fell apart literally. The stock market took a nosedive, and almost overnight, people all over the country lost hundreds, thousands, and millions of dollars.

Runs on the banks were unstoppable. People wanted and needed their money, however little or a lot it was.

The bank back home that JT and NB had founded, the first bank in Douglasville, could not meet its demands. In short order, like thousands of others, it failed and shut down, paying out something like 0.20 cents on the dollar to its depositors. Some paid much less, and others had none to pay. It was a sad and difficult time.

What would everyone do? Go back to farming? Even the Duncan Mercantile in Douglasville, the great store with everything from everywhere, was locked up and shut down.

Aside from the creditors, no one had any money to buy anything with. Everyone was almost penniless. The Great Depression was on us!

* * *

Nowhere, was it more difficult, than for the Hanover family in New York. The stock market had crashed, and folks were jumping out of buildings to their death all over Manhattan and elsewhere simply because they could not adjust themselves to such a reversal of fortune. It was one thing to lose a few dollars in a bad business or a small venture that didn't pan out, but to lose everything, one had worked so hard for, was no laughing matter.

Some of the ships that the Hanovers owned went into receivership, but several were saved. Gradually, over time, they would adjust to the market and rebuild the financial empire they once enjoyed, and JT and NB would be there to help them as they all dug out of the great gaping hole of the Depression.

For a few years, JT and NB and their families would move to New York and establish homes on Long Island.

They would all work together to reestablish themselves, but it would be a long and rocky road!

Prohibition, Pass the Bottle, Drink or Smell, and Groover's Lake

In the meantime, as time waited for no man, as my father would often say, things did happen after a while back home.

Despite the fact that, Congress passed Prohibition in 1920 to curb the alcoholic appetite of the masses, it just didn't take too good. There were all kinds of problems, and crime ran rampant. Speakeasies, illegal drinking places, sprang up all over the country, even here, and people who wanted it got it anyway. Finally, by 1933, everybody had had enough of the whole business of Prohibition, and Congress repealed it. But a lot went on in between. Games like pass the bottle and drink or smell were favorites of the time, and there was a whole lot of moonshining going on, illegal whiskey making!

* * *

By 1930, there was a new game in town, speedboat racing. What? Speedboat racing? Yes, I said speedboat racing!

Groover's Lake, built by John Freeman Groover, had been built as a manmade lake on Beaver Ruin Creek at Lithia Springs, Georgia. It was a fine resort lake of about eighty acres or so with about sixteen vacation cabins built around it. There was a big boathouse and store with a big full-floor dance hall built above on the second floor.

And there were boathouses for fishing boats and for speedboats.

Every Saturday and Sunday afternoons at 2:00 pm was time for speedboat racing at Groover's Lake, home of the *Dixie Dew, Catch Me If You Can, Fast Idle,* and *Water Flasher.* Others too would come and go, leaving their wake behind them.

It was pretty exciting to make your way down to Groover's Lake and traverse the iron and wooden bridge, which went over the spillway and big gorge on Beaver Ruin Creek. It was one lane with rail sidings and very high. You were very careful to keep your Model A Ford on the runner boards of the bridge. Wow, what a sight!

As you pulled across the gorge, you entered into a sort of magical pine forest as you drove over to the big parking lot and beach. Yes, I said beach, a nice big white sandy beach for swimmers and sunbathers. And you ought to have seen some of those bathing suits. Why, some girls were hardly wearing anything on their legs; and by now, the men were beginning to expose their upper torsos. It caught on pretty quick at Coney Island, New York, and here at Lithia Springs, Georgia. People were liberate!.

One of the best features of Groover's Lake was the high jumping tower and cable ride across the water that allowed you to go flying through the air and drop off at the right time to the refreshing cool water below. What a blast!

Boxing was a big sport here also, and summertime was filled with amateur boxing matches, and sometimes a professional bout would culminate from the rigorous training of boxers, such as middleweight title contender Ben Brown, who actually lived at the resort for about two years. In 1939, he would go for the championship bout with Teddy Yarosz, the defending middleweight champion.

Many sparring matches were held on the Boxing Hill, with a real regulation ring and hundreds of spectators on the weekend. And another famous person who frequented Groover's Lake was Virginia Hill from Paulding County. She was the famous girlfriend of gangster Bugsy Siegel. Virginia would show up, usually without Bugsy, but not without a full entourage of bodyguards, who watched her and everybody else like hawks. Virginia loved to dance in the big upper dance hall, which overlooked the lake, and she always had a great time.

On dance nights, the upper sides of the building–windows of sorts–would fold up and be suspended for a full open-air affair and view of the lake. Live bands would play their hearts out, and everybody would carry on like there was no tomorrow. If there wasn't a live band, the jukebox would play vinyl records and blast them out over the whole area. It was a really good jukebox and loud!

On Saturday night, it was the place to be–drinking a cold Coca-Cola or something stronger, holding your best girl real tight, and dancing the night away one more time. It was a swell place!

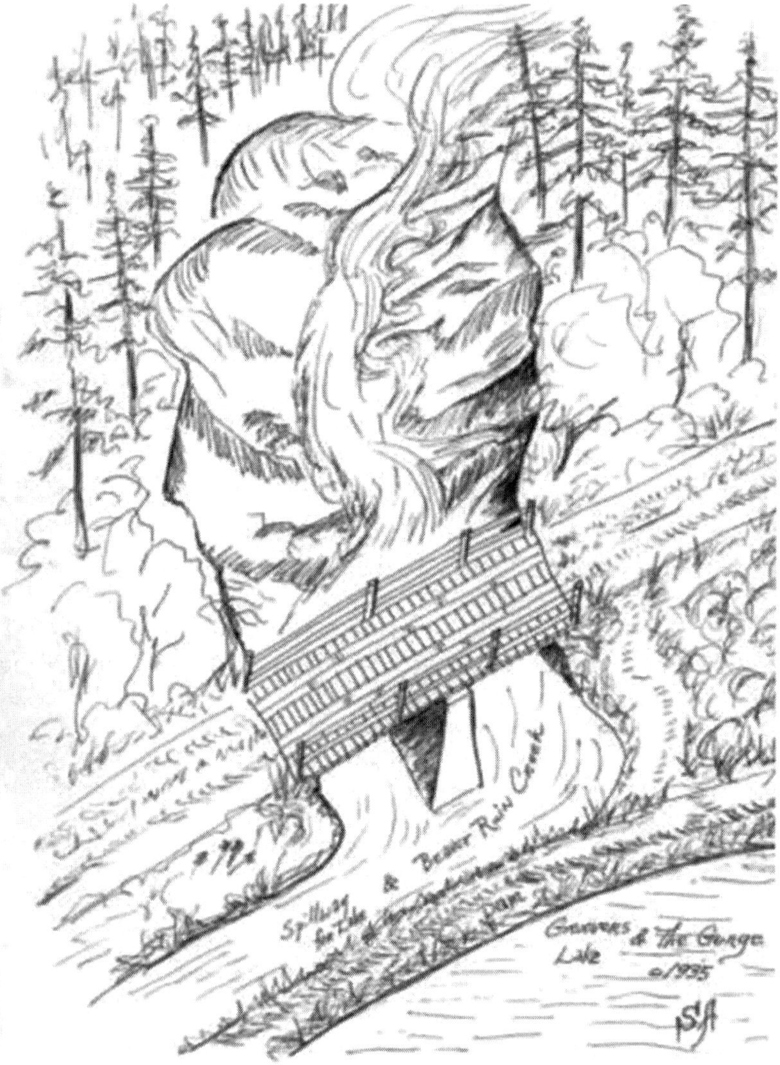

& Beaver
& The Gorge
Lake

Flying the Loop for a Woman Golfer

Tuesday morning caught me early at six. I could barely get out of bed, but it was time to get up and get at 'em.

I had to make a quick flight to Chattanooga–flying the loop, I called it–this morning to pick up a passenger for Bud Johnson, my partner. Why he didn't go was beyond me, but he had some other conflict. He and Linda were going down south to Macon to set up the next air show, I think.

By eight, I was up in the air. I loved my new plane, bright and yellow and all-enclosed cabin and still two wings! A Staggerwing Beechcraft! We were in the gravy now and traveling in high cotton!

The trip to Chattanooga was smooth and routine. As I taxied up to the Beechcraft Hangar and Elmira Air Charter, I shut her down. I wouldn't refuel until I got back to Atlanta. Had plenty of gasoline, enough for four more hours.

I hopped outside the cabin and started walking over to the little terminal office. Outside sat a pristine, dark blue, 1939 Packard automobile taxi, a beautiful automobile.

After sipping down a Hirs Orange Soda, I looked over, and here came a fairly young lady and her two white poodles. *Hmmmmm*, I thought. *What's this all about?*

In a few short moments, she was introducing herself as Louise.

"Hello, Louise, my name is William, and I'll be your pilot today on the trip to Atlanta."

"Oh good, young man, and what about my poodles, Pixie and Dixie? They go everywhere I do. They've never been flying before, but I haven't either, so we're even."

"No problem, Louise. I love dogs, especially flying dogs. Come on, let's get loaded. By the way, what's your last name?"

"Suggs, Louise Suggs. I play golf."

"Yeah?"

"Yes, my daddy is building me a golf course at Lithia Springs, just west of Atlanta."

"No kidding?" I said. "That's where my family is from."

"You don't say?"

"Yeah."

"Well, all right then, we've got something in common. This is going to be a great trip."

"Why don't you just hold the little dogs or let them run loose, if you want to, once we are in the air? I don't think they are going to jump out or anything, not in this new airplane. You won't even feel the wind. It's a real pleasure to travel in. Hey, I see you got your own golf clubs."

"Yes, my daddy made them for me special and taught me how to play too. Are you any good?""Pretty good . . . and getting better all the time. Last year, I won $1,000 and hope to double that this year. You know, the world of women golfing is sort of brand new, and it's beginning to pay some big bucks."

"I'll say."

Soon we were airborne, and the new bird was singing her song all the way to Atlanta. North Georgia sure was pretty this time of year, with all the fall color blanketing the countryside. No wonder I loved flying so darn much!

The poodles were well behaved and sat in Louise's lap most of the time. Every once and a while, they would jump up, put their little feet on the window, and look out for the longest time. It was kinda neat to have some little canine passengers aboard.

Louise and I chitchatted a little about this and that, nothing much. Then she said, "You know, I guess flying is a lot like golf. You have to go from one place to the next, and you have to use your skill to do a good job, if you're going to get a winning score. We usually play eighteen holes, but Daddy's only building me a nine-hole course to practice on. Said that is all the land he has anyway, and that's enough to learn on. He said he took out one million board feet of lumber just out of the fairways on nine and moved all the dirt with a mule and draw pan to build the greens and bunkers. I'm a pretty lucky girl, I guess."

"Yes, you are, Louise."

There was a long pause and some silence as we both thought about golf and flying.

"You know, Louise, one friend of mine said that flying was so weird that you have to first go to an airport, one place you don't want to go to, so you can fly to another place that you don't want to go to so you can go to a place that you do want to go to."

"Wow, I never thought of it like that. I guess he has a point, huh?"

"Well, it's all those hours in between that make up the experience. Hours and hours of boredom, some say, interrupted by moments of sheer terror. Atlanta coming up," I said to Louise.

"Well, this trip didn't take long, and it sure wasn't boring at all," Louise said. "It was wonderful."

"We'll be descending in a few minutes. Better get those golf clubs ready. Ha ha! Pull her back easy, slow. Don't drop the air speed below eighty knots. Easy now, just like sliding your hand up a girl's leg, my instructor had taught me, real slow and easy."

"Wop, wop!" went the front wheels. We were down; in a moment, the tail wheel dropped. *Damn, I thought I had a three-point landing already. But not bad.* I didn't say it out loud, but I was thinking it just the same!

Candler Field was still grass. Guess it would be grass forever as far as I knew, but surely to goodness, one day aviation was going to really catch on.

There was no Chicago/Atlanta Airlines as Uncle Charlie had considered better and had put his money in more real estate in Chicago. However, there was a little shack near the old Blevins Hangar with a board nailed up on top of the door, and it read "Ace Aviation." It was the best thing that me and Bud, and Linda could come up with. One day in the future, we hoped there would be little Ace airplanes scattered all over the country!

"Louise, do you need a ride? Are you going out to Lithia Springs right now?"

"No," she said. "My daddy is going to pick me up, and we are going down on Ponce de Leon to the ballpark. My daddy is the manager of the Atlanta Crackers baseball team, and I think they are playing ball tonight. Wanna go?"

"Nawww. I appreciate it, but I gotta get back to flying again. I think I've got a charter to Columbus this afternoon. Maybe next time. Thanks."

"By the way, Mr. William," she said, "that was a wonderful flight, so pretty and all and smooth. I think I'm going to like flying. My babies liked it too, I can tell from the way they are jumping around. Thanks a bunch. See you on the golf course, huh???"

"Maybe! See you later!"

The Lithia Springs Golf Course

Eighteen holes is a whole golf course, so I guess nine holes was half a golf course. Anyway that, being nine holes, was what Johnny Suggs built at Lithia Springs.

Around the old Lithia Springs themselves, you could now play golf; and if you wanted to play a full game, you just went around twice.

When you finished, you could get some of the refreshing lithia water from the old pump. Wasn't quite like it used to be, but it was still there, along with Frog Rock and the picnic tables scattered here and there.

Aside from the occasional flooding, the course was pretty good, not elaborate but passing. And just like Louise told me, her daddy told me one time that he built the course himself with a mule team and draw pan and that he had harvested more than one million board feet of lumber from the fairways and greens. Quite a bit of an accomplishment, I thought.

The only problem was a highway that went from Atlanta to Birmingham bisected the golf course.

So, when you moved from the eighth hole to the ninth tee, you had to cross the dad-blamed highway to get over there. Then you played your ball up a big high hill, where the Suggs had lived on top; around their house; down the other side of the hill to the ninth green, and then back across the highway over to the number one hole tee. I think golf course building will advance in the future.

Occasionally, we would go down and watch Louise practice and sometimes play a tournament game. Anybody who could play that course as good as she could was bound to be great. She would go on to become one of the greatest woman golfers of all time!

Whatever Happened to Whom?

"Well, I knew you were asking, 'Whatever happened to Ben Jett? And Debbie Langford? And Stephanie Herron and all those folks?'"

I wouldn't know! Never heard from 'em again! No, just kidding!

Many things happened over the next few decades after the Civil War.

As I said, Ben Jett made his way to the big city of Atlanta to find his fame and fortune. After the war, Atlanta was rebuilding and trying to get a new grip on life. Some, like Henry Grady, referred to her as the "rising phoenix." After the great burning was rising out of the ashes of destruction and desolation to a new height of prominence in the New South as he called it.

Ben had a number of talents that would take him far, one of which was his ability to analyze things to take things apart and put things back together. Realizing this potential, he set out to discover just what he could get into.

He was still young at the end of the war, about twenty years old, and in good health. The year was only 1866.

For the next nineteen years, Ben would kind of go from one thing to another. He was really good at the buggy business for a number of years and eventually went into making fine carriages and utility commercial carriers. It was fairly exciting and paid pretty good. Mostly, though, he began to do custom work for special customers, like beautiful carriages with leather and glass, coach lights, and such–real fancy fixings for the wealthy and affluent society.

During this time, he took the notion to try to contact Debbie Langford in Augusta.

Debbie was his brother Steve's old flame, but something had happened, and that flame seemed to have gone low over the years after the war. They never made the effort to meet or get together, so Ben figured all was fair in love and war.

He wrote a letter to Debbie as follows:

August 3, 1867
Miss Debbie Langford, General Delivery, Augusta, Georgia

Dear Debbie,

Hope this letter finds you and finds you well and in good health.

The war is over now, and we have to all get on with the business of living.

My father lost a leg in the war but is otherwise doing fine. My brother William and Levi did not make it back home.

Samuel, Steve, and I survived somehow and were never seriously injured. What miracles happen!

My ma and sister, Anna, were actually deported to the North to work in textile mills instead of in the South. They lived in New Albany, Indiana, until they finally came home at the end of the war. And Anna had a baby, little Charles.

She had married a young man who got killed in the mill in an accident before she left for coming back home. Life can be so sad.

But life can be happy too, and that is why I am writing you to start a new life of happiness.

I have moved to Atlanta and am working in the carriage business. It's not too bad, and I am learning a lot and doing some pretty fine work, if I do say so myself.

My brother Steve is courting some girl named Lucinda now, and they plan to marry next spring. So I figured it would be okay to write to you myself.

Please write and tell me what has happened to you and your family and if you ever hear from cousin Stephanie and the Herrons of Atlanta.

Goodbye for now and Godspeed,

Ben Jett
146 Lullwater Road
Atlanta, Georgia

Exciting Developments

By now, things were pretty hot in carriage sales. Atlanta was booming again. The old rolling mill had been rebuilt and reopened and was now called Atlantic Steel. It was a big business.

By 1885, a new technology school opened on North Georgia Avenue called the Georgia School of Technology. There were only eighty-four students, but Ben Jett was one of them, now at age forty, a little older than most of the young whippersnappers but eager to learn everything he could about mechanics, engineering, and stuff like that. He would go to school in the days and work at night. By 1888, Ben Jett was an official civil engineer and in the first matriculating class of Georgia Tech.

That was the same year that the Sweetwater Park Hotel held its grand opening in Lithia Springs.

Ben had been a part of the architectural design team that worked on and actually drew up the plans for E. W. Marsh and Company, who built the grand hotel. So naturally, Ben knew the design in and out, backward and forward.

As a matter of fact, it was his idea to incorporate a grand ballroom on the second floor above the grand dining room. The engineering required would be the same and would afford a great utility as a social gathering hall for dances and main events.

This grand ballroom would be the showcase special of the Sweetwater Park Hotel, and many lavish parties and dances were held there quite often.

The band would be visiting there from Atlanta, Philadelphia, Boston, and New York and even Vienna, Austria.

The most beautiful thing in both sight and sound the world ever had seen was when the orchestra from Vienna played the Viennese waltz and the "beautiful people" filled the grand ballroom. They danced and danced and danced until dawn!

* * *

By the late 1880s and the 1890s, things were going pretty good for Ben and his family.

He had the good fortune to marry Debbie Langford of Augusta, Georgia, and they eventually had six children!

Yes, Debbie had written back to Ben about six months later, in January 1868.

There was a little confusion for a while about just what all had happened to everyone and the emotions that played such a big part of everyone's lives.

Cousin Stephanie had moved to California–San Francisco to be exact, I believe–and had opened a new restaurant at a place called Fisherman's Wharf. It was bound to be good!

Stephanie had married out there a California man who had struck it rich during the 1849 gold rush. He was about forty-five years old, I guess, not that age mattered, for you only got better with age, until you started to wear out.

In the future, Ben and Debbie would travel a good bit, and they would definitely go to Fisherman's Wharf in San Francisco, California.

As a matter of fact, they traveled all over the country, mostly by Pullman car on the railroads. The railroads were king in those days, just like King Cotton in the South.

Even Alaska wasn't too far away, but part of the way, they had to travel by boat as the rails just didn't go all that far. They liked Alaska and figured it was a pretty good deal for the United States to purchase Alaska from Russia in 1898. But Secretary of the Interior Seward got a lot of criticism, and the deal was generally known as Seward's Folly.

Alaska was a lot of ice, rock, and snow. For what? Ten million dollars? But who knew? One day maybe they would strike oil or gold or polar bear in Alaska. Ben said he would bet money on it. It was, he said, the most miraculous place on the earth!

The Century Turned Fast and Furious

The days around the turn of the century were exciting times in the Lithia Springs locale and throughout the world.

Now I just wanted to clarify one or two things about the actual logistics of what really happened around Salt Springs during that time. It was a little confusing.

The Sweetwater Park Hotel was built at Salt Springs or nearby, now known as Lithia Springs.

The Bowden-Lithia Springs Hotel and/or Ben-Scott Hotel, was built at Cincinnati Junction, now known as Austell.

The Sweetwater Motel was built sometime around the 1930s or '40s on part of the old spring property at the Lithia Springs Golf Course.

Also, at the springs was built a large Lithia Springs swimming pool and Lithia Springs Dance Hall; and across the road adjacent to the other part of the golf course was another development called Pine Crest Park Swimming Pool, Pine Crest Park Skating Rink, and even Pine Crest Park Bowling Alley. It was a pretty exciting place on both sides of the road!

The dance hall would, one day, even host the likes of a leg-wobbling young rock-and-roll singer named Elvis Presley and others like Buddy Holly. Lithia Springs was once again on the map big time. People would come here from miles around and take in the adventure and excitement, and they would dance and dance and dance, sometimes until dawn. Those all-nighters were the best. But now we were getting up into the century a little more, halfway and then some!

* * *

The Lithia Springs Hotel Resort, which also hailed lithia water and touted its miracle qualities, was built at Tallapoosa, Georgia, near the Alabama line. It was built about the same time as and almost identical to the Sweetwater Park Hotel in many ways and lasted until about 1926, when it was torn down, having been abandoned for some years before. It never burned. Twenty-six houses were built from its salvaged lumber!

Tallapoosa had been big on the wine country and glass blowing and bottling for many years after the Hungarian colony at Budapest revolutionized the farming practices of the area from cotton to vineyards. The whole area was a virtual haven for anyone who had anything to do with the wine industry.

The area thrived up until Prohibition in 1920 and the Eighteenth Amendment to the U.S. Constitution. The amendment failed miserably over the next decade and was finally repealed by 1933, but by then, all the damage had been done, and whole towns like Tallapoosa, Georgia, had gone to industrial ruin.

Prohibition, to the wine industry, was a death knell. It was like the boll weevil was to the cotton industry.

It first came from Mexico in 1892, and in the next few years, it completely destroyed the cotton growing in the South. King Cotton had been dethroned, and it was now a historical footnote as an agricultural giant. But all was not lost, and by 1919, a town in Enterprise, Alabama, even erected a gold-plated boll weevil monument and water fountain in the middle of town for all to see as a thank-you for forcing farmers into diversification farming and crop rotation and other more progressive farming techniques. The *Progressive Farmer* became a very popular magazine and circulated widely.

* * *

By 1913 or so, kudzu was introduced to the South from China as the savior of erosion. It was used to combat the terrible, terrible erosion caused across the South by poor farming practices. Soon it would take over the world!!!

Had old Sherman had to deal with creeping old kudzu, he never would have gotten across north Georgia, and Atlanta would have still been safe!

It had originally been introduced to the United States in 1876 by Japan at the centennial celebration of the United States in Philadelphia, Pennsylvania, as a beautiful fast-growing plant in their gardens. From there, it went to Florida gardens and then all over the South by the early part of the twentieth century. Anything that can grow up to eighteen inches a day was bound to go somewhere. And to say the least, it went everywhere. It was even on the farm at home and made for some real problems later!

* * *

Speaking of Prohibition again, another popular location between 1913 and 1933–and later–was Factory Shoals, as the area was known to the locals, just above New Manchester and the mill, all burned out during the Civil War. Nobody returned to this town and area because nobody owned any real estate there. It was all company owned, so really, once burned, there was nothing to come back to. This was the answer to the riddle and mystery of New Manchester. But it was a beautiful area, and the shoals offered much in the way of entertainment.

So on the upper part of the shoals, just about where the old mill race began, the owners at that time either built or leased out the rights to build a two-story open-air dance hall with a two-story double fireplace, one up and one down, all accessible by a small walk over the bridge across the mill race. I think it was built two stories so that if the water got up and flooded the first floor, then you still had the second and still the fireplace. I wouldn't know for sure because I only visited there a couple of times and only once when an actual dance party was going on. It was a bit on the wild side, and beer, liquor, wine, and women all flowed as free as the river.

If you got real amorous, you could spend the night or whatever in one of the several small cabins that had been built on the hillside by the Mennonites and abandoned several years before.

Old man Ralph Brown's daddy built the double chimney and fireplaces himself and talked about it for years later. What a fine job they did! So much for Prohibition. Didn't work here or in Chicago, Atlanta, Factory Shoals, or anywhere else.

I had always heard that, even in the worst of economic times, three things would always sell–alcohol, tobacco, and makeup. And so it did!

During the times of economic depression and alcoholic suppression, people found their solace in other things and other ways and in other places like Factory Shoals, where the river flowed and anything went. With a new pint, a pack of Luckys or two, and a good-looking woman, you could adjust to things in this world accordingly; and in the meantime, you could once again dance the night away at Factory Shoals and let the world go by!

What a hoot!

"Shitbury Shoals
Dance Hall"

Hubert and Inez Get an Electric Stove

So many things had happened during those years. What with the Depression, Prohibition, the Great War to end all wars in Europe, the Spanish-American War, the advent of flight on December 17, 1903, and the arrival of the automobile, the telephone, and electricity. Wow, I didn't know what else could ever happen to change one world to that of another so much, so fast!

The year 1936 brought something else to Lithia Springs and Douglas County. It was the very first electric stove installed at the log cabin home of my good friend and old buddy H. V. "Doc" Branan and his lovely wife, Inez.

Doc was the very first secretary-treasurer of the Douglas County Electric Membership Corporation, simply called the EMC.

This was part of President Roosevelt's New Deal stuff to put the economy back on track and to electrify rural America.

The Tennessee River had been dammed up in a bunch of good places and power plants built to produce electricity, which was distributed all over the southeastern United States, an area somewhat lacking in the newest and latest technology called electricity!

Individual member-owned co-ops were established to facilitate the necessary lines, poles, and equipment for the distribution of this new wonder service.

Just think, a light bulb in the middle of your house. All you had to do was to pull the string, and presto, there was bright white and yellow light. Finally, there was a way to count the flies on your dangling flypaper even at night.

For most often, the light string and flypaper hung together as a matter of convenience and utility!

"Hubert! Get the door open! The men are here with the electric stove!" Mrs. Branan yelled out.

"All right, I'll be right there! Let me get this old stovewood moved out and make a place for it! Hot diggity dog! We're gonna have some good cookin' tonight, just as soon as Inez gets the hang of this thing. Instant fire and instant heat—well, no fire but plenty of heat! Hmmm. This newfangled thing is going to revolutionize cooking and eating, and we got the first one in the whole county. My wife sure is lucky to have me for her husband," Doc said. "But actually, I am really the lucky one because now I don't have to cut any more stovewood—well, maybe for the fireplace, but that don't count."

Hubert was called Doc by almost everyone because he and Inez owned and ran the local and only apothecary or now sometimes called pharmacy in Lithia Springs just up the muddy dirt road, about four miles from their farm on Blairs Bridge Road.

The Branans were turn-of-the-century pioneers in the community, and Doc would put in over forty-nine years with the Railway Express Company before retiring and going into real estate sales with our family business.

Inez would help establish the church system and the Sunday schools for the churches in the whole West Georgia area for the Concord Baptist Association. She was a God-fearing and righteous woman who was not only on God's side but, more than that, God was also on her side.

* * *

And there were other people in the community too like the Harper family. Why, hadn't it been for Nesbit Harper, the railroad first started by the time of the Civil War would have never gotten finished by 1882 and opened eventually to Birmingham and New Orleans. The Harper family lived on the railroad too. Mr. Harper built a beautiful large Victorian-style home overlooking the Western and Atlantic Railroad in front of his house, and it would be there to this day at the end of Harper Drive.

Many a fine dinner was served and enjoyed in their sumptuous dining room of the grand old house. And many a family reunion and church gathering was held on the grounds.

There was a sad note of irony to this story, however, about the railroad; for one day in the early part of 1923, the railroad would take the life of his thirteen-year-old daughter, riding the school bus home, hit by a locomotive at the crossing right in the very front of his house on his street. It was a tragic circumstance that affected all in the community!

Sam Jones Is Preaching Today

The lazy days of summer would come and go, and the winters, springs, and autumns would grace the countryside with all their seasonal glories. The years went by, and time moved on!

* * *

The old Salt Springs United Methodist Church had flourished over the years. Great camp meetings were routinely held on the beautiful oak-laden grounds of the area long before the first wooden church even was built and later destroyed in 1898 by a terrible tornado.

Sometimes as many as 3,500 people would attend camp meeting in the summertime, and again and again, preachers and evangelists like Sam Jones of Cartersville would come and lead the summer revivals.

Sam Jones, you know, was why we had the Ryman Auditorium in Nashville, Tennessee.

Sam led Ryman to Jesus while in tent revival in Nashville early on in his evangelistic career. Ryman, being a real heathen but now saved and having great wealth, told Sam he would never have to preach in a tent again–not in Nashville. So he built him this beautiful building and auditorium, now home to such memorable radio shows as *The Grand Ole Opry*.

This, of course, brought up another thing–the advent of the radio. My, my, my, how this world was a-changin'!

It wasn't long before the Baptists wanted to catch up with the Methodists, and so one Sunday afternoon in the very late 1880s or so, according to my recollection, the elders of Salt Springs Baptist Church and of Oak Grove Baptist Church got together and decided to establish a new, bigger, better, and more centrally located church with a new name.

My father, R. B. Jett, was at that time one of the elders at Oak Grove Baptist up on the hill on the Old Alabama Road, just a couple of miles from our farm.

My mother and father both were real churchgoing people and always took the whole family in for review on Sunday.

This afternoon, they all met to look for and discuss a new location. Up and down the Old Alabama Road they went here and there until finally, about halfway in between the two existing churches, they sat down in a grove of shade trees to rest.

Ma was with them that day, and as they refreshed themselves in that spot of glorious shade, she looked up and said, "What about right here? This would be a wonderful place to build the new church!"

The others agreed, and the new Union Grove Baptist Church was established. My family had been going there off and on for all these years now. It was a fine church, and we have established a fine little cemetery out on the hillside to the north in the back of the church. There on the hillside, in plain view of Kennesaw Mountain, is the final resting place of my dear mother and father on this earth.

New Orleans Comes to Mableton

The year 1923 was big for Mableton, Georgia. For that was the year that Mr. Leonard Williams married Miss Mary "Mami" Lumpkin of New Orleans, Louisiana.

The story began with a love letter, the likes of which only those who had been truly in love can begin to understand.

In the early days of their youth, the youthful, vibrant, and wealthy family of Mami would leave sultry New Orleans in the early summer and make their way to the cool mountains of northern Georgia, in the little valley of Nacoochee near Sautee and Helen. The railroad would take them all the way across the country from the splendor of the French Quarter, their winter home place, to the bucolic countryside and slow pace of the north Georgia mountains and valleys.

Mami (pronounced *may-me*), as a young girl, was first observed by Leonard as he worked around the Sautee Depot, handling baggage and such. She paid him little attention at first but soon caught the twinkle in his eyes and the spark of determination in his attitude. Soon he won her permission to write to her and penned the most beautiful love letter that a young man in love could have possibly engendered. He was a well-educated young man and had obtained a civil engineering degree from Georgia Tech, just like Ben Jett but much later, around 1920.

Mami, as he always called her later, was well educated also, having attended the New Orleans Academy for Young Women and graduating at the top of her class.

When Mami got the letter that morning, she went out into the courtyard of their French Quarter home; and under the lightly tossing Spanish moss from the morning breeze, she read ever so slowly so as to not miss a single word:

September 15, 1922

Miss Mary Lumpkin
182 Lafayette Avenue
New Orleans, Louisiana

My Dearest Mary,

Please forgive me for my undue delay in writing you this letter of admiration and intent. For it begs my heart to express to you the true and exact feelings of my sentiments.

This past summer has been one of the happiest times of my life. For you have opened my eyes in so many ways and touched my heart with the deepest of emotions.

I have never met anyone who even can begin to compare to you, for you are truly incomparable in all ways imaginable.

Thank you for sharing with me the wonderful months of this past holiday season. Your family is as wonderful as you, and I am honored to even know such a fine family as yours.

Please now allow me, without any more hesitation on my part, to be so bold as to ask for your hand in marriage, if you and your family approve. My heart can wait no longer as it was so painful to see you off on the train just this last few days ago.

If you accept, I will plan for us a grand home here in the valley. And unlike the sad Nacoochee, we will travel to the beautiful Yonah Mountain; and rather than jumping in desperation as she did, we will fulfill our great love for the beginning of a lifetime.

Please let me know, by return post, as soon as possible your answer as my heart will be aching until then.

With all my love now and forever,

Leonard

* * *

The next several weeks were tortuous for poor Leonard, but at last, his letter of reply came to him, and he was so happy!

The young couple was married the very next spring at Starlight, the boyhood home of Leonard and the Williams family. And they did take their honeymoon for two weeks by horse and wagon up and upon Yonah Mountain, one of the most beautiful and inspiring places on this green earth. It would be a wonderful beginning for a new life of adventure and excitement!

As a wedding gift from Mary's parents, they were given a one-hundred-acre working farm with everything imaginable on it—beautiful and contemporary large, two-story Victorian house with a veranda porch and turrets on top, a huge cattle and hay barn, a dairy barn, a potato house, a blacksmith shop, a large implement shed, an orchard fruit barn, several fruit orchards, a lake, woods and pasture, a large windmill, several tenant houses, all established and operating!

The one criterion that Mami's father, Mr. Lumpkin, required was that the farm be located close by and convenient to his beloved lithia water, which he had grown to love and depend on for his and his family's health. That was why they ended up in Mableton, Georgia, just up the road from the Mable Plantation, instead of the Nacoochee Valley, but the ties to the valley and to New Orleans would always be strong as the ties of family would always bind us to the places we were from and that we loved so dear.

It was a new time and a new challenge for Leonard or LP as he was sometimes called by Mami. And the changes and challenges for Mami were tremendous also.

As a vivacious budding adult, Mami had been a young and beautiful queen of the Mardi Gras at the mature age of eighteen. She still had the opulently jeweled dress and gown of that auspicious event as well as pictures, scepter, and such. It was a lot for a young lady to follow in her mother's footsteps. Mami and Leonard's children—two girls only, Janie and Mary—would carry on the heirloom heritage of history into their own families and descendants. It would be a rich and unusual heritage to follow!

* * *

Leonard also had a family pedigree to equal that of Mami's, reaching as far back to the president of the United States William Henry Harrison, hero of the revolutionary Battle of Tippecanoe. Then there was U.S. president Benjamin Harrison, who, I believe, served the shortest time as president due to an unexpected downpour of rain on inaugural day and the subsequent onset of pneumonia. Then there was the uncle Noah Webster, who fought with Confederate general Joe Wheeler, the commander of R. B. Jett's cavalry regiment during the Civil War.

Leonard's grandfather had supplied all the brick for and built the original Lumpkin County–now White County, Georgia–Courthouse. The connection with the Lumpkin name I was not sure, but it was very interesting that he would marry a member of the Lumpkin family. Maybe they were distant cousins. This often was the case. The courthouse was still there today.

So, these two families of colossal backgrounds merged like the Atlantic and Pacific Oceans, very similar to the postnatal umbilical cord of the Panama Canal, established about the same time. And like so, their union was just as powerful and meaningful!

* * *

One of the most interesting things about the Williams Victorian home was the "secret garden." The back kitchen door opened onto a flagstone patio that surrounded the well and was shaded completely by a large Georgia live oak in the center area, mysterious and shadily darkened and cooled as a protector for the well and casual entrance area. On the opposite side of the shaded terrace was a boxwood garden with an entrance that opened into the secret collection of colorful flowers, herbs, and such. It was New Orleans all over again–right here in Mableton. It was so beautiful and so reminiscent of the old home. This was where Mami spent special time with her children and her husband as she, no doubt, reminded them that she was different, that they were different, and that they had all come from some other special place. Her own mother, Mama Lena, would not let them forget!

But this was a working farm, and work was what Leonard did from sunup to sundown every day except Sunday, the day of rest. Nobody worked like this man did to provide for his bride and, no doubt, show his deep appreciation for such a fine wedding gift. And well deserving was he, for it was most evident in the way he attended to every detail of the operations of that farm just as the engineer that he was. Later, his children and grandchildren of his namesake would take on the mantle of his diligence and responsibilities, which were far reaching.

* * *

The interesting aspect of all this information was that the daughter Janie would grow up and marry Noble (remember from Noble, France?) Brawnson Ayres, my father Grenoble's older brother. Brawnson and Janie then lived on the farm all their married life and raised five children on that farm in three different homes, aside from the Victorian home, which later burned. My first cousins, in order of age, were Patty, Penny, Christopher "Chris" Harrison (my age), Chip (Noble Brawnson Ayres Jr.), and Len (named after Leonard, his grandfather). As the years went by, we would all grow up on that farm together and a future governor of Georgia too, little Roy Barnes, who lived just down the road!

We'd save some of this for next time. After all, where would the future be without all of us? So Mableton changed, and so did the world!

"Mamie's Secret Garden" by SDA 2018

Thelbert Grenoble, We'll Just Call You Bill

In 1923, April 11, a baby was born to William Ausburn Ayres, son of David "Bud" Ayres and Lorena "Mini" Gordon and named Thelbert Grenoble Ayres, after Grenoble, France. Your guess on the "Thelbert" is as good as mine! I don't know! Later in life, he would always be known as TG or just "Bill," his nickname that he picked up at Western Electric when he was being introduced to the other workers! In the Navy in the Pacific, they called him "Doc." Later, I called him Daddy!

Bill would cut his teeth on airplanes at Vero Beach, Florida, having applied to the United States Navy as a future aviator and being turned down for poor vision. The next best thing was to learn to work on aircraft and what made them fly and to keep them flying during the war effort of WW II in the Pacific, but that was another story.

On April 18, 1925, a girl child would be born to Roy Blanche Wilson and Leroy L. Seignious; her name would be Blanche Virginia Seignious.

Her great-grandfather was Richard B. Jett, who later remarried after his first wife, Virginia, had passed on, having been struck by lightning there on the farm. Nancy, his new wife, even in his older age, bore him a child whom they named Ida Cline Jett. She married my great-grandfather Frank Wilson, and they had a little girl, Roy Blanche Wilson above, who would marry Leroy

L. Seignious from Charleston, and they would have seven children, the last one of which being Blanch Virginia Seignious, my dear mother.

Boy, family history can really get confusing, can't it! And this is just some of them!

Like in your own family, it just went on and on and on, I imagine. Actually, I had heard and highly suspected that we were all related and all, according to the Bible, going back to Adam and Eve. So there you have it in black and white!

So you might ask, "Did your mother marry her cousin? Are you a result of inbreeding?" Well, I didn't think so, but that could explain some of my incongruities and eccentricities. Actually, to make this story come out right, some of the facts had to be changed a little. An author can do that, you know. After all, this was just a good story, and 99 percent of it, less 25 percent, is all completely true!

How William Jett became William Ausburn Ayres was a magic trick to move toward the true identity of my true family line. Maybe he had his name legally changed because he had a nephew, Charlie Callihan Ayres, who had been adopted by David Allen "Bud" Ayres, the late second husband of Anna Jett, who later would bear him ten more children. Lo and behold, it was just too much to keep up with. And my grandmother Lorena was the oldest of eleven children. Honest to goodness, I sure couldn't figure it all out. Anyway, that was the way it was! That is my story, and I'm sticking to it!

* * *

In 1945, January 25, toward the end but not before the end of World War II, Blanche and Bill–TG, Thelbert Grenoble Ayres–would be married.

On September 7, 1946, they would have their first child, William Gordon Ayres.

One July 6, 1948, they would have their second child, Steven Douglas Ayres, me, the author of this here book. Welcome, world!

And we wondered how we ever got here? Born into this big old world? Well, this was how! One day we were just walking around in "Eternity" and "Nothingness," minding our own business; and–BAMB!–We are born, the doctor slaps us on the behind, we start blabbering, and the rest is history!

* * *

Well, there is a lot more to this story still, than meets the eye! It ain't ever over, my uncle Dick would say, until the fat lady sings! And she ain't singed yet–so hold on!

Remembering the Old Days

The swans glided slowly with practiced poise over the glistening water of the reflection pond of Chautauqua Lake. The mist was still rising from the glassy water. The sun was barely peeking through the trees, and bright darts of sunrays shot through the empty spaces and darted out across the pristine landscape.

No one had really been up for very long this morning, and I was taking my customary early morning constitutional walk around the Chautauqua grounds.

It was a good arrangement for me, especially after Lucinda had died last year, and I had been fortunate enough to get this new job, driving the little locomotive *Anna*. It was a real godsend, thanks to my good friend Robert Akers.

Living in a small apartment here on the grounds was especially nice and allowed me to double as a security person at night.

"Hey there, Mr. Jett. Good morning to you," said the old black man John. He was so big and round that he could have doubled for a bale of Georgia cotton—and just as fluffy and just as nice. He worked on the grounds and did odd jobs and such and kept the place clean of any daily debris, tree limbs, and such.

"How's it going, John?" I said.

"Oh, it's going pretty good, Mr. Jett. Got a right smart of things to do today—you know, with all the barbecue and all. Some big shot from Atlanta coming out today to the barbeque, I hear. They have been a cookin' those pigs all night. Oughta be mighty good!"

"Yeah, it ought to be a pretty big day. Mr. Henry Grady is the big shot coming out from Atlanta. Plans to give a big speech at 2:00 p.m. all about the New South," I said.

"Yes, sir, the New South," said John.

"What do you think about the New South, John?"

"Well sir, I don't rightly know, Mr. Jett. Things for me is pretty much just like they was before. I ain't lost no weight or sleep, hardly one ways or the other. He he!"

"Well, John, it's a new age now–new government, new technology, and a new people."

"Yes, sir, I guess so, Mr. Jett, but the good Lord is still the same, and the good food is still the same, both mighty good. Good to me and my family anyway."

"Yes, it is, John. Yes, it is. Well, you have a good day, John, and don't you eat too much of that barbecue now, ya hear!?!"

"Okay, Mr. Jett, and you either!"

* * *

The sun was getting up a little now, and it was about time to go get some breakfast and coffee. After all, my first run with *Anna* was at eight, starting from the hotel depot. Then we'd run every thirty minutes back and forth all day, every day of the week. Last run was at eight in the evening. It was a good job and something I dearly loved, something very different for a guy like Steven Jett. I couldn't complain.

Usually, I would get my breakfast over at the dining hall of the Chautauqua because of convenience and economy.

"Good morning, Mr. Jett," said Dolly.

"Good morning, Dolly. How are you this morning?"

"Oh, I'm fine. Getting ready for the big day today."

"Yes, I know, me too."

"What'll you have this morning?"

"How about a short stack of pancakes, one egg over easy, two pieces of bacon, and some hot coffee?"

"You got it, coming right up," said Dolly in her cute little black-and-white French-type waitress uniform. She was a pretty little thing. But she had three kids too already, all under five years old. Her mama kept them so she could work. Her husband, Dan, worked down at the livery with Charlie, my nephew.

Dan and Charlie, as we called him, kept the livery spick and span. And when the carriages and buggies came in, they would always wipe them down and clean them up from the dust of the road. And they prided themselves on how good they took care of the horse teams. It was a pretty big and awesome responsibility.

Nearly everybody around had some kind of job associated with the Sweetwater Park Hotel, the Chautauqua, the springs and steam baths, or something.

Sister Anna was working down at the springs at the steam baths, and she just loved it. She said that she met all sorts of the nicest people in the world–people from far and near, rich and poor but mostly rich, who would come to get their elixir of cold water and hot, steaming mineral water to soothe their achy muscles and worn bodies.

It was quite an amazing operation, and everything had to be very carefully done so as not to injure anyone. I even had a steam bath myself a couple of times. Can't say it exactly helped, but it sure was relaxing for a while. I could hardly move when I got out. Too much of the good life for me, I'd have to say!

Breakfast went fast, and it was off to fire up little *Anna* and get rolling on the Dummy Line. It was going to be a sure 'nuff big day!

The New South would rise again, and it would be bigger, better, and more prosperous than ever before. Henry Grady said so that day at the big barbecue, July 4, 1888!

And he ought to know because it was only because of him that we had been able to build the open-air Chautauqua auditorium in a record ninety days, one that would seat eight thousand patrons and with a dining hall that would seat one thousand patrons all at the same time. The world was a marvel. The New South was a marvel!

But Henry Grady would not live long enough to see all the greatness he held for his beloved Southland, for he would pass onto the great beyond to meet his Maker very shortly thereafter, a great loss to Lithia Springs, a great loss to Atlanta and Georgia, and an even greater loss to humanity and the South and his fellow man!

"Manchester Mill"
@ 1925

Final Words and Bless Be the Ties That Bind

"Whatever happened to Sweetwater Town?" you might ask. "Or to Campbellton? Or to Dark Corner? Rivertown? Sandtown? Villa Rica? Powder Springs? And a million other places?"

As time passed, some went this way, and some went that way–up, down, over, across, and away!

Ghost towns, some and thriving communities for some of the others. You've heard about them! You just forgot, like everybody else!

One thing for sure, nothing stayed the same! "Change is the only constant," they say, and that was certainly true here!

But there was an interesting story about how Bill Arp, Georgia, got its name, and I do have to share that with you before I go.

Ephraim Pray settled down, before the Civil War, on Dog River in what was now lower Douglas County. He was one of the very first white pioneers of the area, soon built and operated a gristmill on Dog River, and eventually helped establish a church up on the high land, and it was named after him, Pray's Mill Church. It was still there today.

When the settlement grew to be bigger than a handful of people, they got together to put a name on their little community in hopes that maybe there, in that location, would be located the county seat.

"Let's name it after Ephraim Pray, something like Praysville or Praysmill or Praytonville or something like that," they said.

"No, no, no," said Ephraim Pray. "Don't name it after me. Name it after my favorite author, Bill Arp."

So they did, and it stuck!

Bill Arp was actually the pen name for a very widely known satirist writer of the time named Charles Henry Smith, an attorney from Lawrenceville, Georgia.

Charles H. Smith, born in 1826, would grow up to be an attorney; author; mayor of Rome, Georgia; a major in the Confederate army; and a gentleman farmer in Cartersville, Georgia.

While living on his little farm north of Cartersville, he would be the good neighbor of Rebecca Latimer Felton, who would become the first United States woman senator in 1922.

Mrs. Felton would also become an early guardian of the young boy Sam Jones, who was to become the great Southern Baptist evangelist, no doubt through her influence.

Sam Jones would later hold great camp meeting revivals in the old camp grounds in Salt Springs and later, as it was known as Lithia Springs, drawing upwards of 3,500 people for the great events–right here in Douglas County!

I share these connecting events and stories to demonstrate to you, the reader, that we are all connected in some way, one with another. No man, woman, or child is an island unto himself; and no man, woman, or child lives alone without the influences, good and bad, in their lives. Hopefully, the good will always outweigh the bad but not always.

Well, I could tell you some bad stories, some really bad stories, but I just am not! There are too many good things to talk about, and I think we should dwell on the goodness in our hearts and souls.

My grandfather, one of them, taught me if you couldn't say something good about somebody or something, then just keep your mouth closed!

Very often my mouth would be closed, sometimes for quite a while. But then something good happened! And so on we went!

* * *

Our "Legacy," if any, on this earth is to do some good, however we do it and whomever we do it for! It is the only thing of pure and lasting value!

When I think back about this area and all my families and how everything has shaped the way we are, I am reminded of the Great Potter and how He has molded the clay.

Some days, it is too sandy and too dry, and a little water has to be added or taken away. Some clay may be better than others, but in God's hands, all is worked to perfection. For He can take the imperfect and make it perfect. He can take the part and make it whole. And He can take you and me and make us great. . .

Just like He did with Douglas County, Georgia!

THE END

UNDER THE WEDDING TREE

Song of Life

Under the wedding tree,
Vast and gold,
I hear a story, ancient and old,
Of love, of war, of joy and pain,
Of days of living
Amongst the strain,
To struggle, to laugh,
To love, to gain,
To start all over and do it again!

(SDA)

All Hands on Deck

Today was Sunday, December 7, 1941. It was a beautiful day so far, with no rain in sight. The sun rose to the east of Atlanta, Georgia, just like it did yesterday and the day before. But this morning, there was a yellow haze and red swelling of the clouds like you might see out at sea in a forbidding sunrise, one that sailors had known for years. "Red sky at night, sailors delight. Red sky at morning, sailors take warning." In a few hours, it would be time for church. It was my duty to get down to the church and start the early morning fire in the woodburning heater for my father.

My name is Grenoble or, more rightly, Thelbert Grenoble Ayres, but everybody just calls me Grenoble except my mother, Lorena, who most often calls me Thelbert, especially when she is mad or suspect of my whereabouts and wants me to do something and right now. She would go to the door, like this very moment, and let out a long loud, whelping sound, like "Thellllllbert!"

"Yes, ma'am!" I would yell back.

"Get on down to the church right now and get that stove started!" she said.

"Okay!" I would say. And I headed on down to the little white church, where Daddy preached twice a month.

My daddy was an ordained Baptist minister, all right, but he did have a regular job with the United States Postal Service, from which he earned a "real livin'." Most people called my daddy Uncle Willy, his nickname for William Ausburn Ayres. He would give you the shirt off his back if he thought you needed it more than him. He was truly a remarkable man, although I didn't realize it as much back then.

I just thought he was my daddy. He was a very good person to me and all others and also to my mother.

But Daddy was good to a fault, you might say, in my opinion. Once, he had given me a gold coin worth, I think, $5. Now to me, that was like all the money in the world and maybe to him too. But one day Daddy called me up to his side and said, "Grenoble, you remember that coin that I gave to you? That $5 gold piece? We need to give that to the Jones family down on the creek. You know, they are out of work and having a real hard time getting by, and we need to do something to help them out. You understand, don't you, son?"

"Yeah, I guess so," I said in a timid, embarrassed sort of way. I mean, what could I have said? I was really put on the spot.

So, I gave my proud coin back to my daddy so the Joneses could buy some food or whatever they were going to do with my money.

Well, this taught me an early lesson in life, namely, that you could never count on hardly anything for sure. All things were subject to change at any time and any minute.

After a while, the fire in the stove was catching on, and the little empty church began to warm up. I sat down, as was customary, on the empty front pew and picked up a hymnal book lying there. I opened it up to a well-worn page of "Amazing Grace" and began to sing, low at first, almost like a mumble, and then with a little more vibrato; and by a few minutes, I was singing at the top of my voice. What did it matter? No one was there. No one was listening. Then I really belted out the last two verses like all of God's children poured their voices into mine and like I was the only channel to God, delivering praise and glory for all of God's blessings.

By noontime, Daddy was finished preaching, and we were singing the doxology. The doors were flung open, and all the heat escaped the building along with the parishioners. I didn't even remember what Daddy preached this morning, except I knew it was about the Bible. There were two things you could always count on, Bible preaching and prayer.

I was eighteen years old and had already bought my first motorcycle, a beautiful red Indian. It was parked out under the big oak tree in front of the church. I jumped on, like mounting a wild horse; fired her up; and took off for Lori's house (the church pianist), where we all (the preacher's family) had been invited for Sunday dinner.

"Classic" 6/1/91

Cowboys and Indians

It must have been two in the afternoon while sitting in the front parlor, listening to the radio, when we first heard the terrible news.

Pearl Harbor in Hawaii had been attacked by the Japanese. Ships were sinking, people were dying, and things were in a total state of chaos. What happened? Why, just the other day, the Japanese ambassador to the United States had been in Washington DC, saying that everything was all right and peaceful between the United States and Japan. And on top of that, we had been sending them all our scrap metal for years. And now they returned it in bombs? Wow, now things would change again. . .

Remember that coin?. . .

The Call to Duty

Gordon Terrace in west Atlanta was a sleepy little street, modest homes filled with people with modest dreams—good people, to be sure, but not the richest persons around town. Our little home was adequate for me and my mom and dad and two brothers—one older, Brawnson, and one younger, Eldorado, and me, Grenoble, in the middle.

Brawnson was smart and liked anything scientific and complicated. He was into ham radio at an early age and talked to people from all over the world during the course of his lifetime. He would grow up and eventually graduate from Georgia Tech, just like Ben Jett, his great-nephew, had. Brawnson would be an electrical engineer and, as part of the Reserve Officers' Training Corps (ROTC) program, would end up entering the United States Navy as a first lieutenant and would be shipped off to New York City on his first assignment of duty in the next great world war.

Eldorado was just a kid brother, about thirteen years old and too young to join up. He was a most delightful person who was curious about everything except school. He laughed and played with the greatest of ease and seemed to have much more fun than the normal person. And he was talented in his own ways. As he got older, one of his hobbies was raising messenger pigeons.

Some of his pigeons were called "Tumblers." They would go up real high and then roll over like a series of barrel rolls while falling in a sort of free fall toward the ground. One pigeon was a little slow on recovery one time and, before he could come out of the roll, met with Mother Earth! Well, we thought the bird had gone splat! It just laid there, dazed or dead, for a minute or two. Then it raised its head, spread its feathers, shook itself all over pretty good, got to its feet, and then took off again for another round. We called that bird from then on "Suicide Charlie!" In later years, he would bring his pigeons out to the country—to my farm, Honey Acres—and let them go (fly) back to Atlanta. When he got home, there they would be, waiting for him and their supper!

Thelbert Grenoble (TG), a.k.a. "Bill" later by nickname, was the middle road child of the three boys. He was my (Steven's) dad but not yet. The stories I heard about him and by him over the years were remarkable and very memorable, like the time when he was about ten years old and going to build a lake down in Mableton, Georgia, where the family had moved to Floyd Road. He and a little neighbor boy had taken their axes, hatchets, and other tools down to the woods way down on some of the Glore property, and there, they had determined to build them a fine lake along a fine little stream. After a while, he and the other fellow got into a small argument that soon grew large. At its conclusion, my dad picked up his hatchet and went home in disgust. Later at his farm, Honey Acres, Dad would build a very fine six-acre lake for real!

Among other things, Dad had a paper route of thirteen customers in Mableton, Georgia. He delivered the *Atlanta Journal-Constitution*. Now at that time, the *Constitution* came out in the morning, and the *Journal* came out in the evening. My dad was industrious, and he tended this route of newspaper delivery as he did everything else—as though his life depended on it. He was extremely conscientious and honest and had the integrity of Moses. He was like this all his life.

For several days one time, he noticed that he was running a paper short every day. They would be delivered early by truck from Atlanta down at the corner gas station. So Dad decided he was going to get to the bottom of this newspaper thieving, and he got up real early, went down to the drop-off point, and hid in the bushes. Oh yeah, and he took Grandpa's twelve-gauge shotgun too!

When the papers were dropped off that morning, he waited. It wasn't too long before old man Snider, who ran the gas station, came along and slipped one of the papers out of the tied batch so he could take it down to the local café and read the news as he often would do.

About that time, Grenoble popped out of the bushes with the shotgun pointed on Mr. Snider.

"So that's what's been happening to my papers," he said. "Stick 'em up."

"Hey, son, what's happening?" Mr. Snider said.

"You been stealing my newspapers. That's what's happening."

"Well, I'm sorry, son. I didn't think you'd miss just one paper every now and then," Mr. Snider said.

"Well, I do," said Grenoble. "Just put it back and don't do it again ever."

"Okay, okay, okay," said Mr. Snider. "I'm sorry, son. I won't do it again."

And with that, Mr. Snider put the paper back down; and with his hands still in the air, he backed away, got in his truck, and drove off down the road.

No more papers were ever missing again.

Whether that twelve-gauge shotgun was loaded, I wouldn't know, but I'd tell you what–knowing my dad like I did, I am sure it was loaded with double-aught buckshot in both barrels!

* * *

By now, the war was well underway, and nearly every young man was hankering to join up and go fight either the Japs or the Germans. You had your choice, I guess.

Some went to the Atlantic Ocean and to Europe to fight the Germans, and others, like my dad, went to the Pacific Ocean and beyond to fight the Japs.

My dad wanted to be a naval aviator and fly fighters. He would have been terrific too. But as fate would have it, he had less than perfect vision, and so he did the next best thing; and at eighteen years old, he joined the United States Navy.

His first assignment, after boot camp, was at the DeKalb Naval Air Station, Atlanta, Georgia. This would later become Peachtree-DeKalb Airport in future years. His first duty there was guard duty, walking the fenced perimeter of the airport, guarding it against intruders and saboteurs. After a while, on a cold, rainy dark night, he decided that he needed a change, something more challenging. He had heard about some opportunities and decided to put an application in for Aviation Mechanic School in Vero Beach, Florida. He took a preliminary exam, passed with flying colors, and was reassigned to the great Sunshine State in Vero Beach. What a change for a young Southern boy just out of Tech High.

Dad was always a pretty good team player. As a matter of fact, he had played forward on the basketball team in Mableton, where he developed all his quick moves and skill. Aviation Mechanic School would be a blast, and he would learn a lot, he thought. And he did!

His main aircraft at that time were F4Fs, Hellcats, and Bearcats–fighters and torpedo bombers, I think. He really learned everything there was that could be learned in twelve months of school. He thought, at that time, it was all fun and games until he told me about the time that really changed his perspective. It was the day he watched a pilot burn to death after a crash landing, and the plane caught on fire. There was nothing they could do after an unsuccessful rescue attempt. He said he would never forget seeing the black silhouette of the pilot's head and shoulders sitting there in the cockpit, engulfed in broiling yellow flames of burning gasoline and oil. It was an awful sight. He knew then that this was war and not a schoolboy's picnic.

Flying Fortress "B-17
The War in Europe

"Delivery to Ashe"

By now, Dad had bought another motorcycle, a navy surplus model 41 Harley-Davidson. He bought it cheap and repainted it blue with just a paintbrush. Looked pretty cool. This bike had what they called a "suicide clutch" that pivoted up and down on the right side. You had a big lever on the side of the gas tank to change gears, and you had two big ole handlebars a mile wide to hold on to and stabilize your otherwise precarious perch.

Dad's best friend, Red Williams, got one too; and later, they rode around together all over the state of Florida. But before that, they would often ride my dad's motorcycle home to Atlanta from Vero Beach.

They used to tell the story about coming home nonstop while riding double. The one in front would lean way over on the gas tank while holding on to the handlebars, and the one in the back would slide over the front one's back while he would slide backward, handing off the controls, until the whole maneuver was effected. And presto, there you were without ever stopping. I bet they did stop to get gas though.

After Aviation Mechanic School, Dad got orders to ship out for the South Pacific. He had been assigned to the USS *Pine Island*, a seaplane tender based out of San Diego, California. He only had a two-week leave in between.

He went home, and having met during the previous year a beautiful, vivacious young lady at Jacob's Pharmacy after church one day in West End, he married her, my mother, Blanche Seignious, great-granddaughter of Richard B. Jett. After he proposed and my mother accepted, the family had one day to prepare for the wedding, which would be held inside the home of my great-grandparents Frank Wilson and Ida Cline Jett Wilson.

It was a beautiful wedding; it was small, but all the right people were there, and there were ample flowers, candles, cake, and joy. Especially, there must have been joy and excitement. For the very next day, the young newlyweds would depart by train for San Diego, California, their new home, by way of New Orleans. It was a long train ride. But it must have been grand to have been young, just married, leaving home for the first time, going to California, and going off to war. It must also have been overwhelming. Mom was only nineteen years old, and Dad was only twenty-one. What a young age to be beginning so much!

The USS *Pine Island* was waiting in San Diego Harbor to disembark. The sailors had only a few days to report for duty, and mothers, wives, and sweethearts were standing on the docks, waving, cheering, and crying.

As the ship steamed out of the harbor, my mother's stomach sank with foreboding and fear. *What if he never comes back? What if I never see him again? What if? What if? What if?*

But with hope and a cheerful heart, she turned and went back to their small apartment, where she too would begin her long ordeal and time of service to the great cause of the war, waiting and praying.

It just so happened that another couple lived next door, and of all things in this great big world, her name too was Blanche. Her husband too had departed for service. What a blessing, a commonality of coincidence and purposes. They would forge a great friendship that would serve them for the rest of their lives.

The war was really on now, and it was personal!

No Time like the Present

San Diego was a beautiful place with a lot of southern California sunshine and a pleasant breeze off the calm Pacific Ocean. It provided a perfect harbor for military ships and the San Diego Naval Base.

Mother was happy with her new home and excited to be away from her rather large family, who had generally spoiled and doted on her so much. She was the seventh child of a seventh child, a lucky omen according to the stars.

She had four older brothers—Richard, Leroy, John, and Aubrey (Bo)—and two older twin sisters, Ethyl and Rebe. Then Mom, little Blanche, was born. Growing up during the Great Depression was a mite difficult for her, but at her young age, she did not know very much about the world.

Originally, her family lived in a modest house on Stewart Avenue in Atlanta, Georgia. By 1929 or so, at the time of the Great Crash, her grandparents Mr. and Mrs. Frank Wilson bought one and then another adjoining "mansions" in West End of Atlanta located at 1020 and 1024 Gordon Street.

As it would have it, after occupying 1020 Gordon Street, her grandparents—having also bought the house next door at 1024—moved down the street, only two houses up from Joel Chandler Harris, the famous writer of the Uncle Remus tales. He called his home the Wren's Nest all because of a tiny wren who had built in his mailbox.

After Mother's grandparents moved into 1024, her parents and siblings moved into the house at 1020 Gordon Street. She grew up in this big house from about the age of five. This was a large, two-story frame house sitting on a foundation of Stone Mountain granite as was the adjoining home. Both had huge wraparound front porches, wide enough for a cavalry brigade, and large tree-shaded front lawns, with walkways winding their way down to the concrete tile sidewalks on both sides.

There was much leaded glass in all the windows, stonework, tile work, large mahogany staircases, triple inlaid hardwood floors, fireplaces with ornate mantels, huge dining rooms with columns, back staircases, big backyards, and on and on.

With the Depression on, my grandmother Mrs. Richard Blanche Seignious (yes, she was named after her grandfather, Richard B. Jett of *Fallow Are the Fields*) opened her home to boarders. Now she was pretty smart. She knew that, by doing so, she would get all their food ration coupons in exchange for three meals a day and a room to sleep in. It was a pretty good deal, but she earned every nickel and every coupon. My grandfather Leroy Seignious was in the wholesale produce business, so there was always plenty of good food. He grew up on a rice plantation called Lewisfield on the Cooper River in Charleston, South Carolina, with his brother Charles.

Great-Uncle Charles Seignious would go onto Chicago and own the airplane *Puppy Feet*. He would make a fortune in real estate, and his son Witfield, "Uncle Witt," would marry Olga from Russia, an emigrant and evacuee of the great Bolshevik Revolution of 1917. She and her family were high up in the aristocracy of Russia and had many fine things. But they had to flee in the middle of the night, taking only what they could carry or sew into their clothes. Fortune and fate are no respecter of persons. They would settle in Mobile, Alabama, and raise a family of little ones, Jenny, Bo, and Jimmy. They too, of course, would marry and have descendants reaching into our present day.

Well, I drew all this together because it all became the framework of my story and my mother's life. She had a very rich family heritage, and it was quite colorful in many ways.

Even though it was sometimes interesting, Mother–as a young child–often grew weary of all the people, indeed "strangers," in her home, and she had to eat last much of the time. She never went hungry, but she did pine for the attention of her mother, father, and siblings among all the constant conditions of invasion on family privacy. She would, however, learn to deal with it and adjust.

At the age of five, she was first introduced to aviation and Uncle Charlie's airplane, *Puppy Feet*, in 1929 at Blevins Hangar, Atlanta Airport, the old Candler Field. Little did she know then that much of her life as an adult would be surrounded and influenced by aviation, although she herself would never learn to fly.

When Blanche was about ten years old, she experienced one of the first great setbacks of her life when her older brother John died from an old football injury to his knee when infection had set in. It was a typical sort of infection, not uncommon, but blood poisoning was always a danger, and it was just before the miracle of penicillin was available. Losing her brother was a great and significant loss to all.

John had been deaf for many years at an early age, and Blanche had remembered all the trips to visit him at the School for the Deaf in Cave Spring, Georgia. A beautiful and magical place, it had afforded young John the opportunity to learn how to live with and overcome his disability; and indeed, he and all his family had learned sign language so as to be able to communicate.

Years later when visiting this magical place, I myself would always think of Uncle John and how, vicariously, I too was attached to this miracle place tucked away in north Georgia just northwest of Cedartown. Many visits would be made over the years even still, and we always spoke of Uncle John.

Despite losing her brother, Mother lived a good life growing up, one of austerity dashed with opulence, good taste, and Southern aristocracy. Every week Mom and her twin sisters, Ethyl and Rebe, would all walk downtown and go shopping at Rich's and other fine stores, go to a movie perhaps, and maybe have the luncheon at the Magnolia Room at Rich's. It was a grand life for a spoiled little girl. And privilege had its benefits, and at the young age of fourteen, in 1939, Blanche was one of the fortunate people to attend the second night premiere of *Gone with the Wind* at the infamous Loews Grand Theater in Downtown Atlanta. She wore a brand-new pair of red high heeled shoes! Little did she know that Grenoble, her future husband, at sixteen years old, was sitting across the street atop the Carnegie Library Building, watching all the fanfare and festivities from his lofty perch. It was an amazing event to be a part of in any way!

And to top it all off, her big brother Bo–who was a budding young photographer–took color pictures of the event with all the celebrities, including Vivien Leigh, Margaret Mitchell, David Selznick, Clark Gable, Olivia de Havilland, and all the others. He later sold these in sets and made himself enough money to buy a new car, his first. Today we still have sets of those pictures, and they are real collector's items of *Gone with the Wind* memorabilia.

A graduate of Joe Brown Elementary School and Girls' High of Atlanta, Mother learned to play the piano and was a majorette, twirling the baton like there was no tomorrow. But tomorrow there would be, and after high school, she got a job with the telephone company and went to night school to advance her secretarial skills with typing and office management. Mom grew up a good churchgoer in West End Presbyterian just up from the Gordon Street Baptist

Church, my dad's church. In the middle was Jacob's Drug Store, where on a pretty Sunday afternoon she had met my dad!

It had been several weeks now since her beloved Bill had sailed away out of San Diego Harbor. It was about time that she heard from him. Was he okay? Was he still alive?—all the questions you ask yourself when you were the one left behind. And then one day, one beautiful, wonderful day, a letter came to her door!

She would rejoice in the knowledge that Dad was okay and dream of the time when he could come home once again to her loving arms.

Cruising the Pacific with Uncle Sam

The day was cold, colder than usual. Most of the planes were still out, but two had returned already from their twelve-hour sorties. Four PBY Catalina reconnaissance aircraft were still cruising out there somewhere in the Pacific.

Dad's crew serviced and worked on these aircraft from the tender ship at sea. They were a sort of floating fixed-base operator (FBO) in the middle of the ocean. These planes were involved mostly in search, surveillance, and rescue. They were magnificent in their two-engine design and remarkable in their abilities.

This was where Dad said, "You learned not to drop anything because if you did, it was just gone." So working out on the water especially taught him some extra lessons about being an aviation mechanic!

The USS *Pine Island* had a very large hangar built as a part of the ship, which was large enough to load and house two PBYs or two PBMs (Mariners) at a time indoors. There were large cranes on the ship that were able to pick up the aircraft from the sea up to the ship and vice versa when ready to go back into service. They would always take off and land on the ocean, unless of course there was a dryland runway or airfield available because they were amphibious. Later as a child, I marveled about how amazing and exciting all this must have been. My brother Gordon even built a plastic scale model of the very ship, which we kept on the fireplace mantel. There were two sister ships to this one, the USS *Norton Sound* and the USS *Currytuck*. Sixty years later, my dad's Sunday school teacher– Mr. Harry Allgood–would tell stories of how he was on the crew of the USS *Currytuck* and how they steamed into exploration into Antarctica after the war.

It was a common bond of seamanship and brotherhood, which was unsurpassed. Both men were just kids at the time!

At 8:32 p.m., the last aircraft was back in and ready for refueling and servicing. Dad and the crew scrambled around, getting all the jobs done, while the flight crew got some much needed rest in preparation for the next time out. These flights were and had been absolutely critical to the successful operation of the U.S. Navy in the Pacific theater. It was only in May of 1942 that the pilot and crew of a PBY Catalina had successfully first spotted the entire Japanese fleet, which was centered on the island of Midway, alerting the allies and setting the stage for one of the biggest and most significant sea battles in all history. One that ended, I might add, in their solid defeat!

To me, my dad was a hero just as much as any man, and I knew that it was because of what he did that we won the war. Any son would not think less!

* * *

The two atomic bombs, one on Hiroshima and the other on Nagasaki, would finish the job, and Dad would do damage survey work for the U.S. Navy on both. It was bad!

For several weeks after the war, Mother waited to hear a response from Bill. Was he okay? Was the ship okay? Where were they now? Then one day about midmorning, the mailman was making his rounds as usual when Blanche saw Robert waving a piece of paper in the air as he approached. With joy and excitement, she thought this must be the long-awaited letter! And it was!

With much anticipation, Blanche carefully opened the airmail letter from Bill (Dad's nickname), and it read as follows:

T. G. Ayres, AMM2/c
USS *Pine Island* (AV-12)
Div. V2 % FPO
San Francisco, Calif.

                                                                    Mrs. T. G. Ayres
                                                    1024 Gordon St. SW
                                                      Atlanta, Georgia

September 28, 1945

My Dearest Blanche,

Hi, chum. We made it here about eight o'clock this morning. This bay has only a very small opening to the sea, and we're way up in one end of it. They're quite a few other ships up in the other end, and there's a fair-sized town there.

When the knotty pine swings round toward land, it looks like you can almost throw a rock to the shore. It is really a very small bay compared with the one at Okinawa. All around, the hills rise steep at the water's edge, and there's little patches of farmland all over the hills. There's quite a few small Jap fishing boats around.

Our planes are already here, and we will operate from the ship here for as long as we're here, I suppose, and I don't have any idea how long that'll be.

The weather is grand so far. It's just cool enough to make sitting in the sun feel good. Gives a guy much more pep.

No one can go ashore, not even the captain, yet. May be able to later on. We're not using the rubber boats anymore, so I guess we won't be able to make our own trips over. There won't be any storm worry here because we're protected all around. So don't worry about that.

This cool air has made everyone feel wonderful today–sure will be nice sleeping if I had you, hon.

Sometimes it's hard to keep faith that I'll be with you by Christmas, but God knows how much I want to be. Just have to leave it in his hands–His will be done.

Let me remind you again how I love you, and I always will. You're the most wonderful thing I have.

Always Your,

Bill

* * *

The war was finally over, and my dad and mother were some of the lucky ones. Dad had made it through all in one piece both in mind and body. Many lost everything. Fathers, sons, daughters, brothers, sisters, and especially mothers suffered great personal loss. This was the Second World War, but it would bring peace to the world for only a time. There would be other wars in the not too distant future, in other far and exotic places with names we could hardly pronounce; but for now, there would be a time of rejoicing.

Seaplane Tender
~ War in the Pacific ~

The Boys Come Home

On September 2, 1945, the Japanese signed a formal surrender to Gen. Douglas C. MacArthur, aboard the USS *Missouri*. By October 7, 1945, over one million Japanese soldiers would surrender in Peking, China. Almost immediately, the occupation of Japan began, and the world was changing again.

About this same time, the war in Europe was ending with the solid defeat of the Germans. This was a complex war in many ways, and the ending of it was complex in many ways also. Adolf Hitler, the leader of the Germans, supposedly committed suicide in his private bunker just before being personally apprehended.

The Holocaust too was over. About five million Jews had been mysteriously and systematically singled out in Europe by the Germans and been sent to massive concentration camps, where they were lethally gassed, their bodies burned in crematories. Men, women, and children, old and young–the talented, the educated, the beautiful, and the innocent, one and all–were sent to their untimely deaths in a horrendous effort to strike them from the earth. Man's inhumanity to humanity was terrible and devastating in a way that would never be forgotten.

* * *

From all over the world, U.S. soldiers began coming home slowly but surely. It was a time of great rejoicing! Atlanta, Georgia, would very soon again be bustling with the renewed activities of the returning soldiers. Among them were Grenoble and his young wife, Blanche.

It wasn't long before Grenoble got a good job with Western Electric in Atlanta. He would ride his motorcycle to work every day and bypass all the slow traffic by nook and crook and have feats like going up between standing traffic to get through, until one day he got his handlebars stuck between two cars. Then he figured he had better slow down and drive more like normal people!

One day he was at work looking out the back window across several railroad tracks that ran behind the building. About that time, he saw a train coming down the line and a woman out there walking on the tracks with her back to the oncoming train. He tried to call out to her, to warn her to get off the tracks, but she must have been either deaf or out of hearing range or something, for she never even looked up. There was nothing more he could do, and within seconds, the train ran over her and cut her in two. It was a terrible thing to see and especially not be able to prevent. My dad would never forget it, and it would be one of the more memorable stories he ever told over the years.

Finally, one day he decided that he wanted to be "outside" in the fresh air and that maybe he would go back into aviation, this time civilian. So he applied for a job as an aviation mechanic with Beechcraft in Atlanta, who at that time was affiliated with Southern Airways of Atlanta Airport. I didn't know exactly the business details, but they shared the same big hangar out at the airport just off Virginia Avenue, the old Candler Automotive Racetrack Field as it was once called, now used mostly for airplanes. In 1929, the city of Atlanta had taken a lease on the original field; and by 1950, it was owned lock, stock, and barrel by the city. It was destined to become the busiest airport in the world!

My brother Gordon and I would go out to the airport when we were young, and I remembered just how big the hangar seemed to be. It was huge! And at that time, there was still a north/south runway as well as east/west runways. We marveled at the large modern terminal building with its elevated observation deck. Wow, what a place! It all was just magical. My brother and I were certainly introduced to airports at an early age, and we loved them ever since. One day I would build my own!

During this time, we lived at 1024 Gordon Street SW, Atlanta, Georgia, the former home of my grandparents and before them of my great-grandparents. After the war, Dad bought the house for him and Mom on the GI Bill, which guaranteed the loan against the property. All the grandparents and greats had moved next door in the adjoining house by that time at 1020 Gordon Street. Actually, the house had first been sold to my mother's older brother Uncle Dick, and my dad and mom bought it from him. They kept an apartment there for a short time and later moved out, allowing Mom and Dad to convert the entire house into multiple apartments. It was a big house, and I think, including our own living quarters, there were five apartments altogether. So much for the big "mansion." Now it was drawn and quartered and even "fifthed." But it was a business venture and the first real estate deal of the family!

Behind the house, we had a big backyard; and in that yard, we had about five or more beehives–yes, beehives. Part of the yard was very sandy, and I would play in that white sand with a rubber Donald Duck car, which was my favorite at four and five years old. I would play, and Dad would, once a year, "rob" the bees of the honey. We had a large round green metal centrifugal honey extractor. You would put the frames into the extractor, and it would whirl them around, emptying the honey out and into the bottom, where it would be drained out into honey jars. They would be sealed, and we would place on the glass jars our own label, "Honey Acres Farm." Every year this was how we made our vacation money, that and selling purebred black cocker spaniel puppies produced by Susie, our dog.

Mine was an enterprising family from way back. And whenever or wherever there was an opportunity to make some money, we were doing it except I wasn't going to have anything to do with those bees. I told my dad when he challenged me to help, "I am a man, but I ain't going to go near those bees." I was only five, and so he made an exception, but it would be one of only a few over the coming years!

There were so many childhood memories that one had over the years. Mine were segmented according to where I lived at the time and made it rather easy to classify and remember in my own mind many things that otherwise may well have been forgotten–things like making paper cutout airplanes by the tens and hundreds and creating complete air forces of my own design, things like the Lionel model railroad my dad built for and with us. It would hinge down from the wall, we would play, and then we would hinge it back up. And it was big, four by eight feet with fake grass and roads and everything. There were things like listening to "The Little Engine That Could." "Toot-toot! I think I can, I think I can, I think I can." Remember? You probably listened to it too. It was a great motivator and teacher at a formative early age. It taught me not to give up when things got hard and difficult.

And then there were the little newspapers that I would create before I could even read or write. I would draw pictures of the news of the day and scribble words underneath, big scribbling for headlines and little scribbling for the details. Then I would make copies and give them to people! Little writers start early!

My home and early formative years were wonderful. A toy Cadillac for Christmas and other toy work trucks would inspire me in many directions over the oncoming years of my life. The big round sugar cookies for snack time were my favorite remembrance of kindergarten at People Street Elementary School in West End of Atlanta and the many other toys and the fun of playing or learning to play with other little boys and girls. I thank my mom and dad for giving me so much inspiration at such an early part of my life. It was a good start!

Then the time came, and we moved to the country. Daddy had always dreamed of owning his own farm, and now he would!

Welcome to the Farm

The old farm that my dad bought was in pretty poor shape in 1952. No one had worked it in years. Indeed, no one had lived there even in a number of years. It was old even then, well over one hundred years, but who was counting? We did not move out to the farm for about a year or so after my parents bought it. It was going to take a lot of work to even make the house livable. Besides, I was still only five years old and had to complete my kindergarten year at People Street Elementary School.

We had been living in a rather lavish and elegant two-story mansion of sorts in West End of Atlanta, at 1024 Gordon Street SW, next door to my grandparents, who had purchased the two houses back during the time of the Great Depression when they were dirt cheap by comparison. So, my mother–the youngest of seven children–was raised, you might say, in the lap of luxury. Now my mother and her family were moving to the "sticks" as my grandmother called the farm.

My grandmother's grandfather was Richard B. Jett or R. B. Jett as he was most often known. His father was named Steven Jett so he named his youngest son, Steven, and the family, one day, would be the subject of some of my later writing about this very farm. My grandmother Mrs. L. L. Seignious would later entrust to me, as ongoing historian of this family, an entire box of letters and diaries written between her grandfather and her grandmother during the American Civil War. I would treasure and forever protect those literary gems and attempt to preserve them for posterity.

Four Rooms and A Path! & Running Water!

"No Place Like Home"

That next summer, after making the old farmhouse somewhat livable, we moved to the farm in Douglas County, Georgia. I would, that fall, attend first grade at Lithia Springs Elementary School and each year thereafter for the next seven years. Along the way, the name would be changed to Annette Winn Elementary School, after our principal, a wonderful lady and proud educator.

Lithia Springs, Georgia, formerly known as Salt Springs and before that Deer Lick by the Indians, was a sleepy little town with one caution light at the main intersection of U.S. Highway 78–Bankhead Highway and North and South Sweetwater Roads. Large elm trees lined the highway, bridged by bench boards in between for sitting on by the old men and whoever else cared to watch the world go by–people like Uncle Bee, the old railroad man, and Uncle Luke, who had painted his car a different color every year, and old man Kilgore, who ran the local general store, and others. I often thought that maybe one day I might earn an esteemed seat on that council of wisdom, but alas, the trees one day were cut down to widen the road, and the council of wisdom took a back seat under some other old trees down the way, never to be the same again.

"Council of Wisdom"
©1954 Lithia Springs, Georgia
Steve Ayres 2015

The town had pretty much laid dormant since the burning of the Sweetwater Park Hotel in 1912. Not much had happened. The Chautauqua was gone too. Manchester Mill and New Manchester Town had been burned, and only ruins remained. Sweetwater Town was gone. Sandtown was gone. But Douglasville, founded in 1870, was thriving as the county seat; and Villa Rica was holding its own, almost, as was the town of Temple and so on.

The Civil War had come and gone, and most of the farm was still standing. It had survived the Spanish-American War, World War I, World War II, and the Korean War already. Many other conflicts would come and go in my lifetime, but our family farm remained constant, a representative of a simpler time. No American was untouched during these times. The farm was, in many ways, typical of the American way of life, at least in the country if not in the city. Peaceful and quiet, it was a wonderful place to spend a childhood and grow up.

Gordon was almost two years my senior. He was a wonderful brother, my only, and we had no sisters. We were forever playing pranks on each other—but mostly me on him as I was somewhat of a pest, I imagine, but he was tolerant, to a point. There was the one time he got a gun after me, but I surrendered before he could shoot me. Gordon and I would spend countless hours and days drifting in and out of reality as we ran and played throughout the day.

The farmhouse itself was small. It had two bedrooms and one bath with a shower only, living room, and kitchen dining area. The bedrooms were only nine by seven feet, one I shared with Gordon until I was fifteen years old when we built onto the house. My mother and dad shared the other tiny bedroom as the master suite. I mean, it was cozy. We had two fireplaces for heat and cooking if needed. An oil floor furnace was added for heat and windows for air-conditioning, and we had a nice screened front porch. We always said we had just a little bit of room on the inside but a whole lot of room on the outside, about 165 acres, give or take. Outside was where we stayed most of the time!

After several years, we had fencing up, and we were running four to five head of cows, white-faced Herefords, a particular hearty breed of cows somewhat new in those days. Later, the herd would get up to fifteen or twenty during calving time with a great, big bull to crown the herd.

Horses also became a part of the scene, and we learned to ride really good. When we played cowboys and Indians, the Indians had to ride bareback—no saddles, no blankets. So I became an expert at bareback riding, among other things like hunting and fishing, across hills, dales, lakes, and creeks all in the name of good, clean fun.

The first planting my dad did on the farm was of sericea lespedeza, a stalklike grass very tough and determined to live and thrive on very poor, cotton-cultivated, deprived red clay Georgia soil. It was otherwise so poor that the only other thrivable plant on the farm was kudzu, which was the terror of the biological plant world. It would cover your house up if you let it. And the only way to kill it back was to let your livestock, if you had any, eat it back to oblivion. Then you had a fightin' chance with it!

The school bus ran within one mile of our house, and we walked that mile both morning and evening, cold or hot, rain or shine, snow or not. And we never missed a day of school unless we were deathly sick. The bus then ran another two miles to school, where we would play on the playground until the bell was rung, signaling the beginning of another day of learning and big dried lima beans for lunch.

But school wasn't all bad, and there, I found my love of learning and had *some* wonderful teachers who would become lifelong mentors and friends–friends like Mrs. Vivian Cranford, my sixth-grade teacher who would greatly influence my life, along with her husband, James (Jim), who would later introduce me to the Masonic order as I became a Master Mason at Battle Hill Lodge number 523, and Mrs. Annette Winn, our principal, who would share with us her beautiful slides from her trip to Europe and who would inspire us to travel and see the world. And I did, just like her. I treasured and, to this day, appreciate those early seeds of influence and inspiration for our growing young minds–to let us know and tell us that we could do and become whoever we wanted to be and at the same time be proud, educated citizens of the world. And we did!

On the farm, I learned many skills like hunting, fishing, tracking, camping, boating, animal husbandry, and a million other things. I would credit my dad, my mother, my brother, and my grandfather in particular among many others.

I learned courage and integrity from my father, love and trust from my mother, patience and self-control from my grandfather, and self-worth and adventure from my brother. We all shared a grand life together there on the farm.

John Timko — "All — At-Rest"
on the farm

But my dad was in aviation for a living, and besides the farm, I grew up around airplanes and aviation. I spent considerable time, now and again, at the early Atlanta Airport and Charlie Brown–Fulton County Airport. Later, I would keep airplanes there and learn to fly myself.

After the war, Dad was on contract with Beechcraft and Southern Airways at Atlanta Airport. Later, we–by contract–would move for one year to Fort Bragg, North Carolina, and then back to the farm. Then another year, we moved to Fort Rucker at Enterprise, Alabama, and then back to the farm for good. While Dad was on civilian contracts to the military, I would grow up around helicopters and be exposed to many new and upcoming flying devices like the gyrocopters of Igor Bensen and such. Once while at Fort Bragg, I witnessed a three-thousand-man paratrooper mass jump from Flying Boxcars. It was an awesome sight and one not usually witnessed during peacetime. I would never forget it!

Then there were the "Flying Clowns" at Fort Rucker–H-34 helicopters painted up like clowns and doing clown dance maneuvers. It was awesome!

And to think, I later married one of the few women civilians to ever fly in the Goodyear blimp, my wonderful wife, Beth.

But back to the farm as we always went home to the woods and solitude once more. The farm kept improving as we kept busy, first this and then that and always the fencing and fighting kudzu, bitterweed, ice storms, forest fires, snowstorms, tornadoes, droughts, and rains that lasted for days and days and days. It was a never-ending cycle of guess-what-was-going-to-happen-next!

While all this proceeded, my brother and I went to Douglas County High School, where we were each, in our separate senior year, by some measure, voted by the faculties as Senior Citizen of the Year. My folks were real proud and rightly so, I think. I would give them all the credit, not us!

During the same time, my dad and some other men founded and started Aero Sales Inc. at Charlie Brown Field–Fulton County Airport. While there, they built the very first large hangar for aircraft sales and maintenance. For a very cool $100K, you could purchase a twin brand-new Aero Commander 560–the executive business aircraft of the day–to travel in luxury and speed wherever you wanted to go. Like the airplanes, the building was immaculate, state of the art, with my dad serving as operations manager. They had a beautiful lobby with an Aero Commander inlaid in the tile floor, and men's and ladies' restrooms with little colored plastic airplane-type icons for boys and girls. Pretty cool. They also had their own radio shop and sales offices and everything else you could imagine. I was so proud of my dad and his part in this exciting business. I grew up around there in his shadow and met some of the flying greats like Frank Tallman, the stunt pilot; Steve Wittman of Wittman Field at Oshkosh, Wisconsin; and Bob Hoover of Shrike Commander fame and others!

My most impressionable time there was at Christmas, one year, when Santa Claus, red suit and all, and gifts for everyone, arrived in a V-tail Bonanza. It was pretty exciting. Later, I would own a V-tail Bonanza myself!

And there was the client, a pilot, who flew in his underwear. I saw him one time remove his trousers as he was getting in his airplane in the summertime to take off. It was a lot cooler, so he said, and he was wearing only boxers!

And there was the chicken farmer Mr. Vansant, who flew out of his own two-thousand-foot pasture airfield and would come in with manure on the belly of his Aero Commander. That was one exciting place, and I loved every minute of it. While there, our family would buy our first airplane, a Piper PA-12 Super Cruiser, N4900M, which I would help paint a cream color trimmed in Bahama blue and paint the N numbers on myself. Double "O" Moma, some would call it. Our good friend, Reese Munch, would assist in the project in exchange for flying time. We were rolling in aviation!

About the same time, my mother decided she wanted to go into the hobby and gift business, so she opened up in Lithia Springs Blanche's Hobby and Gift Shop, only fifty years ahead of its time. She had a thriving little business for about two to three years, and we loved it. As kids, my brother and I got to go with her to the toy warehouses in Atlanta every Wednesday when we were not in school. We thought we had died and gone to toy heaven! It was unbelievable! At Christmastime, we often would get special items that had not sold during the Christmas season—or you know, maybe Mom just marked them Sold. But I believe we were awarded from what we did not sell. Anyway, we didn't care, and those were the most exciting years ever!

Today my real estate office and desk would be on the very site where, fifty-five years ago, I often played in the dirt next to my mother's little hobby and gift shop. Not many people can say that!

The farm was still only three miles west, and often we would walk or run home from the hobby store. My other grandparents' home, my dad's parents, was only a couple of blocks away, and we would often go there for various reasons, including the cutting of grass. Thirty minutes on, thirty minutes off, me and my brother—it was a great duo. All was followed up by delicious peanut butter and banana sandwiches with mayonnaise, a moon pie, and a Coke while watching Johnny Carson on *To Tell the Truth*. The TV screen was smaller than my dinner tray, a real antique today!

In time, my brother and I left the farm to pursue higher education, my brother, Gordon, in 1964 and me in 1966 from Douglas County High School. Gordon was senior class vice president and president of the Beta Club. I was senior class president and president of the student council. We got a good public education in the Douglas County public school system. We were both off to Emory University for the next chapters in our lives. And the farm kept farming. Mom and Dad were soon to be empty nesters!

"Welcome to Tightwad"
SH

Just like Early Litha Springs, Lyndon, jane

Country Roads and Times

It is early March 2010, day of the fifth. The sun is shining bright, and it is a brisk thirty-four degrees or so by now. The frost heaves were heavy again this morning, meaning we had a pretty cold night.

When I was a kid, it was so great to stomp on the frost heaves early in the morning on the way to catch the school bus about a mile away from home. We would walk every day, rain, snow, sleet, or shine; cold or hot; beautiful or not. Then in the afternoon, we would walk back home. It made you feel like a giant to trample the delicate ice crystals that had spewed up like little miniature cities the night before. "Crunch, crunch, crunch" went the little metropolises!

Along the road, there were *big* deep ditches, big enough to imagine our own little grand canyons along the way, big enough after school, and deep enough and private enough to take an impromptu nature break if we "couldn't wait" until we got home. For some reason, those ditches were awesome and impressive. You'd probably remember that kind yourself if you grew up out in a very rural area as a child.

The roads had no gravel, just dirt! Or just mud–in the bad weather! Gravel on the roads was a later modern convenience. The roads and revenue commissioners did not have the luxury of budget for gravel.

Bridges were a luxury, and we had an old wooden bridge on our road, held in place by steel cables so that it wouldn't wash away at the first deluge. Our bridge went across Gothards Creek on the way to McTyre Cotton Gin. So, the early name of our road was McTyre Road, and earlier, maybe Sleepy Hollow Rd. Later, when the Lake Greystone was built by George Shaffer in the 1930s or so, the name changed to Lake Greystone Road.

"Going Home"

Early Ford on Gutshalls Creek

By the way, old George was a curious man. First of all, he was Catholic. In those days, that made him strange in these parts. Second of all, he was originally from Canada. That made him a foreigner, sort of. He was a sign painter/artist by trade and a good early example for me of an entrepreneur, probably the first one I really knew anything about.

He built about a twelve-acre lake and another lake about five acres above it. He built several smaller shallow, stock ponds and a fish hatchery house for raising minnows. Then he would release them first to the smaller ponds, then to the larger one, and finally into the big commercial fishing lakes. It was quite an operation, I thought. And he did all his earthwork excavation, lake and pond building, and so on with a small Ford tractor with a scoop and draw pan. Imagine building not one but two large dams and then some with only that equipment. It was truly amazing! And he built several little houses and such around the property, including his own little lakeside house/office/headquarters with screened-in porch and hammock overlooking the lake. Also, he had a nice little fountain and pond along his driveway and boathouse. And he built large pillars at his entrance with electric lights and little statues of black boys in red coveralls holding fishing poles. It was quite impressive!

Fishing was his business. Big bass and bream came out of that lake every day. The big lake was the main fishing lake, and the one above, I believe, was like a reserve lake, with growing fish no doubt. For a reasonable small fee, you could fish all day or half a day and catch so many pounds. You could rent a boat and buy or rent fishing poles, tackle, and so on. You could buy bait and minnows and get you a cold drink and a pack of crackers. It was pretty neat. All the while, George might be hand-painting the signage on a pretty new red truck that said "Mitchell Appliances, Douglasville, Georgia," or some other piece of art. What a way to make yourself a nice, quiet, and comfortable living, the best example of entrepreneurship I had ever witnessed and a fine one even to this day. He owned the land, he owned the lake, and he owned his own home, all free and clear with no mortgage, just taxes to pay unfortunately. But more than anything else, he owned his own self, and I saw that and never forgot it!

McTyre Cotton Gin

"Ginning Time"
FM

College Bound

It was 1966 and time for graduation from Douglas County High School. It had been a very eventful senior year, and my life had been changed forever!

March 21, 1966, spring break of my senior year, was the day we got the news about my brother, Gordon. I had been home alone, not an unusual thing, with Mother and Dad working the real estate business all the time, and I heard the telephone ring. I think it was on a Saturday.

"This is Captain Chambers calling from the DeFuniak, Florida, Funeral Home," the caller said.

"Yes," I said.

"Is this the home and family of William Gordon Ayres?" Captain Chambers asked.

"Yes, sir, it is," I said. "I am his brother."

"Well, son, there has been an accident. Is your mother or dad at home? Could I speak with one of them?" he said.

"No, sir, they are not here. I am the only one here. I am his younger brother. What has happened? You can tell me, if you would," I said.

"Well, like I said, there has been an accident, and we have your brother's body here at the funeral home in DeFuniak Springs, Florida."

"DeFuniak Springs, Florida?" I repeated. "What happened?"

"Your brother drowned down in Morrison Springs near here while he and some other boys were cave diving. There were three of them all together. We have notified the other families."

I was numb. I could barely speak or even stand up. How could I bear this news here by myself? Why me? Why did I have to be the first person to contact? I couldn't just call Mom and Dad and tell them what had happened. So I decided to call my uncle Brawnson, my dad's brother, and his wife, my aunt Janie. They immediately came up to our house from Mableton.

It wasn't too long later that Mom and Dad came home from their work, and they learned the sad news. It was awful. It was more than awful. It was the saddest day of my life.

It took a long time to try to adjust to this new set of circumstances in the lives of all of us.

The funeral was sad, of course, and many people got out of school to attend my brother's service. It was a bright, sunny day much like today. The air was crisp with newfound spring green grass and flowers starting to bloom. It was like the daffodils were saying goodbye to Gordon, my dear, beloved brother.

Gordon was buried next to our grandfather Ayres in the Ayres family plot in Westview Cemetery in Atlanta, Georgia. Resting there also was my uncle Eldorado Ayres, my father's younger brother, who had committed suicide by gun just about a year earlier. Financial problems, depression, marital problems, and drinking had pushed him outside the limits of forbearance. He too was a young and good man, gone before his time.

The loss of my brother forever scarred the last days of my high school experience. He had been pre-med at Emory University, almost at the end of his sophomore year.

I too was headed for Emory University as I had been accepted at its founding source at Oxford–or Oxford College of Emory University as it was also known–in the little town of Oxford, Georgia. In the 1930s, Asa Candler had given a large financial gift to Emory in exchange for the board of trustees agreeing to move the main campus about fifty miles west to Atlanta. But the original old campus was kept and enshrined as Emory's Junior College of two years, and it awarded its own associate's degree upon graduation. Then you went right into your third year on the Atlanta campus of Emory University, or you could decide to go elsewhere as some students did.

By 1970, I had completed four years of hard-core academia and had earned my associate's degree and a bachelor of business administration degree, all from Emory University. My parents were very proud of me, and so was I. On the day I graduated, my mom and dad presented me with a check for $1,000. It was a lot of money. This was even after they had paid all my tuition, room, and board for the past four years. They had kept their part of the bargain, and I had kept mine. I was so lucky to have such good and wonderful parents. And I would often thank them later for giving me the opportunity of a good, quality education. They had always held high standards for us boys, and we, now I, had a lot to live up to!

Those first two years at Oxford College of Emory University were like magic. They were two of the most wonderful years of my life. There were so many things that made my life at Oxford, Georgia, so special.

First, there was the quad, covered with towering old shade trees, shading crisscrossed walkways that went like celestial paths through the universe to special places of learning, understanding, and revelation of knowledge.

Then there were the buildings of old, built more than one hundred years before, most of them still serving the academic needs of new, fledgling students like me.

There was the old Seney Tower and Administration Building, where Mr. Tarkenton, the father of the famous football player Fran Tarkenton, was the registrar. And the belfry housed the grand old bell given to Emory by Queen Victoria in 1886 or so. Its ringing was academic resonance of the sweetest sound I had ever heard. I knew I was there in the crucible of my beginning of a lifelong pursuit of knowledge and excellence in all things. As I looked back, I knew that I marveled at the opportunities that lay before me.

And there were so many other things, not to mention Dickey Dorm, where I was assigned to living quarters for the next two years. In honor of Professor Dickey, one of the outstanding old professors, we still bore the brunt of teasing and pundits over the years. But we were right across the street from the brand-new girls' dormitory and the new cafeteria and student center. So, there were advantages to be had.

Also, there was the old Confederate graveyard where soldiers of the great war spent their last days in an Emory hospital and gently passed on to their eternity.

And there was the enclosed, heated swimming pool just about sixty feet away from the old gymnasium, to which in wintertime we traversed through deep snow from our locker rooms. Today, of course, all that has changed, and there is every conceivable modern convenience.

I learned to play tennis on real red clay tennis courts that were absolutely marvelous. And I learned to love the fast-paced sport.

And there was Air Force ROTC, of which I became a part, and I wore the uniform of this country as an air force cadet and became a proud member of the rifle drill team. But my military service would be cut short, and later, I would receive my draft lottery number of 327 for the sixth day of July. Vietnam would go on without me as numbers that high would never be called.

At Emory, my eyes were opened to so many things, like Delta Tau Delta, my brother's fraternity, where he had been vice president. Now it was the choice fraternity of myself, my first cousin Chris, and half a dozen great friends from Oxford. We lived on campus in Atlanta and had some of the best times of our lives at the Delt house on fraternity row.

I'd never forget one particular party of many where we had Poonanny and the Stormers and the Tornados. It was one wild and crazy party–barely manageable and totally out of site. The Shelter, as it was called, really rocked that weekend!

Then there were Dooley days, when the spirit of Dooley–a skeleton of the oldest living-dead student, professor, dean, or whatever he really was–could come into and dismiss your class, cause a ruckus, or generally upset or inspire the student ensemble, wherever he might show up! He was the embodiment of the "Spirit of Emory" and lived or died by that passion. Who at Emory would not remember Dooley?

Alas, the years did pass. I was married my senior year in 1969. It could have been a mistake, but it was not, for it was life yearning to live and to live free by the spirit. But there would be ramifications, unavoidable ramifications.

On December 28, 1969, Sunday at 3:00 p.m., I married Karen Sue Hoeflich, the girl of my dreams, or so I thought at the time. It was Christmas holidays from school, and there was this wonderful time of opportunity to get married. We had planned it since back in the fall.

She and the preacher's daughter, Nancy, used to come to my family farm every week and sometimes twice a week or more to ride and exercise the family horses. I had generally ignored them for quite a while until one day at the end of my junior year, when I came home for the summer. That day and that summer changed my life forever!

The day of our wedding, the well at our farm failed, and I had to take a bath in the lake. Had I been wiser, I might have taken this as a sign; but at the time, it was just an inconvenience along the road to matrimony. By two thirty, it was sunny and bright; and friends, family, fraternity brothers, even Jan Montgomery–our chapter sweetheart–had arrived at the little white-framed Lithia Springs United Methodist Church. The Reverend Lloyd Jackson did the honors. My father was my best man, and Robert Foxworthy and Mel Purcel, my big brother, stood by my side.

We married that sunny Sunday in December, and we embarked on new adventures for us both. Karen was a beautiful bride and would be a wonderful wife during those early years.

To make a long story short, I finished college at Emory. Karen had finished high school and was the salutatorian and chief speaker for her class at graduation that spring in 1969. I would never forget her speech, which was concerning the circumstances of life and how we should be the "Makers of Circumstances!" I was impressed and in love!

The Law

Law school called next in the fall of 1970. We endured this first year in Macon, Georgia. I studied the law, and Karen worked for a law firm so we could eat and pay the rent on our carriage house apartment, a small horse barn and carriage house converted into small apartments. We had the downstairs, and Micky (a girl, his wife) and Jim Terry had the upstairs. He was a Captain, later promoted to Major, in the Marine Corps. Jim had barely survived Vietnam and was now a pursuer of a legal education. We had some good times, and we had some rough times, like the night the law library burned, and we all had to form a book bucket brigade to evacuate as many volumes of law books as we could before the fire engulfed them. That was, I think, in the fall of 1970 or winter of 1971.

By year's end, we had both completed our freshman year of law school at Walter F. George School of Law of Mercer University, Macon, Georgia. Jim would go on, finish, and become an outstanding lawyer with the judge advocate general's corps. I would essentially terminate my lifelong dream to save my failing marriage. I would not go back to law school but rather move myself into the arms of the family real estate business and would eventually become a real estate broker!

The law was and always would be a great love of mine. I knew I wanted to be a lawyer since on the playground in the seventh grade at Annette Winn Elementary School. I couldn't remember why, but it was like a revelation to me. Along the way, I would receive other revelations about life. Some I had not counted on!

For two years or so, I had enjoyed the good fortune to work for one of the top law firms in the country, King and Spalding in Atlanta, Georgia. It was a tremendous opportunity beginning on the day I was hired by Mr. Richard Denny, who introduced me to Mr. Buddy Fickling, who introduced me to a Multigraph Multilith 2550 printing machine. I would be the printer of all the legal documents produced by the entire firm at that time in 1968. We were housed in the original Trust Co. of Georgia Building in Downtown Atlanta. I took great pride in my work and applied my artistic skills in producing the clearest, sharpest images and documents that could be produced. It was an important position, and I learned a lot!

Later, I worked my way up some from the printing and mail room to making the occasional out-of-town trip for some of the attorneys who especially trusted my work and integrity.

Once, I made a first-class champagne flight–we always flew first class– to Washington DC to file prospectuses with the Securities and Exchange Commission. Anyone, I guess, could have done it, but they chose me. All in one day, I got back home that evening at about seven thirty, in time to meet my girlfriend and future wife, Karen, to go to a party together at one of her friends' houses. We went, and all evening, I basked in the glory of the day and night of being on top of the world. I was only nineteen years old, and the world, I thought, had indeed smiled on me!

My friends at King and Spalding were truly wonderful and helped me gain entrance to law school that next fall. As a token of esteem and appreciation, they gave me a wonderful Samsonite briefcase for law school, which I soon put to good use and still have to this day. Had things turned out differently, I believe there would have been a good future for me among all my new friends– friends who would remain with me for a lifetime!

But now it was time to study real estate brokerage!

Returning to My Roots

In 1971, I left law school and went home to Lithia Springs, Georgia. In some ways, I felt like a failure; but in other ways, I felt totally relieved–relieved that now I could work instead of just study, that I could really earn some serious money. And although I had always worked part time or more, now I could really concentrate on working entirely to establish a career–a new career in the real estate business!

My mother and dad had formed Ayres Realty Co. in 1960 after Mom had given up on the hobby and gift shop business, and Dad and his partners, feeling the pinch of financial difficulties from overpromotion and overspending, had sold their aviation business of Aero Sales Inc. to Big Brother Aircraft.

It was a new day for them, and ten years into the business, it was a new day for me. Even though I had been an accounting major, I had done and still did bookkeeping and accounting for them; I was first licensed to sell real estate in 1971, I think in December. It was a good Christmas present, but it wasn't free!

For the next year, I had decided that if I could earn $1,000 per month, I would make $12,000 for the year, a respectable figure, I thought. At least I could pay my bills. Also, my dad said I would be paid a bonus of 10 percent on earned commissions, but I would have to sell like any other salesman for three years, completing my apprenticeship, until I could qualify for the broker's examination. This I did. The first year, apprenticeship or not, I earned almost exactly $12,000 and a little over in commissions, plus earned my 10 percent bonus. It was a good year. The next two years were equally good. I was on my way. By end of year three, I had taken, passed, and earned my real estate broker's license. Now I was ready to take over the company and relieve old Dad!

Mom and Dad loved to travel, so my getting a broker's license really freed them up a lot over the next several decades. All through the '70s, the '80s, and the '90s, Mom and Dad would travel all over the world. They went to Europe, the Middle East, the Holy Land, and all over the United States, including driving the Alcan Highway to Alaska and to the Yucatan in Mexico. And they would cruise in the Bahamas and Bermuda and through the Panama Canal. They became riverboat gamblers on the Delta Queen on the Mississippi River, the Tennessee River, and others. I didn't think they really gambled; they were too tight for that. But they always had a really good time!

All this time, they gave me free rein over the real estate business as they had turned it pretty much over to me.

I lived, struggled, thrived, and survived with the business over the next forty years or so. There were many ups and downs and many challenges along the way. Today Ayres Realty Co. has been in business for almost sixty years, and we are continuing through the efforts of our own children!

The Real Estate Business

Franchises were big in my early days of real estate. And it seemed that everyone was getting on the bandwagon. We didn't want to be left behind, so we negotiated for a Realty World franchise to bring us into the modern age. Mom-and-pop businesses like ours were going out of style and out of business. The new thing–the hot thing–was to have a nationwide franchise with radio and TV advertising. Maximize the advertising dollar and get TV and national recognition!

It was a grand undertaking, but it was difficult to get everyone on board, especially relatives of the old school. What with new blazer jackets, blue shirts, red striped ties, and such, we were the epitome of fashion and a sign of the new times!

Our old signs were not good enough or fancy enough, of course, so we had to start using these expensive big bulky wooden posts from which to hang the stylish new color signs. And we had to dig the holes to put them in the ground, oftentimes in the beautiful lawns of homes unencumbered by such due diligence as ours, but we would not deprive us and our clients of the biggest and the best that the industry had to offer!

This continued for several years. By then, the franchise had experienced several major upheavals, and we had all the firewood in wooden posts and signs that we could handle. The writing was on the wall. Being big and better and more expensive wasn't all it had been cracked up to be. But we did have the most beautiful picture board and office you had ever seen. We were even voted the best in our region. Things couldn't be all that bad, but alas, the real estate franchise world was just not our cup of tea!

Soon we were out of the franchise world and back into our own. It felt a little naked, but in a way, it felt good to be back to basics.

By now, my lovely wife and I were divorced and parting real estate ways. She got the five horses, and I got the airplane in what we called the "great divide." We both got our little girl, Heather, although her mother would have custody until she was fourteen. Then she could choose on her own. That was another story.

So now, here I was, a single man working the real estate business; and on top of that, I had just purchased a franchise in the personal motivation business called Success Motivation Institute (SMI), headquartered in, of all places, Waco, Texas, home of Dr. Pepper, my favorite drink!

Dad took me to the Atlanta Airport that day, just him and me. It was exciting to me to be going off to Texas to find myself and fortune, but it was sad for him because he knew my life was taking a new direction. Later, one time, he said that my involvement with SMI was the worst thing that ever happened to me because it took my concentration off the real estate business. But I think it was the best and most wonderful thing that ever happened to me because it opened so many more doors of opportunity and expanded my thinking so much.

At any rate, that day, he was sad as he bid me farewell, and we both left the boarding gate in opposite directions. I felt guilty, but I had to go. I had to see what else was out there!

Personal Engineering Company was the name of my company, and I learned to sell $600 personal motivation programs to people who didn't even want them, much less need them. But I was good, and I had the best instructors in the world at SMI.

Paul Meyer was an awesome man and founder of SMI. He taught us, like him, how to crawl over broken glass to obtain our ambitions and sell programs. Probably no other training in my life gave me the tools and skills to be a personal engineer of people, including myself.

After a few years, my time with SMI took a back seat to my ongoing real estate business, which I never really gave up on. Within time, I was really going at full steam ahead.

It was about that time I met Beth, the woman who would become my second wife and the love of my life. We met quite accidentally at the World of Wheels Car Show in Atlanta, Georgia, in 1978. I had had a date to cancel that night, and so I went with a male friend of mine to the car show just to have something to do. Beth had gone with her sister, Brenda, because a friend of Brenda's–Jackie from Douglas County–was exhibiting a car. I couldn't remember the car so much, but it was an absolute miracle that Beth and I literally stumbled into each other in front of Jacky's car. I looked in amazement at the beautiful tall girl with long blond hair in a burgundy suit, top coat, and high-heeled boots. Wow, what a dazzler! How lucky for me!

I immediately excused myself and apologized for running into her, and she just as quickly did the same. After a few words and pleasantries, I asked her if she would like to walk around with me some and see some of the cars. "Okay," she said. And we were slowly off and looking. I was on cloud nine!

In a little while, my friend Bill Eidson and I asked Beth and Brenda if they would like to go to the Burt Reynolds Club there at the World Congress Center. They couldn't decide if we were going to abduct them or what, so they declined. But I did ask Beth for her phone number and told her maybe I would call her sometime. So she took the risk and gave me her real, not made-up, number; and two weeks later, I took the bold move to call her.

Our first date was awesome! When I got to her home in Smyrna, Georgia, she opened the front door. She had cut her beautiful long blond hair, and now it was sort of shoulder length or less and done up somehow in a new hairdo. It looked so different, but great! She said, "Come on in." And I did. She looked so beautiful and was absolutely fascinating in every way!

"Oh, I see you have a piano," I said as I glanced around the living room. This was a big plus.

"Yeah," she said.

"Do you play?" I asked.

"A little," she replied.

"So play me a tune?" I asked. And she did. She was good, and she could read music like a pro. Amazing!

"And do you play?" she asked.

"A little," I said.

"Play something," she said.

So, I did a little number I had learned by ear and gave it my best shot. And she acted so amazed at my playing!

Our first date out that night was for Chinese. And the matter of it was I didn't even like Chinese cuisine. But I did now and have ever since. That very night as I looked across the table, I watched this beautiful, magical woman and said to myself, *This is the woman I am going to marry.* I wasn't looking for love, but it found me and would not let go. The rest was history!

It was so amazing! Now, after thirty-three years, (now forty-one plus) we still looked into the sparkle of each other's eyes and still laughed at nonsensical things. We have two wonderful grown children ourselves and three granddaughters. And Beth, now a real estate broker herself, for over thirty-five years, runs the family business as managing broker and me as principal broker. We became a dynamic duo, you might say, and we loved the business, our family, and all the people who worked with us. Life was and is good!

We are still going in the real estate business, this year marking fifty-nine years of "bringing homes and families together." Jennifer Henniger came up with that catchy slogan, which really captures what we have strived to do over all these years. We have been so blessed with good people like Jennifer; Bethany; Stephanie, our daughter; Benjamin, our son; and Heather, our daughter by my first marriage. All were well educated, and we were all on our way to success. Thank you, all!

Friends Near and Far

Speaking of Chinese, I would be remiss if I didn't tell you about my parents "adopting" my Chinese brother, Allen Kuo, and his lovely wife, Anna Kuo as a daughter.

They owned the newly established local Chinese restaurant, the Dragon Gardens, and it was the closest we ever came to owning a Chinese restaurant ourselves, for we never ever paid for a single meal. Somehow my family became intrinsically linked, either by design or fate, with theirs; and before you knew it, we were spending holidays together and all kind of special time.

My parents were most attached and me and my family too by default, sort of, and then we too were all caught up in an international relationship of intrigue and hospitality.

Over the ensuing years, we would be close with not only Allen and Anna but also their newborn children, Jennifer and Henry; their nephews Tony, Wayne, and Gary; and their parents from Taiwan and the former Nationalist China, of which Allen's father was a former general in the Nationalist army. They had all gone to Taiwan when China became Communist.

A particular memory was of one clear but snow-covered day of Christmas in around 1985, when it was so cold that the lake at our farm was frozen over. We'd had about four inches of snow, and we all showed up at the family farm for Christmas dinner and visitation. The first place all the kids went to was out in the middle of a six-acre frozen lake. And I was so worried when some of the ice began to crack. Fortunately, we got everyone separated and back to safety!

This highly unusual family aberration would continue for some time and once even took a precedence over Father's Day, when my folks took off with them instead of me and my family. It was most unusual and often difficult to understand.

Later, as things would have it, Allen and Anna would get a divorce. She would move to Vancouver, Canada, and he would move to New York. The nephews would go back to Taiwan, and the parents all eventually died out. It was all so weird. What can I say? There was a lot to this story, more than I can share with you here, but enclosed see a copy of the letter from Anna's parents to my mother and dad.

Today we are all still friends, and even though in remote contact, I am sure there will always be a sort of special bond that will always be there. They would be forever welcomed in my home, for they were our counterpoints across the sea–the sea of geography, time, and space!

March 26, 1991

Dear godparents of my daughter Anna:

We received your nice letter and card some time ago. Because of certain matters taking up much of my time, I have not been able to write to you until now. Please forgive us.

My wife and I are very happy to know that both of you like and valued our daughter Anna enough to accept her as your goddaughter. Since you have such deep appreciation for her, it is our honor and wish that you will treat her as your own child as this will give us much peace of mind and comfort. Should there be a time when she needs counseling, please do not hesitate to counsel her. My wife and I do feel it is in Anna's good fortune to be able to be adopted into the family of such an affectionate couple as yourselves.

We are looking forward for an opportunity in 1992 to visit Atlanta, when we can meet together with you again. It is still too early to make arrangements, but we will certainly keep you informed.

May good health and happiness be with you always.

Sincerely yours,

Jih-wun and Chuen Sheu

* * *

And not to be outdone by the Chinese, there was our good Japanese friend, Kasaburo Ito. Mr. Ito, as we called him, was one of our early international clients when he came to Lithia Springs and Douglas County, Georgia. He owned and operated the very successful Japanese restaurant Wisteria Gardens in Jonesboro, just south of Atlanta.

He was a land investor and developer who would befriend and beguile my mom and dad and me. Each time he visited our home or business, he would come bearing gifts and tokens of appreciation and generosity. You know, we can learn a lot from our international friends!

Wisteria Lane in Lithia Springs was his street that my mother named for some of his land development. He did well, and when I went to Europe, I visited Mr. Ito in Manhattan, New York City, where he lived at that time. I enjoyed a wonderful breakfast with him as he wished me off to Europe for a three-week trip. He also presented me with a very nice pair of pajamas. How thoughtful! Our international horizons were expanding!

* * *

Then last but not least was our good friend and client from Bolivia, South America, J.A.Arquedas, a man who purchased everything from needles to locomotives and who once served as the Bolivian ambassador to the fledgling League of Nations, led by President Woodrow Wilson, in around 1914 or so.

I sold land for Mr. Arquedas in Douglas County, a nice beautiful wooded land in the country that was subdivided and parceled out.

During the course of this time, I (we) would forge a uniquely strong relationship with Mr. Arquedas, and we would have the privilege to visit with him in his uniquely imaginative self-built estate in Lawrenceville, Georgia. Remember, Bill Arp–a Douglas County namesake–was from Lawrenceville.

His home was marvelous with pools and fountains, Steinway player piano, electric movie screens (before their time), special meat and locker pantries, in-floor radiant heating, and so many things foreign to us at the time. A special feature in his kitchen was backlit slides of friends, family, and the world surrounding his cabinets. How neat! How fun!

Over the years, we enjoyed a great relationship with this very special man. Upon closing his last transaction, he wrote to us the following letter:

August 4, 1973

Dear Mrs. Ayres:

I wish to acknowledge receipt of the check and statement you were kind to send me. This brings to a close the two transactions I was privileged to conduct with you, and it is my opportunity to tell you that I was very fortunate when mere chance put me in contact with your firm.

I have bought and sold many properties here and in New York and never have I dealt with a realty company as capable, efficient, trustworthy, and pleasant as yours. I particularly enjoyed the privilege of dealing personally with you and your very talented and artistic son, to whom I ask you to convey my congratulations for his best and most important creation, your first granddaughter.

Should you and yours ever find yourselves driving in these parts, please come in and have a drink or a bite to eat with me.

Most sincerely,

J. A. Arguedas

My parents always reminded me that the real estate business was a people business. We served people, and we helped them solve their problems. I would never forget this great lesson!

A Family of Entrepreneurs

We had always worked for ourselves doing one thing or another, it seemed. At least we had always worked!

Early on in my life, my earliest recollection of business was the family raising of honey!–Bee Honey! All the early vacation money was earned from the raising of bees, gathering the honey, and selling it under our own label. Dad had about ten hives or so at that time, and I was three to five years old. They were close by in our backyard, where I would play with my Donald Duck car around the big old oak tree.

Dad would have the old smoker going to numb and distract the bees, and the next thing you knew, he would be removing the frames of delicious fresh golden honey from the hives. He would then cut the honeycomb off the frames with a hot electric knife, and then it would be cut up into nice neat pieces to put in quart jars with other pure honey.

Some frames were put into a centrifugal extractor to throw out the honey, and then it was drained off without comb right into the honey jars. They were labeled, cleaned, and ready to go–nature's wonder. It was the only predigested food we eat–and love!

Well, the honeybees went with us to the farm, and we always raised honey. In fact, of course, we had to name the farm–what else?–Honey Acres. It was, for us, our pot of gold at the end of the rainbow. And we produce it to this day!

Our family honey label

Other business ventures came our way as well, things like my mobile car wash I started when I was about fourteen years old. Not yet having a driver's license, I hitched up the horse and buggy we had; grabbed my water hoses, buckets, soap, and rags; and took off down the country roads of our area, washing people's cars and smartly, I thought, using their own water to boot. Then there was grass cutting, a young man's stable venture, for there was always grass to cut!

And we were selling, buying, and horse trading whenever we could. My first commission sales were those I made for my brother to sell the "pony cart" he had built out of my granddaddy's old Model A. I sold it for $35.00 with an earned commission of $3.50, my very first. Then later, there was the banjo I sold for him for a $5.00 commission and a few other things. I liked the selling business and would grow up to, one day, earn a full-time living doing just that!

Along the way, I sold everything from *Collier's Encyclopedias* even on the dime-a-day plan–which really did not exist, I discovered–to Electrolux vacuum cleaners. "Nothing sucks like an Electrolux."

My selling came naturally to me as my mother, early on, had set a real good example by selling our dead horse–yes, our dead horse. It had died rather unexpectedly of the colic right in our front yard at the farm. It was a big horse, at least sixteen hands, and a problem! Mother thought real hard and, being the smart businesswoman she was, decided to call Farmer Brown. He lived over across Gothards Creek and had a big pack of hunting hounds.

"Mr. Brown," she said, "I have something you need. Do you still have all your hound dogs you have to feed?"

"Yeah," he said.

"Well, I had a horse to die over here in my front yard. And if you want to come over and get him to feed to your dogs, I'll sell him to you for $10."

"Yeah?" he said, and no doubt, he must have been scratching his head, figuring up how much dog food that might be and how much money he could save and so on. "Okay, I'll be over there first thing in the morning to get it." And he was.

He gave my mother the $10, and the dead horse (Major) was gone. We thought our mother was the smartest person we knew! Who else could sell a dead horse!?! That lesson stuck!

So, sales became an important part of the lives of all my family. For the most part, it would end up being real estate sales!

Along the way, however, there would be a number of other jobs and learning experiences, like pumping gas at the Sinclair Service Station and washing cars there on Saturdays; picking tomatoes for my uncle Clark, who was a truck farmer, and planting tomato slips; and catching chickens for Edward Johnson at four in the morning–now that was hard work, catching five thousand chickens by hand. We would walk up the road and up the hill in the dark to his chicken houses, work until up into the morning after sunrise, and catch and throw all those chickens into crates and onto big trucks!

Then there was my job at the Lithia Springs Rexall Pharmacy, where I was a soda jerk, stock clerk, sweeper, cleaner, cook on the short order grill, and anything else that Dr. Bob Milner could think of. I worked after school in high school every day from 4:30 p.m. to 9:30 p.m. and in the summertime 13½-hour days for $0.75 per hour. I learned a lot, including that big spoons are for men, and little spoons are for women and children. Dr. Milner was and still is a good man, who became one of my dad's best friends and mine. We all hunted and fished together for years!

Once, my dad told me, "Oh, we're not such best friends. We just tolerate each other!" Well, I guess that was what best friends did; we tolerated each other. But what would life be like without good friends?

Later as the years passed and I got older, I got a job with the law firm of King and Spalding, which I dearly loved. I did printing, supply accounting, and some high-class gofer work as I called it. Today it was called clerking and paralegal. I worked hard and gained invaluable experience and great insights into the legal profession, for which at the time I was headed.

Deerlick Trading Post was another of my efforts when I tried a lick at the antique business. I loved it, and every Tuesday night at seven thirty, I'd always be at Gold's Antiques and Auction on Lee Street in Atlanta, buying another truckload of stuff coming out of Europe or somewhere.

Once I purchased a two-horse enclosed antique peddler's wagon with doors, drawers, and cubbyholes all over it. It was a wonder. I paid $1,000 for it and used it in parades and as an attraction for my Highway 78 antique business. We made lots of money, about $300, I think. Ha ha! But we had a lot of fun!

Once, I had bought a three-quarter-ton 1937 Chevrolet pickup truck, which I had just purchased a little before sundown. On the way home in the dark, I had a fire in the ignition wires that really livened things up to say the least. Fortunately, I was able to get it subdued before the whole truck blew up, but it was exciting!

Then there was the old horse buggy that I bought in Indiana and brought back home on top of the car on the $5 boat racks the old lady sold me. The idea was to hoist up the buggy in the barn and drive the car up under it, removing the wheels to put in the trunk and putting the pulling shafts on top; and presto, you have an instant buggy mover from one state to another. I did great with it, until I pulled into an A&W root beer awning for supper!

"I'll have two hamburgers, two root beers, a hammer, and a screwdriver," I said. I fixed it, and I was on my way again!

I also have to mention the forty-eight-foot houseboat I bought for $275 and two fish dinners. For the longest time, this home-built houseboat–fourteen feet wide and forty-eight feet in length–had set up on the highway. I watched it forever coming and going. At first, they wanted a fortune for it, then a small fortune, and then a ransom; it got cheaper, cheaper, and cheaper until finally, one day, I could not resist. The owner *had* to remove it in so many days or else, so I had bought it for a song and two free fish dinners for me and my mom, who went with me across Atlanta to pay the fish restaurant owner who owned it. I wrote up the bill of sale, ate up, and was the proud owner of a new white elephant!

It cost me $250 just to move it to my home in the backyard, where I remodeled and painted it and then looked at it for the next six months.

Finally, I sold it for $2,000 cash, a 125cc Honda motorcycle, and a go-kart in trade, and the new owner had to come and get it. It was a good trade. Later, Dad saw it up on Lake Lanier, where the owner used it for a floating playhouse for the kids. The Corps of Engineers had required him to fill the entire hull with Styrofoam so it wouldn't sink. It was pretty cool and one of the more unusual things I had been involved with!

After that and along the way, there had been cars, motorcycles, airplanes, swimming pools, tractors, horses, cows, go-karts, wagons and buggies, real estate, you name it!

Also, being an artist, I had bought and sold a good bit of artwork–paintings of all kinds and drawings, pen, and ink that I sold through *Southern Living* magazine as old South prints. And when Six Flags over Georgia opened, I worked there as a caricature artist doing cartoon-type portraits. In college, I made extra spending money doing commission oil and watercolor paintings. Somewhere there was an oil painting called *American Gothic Unclothed*, which was my most risqué painting–top only. If you can find it, it might be worth some money one day. At the time, it bought me a few hamburgers, some gas, and some date money.

So many things we learn to do as we all strive to earn a living and make our way through this world. I feel like I have done it all, but I know I haven't. There is so much more out there untouched and unexplored–perhaps one day!

Growing Up in Aviation, A Hobby Store, Farming, and Real Estate

I don't know which way is up sometimes when I examine the exposure of things I experienced as a kid! I could have gone off in any direction, and indeed, I think that sometimes I did just that. But, any direction turned out to be all directions because I tried it all!

All of it had been so much fun! Being around airplanes early on was such a privilege as well as having the opportunity to fly at an early age. Wow! Oftentimes when I, or we, had to go somewhere, my dad would take us in our "private" airplane, not a jet, mind you–this was a long time ago–but our own airplane nevertheless. I thought we were rich! We had a speedboat too! And I was very humble and a little embarrassed at times that we had so much!

At Georgia Southern College in 1964, the kids asked me how I got down to the summer camp for high school student council presidents.

"Oh, my dad dropped me off in our airplane," I said casually, like, *Well, doesn't everybody travel that way?* He quite literally let me out at the airport with the engine still running, turned around, and took off back for home while I watched. He was off on another adventure himself, and so was I. Fortunately, it was a short walk over to the college!

I too would do some similar things when I became a student pilot at age twenty-four. It would take me about five years to earn my private license, but I had bought my own plane to learn in, N87034, a beautiful little blue and white

415-C Ercoupe. It had blue-tinted plexiglass and a sunburst paint scheme. It was a beauty, and now all I had to do was hire a flight instructor to teach me how to fly it. After learning also to hand-prop it because of dead batteries, I found me an instructor, Walter Barnes from Cartersville, Georgia. He was a crop duster by profession and a pilot's pilot and the only FBO at Cartersville Airport in those days. The hangar he used was held up by fifty-five-gallon drums stacked to the ceiling and a roof put on top and something like walls, but not quite, on the sides. It was quite a sight, I must say. But they had gas, a good runway, and plenty of cotton fields to land in if you needed them. And $35 an hour was a good rate for Mr. Barnes, and we could go over the power lines instead of under them. He taught me well. It was a pay as you go plan, as you had the time!

Flying the board

And then there was Mr. Dan Emin, who instructed for the Georgia State Patrol, who finished me up on my training and finally made me into a real private pilot!

In 1978, I took my check ride in my airplane–the 1946 Ercoupe with no rudder pedals–with Mr. Bill Mobley, the flight examiner. We did the usual stuff–stalls, turns, navigation, and so on. And when finally we came back into Charlie Brown Airport on runway 14, he said, "Here, let me have it. I want to see if I can land this thing with no rudder pedals!"

He brought her on down, living through his own wonderment and apprehension of how you could actually fly without rudder pedals, until he set her on the runway itself, and then said, "Now you can have it. You're all right."

To this day, I never demonstrated a qualified landing myself, and I guess he still didn't know if I can land an airplane. The Ercoupe was still a marvelous airplane. It practically landed itself–with an instructor, that is!

* * *

Blanche's Hobby and Gift Shop sure was fun to grow up with too! Hamburgers from Pop and Clara's, the local pool hall and café, were best eaten on my mother's sales counter, where she kept two big rolls of all-occasion gift-wrapping paper. This was always part of the deal if you wanted free gift wrap. What a great idea!

"Ten, two, and four" was the sales slogan for Dr. Pepper, which was sold ice cold right down the street two doors down at Mrs. C. W. Bennett's Grocery. For the longest time, you could still buy gasoline and kerosene for your oil lamps and other things. It was the most fascinating old country general store you had ever seen with Lucky Strike cigarettes, hoop cheese, fresh meats, and ice-cold drinks. According to old Doc Branan, a reliable resource, Mr. Bennett would buy all the rabbits you could bring him for ten cents apiece. He would resell them for a little profit, and everybody got some really good meat!

My first sailboat

After Mr. Bennett and his son died during the middle of the century, the two-door old 1949 Ford sat under the drive-through porch for years and years. Mrs. Bennett would not sell it for nothing, no amount of money. There must have been thousands of inquiries about that car. Now the car was gone, and the old store was barely still standing behind a For Sale sign. Times did change!

At Christmastime, we would get all the toys that Mother was unable to sell during the busy holiday season. She did pretty well, but she was way ahead of her time for our area!

* * *

Farming was a good place to learn everything you couldn't learn anywhere else. The responsibilities on a farm were far and wide, from slopping the hogs, feeding the chickens, milking the cows, tending the horses, haying, planting, harvesting, woods management, lake management, gardening, wildlife management, you name it.

On the farm, we also learned to hunt, fish, and provide food for the table. We dressed and ate what we brought in from the woods, fields, streams, and lakes. We ate a lot of squirrel and dumplings–fried squirrel, fried rabbit (my favorite), turtle, opossum, dove, quail, deer (venison), fish (bass and bream mainly), and anything else we could bring in. Put grits and fresh corn bread with it, and you would have a mighty good meal!

So living on a farm involved a little bit of so many different things. I was very impressed one day when my brother and I had failed to cut the yard grass one fine summer day. When Dad got home, he asked us why we had not cut the grass like we were supposed to. We said it was just too pretty a day, and we had wasted away all the day playing and doing other things.

"Well," he said, "get out your flashlights, get outside, and get it cut." And we did–but not without argument.

"Why don't we just hire somebody to cut our grass?" I asked Dad.

"You know, son, hiring someone to cut your grass is like hiring someone to breathe for you." But I thought he said "*breed* for you." And being raised on a farm, I knew what that meant. Needless to say, I didn't ask anything else. And I thought about that–how important it was to cut your own grass for a long time that night!

* * *

Growing up in the real estate business was sometimes difficult because my parents were very busy and often out on appointments. There were contracts to prepare, papers to sign, deeds to obtain, people to interview, property to show, surveys to check, and telephone calls to answer!

But when we went home, Dad and I would head to the lake and fish until dark. Well, Dad would fish, and I would paddle the boat for hours on end till it was dark. That was the best fishing time, and it gave my dad a good break. Mom would catch the telephone calls during this time while she prepared supper, which was quite an effort for her—she did great and was very efficient. When we came back up from the lake, we would eat supper; and after we ate, Dad would often be back on the phone, answering calls and inquiries and other things. It was a busy time, but I really learned to paddle like an Indian using every quiet feathered paddle technique, never hitting the boat, and learned all about fly-fishing and every other kind done in fresh water. Dad was the best fisherman I ever knew, and he taught me a lot about fishing, hunting, farming, and life in general!—and about cutting your own grass!

He was also a licensed commercial pilot and certified aviation mechanic. He taught me about flying, how to take care of your tools, and how important it was to have the right tool for the right job. He was pretty near a perfectionist in many ways, and "good enough" was often hard to find. He was smart and knew everything, I loved him dearly, and I miss him today like my best friend.

Mother was smart too and was a very large part of the success of our family real estate business. Starting out in 1960, she and Dad shared a telephone through a hole in the wall with the sign company next door, A-1 Sign Company, owned by George Shaffer, our neighbor who built Lake Greystone. If one or the other was out, you had built-in answering service and only half a telephone bill on one line. My, how the business had changed!

All contracts for listings and commissions were taken on a small, 3"× 5" preprinted card that you carried in your shirt pocket. Listing information on one side and commission sales agreement on the other!

When you wrote a sales contract, it most often was a single-sheet contract. All you needed was a carbon copy or two. And we had a manual old Underwood typewriter that looked like it belonged in the Smithsonian and probably is there today. And nobody knew how to type in those days because kids did not grow up with computers and keyboards. Mom used the "hunt and peck" system like most other people, but she was pretty fast. She would make sure that I learned to type in high school (98 = A). I was good, I think, because I played the piano. And when I graduated, of course, I was awarded a brand-new Olivetti-Underwood Studio 44 manual typewriter with hard case, on which, I aptly applied myself for the next five years of college and law school. I still have it but have moved on to a computer now, thank goodness! Big improvement!

All in all, the real estate business was and has been very good for my family. There has been ups and downs for sure, but overall, it has been a wonderful undertaking. And I and my family have been richly blessed! Thank you, God!

Andrew Carnegie said, "More fortunes have been made in real estate than in all industries combined!" And we should all remember that... Under all is the land!

We are still going after fifty-nine years!

* * *

Another lesson not to be forgotten, taught by my dad, was that of "Educational Loafing." This was what you did when you had some free time. You'd go get a cup of coffee somewhere, you'd stop and look at the tractor for sale, you'd buy some corn from Farmer Brown, or you'd just go visit some of the businesses or friends in the area. You did this to learn and share and to expose yourself to opportunity (i.e., loafing with a purpose). It worked, and it was fun and you often came upon the most amazing things!

Taking on a Family

Family was very important! It had always been important to me, and I wanted my own family, but sometimes you really had to work at it hard! I don't know why things happen the way they do, but they do. And sometimes you have to try and try again to obtain your dreams and ideals. It took me twice myself, and in two tries, I think I got it right!

It was December 28, 1969, 3:00 p.m., at the Lithia Springs United Methodist Church. It was her church, but I had spent a lot of time there over the years for various reasons, but this time would be my first altar call for marriage.

Karen Sue Hoeflich would become my wife on this beautiful sunshiny day, three days after Christmas. The details I had shared earlier in this story, so now I would concentrate on the concept of taking on a family. Although this marriage did not end well, it did begin–like many things–very well and was certainly an exciting event in my life and hers!

After the traditional church service of matrimony, we left the church and all our friends and families, got into our little black 1960 Volkswagen Beetle, and were off to see the wizard of marital bliss!

We honeymooned in the gorgeous north Georgia mountains, in particular Vogel State Park. There was a nice little log cabin there with a cozy warm fireplace, and there was December snow on the ground. It was a winter wonderland just for us. Life was good!

After a few days, we made our way across the mountains, driving under Bridal Veil Falls on our way to Lake Toxaway, North Carolina, where we visited with the Johnson family. David Johnson, my first roommate (dorm mate) at Emory, lived there with his mountain family. They had a nice little home nestled in the hills on a small mountain pond overlooking the valley below.

They were mountain people from Appalachia through and through. Years before, David's father had built a beautiful home on Lake Toxaway–a resort lake–for Mr. Richardson of Atlanta, who had married the sister of Mayor Ivan Allen of Atlanta.

The families were very well off, and as a token of his appreciation to the Johnson family, he had sent Bud David's older brother–to Georgia Tech and now David to Emory University. On top of that, he purchased for them several new cars for graduations and such. Among them was a brand-new Pontiac GTO with a four on the floor he bought for David for completing his first year at Emory. It was a green beauty. Within two weeks, David–being the wild child he was–totaled the GTO (Gran Turismo Omologato, Italian for "ready to race"), and it was no more ready to race!

So then, Mr. Richardson said, "Son, I am not going to get you another four-speed. You can only have a three-speed." So then David got this shiny brand-new gold Chevrolet Camaro with a three-speed in the floor. That car David and I just about wore out on the mountain roads around his home and elsewhere!

Anyway, life in the mountains was good, and we all became intertwined in our ongoing lives as the years rolled on.

David's father had served in the army in World War II and was there and took part in the Normandy Invasion on D-Day on Omaha Beach. I was impressed about that, but you could never get Mr. Johnson to talk about it. Must have been some terrible memories to carry with you all your life. I remembered him as a very big man with very large hands–hands that had done a lot of hard work and hands that had fought a war on the other side of the Atlantic. I didn't push, but I was curious!

David would leave Emory after that first year and join the U.S. Army Special Forces in preparation for Vietnam. It was 1967 at that time when David was supposed to ship out the next day. That night, he suffered brain aneurysm and was rushed to the hospital, where for ten hours he struggled for his life. While on the operating table, the hospital–including the emergency room–experienced a total power failure and had to go on emergency battery backup! He almost died but didn't!

The doctors told him later that there had only been one chance in one hundred thousand that he would have survived. It was a miracle, but they also told him that he would never be able to walk again. It was not good news. By then, he was married to Linda from back home. Romance and love were so strong, you know, and you just can't keep a good man down!

For the next several years while I was at Emory, I would visit David regularly at the VA hospital on Clairmont Road, out near Emory. I would take him models to build to occupy his time and mind.

One day I went out, and David said he could walk. "Let's see," I said.

So he slowly but surely got out of bed, and with some help, we stumbled down the hallway. It was the beginning of a grand recovery. It wasn't long before David walked out of that hospital and walked away with Linda into their future. David went to seminary school and became a minister, and at last count, he and Linda had two beautiful children. They later visited my home, and we all had the best time swimming in the pool, cooking out, and playing with the children!

By then, I had been divorced, remarried, graduated college, left law school, had three children myself, and was in the real estate business. And all that was another story. My, how time flies!

* * *

On July 1, 1978, on a very hot summer day, I married Elizabeth Hill, whom I was engaged to for one week. We had dated for about six months since we had unexpectedly met at the World of Wheels Car Show in Atlanta!

Beth, my lovely Beth, and I had now been married for thirty-three-plus wonderful years. She too had been married and divorced after about five years, much like in my case. We came to the marriage altar as more mature, wiser older but still young adults. She had no children, and I had Heather, who was about five years old. She and I both took the leap of faith together!

I had almost broken up with her on a Sunday night because I was so scared about getting in deeper into our relationship. I was scared to death—and stupid!

By the next morning on Monday, I was miserable. I could not live with myself!

I called Beth at work. She was executive secretary to the personnel manager at Goodyear Tire and Rubber Co., a very high and flattering position to have obtained. I told her I was miserable and ask her if I could please meet her for lunch that day. She said yes, and I hurried off to Atlanta.

We went to Lum's Restaurant, home at that time of some of the best gourmet hot dogs in town. Wow, big spender! But Lum's was a nice quiet place that we both liked, with a nice, laid-back little atmosphere. It was the perfect place—the perfect place to ask Beth if she would marry me. To my delight and somewhat surprise, she said, "Yes. But when?"

"How about Saturday?" I said.

"What? This Saturday? . . . Okay," she said. "We will have to tell our families, and we'll have a nice small family wedding, just family and us."

"Great," I said. "Thank you so much. I love you so much, Beth, and I want to spend the rest of my life with you!"

"I love you too," she said. "And you will never find another who loves you the way I do and as much as I do!"

We were both so excited and then back to work or what we could do of work. We had a wedding to plan!!!–and not much time!

At first, we were going to elope, go to Callaway Gardens, and be married in the beautiful little chapel there on the pond. We had both visited there before, and we knew it would be perfect. But we didn't want to leave our families out of this joyous occasion. And they wanted to be a part of it!

So in the short run, my mother said she would put the wedding on at home on the farm, and we could be married in the yard under the big oak tree! Under the wedding tree–it was perfect!!!

Reverend–no, not reverend but rather Judge Robert Noland–family attorney, newly elected Douglas County superior court judge–agreed to do the honors. We were only the second couple he had ever married, and he wanted to be sure, he said, to "Use the right glue and enough of it!" Apparently, he did. His lovely wife, Betty, attended and helped him with the particulars and also graced us with her presence. We love them both!

Our families and close friends gathered on very short notice. Little Heather was the flower girl and stood with us, and a new book began for each and every one of us–a new book of love, life, and pursuit of happiness! Was this America and the land of opportunity or what!?!

By two o'clock pm, we were man and wife! By three o'clock, we had eaten the melted wedding cake, taken pictures, kissed everybody there, said our goodbyes, and were off to our new lives! Wow, what a rush! What a marvelous and wonderful experience! How exciting!!!

Our honeymoon took us by way of Atlanta and onto Savannah for several days of fun and games. We stayed at the old but luxurious Oglethorpe Inn in Savannah and took in some of the sites of that grand marquess city. It was a fabulous new beginning for two still young kids. At least we felt like kids, and we were definitely in love!

By the time we returned home, we adjusted ourselves to get back into the groove of work and making a living. We had much additional talking and planning to do. It would not always be an easy task, but we were up to it, and the future was ours and whatever we could make of it. And make of it we did!

* * *

Marrying Beth was the best thing I ever did! I am so thankful!!!

Finding Myself and My Place in the Business World

Finding one's self is not always easy. Who was I? Whom had I become? Who would I be in this old world? How would I relate to all the opportunities that surrounded me?

Business, I decided, would be my forte! Business of all kinds! I would, above all, be a businessman! This entailed a lot of concepts, but I was well prepared.

With a four-year degree in accounting, and a BBA from one of the leading universities, and with a year of legal training under my belt, and a fresh real estate license on the wall, I was ready to go!

A good arrangement was made with my Dad as broker of Ayres Realty Co., the family business, and Mother agreed.

I started out doing their bookkeeping while still at Emory in exchange for rent on one of their houses. Karen and I lived at 3351 Bankhead Highway, Lithia Springs, Georgia. I had remodeled the house myself and was intimately familiar with all its aspects.

I was riding a motorcycle at the time for some basic transportation, and the VW was our luxury car. At night, not trusting the neighborhood on the main highway, I would roll my motorcycle into the living room for safekeeping. In the morning, out it would go.

I learned that you could "rent" art, pictures, and such from the Carnegie Library downtown, so I graced our home with six-month rotating prints of the great art of the world, like Remington, Russell, Renoir, and others. It was a fun way to decorate and cheap–like nothing!

All our furniture was early American; "junk," I believe, pretty well described it. We never bought a new piece of furniture that I can remember. The only new thing we bought was a $149 black-and-white TV, which we had saved up for over the summer before we were married. It was quite a prize!

Later, having a small antique store on the side, we would acquire quite a few nice old pieces of antique furniture, including chairs, sofas, chests, and even a beautiful carved cherrywood upright piano. Times were improving, and so was the money. We were never rich but eating every day!

During the law school year, we lived in a barn apartment and then another small apartment in Austell, Georgia, on Euclid Street. Then finally, we got our first house that we owned. Actually, to be honest, Mom and Dad helped us buy it at 3252 Creel Drive, a nice little, two-bedroom den with one bath, an all-brick home for $15,400, and it had a single carport and patio.

That summer, I decided that I wanted a fireplace. So I took in the single carport for a nice expanded, sunken den, and I built myself a beautiful stone fireplace. I taught myself stonework skills from library books. The very first winter, we had a four-inch snow, and we felt so cozy and secure and enjoyed the fireplace so much. It was a blessing beyond words!

I also built a large sundeck on the back, accessed by glass sliding doors off the den. There were many nice features incorporated, like exposed cedar beams in the ceiling, posts and rails separating the den and dining room, and a nice credenza with storage and bookshelves. We had a raised hearth for the six-foot fireplace with a three-by-four-foot firebox, ash dump, and damper and a washer-dryer closet in the corner. It was a work of art. And I was so proud of it all!

Then later, I built "ye old toolshed" in the backyard. I dug the foundation, laid the block, and did all the framing, painting, and roofing. It was a labor of love, of which I was so proud because it was all built from salvaged materials. It served me well!

All this while, I was listing and selling real estate for a living. Remodeling and building was my hobby, and a good hobby it was! By the following year, in July of 1973, my oldest daughter, Heather, was born, and the family was growing. Being in real estate, it was time to make a move on the market.

By the next spring, we had sold the little new place for $28,000, including a 1957 red and white Ford convertible in trade. My friend David Peek was the proud new owner!

By summertime, we had built a brand-new house on an acre of land gifted by my parents on Lake Greystone Road, built by F. M. Womack and Son, finest builders in the area at that time. They did a great job. And this time, I put in two all masonry fireplaces, one stone and one brick. And I put in a library of my own!

"Closed on Sunday"

Ye Old Tool Shed

My wife and I, both being artists, loved color, so we put a different color carpet in every room in the house! It was awesome! Also, a sunken living room with the stone fireplace and more exposed, rough-cut cedarwood beams and a half-story upstairs. Three bedrooms and two colorful baths complimented the other special features we put in. It was indeed a thrill! A turnkey project! All we had to do was move in!

Later, we would build a hitching rail right in the backyard for the eventual five horses we would have. We had some good times, but it wasn't all paradise back on the ranch, and soon my world would all come toppling down!!!

* * *

Reasons for divorce don't always matter. It happens. We all know that from experience. But how we handle an upset like that can make all the difference in the world. To be compatible and civil is the best way to go, if you have to go through it.

Somehow, we got through it, and life moved on in other directions. She moved back home, and I later sold the house, for it was too sad to be there then. Actually, I traded my house to Barney Word, and I took his house on Fitzgerald Street in Lithia Springs, which I later sold to Donna Florence, another friend.

Fitzgerald Street put me off to a fresh start, but it was difficult starting over again. With visitation and shared time with my young daughter, my life took on a new routine of Wednesdays at 12:00 to 6:00 p.m. and every other weekend for some years, along with child support and occasional emotional baggage to deal with. It wasn't easy!

* * *

All this time, I kept selling real estate. At least I was going through the motions.

* * *

Success had found me in several other ways, if not marriage. By the time I was twenty-five in 1974, I was President of the Lithia Springs Ruritan Club, where I first met Mr. Newt Gingrich, our guest speaker one night. He looked at me and I at him, and he said, "Hey, we're wearing exactly the same suit. That's neat!" We were instant friends and have been ever since. Of course, Newt would go on to become speaker of the House of Representatives of the United States. And he may become our next president in 2012. We would see. I wish him luck!

Also, the same year, I had been fortunate enough to be elected President of the Douglas County Chamber of Commerce and, that year, hired the very first paid person for the chamber, our new secretary, Shirley.

Mr. Jim Gisi, a northern transplant, had been our first and free executive director for some time until his death. He was a selfless, giving, faithful, dedicated person to the Douglas County Chamber of Commerce, and we can be very thankful for his early involvement. He became a very dear and personal friend over the years. He was buried in the mausoleum at West View Cemetery in Atlanta, Georgia. I still miss him!

After being President, I wanted to do something just for fun and enjoyment. So I produced and later won an award from the chamber for creating a wonderful color slide program about the county. The slideshow used 360 slides, changing every five seconds, with music scored from the *Grand Canyon Suite*, I believe the Ray Conniff Orchestra. The copy was written by me and narrated by a professional disc jockey for WXIA radio station over on Westside Road, then owned by my neighbor George Purdy.

All in all, it was a great success and was used every place possible over the next several years to promote Douglas County, including at the opening of the Georgia World Congress Center in Atlanta the following year. It was fun, upbeat, and inspiring to see the beautiful pictures shot on 400-speed Ektachrome film, with a 135 Instamatic camera. I always said that good camerawork was good film, good lighting, and good composition!

* * *

Also, by 1978, I had been elected as President of the West Georgia Board of Realtors and that year became a state director for the State Board of Realtors of Georgia.

Well, there were a lot of people who had held these and many more important positions, but I was proud to have served my peer groups, and it was good to know that I had earned their respect. For that, I was most particularly thankful. And all this time, I was still selling real estate! Contacts didn't hurt!

* * *

By now, I had also learned to fly; bought a small airplane, a 1946 Ercoupe 415-C; and had my first–and only, I hope–forced landing down in South Georgia. And that was another story! But I was finding myself and who I was!

How to Make and Lose a Few Million Dollars

By now, real estate and I were on the same page, and we were on a roll!

I was buying and selling everything I could to make a dollar on–land, mostly, because it allowed me to be outdoors more, and I loved walking in the woods, working survey lines, dividing properties and being creative about making deals. It was fun too!

In the summer of 1981, my wife, Beth, and I traveled to Daytona Beach, Florida, to attend a seminar by Jim Stephens, a landman from Texas. Beth was very pregnant with our first child, Stephanie, and I thought she was going to blow at any time! But it was early yet, thank goodness!

At that seminar, we learned the secrets of making money with land, at least like in Texas. The concepts were good and solid, and Mr. Stephens had convinced us that he knew what he was talking about as a very unpretentious country boy who had made good, dealing in land and acreage in particular. Now he was older and had his own jet! I was impressed!

Of all people, we (my wife and I)–as the only licensed real estate broker and wife–won the big door prize, which was a hands-on assist in making our first big deal. It was fate! We came back home that summer and, within thirty days, bought a large tract of land in Douglas County from an owner incidentally residing in Texas, not Mr. Stephens!

Within those thirty days, we were able to purchase, survey, and presell the first tract; do a double closing; sell the second bigger tract; and option out the third and largest tract. We were done!

It took guts, finesse, fortitude, and determination to make it all happen. But we followed the book and plan, and the rest was history!

Today that 113 acres on Ephesus Church Road is the home of the Shiloh Children's Home, founded and established by Reverend Harold Howard and his son Reverend Happy Howard–visionaries for Douglas County and countless children who otherwise would be without!

From that day on, we were off and running from one deal to another. We, over the years, would purchase raw land deals, gristmills, log cabins, entire mountains, airfields and aviation properties, mobile home parks, historical properties, houses of all descriptions, and business properties too.

And we would live in many of these places as we raised our family through the years!

When Stephanie, our first daughter, was born, we lived in a nice brick ranch home with a pool that we ultimately moved into three times and away from three times. Imagine that!

When our son Ben was born, we lived in an old gristmill known as the Abernathy Mill up on the Big Tallapoosa River. We had one of the most memorable Christmases ever there, with a large snow falling on Christmas Eve. My mom, dad, and aunt Rebe–my mother's sister–were with us that Christmas, and it was the loveliest of times with the grand old fireplace and such. The mill was certainly a unique living experience for us as it had been previously remodeled into a private residence with central heat and air conditioning, silent flush commodes, and such by Dr. Julius Hughes, a retired dentist. Dr. Hughes had come on hard times, and incidentally, the old mill had stood vacant and abandoned for about three years when we came along.

My good friend–indeed my best friend in all the world–Jerry Frith and I first discovered the grown-up, abandoned place. We were awestruck by its condition and potential, the big Mill House itself, sitting as it did with two guesthouses, a 20' × 40' in-ground swimming pool, a small pond, and 3,000 ft. of rainbow trout river frontage, all on 23 acres of land!

"Jerry," I said, "how 'bout I buy it and you and your family move in and fix it up?"

"Okay, that's a deal," he said.

Well, to make a long story short, I made a very low offer on it and almost hoped they wouldn't take it–but they did. Yikes! And I had a tiger by the tail!

Jerry and his family never did move in, and Beth asked me one day what we were going to do with the mill.

"I guess we are going to move to the country," I said. And we did!

This Was Home

For six months, we didn't even get a telephone, and this was before the time when everyone had cell phones. We decided that if anyone wanted to see or talk to us, they could just come out to see us or write us a letter! It was sheer bliss! There were water shoals right outside the house! Rainbow trout and ambiance galore! It was the most beautiful and unique home we ever lived in, with all the architectural enhancements, including the millstones, wheels, shafts, and stonework, all on five different living levels! But there was a lot of work or rework to be done to bring it up to par, and we loved every minute of it, including the twenty-three copper pipe repairs I made personally. And when I had repaired the master bath plumbing, I turned the water on in the sink, and the water came out of the bathtub, I swear! I still don't know how! But, real plumber I was not, obviously!!!

The old mill would eventually burn to the ground, and we would sell the property, but we sure had some good times there! Fortunately, we did not live there at that time and the occupants were not injured! Thank goodness!

* * *

Real estate kept a-coming and a-going! We continued to make deals wherever and whenever we could!

We even bought a mountain near Bremen and developed it. We put a road on it so I could drive my Cadillac all the way up to the top, around a circle, and back down! It was a good way to show it and the tracts we divided up!

And we bought property we developed into an aviation community, in which we were still involved. We called it Ayresouth Fly-In Community for the flying enthusiast. Live and fly in your very own home, lot, and runway! Come in your front door, go out the back, get in your airplane, and be in Panama City, Florida, in two and a half hours! Nonstop!

A two-story log home caught our attention a few years later, and we moved to that farm and ultimately bought up about seventy-five acres or so. Mill Branch Farm we called it. It was like living in a state park where you came into the property over this little bridge and stream so picturesque, the pasture opened up, and there was the log cabin sitting on the hill in the distance! It was magical!

One of our best winters was spent there sliding down the long driveway hill on a four-inch snow. We used almost every piece of plastic off our old chicken house, making snow sleds those few days, until we and the kids, all three, were completely worn out! We loved that old log home! So when the 1990 recession hit us like a tsunami, everything for us just stopped but not our obligations!!! And we did have plenty by that time!!!

We were already involved with a large, three-hundred-acre tract of commercial and industrial land in Newnan, Coweta County. We had sold a good bit of it but were still struggling with the rest, and it was heavily financed.

Abernathy Mill

We had an auction sale with Roswell Realty and Auction Co. in an attempt to liquidate the holding and the debt. Three registered bidders came and signed up for this sale. Of course, with only three bidders, it was so low that all we could do was to have a "no sale," and back up, and punt!

It was one of the most disappointing times of our lives, and times would be tough and would get tougher. We moved to the old Bowden house we owned at the time of the grave-robbing family during the Civil War. The house also served as post office for Salt Springs as far back as 1850. Time was going backward, it seemed, and we were too!

In the next year or so, we regrouped, somehow survived, and never declared bankruptcy! I was always taught to pay your bills, and so we did, over a million dollars' worth! It took us over four million in equities to pay off one million of debt–four for one, you know. It was not easy, and it was a very humbling experience!

Had it not been for the stalwartness of my family, my wife and children, their love, understanding, and willingness to readjust, we would never have made it. But we did, and it wasn't too long before we were once again on the road to recovery. But it would take a while and much personal sacrifice!

* * *

After we left the Bowden house, we moved, of all places, back to Lake Greystone Road, the little house I had built back in 1973 or so.

Barney Word and his wife, Carolyn, had lived there still and had raised their two boys, Steven and Sam, there. They were moving on, so I took the opportunity to be near my parents, in fact next door. It was time to move closer to them and home as they were advancing in years. So "Red Bird Farm," as we called it, would be our new home for the next fifteen years or so, where our kids would all finish growing up!

One by one, they would be married–like me and Beth–under the old wedding tree, and life would move forward!

* * *

In the meantime, Beth and I had bought a V-tailed Beechcraft Bonanza–1947 S-35 model–with my good friend Jerry, and we (Jerry and I) would fly it across the Rocky Mountains back home to Georgia. We had been partners in a Christian flying missionary project called Wings over the Mountains, but it was over now. Jerry and I would start a new and exciting business called American Graphics Engineering Company. We would do business in seven states while we researched and built up a new prototype cut-and-glue labeling machine, the AGE.15000, for the graphic arts industry. We would even sell and collect for the first machine but, alas, could not perfect our design and deliver, and the business folded after losing a lot of my money. I decided enough was enough!

We kept the stove fire burning!

At one time, Jerry and I even had (not sure if by accident or similar taste) matching cars–same color, style, and year, Buick Electra diesel station wagons. It had to be a sign! Both cars went bad, but our friendship remained. There was certainly something to be said about friendships over the years, and despite our ups and downs, we had always remained as steadfast friends!

* * *

And I kept selling real estate all this time! And the world kept turning–only faster!

Douglas County Makes a Wave—The Big Kahuna

How to convert a major hospital into a big hardware store–lesson no. 126 on the "Road to Learning and the Environmental Treadmill of Economic Development" was about this!

First, you or somebody–in this case the Seventh-Day Adventist Church, Mr. and Mrs. Carter–would buy a prime piece of real estate next to the interstate in Lithia Springs and then proceed to build the finest, most modern round hospital in the world. You then staff it with the best medical staff in the world along with all the modern equipment of the day and open the doors for business!

Then–and but, I might add–you'd tell them they cannot have their usual hot coffee in the mornings or their beloved ground-meat hamburgers and a few other things, but they can have all the soy-based meat they wanted and a few other things they really didn't give a pea turkey about or for.

You'd run this business like a tyrannical boarding school for a few years until, one day, somebody would say, "Hey, who's gonna pay this big light bill?"

"Not me," said the hamburger-eating, coffee-drinking, cigar-smoking son-of-a-gun customer with the broken leg, "because I am going somewhere else so I can get all the not-so-good-for-me depravities of life that I just ain't gonna do without."

So, with that motto trumpeted for a few years, they soon had to turn off the beautiful, Rome-like fountain at the front door and put up a "For Sale" sign!

But this place was so big and so elaborate and had in it so many bedpans to empty, among other things, that nobody wanted to lay claim to such a jewel as a twelve-story seventeen-million-dollar behemoth that needed the grass cut, the light bulbs replaced, and the bedpans emptied!

I even took my son there one time when he had a motorcycle accident and busted his arm up. He was ten. His motorcycle, a Honda 70, was one. And the bill was about $350 or so. It was basically a good, even great, hospital!

Part of my responsibilities at that time, through the Chamber of Commerce, was teaching at the hospital a new employee orientation seminar to introduce them to the area and the county. It was fun, and I enjoyed it. It was a very upbeat and rewarding experience, and I met a lot of great folks.

But alas, one day the property had been up for sale for a long time with no newcomers to turn the water fountain back on. I loved that fountain! It was so beautiful and constantly reminded me of Rome, Italy, where I had once visited!

A big, six-foot-high chain-link fence now surrounded the premises. It was an eyesore, a real ghost of the past, and an eerie harbinger of the future!

Finally, a little hardware and home improvement company called Home Depot came along and basically said they would buy the land and build a new edifice if the seller would tear down the old and deliver the land in buildable condition!

They did, and it was, and it is today, what it is!!!

* * *

What bright light in yonder window shines? Shakespeare might have asked. *Is it a hospital of great regal design and grandeur? Or is it another Home Depot? A hardware store to be sure but much more, of course. Why, you can find anything your little heart desires in there. Only thing you can't find is your little heart. Your little hearts went like the blowing of the wind to another time and another place, never to return again!!!*

And I still like my coffee with a little cream and sugar, don't you?

The Secret of Arbor Place Mall

It wasn't supposed to happen like this. It just goes to show what big money and politics can do when they get together!

Early on, let's say in the early and midseventies of the late great last century, elaborate plans were underway to build an extravagant shopping mall right here in Douglas County but not where it would be today. It was to be built on the best ground old Douglas County had, in my opinion, right in the middle of the old Silver Creek Ranch. Now you might ask, "Where the heck was that?"

Just over the creek, Sweetwater Creek, that is, from Old Salt Springs was about a four-hundred-acre ranch known as Silver Creek Ranch. It was almost encircled, at least on three sides, by Sweetwater Creek. There were no roads there, no buildings, no houses, or anything significant, save a few old sheds and an old house and barn on the ranch. Old Alabama Road, the main drag, looked at it from the east side as it came across from Old Sweetwater Town (New Maxham Road area) along the east side of Sweetwater Creek up to Old Salt Springs. My daddy said that, at that point, there was an old traveling gypsy camp in a glade of trees on the riverbank and a swinging footbridge that traversed the creek (now Highway 6 or Thornton Road). That was all!

Today there is a four-lane highway and bridge there! It is called Thornton Road after Thornton Chevrolet, the first business to locate there down toward the I-20 end. So now a nice big road went right down through the middle of Silver Creek Ranch. At one point, the land went up for sale, and my daddy said he could have bought the entire four hundred acres or so for $185,000. But that was a lot! Especially in those days! He was a little short on the moola but had a great insight for the future!

Not long thereafter, the land was acquired by the Atlanta Braves Baseball Organization. It seemed certain, by rumor, that the farm would become a winter or summer training facility of some kind, and this would be great. But alas, this did not happen, and the land remained relatively unused and undeveloped—until somewhere along 1970 or so, when a big outfit developer from Australia came along and realized the great potential this land had for the placement of a regional mall. Hooker-Barnes was soon the new owner and soon-to-be developer of this mammoth new undertaking! Boy, once again, Lithia Springs, Salt Springs, Deerlick, or whatever you called it was going to be back on the map—and big time!

Sir Leslie Hooker and Mr. Barnes had some great plans for their new mall! Working alongside the local Douglas County Chamber of Commerce and the local business community, enthusiasm was growing wildly. They even decided to throw what you might call a "down under" party. That was Australian for "let's get this newfangled show on the road as time's a-wastin'." A big party and reception was set, which I personally attended, along with every other businessperson in town and two real, live kangaroos bouncing around the party floor, free as two jaybirds. It was quite comical and very Aussie—and a lot of fun!!!

But the unexpected happened just when you didn't expect it, of course. Within just a very short time, Sir Leslie Hooker, the big moneybag from Australia, and his American counterpart, Mr. Barnes, both passed away in a rather untimely manner, leaving this grand scheme to also soon realize its own timely demise. There was no resuscitation for this calamity of events. It was the end of the line!!!

Today that very land would be known as Westfork Industrial Park and was bisected by the very busy and very successful Thornton Road and Maxham Road and connected to Interstate 20 West!

* * *

Plans for a large regional mall went stagnant for many years afterwards. The momentum was lost, and it took many years to overcome the fact that the timing and money for a large regional mall was just very slow in coming round again!

But it did finally—in Douglasville, in one of the most unexpected locations you could imagine, right on top of the middle of Anneewakee Creek and the city reservoir, the main water supply for the city of Douglasville, Georgia, our county seat! But there was something unique about this location, besides being a major wetland area—it was next to the interstate. Voilà! It was magic! All you had to do was put in 1,500 feet of tunnel for Annawakee Creek, shift the wetlands downstream, and build the mall on top, parking lot and all. And they did!!! They—we wouldn't specify—built this beautiful gigantic regional mall, Arbor Place Mall, right in the very most unlikely place to build a mall you ever did see! In the finer recesses of the mall proper, they even paid a sort of tribute to the history of the wetlands and how they were recovered and enlarged downstream, how wonderful it would be today, how happy all the beautiful wildlife would be, and what a fine home it would be today for these animals!

Hardly anybody knew the real secret of the mall; furthermore, I didn't think very many people really cared. What was important was that *they* got the mall where they wanted it, next to the interstate, along with ten thousand parking spaces or so. No small feat for a conservatively conscious society "obsessed" with doing the right thing environmentally! Yeow!!!

I am still scratching my head on this one! Meanwhile, I am one of Borders Bookstore's best customers, and their coffee is not bad either! C'est la vie!!!

* * *

Now Borders is gone, having met an economic demise, and we are still searching for that elusive cup of coffee, along with our books!!!

The Shock of September 11, 2001, and Other Times

In July and August of 2001, my son Ben and I had just completed almost a five-thousand-mile, three-week odyssey jeep trip from Georgia to Montana by way of Oshkosh, Wisconsin, and the Experimental Aircraft Association International Fly-In.

About the middle of July, we loaded Ben's 1998 Jeep Wrangler with everything we could for camping and traveling, including the Bible for protection, a big bowie knife for comfort, and an entire sack of delicious, nutritious, Vidalia onions! Yum! We set out on a strange trip to Oshkosh and to see the northwestern United States, at least as much of it as we could during our allotted time and money.

At the fly-in, we camped next door to the NASA team from Houston, Texas. While Ben and I were eating our beanie weenies and Vidalia onions, they were having catered food brought in and their own private chefs. They offered for us to join them on one occasion, and I wished we had, but the company of astronauts that day was just a little overwhelming, especially when they got a telephone call from one of their buddies in outer space. We could always tell the location of our campsite in Camp Schuler, among forty-thousand-plus campers, by the high-flying flag of Texas, the Bonnie Blue Flag. So we never got lost. Upon leaving the spectacular event of Oshkosh at Steve Wittman Field, we made our way across the state to Madison and then to Spring Green, Wisconsin, home of the House on the Rock and Taliesin, three-time home of Frank Lloyd Wright, which incidentally burned twice!

The House on the Rock was the most amazing place! Built on a rock pinnacle, so many people were curious of Alex Jordan's strange home (he never lived there) that his father told him he should start charging a small fee to show it. One thing led to another and another and another, and before you or he knew it, there were buildings all over the place housing worldwide collections of everything imaginable. It was an amazing place to see!!!

Equally intriguing was Taliesin, home of Frank Lloyd Wright, built in the Wyoming Valley, where he grew up at his grandparents farm and where he was buried at the Unitarian church he later designed. The story behind it all is legend, and while there, I wrote a song–a ballad really–"The Ballad of Frank Lloyd Wright, the Great Architect." You may hear it on the radio one day!

Then we were off to many other exciting places like Devils Tower, where we played golf one beautiful day; the carving of Crazy Horse; Mount Rushmore; Jewel Cave; Deadwood, South Dakota; Sturgis and the big bike rally; and the Little Bighorn in Montana!

At that time, my good friend Jerry–having lived in Idaho before with his first wife, Jean–now lived in Newell, South Dakota, near Sturgis and the Belle Fourche Reservoir. He had a new wife, Susan, and a daughter, Leighanna, and they owned a six-hundred-acre ranch just outside town with all the trimmings of barns, water canal, nice home, the works. He grew hay, had and managed cattle and horses, and generally lived the good life!

Ben and I stayed with them for three days and used the ranch as a base headquarters as we went out and ran around the country!

Jerry's son, also named Ben, lived up there too, and he hung out with us some. It was a lovely place but very windy and cold in the wintertime. After three years of that, they had to come back to Georgia and warmer weather!

While there, though, Sturgis and the big bike rally were in full throttle. Three hundred thousand people descended on that tiny city, and most of them were on motorcycles. It was crazy but fun! Ben and I were, of course, there by jeep, but no one really knew, and no one cared. It was just all one big blowout. It inspired us all to get new Harley-Davidsons when we got back home, and we did!!!

The trip was absolutely one of a lifetime for Ben and me! By the time we got back, we had developed a whole new respect for a father/son relationship. We had learned about each other and ourselves. We were not the same two people–we were transformed into two maniac roving cowboys who just came in from out on the range! Neither I nor Ben would take a million dollars for that experience. Later, on another trip, we would visit the southeastern United States. We had just gotten settled back in when, in the morning of September 11, 2001, we–like all America–heard and actually saw on TV the terrible news. Two airliners hijacked and flown by Muslim radicals of al-Qaeda had crashed into the Twin Towers in Lower Manhattan of New York City. Within minutes, almost the two buildings were totally destroyed and only a pile of rubble! They had collapsed because of the excessive heat of the fuel spill and fire, literally melting the steel superstructure and collapsing under its own weight. About three thousand Americans died that day. Another airliner went down into the Pentagon in Washington DC, and another thwarted effort with an airliner in Pennsylvania was believed to be headed for the White House. Several hundred heroes perished there also in a Pennsylvania field as the passengers stormed two hijackers, and they all crashed into a vacant field!

America was under attack! We were at war!!! Or soon would be or something. It was so confusing that it took a while to figure it all out!

Ultimately, we attacked Iraq for having weapons of mass destruction and harboring al-Qaeda and the radical Muslims of the Taliban under Saddam Hussein. We would initiate an invasion of Iraq and capture, try, and execute Saddam Hussein, and the Iraq War was on.

Finally, it was over, and we moved into Afghanistan, where the Russians had failed earlier because of the mountains and rugged terrain. Now we fought on in an effort to localize and eliminate for good the Taliban and al-Qaeda in Afghanistan, Pakistan, and anywhere else they were hiding out.

Homeland Security was greatly heightened and remained on high alert. This country and the entire world would never be the same.

A new strain of living had developed between Muslims and non-Muslims here and throughout the world, not unlike the great Crusades of the past, where millions died fighting over the Holy Land all in the name of religion.

What was so good about any group that sought to annihilate everyone else that didn't agree with them?

We must learn to be tolerant and develop forbearance for one another, without which, then, there would never be any peace again!!!

* * *

The next thing my family did was to go out and buy more guns and ammunition! We knew there was going to be a war here before we could be adequately prepared. Today we stay prepared, and unfortunately, all Americans should remain alert and prepared!!!

* * *

Recently, on September 11, 2011, this year, after ten years, a fitting memorial was dedicated on that very site and the others, lest we forget.

Now, in the year 2019, One World Tower, has risen in the new skyline over Manhatten, demonstrating our resolve and resealance for a new age!!!

The Flood of 2009

It was September 22, 2009, Tuesday afternoon at three twenty. The sun was shining in a mostly blue sky, punctuated with renegade white cumulus clouds. The big storms were over. Occasionally, you'd even see an airplane or helicopter sightseeing over the newfound water wonderland.

For almost two days now, I had been in doubt regarding the dry safety of our other real estate branch office on Thornton Way, just off Thornton Road. My wife and staff had most recently taken over that location after the previous owners had left. Now it was our ball game!

My old and main office was up in old Lithia Springs on solid high ground next door to the bank. It was convenient and well protected from most elements save the occasional car that crashed through the end wall of my building or the occasional tornado that destroyed the Methodist church across the highway and railroad in 1898. Of course, we were not here then, thank goodness, but now it was flooding!

Not in all my sixty-one years had I witnessed such a devastating flood in this area. You just wouldn't believe it unless you saw it with your own eyes!

Sweet, lazy old Sweetwater Creek twisted and turned all around this entire area of Douglas County and, indeed, much of the West Georgia area, including Paulding and west Cobb Counties. It almost encircled Austell, Georgia, on its way to Sweetwater Creek Wilderness State Park and down to the Chattahoochee River. Today I tried to go down to our other office, but all the access roads were flooded. At the main drag intersection of U.S. Highway

78 and Thornton Road, traffic was cut off in two directions, east and south. You could either turn around or turn left and go up to Humphries Hill, where you were faced with a similar dilemma. And it was like this all over, with major and minor traffic arteries flooded and underwater, bridges washed away, roads washed out, trees down, and so on.

Seven persons had already lost their lives as of this writing in the past day and a half, four in Douglas County alone. It was bad!

The floods were no respecter of person or property. Clarkdale Elementary School was inundated with about eight feet or more of water, and all the children had to be evacuated. Houses, homes, and businesses were buried beneath the water either completely or partially. Seventeen counties in the Atlanta metro area have been declared disaster areas. Most counties got five to ten inches of rain in twenty-four hours. The worst areas—including parts of Douglas, Paulding, and Cobb Counties—received fifteen to eighteen inches of rain in twenty-four hours. The old one-hundred-year flood level had just bumped itself up considerably. Now it was a five-hundred-year flood level!!!

Now we might want to speculate on why this occurred, if you got to scratch your head hard enough. With the excessive drought we had just been through the past couple of years, when all the lakes, rivers, and streams dried up, this was just payback, a correction in the tables of nature as an economist might word it. After all, they said an economist and a meteorologist were the only people who can be wrong all the time and still have a job. I believe that to be true with my years of observation. However, somehow God—in his infinite wisdom—decided we needed a little extra water; and by golly, we got it!!!

Most of the water levels had just crested within the last hour or so at some extreme unprecedented high level. It was going down slowly. It may take days; nobody really knew. But one thing was for sure—nobody was going to be doing any rain dances anytime soon unless it was backwards, and that was the truth!

And I still didn't know if the new office was submarine, subterranean, or just gone. Maybe like a lot of others, I'd find out tomorrow!

* * *

As a postscript to the above, it turned out that the other office was safe! The water had come within a few feet of the door and ultimately receded! Boy, were we lucky! Others were not!!!

Old Barns and Weddings

Well, let me tell you about the barn—I mean, *the* "Barn!"

It started out as just a new version of an old idea. We had always had a barn on the farm, sort of. Actually, it was a larger corncrib converted into a cow and horse barn. It had an elevated floor about two feet high or so on brick pillars with two doors and a divider in the middle. It had a gabled roof of tin with long hinged fold-down windows on the sides for providing maximum ventilation.

We modernized the corncrib by building a hay manger shed on the northwest side, a lean-to cowshed on the southeast side with a couple of stalls, a chicken pen yard on the northerly side, and a small coral with a loading ramp for cattle on the southwesterly side. It was grand in a sort of way. It was everything we needed, and it was an adequate distance from the house. My brother, Gordon, and I dug a ditch for a waterline to the barn after what seemed like many years of hand-hauling water. Two five-gallon buckets or so of equal weight were best and kept one balanced. I always said that was the reason my arms were so long, thirty-five to thirty-six inches, and my shoulders were so broad.

We had a couple of milk cows from time to time, and Gordon always did the milking. One time he got gored pretty bad when Daisy threw her horned head toward him, I think to catch a cow fly. Didn't break the skin, but it bruised him up pretty good. Daisy was a beautiful Guernsey milk cow. Once, we had a Jersey milk cow; and boy, could she give the milk. It was common for us to go through a gallon of milk almost at one sitting for dinner. Mmmm, good fresh milk from the farm. Went good with those fresh chicken eggs for breakfast too.

"Lets go gals!"

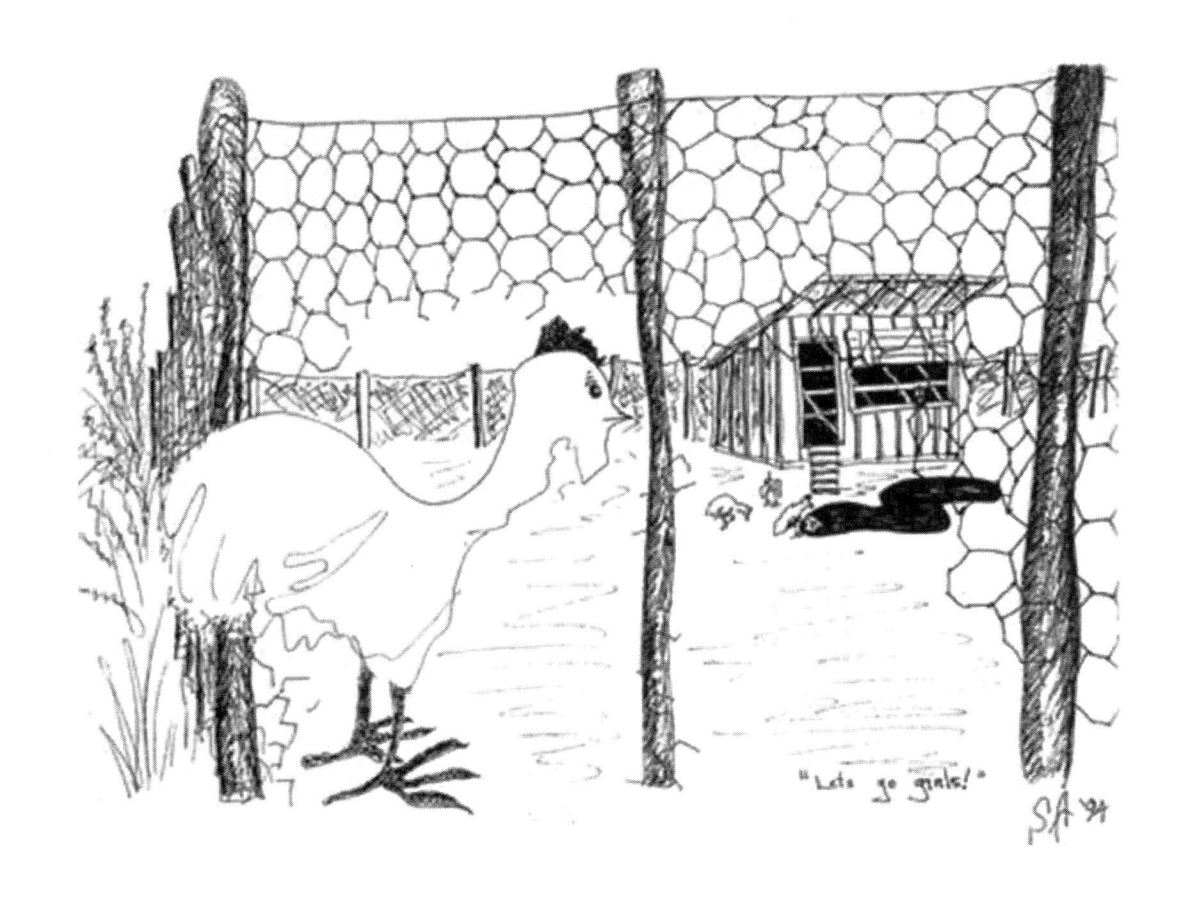

So that was pretty much our barn for as long as I can remember. However, before my generation, there had been a large livestock barn on the farm, which had burned to the ground in around 1936. One barn party too many, I think!

Also, there had been a log smokehouse for ham and bacon directly behind the house, an outside well shed over the well, and a privy outhouse. Yeah, we were modern with two bedrooms and one path. And we had running water–you ran and got it! It wasn't long before we added a pump to the well and real indoor plumbing–simple but sufficient. We tore down the dilapidated log smokehouse, renovated the old farmstead home, and started over with a new generation of living!

I always said we had just a little room on the inside of the house, but we had a lot of room on the outside! It was and still is a wonderful home. I live there today once again with my wife, Beth, after being away over the years and living in many other wonderful and interesting places.

The common thread here is that we have had the joy of four weddings over the years right here on the farm!!!

The first was on July 1, 1978, when my wife, Beth, and I were married in the front yard underneath the giant ancient oak, hence known as "The Wedding Tree." And ever since, one by one, all our children–two girls and a son–have married their beloved under and around that same old oak wedding tree. What a blessing of unknown proportions! It was a joy to be married here myself, a small gathering of family and close friends. No time for much planning or written invitations but beautiful nonetheless. And now we were going on thirty-three years. Wow! (Now forty-two years – Wowsers!!!)

Then our oldest daughter, Heather, married Matt McKay from Bremen, Georgia, on September 7, 1996. Heather is my daughter with my first wife, Karen, born in July of 1973. Heather was only five years old when Beth and I married and started this new tradition. Now she was all grown up and getting married herself after finishing college at the University of Georgia in Athens.

Her wedding was magnificent and sweet. It brought back sweet memories of many years ago. The weather was fine and clear. A gazebo had been built under the wedding tree, and this was where they were wed by Reverend Dr. Robert L. Whitmire, pastor of our church at Lithia Springs First Baptist. His sweet wife, Roxanne, attended and assisted. We loved them both dearly!

The marriage has been a great success, and they now have a little girl, Samantha, just six years old at present, who is the love of our life. She is a McKay, but she has very deep "Ayres" roots! Just ask the old wedding tree!

In 2003, September 20, our beautiful daughter Stephanie married the handsome Andrew Godfrey, whose mother is Judie Nails Godfrey, having married Edwin, her lifelong sweetheart. Judy and I and an entire small class of friends went to school together in Douglas County for grades 1 to 12 and graduated together in 1966—class of '66. It was and is a joy to know that our legacy lives on in the lives of our children!!!

Stephanie and Andrew were married in the front yard under the wedding tree. It was the most beautiful autumn day ever to behold! The leaves were brown and gold, and it was like a paradise of color!!! How blessed we are!!!

The Reverend Dr. Robert L. Whitmire and his lovely wife, Roxanne, again did the honors. He did such a beautiful and meaningful ceremony. The joy that day was spectacular, and once again, I had the profound pleasure and satisfaction of walking another daughter down the aisle to give her away. It was hard! It was difficult! It was kinda sad! But you know what? It was a joyous thing, and tears welled up in my eyes when the preacher said, "Who gives this bride?"

And I said, "Her mother, me, and her brother." She was so beautiful!

Today Stephanie and Andrew had come a long way, having owned a couple of homes and having lived as far away as Villa Rica. We were now glad to have them back home in Lithia Springs, Georgia, along with their two little "granddogs"; we called them, Sadie Mae and Nellie Belle, two amazing, vivacious miniature schnauzers. They keep them and us busy!

Then one day our bachelor son, Benjamin, decided he was going to tie the knot!

A young lady by the name of Amanda Mathis and her little girl of two years old had captured his heart while meeting in college at Kennesaw State University. They had a couple of classes together and, I believe, shared some homework assignments. They both knew a good thing when they found it.

Ben had been a world traveler, even by his young age, and had been the pick of the litter when it came to boys. Not only had he traveled extensively but he also had early entrepreneurial skills that led him to start his own business in the computer field and other areas. He was and is a smart fellow with a good, level head on his broad shoulders and six-foot-four frame. He was a man's man as I liked to say!

Amanda was a marvel of the feminine mystique. She was beautiful, loving, trustworthy, and a great cook. Her little girl, Alivia or Ali as we called her, was what sealed the deal with her and Ben.

From the start, it was a package deal, and Ben knew how lucky he was to be getting two for one! The day of their wedding was November 22, 2008, at two o'clock, another beautiful fall day with bright colors and sunshine. The old wedding tree, which sadly had to be cut down a few years before, was now a memorialized stump, immortalized by the poem "The Wedding Tree." The ceremony was held just across the yard under the big old chestnut tree as it was the honoree that year. The old oak stump stood sentinel and silent guard to the auspicious occasion. Honors were performed once again by the Reverend Dr. Robert L. Whitmire and his lovely wife, Roxanne, who was his constant companion, except on the golf course, I think. Dr. Whitmire's words were reverent and magical as he recalled all the previous weddings on this hallowed ground. He sealed the ceremony with words of love, humility, and God's everlasting goodness to mankind—and the joyous nature of marriage!!!

Ali was the flower girl, and she took particular pride and joy in being an important part of the celebration!

Afterward, there was a reception in a great, big rented tent out in the middle of the pasture, where all the festivities were held, complete with dance floor and lots of good food and drink! What a party ensued!!!

Just before dark, a helicopter landed in the pasture; and shortly thereafter, Ben and Amanda left the farm in an aerial escape as darkness began to fall on Honey Acres. It was unbelievable and very memorable. I'd never forget it. They were on their way to Atlanta Airport and the next day to California and Yosemite National Park for their honeymoon—a long way from Lake Greystone Road. Their life together had really taken off!!!

Now things had settled down just a little bit—a new home or two, a new business or two, and a new grandchild, Emmeline Elizabeth Ayres. She was the striking image of her daddy and a blessing to us all!

Ali was the joy of our lives and quite the young aviator, having flown with her grandfather Walt Mathis in his private plane when she was only five years old and since. She knew all the ups and downs and had had some rather good experience at her young age. Since both her grandfathers were private pilots and had airplanes, she can't miss! Well, the story of the barn was like the story of our life. It was a long story, and we were still getting around to it. It had been quite an adventure along the way. Perhaps we would move on in another part and talk about the "new" barn. It was a dilly! So next time, meet me at the barn, and I'll tell you all about how to make an old dream come true!!!

The New Barn and More

Old dreams do come true–it just takes time, determination, and money! The new barn was one of those kinds of dreams!

For some time, we had planned for a new barn. Dad had passed on May 28, 2008, essentially from old age at eighty-five, and we were still reeling from his passing. He could have built a barn had he seen the need, but he didn't, and now it was up to me, my wife, and my mother. We were working with a builder who had built a cabin for us on the lake. He had done a pretty good job too!

As we progressed, I drew out a plan for a barn on a napkin, and Mother drew a conceptual picture or two. I even went down to Franklin, Georgia, to see another barn he had built. He did a good job, but it cost a lot of money!

We were looking to spend a lot less than he quoted, so it probably couldn't be done, and he knew it. I imagined that was why he became more and more difficult to reach and get any response.

We got anxious, and then the unexpected happened. Mother passed away quietly on October 5, 2009, at eighty-four, and she had been so intent on getting the barn started. It was too late for her, but we were determined to turn that plan into a reality!

After mother's funeral, I was expressing to Jerry about our frustration over building the new barn.

"I'll build you a new barn if you want me to. I would love to put my mark on this old farm if there is a way," he said.

"When can you start?" I asked.

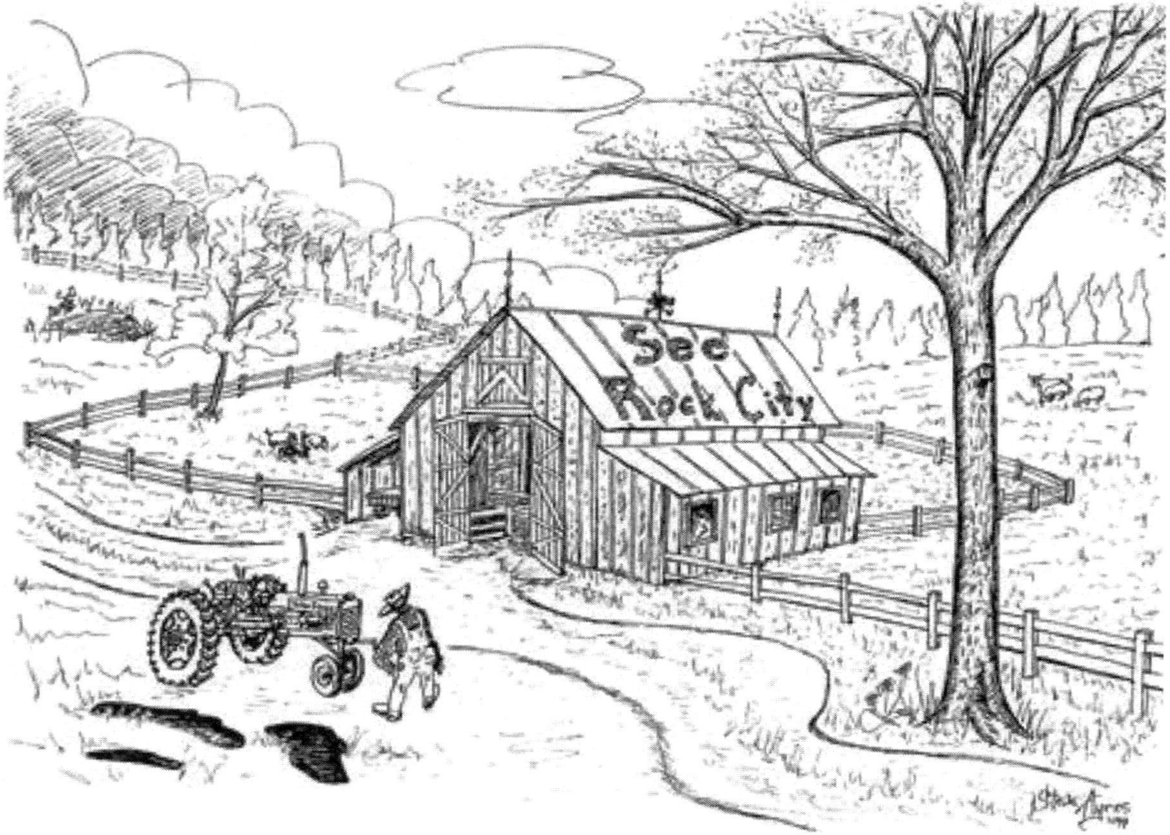
See
Rock City

"Is Monday too soon?" he said.

"No, perfect. You're hired."

And we started the new barn on Monday morning at eight o'clock! We had the site already picked out, and we had the plan on a napkin and a few sheets of paper, what more did you did!?!

Beth and I wanted to revitalize the old farm after years of inattention and dormancy. Mom and Dad had been satisfied, but now it was to be our home. We wanted to make the farm feel alive again for our kids and the grandchildren. We wanted to have horses again and cows and chickens and goats and a place people, friends and family could gather and have fun and fellowship like no other place on earth! And we wanted to put the "Honey" back in Honey Acres too!

Finally, toward the end of February 2010, Jerry A. Frith, master barn builder, and his son Daniel Frith, junior master barn builder, had built for us the most magnificent barn in northwest Georgia! I'd been told by more than one person just the very same!!!

It was a beauty with seven 12' × 12' horse stalls, a washroom with hot and cold running water, a tack room/office with picture window and refrigerator, a 14' × 60' grand hallway to front and back, a staircase room and passageway to a 12' × 60' open-air, covered gathering porch with rocking chairs and picnic tables, another 12' × 60' side shed on the opposite side, and a hay loft that would probably hold three thousand bales of hay or three hundred square dancers! All was wired and plumbed with lights and four ceiling fans on the porch and running water. It was built from ponderosa pine–roughly cut, one side exposed, board and bated, and now left in the natural wood color for the time being. It is the pride of the farm!!!

On Easter Sunday in 2010, we hosted seventy-five people for Easter dinner and an egg hunt! On Mother's Day, we had another big crowd and several times since! We were so proud of the barn and of Jerry and Daniel for building it for us. It did cost just a bit over our original budget, but we thought it was worth it to make the dream into reality!

We also wanted to build a nice new swimming pool for everyone to enjoy, and we did with the able help of Brown's Pools of Douglasville, Georgia. We chose an oasis style and even added a customized water feature using old millstones from Carroll County furnished by Ben that he had purchased from an old estate. The whole family has really enjoyed this addition to the farm, especially on those hot summer days! We also added about five miles of riding trails for the horses and an airfield for my Piper PA-12 Super Cruiser!

The old farm had really been transformed, but we were still working on it. Seeding and other projects like fencing seemed to go on forever, and

I suspected they would for some time. But we already had chickens laying sometimes eight eggs per day, as well as dogs, cats, horses, goats, cows, and now a pig. What was a farm without hogs, right? And the honeybees were reestablished. Last summer, the bees produced over 100 lbs. of honey. Life was getting sweeter by the day. Thank you, God, for all your blessings!!!

4 Alivia Mathis 4-14-09

My Grandpa Steve liv
in a big red house on a
peaceful farm. We like to
go on hikes. Sometimes
we find animal tracks. We
even found owl pelets.
I like to go fishing too.
My Grandpa Steve knows
a lot about the farm.
My Grandpa Steve is as
wise as an owl.
By Alivia Mathis

wise as an owl

wise _____ as an owl

"The New Old Homeplace"
BJF 2011

Adventures on Motorcycles

Somehow, I would be remiss if I did not include some commentary on motorcycles!

The two-wheeled wonders came along early in my life while I was still in college. My personal primary transportation for a period of time was a 125cc Sears Allstate Motorcycle with a kick start, a true and legal street bike that delivered 129 miles per gallon on regular gasoline! Wow!

When I first got this motorcycle, I was still at Emory University, so I took it down to Candler Lake Park on the Emory campus and taught myself figure eights, left and right turns, balancing, stopping, starting, and so on. It was a real training exercise. Finally, I felt as though I was ready to take on the real world and real-world traffic. And that, on a motorcycle, can be very intimidating, especially in Atlanta! But one thing led to another and another!

On my first trip home to the farm, however, I was coming down one of the local dirt, gravel roads. Just about a mile from home, I hit some bad ruts and gravel, and–swoosh!–down I went like a flipped pancake. A car came along just about that time, and a nice lady got out and asked if I was all right. I said I was, got up, and thanked her for stopping. Aside from a few scrapes, minor scratches, and a little bruised ego, I was okay. I picked up the bike, kick-started it again, and was on my way. Never again did I look at loose gravel the same way. It was a valuable lesson. As time passed, the bikes changed with the years from Hondas to Kawasakis to Yamahas to Harleys. There were several along the way!

One of my last big bikes was a beautiful Honda Silver Wing. Not to be confused with the Gold Wing! It had all the bells and whistles and was a shaft drive. The kids loved to ride on it when they were little. But somehow it just never felt like *my* bike. I think it was because it sat with a high center of gravity. At any rate, I finally sold it and moved on.

In more recent years in around 2004 or so, my son-in-law Andrew bought a brand-spanking-new Harley-Davidson Night Rider. He was so cool! He would later acquire several others and keep moving up the line until he had several big touring bikes! He and my daughter Stephanie would make long (two-thousand-mile) vacation trips on their motorcycles and leave us all gasping at their adventures!!!

It wasn't long before the fever bit my son, Ben, and he purchased a brand-new Harley-Davidson Deluxe in 2004. Blue and white, it was the cat's meow. It was a real hog and absolutely gorgeous!!!

Old Dad here was having a little motorcycle withdrawal himself, and drooling over their beautiful big machines did not help!

On Halloween Day in 2005, old Dad bought his own 2006 Heritage Softail Classic–a fire-engine red with charcoal trim, saddlebags, windshield, and the works. It was a real beauty! My dad too would have been proud! Now I would be able to chaperone the kids on my own bike again and get in on some of the fun!!!

Over the years, we all have made many adventurous rides all over the country. It has been a thrill a minute, a fantastic hobby and passion and I would not trade it for the world!!!

Most recently, my wife, Beth, and I made a three-day trip in the beautiful fall weather to Dollywood at Pigeon Forge, Tennessee. As motorcycle parking was at the very front in the parking lot, we were able to park right next to the entrance and just walk in. We had a great time seeing all the sights and finally departed about dark for the Old Mill Restaurant, where we had a sumptuous meal!

The next morning, we had a big breakfast by a roaring fire and then loaded up on our Harley to head for the hills of the Great Smoky Mountains. A cold front was moving in, and the weather was changing. By about noontime, it began to rain, and we rode the next five hours all the way home in a cold, soaking, off-and-on rain. When we rolled in, we were exhausted but in a good way, and we were finally home. Neither one of us would take a million dollars for that trip!!!

The bonds of love, togetherness, and friendship that you experience on a motorcycle are like no other. It is hard to explain. You just have to be there and be a part of it. I am so thankful for all the good times and experiences we have had riding alone, together, and with groups of riders who shared this common bond–groups like the Austell Friendship Riders, the Traveling Masonic Men, Harley Owners Group (HOG), and many others. Thank you, all, for enriching our lives with a sense and thrill of adventure that has been like no other! "Kick stands up at 9:00 a.m. Don't be late! We're moving out! Ride safe and ride often!!!"

Adventures with Airplanes

It was Monday morning, April 10, 1985, almost eight o'clock, when I picked up Jerry Frith, my old-time friend. Some time had passed since we had first entered a partnership to purchase a 1947 V-tail Bonanza for the flying missionary ministry founded by Jerry, called Wings over the Mountains.

Caleb, a biblical name meaning "God's right arm," was the name of Jerry's first airplane, a Stinson Voyager tail dragger. It had served him well as he worked his territory out of Coeur d'Alene, Idaho. Settled in the land of the Nez Percé Indians on the plateau between the Cascade Mountains to the west and the Rocky Mountains to the east, it was and is a beautiful land of spectacular scenery, with rivers and plains surrounded by mountains.

One day Jerry was out flying, and the weather began to deteriorate. Snow was in the forecast, and the cloud ceilings began to plummet. Before long, he found himself closed in up a box canyon. There was snow on the ground and drifts several feet high already. He spotted a small farm and open area. It wasn't the greatest place to land, but it was better than the alternative. So, he brought old *Caleb* down for a soft field landing. Just when everything looked pretty good, and he was pretty sure he had made it, down went the landing gear in the new fresh snow, and before he could do anything else, *Caleb* flipped up on his nose and over inverted! Ouch!!! Now there was only silence as the engine shut down, and the reality set in. Jerry unbuckled his seat belt, fell out of the cockpit upside down, and began to examine the damage. He was fine, but the airplane was not. For all practical purposes, it was rather severely damaged and might not see the sky again, at least for a while!

Jerry looked around, and seeing a faint light in the window of the yonder farmhouse, he began making his way across the snow-covered cornfields in the late evening.

Upon arriving at the front door, he knocked, and soon a little old lady and her farmer husband opened the door. They were somewhat startled to have a visitor at this hour and during a snowstorm too.

After drying off by a warm fire and having explained the reason for his impromptu visit, they would all sit down for a nice hot supper.

"I didn't know why," the old lady said. "But God just told me to put on an extra piece of meat tonight. So I put an extra one in the skillet."

"I sure do appreciate it and y'all's hospitality," Jerry said.

"You can stay over with us tonight in the extra room and see about your airplane tomorrow. Get yourself a good night's rest," said the old farmer.

So that night, Jerry got a good meal, a hot shower, and a good night's rest. Tomorrow would be another day!

As it turned out, the insurance company "totaled" the airplane. Just too expensive to fix for their taste. It was another lame bird to be laid on the scrap heap of unflyable airplanes. But as the old saying went, "Any landing that you can walk away from is a good landing." Jerry would fly again, even if *Caleb* didn't!

A few weeks had passed when Jerry called me up all excited on the phone from Idaho.

"Steve, this is ole Jerry. Guess what?" he said.

"What's up, old friend?"

"You know they totaled the Stinson, but I've got just enough with the insurance money, and if you will go in halves with me, I found the perfect airplane," Jerry said.

"Yeah?" I said with anticipation. "Tell me about it."

"It's a 1947 V-tail Model 35 Beechcraft Bonanza, serial no. 439, one of the first five hundred ever built, N3834V. It's a beauty. It's owned by a Pentecostal preacher who flies it in his tennis shoes with his feet propped up on the instrument panel. It's a little rough, but I think we can fix it up. It's really in pretty good shape."

"Famous last words," I said. "But yeah, that's pretty exciting."

"I know how you said that you had always wanted a V-tail Bonanza, so now's your chance. I'll even send you a set of keys," Jerry said.

"Yeah, a set of keys to an airplane almost three thousand miles away. Wow," I replied.

"Just send me a check for [all the money in the world], and I'll take care of the rest. We'll put it in both names."

"Let me think about it, talk to Beth, and I'll call you first thing in the morning," I told him.

"Okay, old pal. I'll listen out for you in the morning," he said.

The next morning, I called Jerry and told him we were in and to go ahead. I sent him a check, and the rest was history!

* * *

To make a long story short, sometime later, Jerry and I ended our involvement and closed down Wings over the Mountains. I had always thought about being a flying missionary and, because of Jerry, had come very close, at least from a financially supportive position as a businessman benefactor. Now that era had come to a close.

Jerry would move back to Georgia, we would do some horse trading on real estate, and somehow I would end up owning the Bonanza outright by myself. It was still up in Idaho!

After some time had passed, I said to Jerry one day, "You know, we've got to go up and get that airplane and bring it home."

"Yep, we really need to," he said. "Let's go get it."

"So if I pay all the expenses and everything, will you come fly it with me and help me bring it home?" I asked.

"You bet," he said.

So not too long later, we planned the trip, and we were off to Idaho!!!

* * *

The first day out was pretty intense. We took a commercial flight on Delta out of Atlanta direct to Denver, Colorado. It was snowing! There, we transferred and hooked up with Frontier Airlines from Denver to Spokane, Washington. Of course, the airlines lost our two non-carry-on bags, and they would have to forward them to us. We rented a car and drove from Spokane to Coeur d'Alene, Idaho, where we were to pick up the Bonanza.

At the municipal airport, the old bird sat forlornly out on the south end of the ramp and runway, but there she was. Jerry had parked an old throwaway car next to her for contingent transportation. It didn't work, of course, but there were a few valuable things in the rat-infested trunk, like jumper cables for the airplane!

We opened the airplane up and began an inspection. My eyebrows were high on my face by now, and I thought, *What in the world had I gotten us into?* And a light snow was now beginning to fall.

The battery was dead, having set for a number of months, but the airplane fortunately was still in annual, just barely; it was soon to expire. We checked the oil and did a thorough preflight, jumped her off with an auxillary power unit, went down to the FBO, gassed her up, and fixed the brakes with some new fluid and a few kicks to the tires, and Jerry was down the taxiway for the active. To be current in the retract, he would have to do three takeoffs and landings with full retracts of the gear and back to be legal with the FAA.

It was like a miracle to see it lift off the ground and fly like the bird it was. It had that unmistakable sound of a Beechcraft Bonanza, and it was showing its stuff!

Oh yeah, we had to jump it off to get it started and nearly every time thereafter, until we finally bought a new battery in Topeka, Kansas. But that was much later.

When Jerry brought her back around and in, he taxied up and said, "Okay, let's go."

I threw our bags in and climbed aboard as copilot in the right seat, and we taxied out. It was still snowing, but there was about a 5,000 or 6,000 ft. ceiling, and we were on our way south, down to Lewiston, Idaho, where we would temporarily be based at John Black's house. John was a good friend, a flight instructor, and lived raising his family in Lewiston. We flew down the 3,000 ft. elevation of Nez Percé Plateau South until it dropped off at the confluence of the Clearwater River and the Snake River like a big hole in the earth. There was the Lewiston Airport at 741 ft. elevation or thereabouts welcoming us Georgia boys for a visit. It was a beautiful sight!

It was now twilight, almost dark, and that concluded the first day of our trip–for me. Jerry would end up taking another airplane from the flying club, a Cessna 150, I think, and make a night flight back to Coeur d'Alene to visit some old friends. That would conclude the first day for him. Man! And we had just gotten started!!!.

* * *

The next day, John asked me, "Steve, how would you like to take our club's floatplane, a Luscombe 8E, off the Snake River down at the marina, and we'll fly down through Hells Canyon?"

"All right," I said. "That sounds exciting!"

Now, Hells Canyon is the deepest canyon in the Unites States. It is over seven thousand feet from base to rim, even deeper than the Grand Canyon. This was going to be an exciting adventure of a lifetime and, honestly, pretty dangerous, especially at seven hundred feet over the Snake River; but hey, we did have a floatplane. Because John was a certified flight instructor, he said, "You take the left seat as pilot in command, and you can log the time toward your seaplane rating." That morning, I logged three hours seaplane time. Wow!

At first, we couldn't get airborne off the Snake River in the little Luscombe 8E. We must have run four thousand feet, so John said, "Let's turn around and try it the other way. Maybe we can catch some wind." So, we did, and finally, after about three thousand feet, we lifted off and headed upriver toward and shortly into the Hells Canyon. It was awesome flying the stick-and-rudder airplane left and right and down through the canyon walls, just like going down nature's hallway over the beautiful Snake River. At one point, we landed on the river, paddled over to a sand bar, and got out to stretch our legs and look at some old, ancient Chinese-built rock wall fences. We saw curly-horned Dall sheep and wild deer. It was amazing!

We got back in the airplane, paddled out a little into the river, and took off again, proceeding on down the canyon to where the Salmon River intersected the Snake River. There, we did a big swooping turn back to the north, back down the Snake, and finally all the way back down to Lewiston, Idaho, and Clarkston, Washington, twin cities, where we did a little sightseeing over these two auspicious historical cities separated by the Snake River, made famous by three great Americans–Lewis, Clark, and Sacagawea. Without their expedition, fortified with tenacity and courage, we would not be enjoying this vast territory of the northwestern United States today!

I hereby would like to say "Thank You" to them and to John Black for this great adventure! Wow!!!

* * *

In a couple of days, our bags finally arrived at Lewiston Airport. It was good to have some fresh clothes and our warm coats now that the weather was a little chilly.

For the next several days, we were assessing our options with the weather and trying to prepare the Bonanza for a transcontinental flight across the Rocky Mountains and to the eastern United States. It was no small challenge!

We flew over to Grangeville, Idaho, where another friend, Ron Caruso, had a nice little hangar on a cinder strip where we could work on 34V. While there, we changed the oil, complied with several AD (airworthiness directives) notes on the airplane, replaced a nonworking oil temperature gauge, and put new four-inch registration letters and numbers on each side of the fuselage because Jerry had recently painted the bird a beautiful red, white, and blue. He did a great job, and the airplane really looked all American. It was sharp, with a number of late-model modifications having been added!

We took off that evening right at dusk and made a wonderful low altitude, moonlight flight, over snow covered wilderness, dotted with little lit up farmhouses and barns, back to Lewiston Airport. It was a very memorable flight!

The next day, we went up for a look, did some "scud running" of sorts, and found the ceilings too low and the upper terrain all covered with snow. The weather was not cooperating. We did a 180 and went back to Lewiston. A day or so later, we took the Bonanza out and had to fly 150 miles one way to Yakima, Washington, nearly on the West Coast, to pull and repair our radios. There, we obtained some new crystals for our radios (yes, they really used crystals) and had some avionics work done in preparation for the long haul. We were there, almost right at Mount Saint Helens, just two weeks before she blew her top! I was glad we were early!!!

Now we were 150 miles back up the Clearwater River easterly to Lewiston again. While we were in Yakima, we had a mechanic look over and check out our ailerons, which were magnesium covered on aluminum ribs. It had something to do with the war effort, I think, and the fact that earlier models even had fabric cover on the ailerons. However, there was this thing in chemistry known as electrolysis by dissimilar metals. Our airplane had this problem, and the right aileron in particular was in a pretty bad shape as far as corrosion was concerned. The mechanic in Yakima said, "I sure wouldn't fly it all across the United States like that. But it's your airplane."

I really pretty much agreed with him, but I also had to make some judicial decisions if we were to ever get 34V back home.

"I'm going to be watching it real close," I said, "because it's going to be on my side."

And I did watch it carefully, telling myself that this was just like a ferry trip to get it back home, and then we could do all kind of work on it.

In a few days, the weather broke, we said our goodbyes, and we headed back north to Coeur d'Alene, turned east toward the Rockies, and headed for the Bozeman/Missoula Pass and into Montana. At 9,500 ft., we made the passage east through the Great Rocky Mountains and into the heart of America. It was absolutely stunning flying your own airplane across and through these great sentinels rising 10,000, 12,000, and 14,000 feet or so, all covered with a spring snow and now glistening in the bright April sunshine. We were aviators, sure 'nuff–careful to be sure but fortunate beyond words to share such a marvelous experience. There was a bond of unbreakable ties for me and Jerry, not unlike Lewis and Clark, only we were going backward over a hundred years later with the most modern of technology in travel. Still quite a buzz!!!

* * *

The trip continued through Montana, Wyoming, Nebraska, Kansas, Arkansas, Tennessee, and Alabama and home to Georgia. With several stops, days and nights, we finally made it to Brown Field–Fulton County Airport. There, waiting to greet us as we landed and rolled up on the tarmac, was all my family—my wife, Beth, and the kids and my mom and dad. What a welcome home committee! Tears welled up in my eyes as we taxied around to a stop and got out. It had been a hard, exciting, eventful, and emotional long trip. Really, really amazing! It was some of the most intensive flying I had ever done, and I was only the copilot. Thanks to Jerry as PIC (pilot in command), we had made one heck of a trip, one we would long remember!!!

* * *

Later after that, Jerry would go on and embark on quite a little career in flying all over the country (eastern United States mostly), and I would settle back into real estate and building little airports—and still flying also!

Over time, we would have many other flying adventures, too many to recount here at this writing. Aviation would become and remain a part of our involvement and lives for a long time to come and even now!

But we would always remember N3834V (*Victor for Victory*) and how it transformed our lives and changed us from caterpillars to real butterflies that springtime day we crossed the Rocky Mountains. Thank you, Jerry, for a job well done.!!!

Grandpa's First landing On the Farm
November 19, 2013 – A Boy's Dream
Since Childhood – 2:00 PM

By Steven "Steve" D. Ayers – At Age 65

Flying over the farm seemed, by now, like a natural thing. For many years I had flown out to fly over our own little farm. The surrounding landscape was natural and familiar for I had see it many times form below and above. Chasing cows and riding horses over so many years had helped me learn every nook and crook, creek and tree line. It was my boyhood "Stomping Ground" as they say.

My key indentifier for lining up on the new South Runway was a large old "Square" barn about one mile off the north end of the approach. This is the only large square barn I ever knew of, in the area, and it being so unique and in the exact position it was, made an ideal point to turn base to final approach. As long as I could see it, I knew exactly where I was.

There it was, big as life, as long as you knew what you were looking at! Base to final, ninety degree turn, here we come, already on carburetor heat, throttled back to fifteen hundred rpms, two thousand feet MSL (about a thousand over the earth-actual ground level) and descending approximately 200 feet per minute at 80mph.

Now, watching the air speed very carefully, gently raising the nose to reduce air speed down to 70, then to 65, then to 62 – and 30 degree flaps – over the trees 83 feet tall on that end – noting a little bit extra energy level, I thought I should put in the other 10 degrees flaps (probably shouldn't have) to 40, my max – while simultaneously reducing power to idle and sharply pushing the yoke forward (should have pulled aft) to put the nose down toward the runway, having just cleared the tall trees – by doing so I had inadvertently "increased" my energy level by probably 10 – 20%. (That's why, I should have pulled the yoke aft, to help dissipate the energy level and come down more like a bird) being careful not to stall.

By now, I was 25% down the 2,000ft runway, and was approaching the flare position –as I flared carefully by drawing back the yoke – I began to float just above the runway- and I floated – and I floated – and I floated (I should have dumped the flaps, but didn't) – by now, I was 3 / 4 way down the runway, with about 500ft remaining – I had already mentally prepared myself, that if I did not settle down to the ground, I would have to fly into the fence at the end – there was no go around – no possibility – I was totally committed – then in 200 more feet I touched down, so easy and smooth – I had maybe 300 ft to get stopped – I immediately hit the brakes, heavily and intermittently – dumped up the electric flaps to increase the braking capacity and continued to ride it out – perhaps doing a ground loop, if necessary to avoid the end fence – but I did not have to, thank goodness – I finally stopped within about 30 feet of the end of the 2,000 ft runway. That old fence was mighty close, but looking pretty good since I was STOPPED. Whewwwww…. Was I relieved!!!

My adrenaline was running pretty good about this point of my adventure! I was pretty excited and the little Cessna 150-F, "Tweety Bird," painted red and white, had done her thing remarkably well! November 6 – 6 – 4 – 3 Foxtrot had really brought me home, for real!

My only real witnesses that day to this awesome event, were my farm helpers, Bryan and David, who were working on the upper part of our new chimney on the library and who were at and up on the runway, on and on, and on and wondering if I ever was going to stop!!!

They hurried on down to the very close by, adjoining airfield, right next to the house, and gave me a hearty welcome as I taxied up to the old flight shack and shut her down. It had been "Some more" thrilling experience, maybe once in a lifetime, maybe there would be more, but for now, I took a big exhale of air and thanked mu lucky stares, that I had just done something amazing, the very unlikely and had actually lived to tell about it!!!

Sometime much later, I would attempt to take off, from the farm, another first for me, but that too is another story!!!

April 10, 2015 – SDA – Now Aged 66

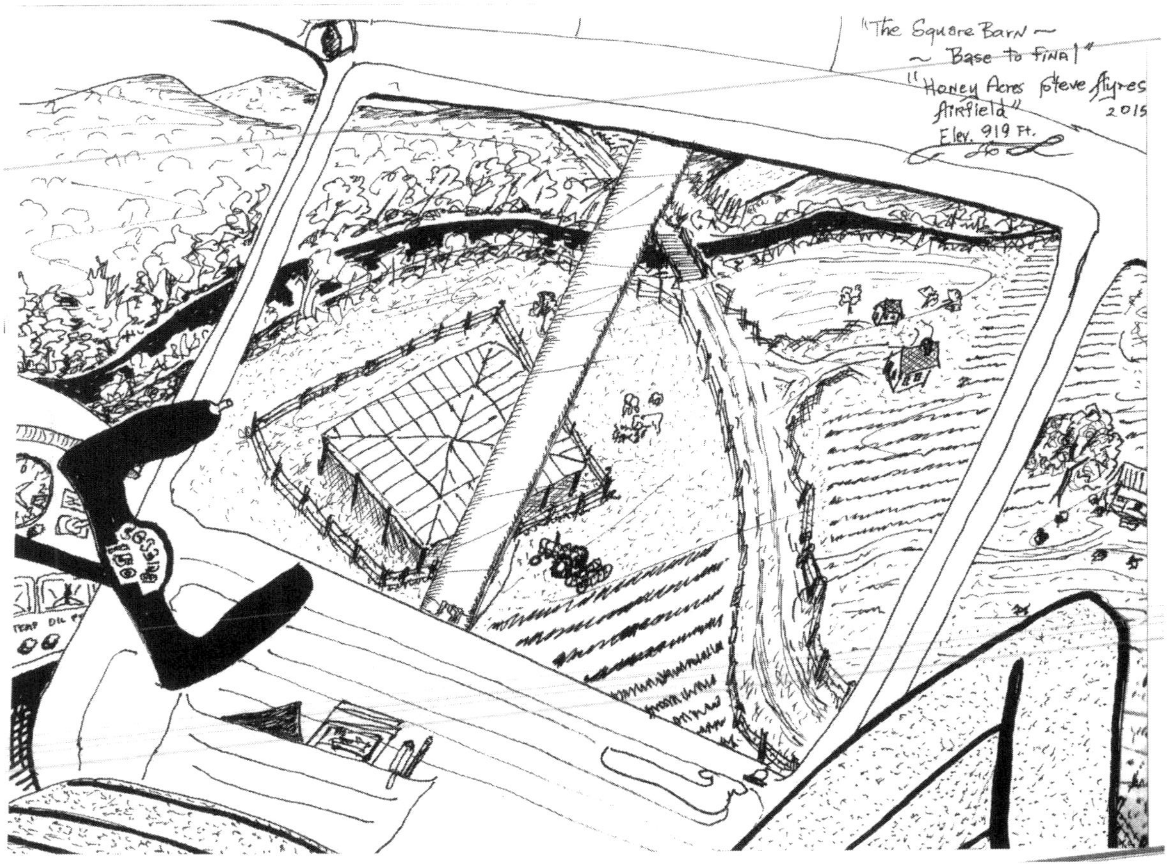

"The Square Barn" —
~ Base to Final ~
"Honey Acres" Steve Ayres
Airfield
Elev. 919 Ft.
2015

Let Freedom Ring: What a Day to Be Free!

Today was July 4, 2010, Independence Day in the United States of America, land of the free and home of the brave!

I woke up early this morning on the beaches of Amelia Island at Fernandina Beach, Florida, USA, the Earth, the universe. What a day of sunshine and glory as the waves of the Atlantic Ocean came rolling in and the rays of early morning light came into my bedroom, kissing me and my wife all over with sweet warm sunshine. The aroma of freshly brewed coffee floated through the cool air of the air-conditioning and the radio. WKTZ, Jones College Radio out of Jacksonville, Florida, was playing patriotic music, beautiful renditions of "The Star-Spangled Banner" and "God Bless America." It was a good day to be alive and on vacation!

Vacation with family was an awesome event. We usually did this once a year in the summer with all the kids, grandchildren, and grandparents, if they can come. We'd been doing this for years as I knew you probably had with your family.

Now we were the grandparents, and we were the ones to lead the way. It was such a joy and a pleasure to spend this happy time together, if for no other reason than it gave us time to talk, visit, eat, sleep, and play relatively unencumbered by the daily grind of unfinished tasks and toils. This year, however, was different. The Gulf of Mexico was "closed" due to the BP oil spill. The beautiful white sandy beaches of the gulf were black and tarnished with the ruinous unrefined oil and tar of an uncapped, gushing offshore oil well. The initial oil rig explosion killed many workers, and our hearts went out to their families for their losses. Finally, on about day 154, the well was successfully capped; but by then, the damage had been done.

Worse even than the Exxon Valdez in 1989 in Alaska, this would become one of the worst environmental disasters ever to happen in the United States and North America!

So, the beaches we loved and visited for years were unsuited for us and thousands, maybe even millions, of others who had patronized them all our lives. This year, we had to find and go, if we could, somewhere else. For days, we had waited for the bad news; and finally, just weeks before our scheduled reservation, we canceled the Gulf Beach condos we had rented. We would need to stay in a reasonable travel distance from Atlanta, so we started looking on the Atlantic coast. Finally, we found and settled on the quaint and beautiful beaches of Fernandina Beach, Florida, on Amelia Island, named for the beautiful Amelia, the youngest daughter of King George II. It was so named by James Oglethorpe, founder of Georgia around 1774. It was an island that would become the playground of many joyous visitors over the next several hundred years, including me and my family!

Oddly enough, the town was named Fernandina by the then governor of the Spanish territory in honor of the fallen monarch of Spain, Ferdinand VII. They wanted him in exile to come here, but alas, he had other plans!

While I do fly real airplanes, for fun and practice, I fly my Flight Simulator X by Microsoft, a marvelous software product on my personal computer. Only the night before, I had flown my Flight Simulator Bonanza–N5119H, a V-tail just like I had previously owned–from Charlie Brown (Fulton County Airport, Atlanta, Georgia) to Fernandina Beach Municipal Airport. Time en route was one hour twenty-four minutes at 5,500 feet MSL, a late-afternoon flight through simulated real-time weather conditions. The beautiful turquoise and white V-tail Beechcraft sailed across the skies like the gallant lady she was in record time and style. How much fun can a computer be? A lot, let me tell you. I had made real flights like this before to Florida and other places but not while drinking my coffee and catching a nap while on autopilot. Modern technology and the blending of American freedom was a beautiful and wondrous thing. We are so blessed to live in this country, the land of the free and the home of the brave!

It is a country where little children can grow up to be whatever they want to be. A kid like me who rode a horse across the pasture of his boyhood farm, all the while flying a toy airplane, today flew his own airplane across America! A little boy who today is building his very own airfield on that very farm in that very pasture!

America is great, and we have so much to be thankful for! As I pondered the thoughts of the morning, I was reading a new book I picked up just yesterday entitled *Lady Liberty: A Biography* by Doreen Rappaport and Matt Tavares. As part of the story of the Statue of Liberty, I was very mentally engaged to remember the words of Emma Lazarus, a poet from New York City, written in November 1883, engraved on the tablet held by Lady Liberty:

Give me your tired, your poor, your huddled masses, yearning to breathe free, the wretched refuse of your teeming shore. Send these, the homeless, tempest tost to me: I lift my lamp beside the golden door!

In 1968, on my way to Europe from America, I read those words as I visited the lady on Liberty Island. I climbed up to her stretching arm, walked through the grand crown gracing her head, and looked out her windows on New York Harbor and the world. I was nineteen years old, a young product and progeny of this country we called America. I was looking back to France, the motherland of this precious gift. In a few days, I would walk the streets of France and retrace some of the steps of my ancestors. My grandfather and my mother were named Seignious, as French as you can get. My father and his side, Ayres, were from Scotland and England!

This morning, I was moved to tears as I was reading those words by Emma as my own granddaughter Emmeline, aged one, played across the floor. In two days, I would be sixty-two and eligible for social security in the marvelous United States of America. I can't help but wonder what great things little Emme would do and behold in her lifetime! My prayer was that God would bless her even as he had blessed me and all my other family and that Lady Liberty would continue to stand as a beacon of freedom not only to this land but also to all the world! Happy Fourth of July 2010, and may the future be bright!!!

Silent Night — *Midnight Snow*

The Benediction and Convocation

In these last few years, time had moved pretty fast. As I have reflected about the past, many thoughts and observations have come to mind. No doubt, you too, have done the same.

While giving our thanks and blessings for all our past, we also need a calling together of the cumulative spirit of man to remind ourselves, once again, that we are only human and that God is God and that it is He who has made us and not we ourselves. May the blessings of God be upon us in all we do and in all we undertake in our individual lives. So that, at the end of our journey, we may be welcomed into the loving arms of our Lord and Savior, Jesus Christ, and may we abide with Him forever. Amen.

And now, for me, something needed to be done to create a closure for the past and a new beginning for the future, so I decided to write a book about my life experiences and remembrances, a novel perhaps. It would certainly be about history and the many glorious years of the days gone by and also about those to follow...

It would be based on my ancestral letters and the family farm where I grew up... and so I begin my story...

I grew up in the low hills of northwest Georgia. It was a time when the world was much smaller than it is now. Days and weeks seemed to last forever, and the entire universe centered around the family farm. The year I was born was 1846, in the month of July, day of the sixth... It was the beginning of *Fallow Are the Fields*.

And the moving finger, having writ, moves on!

The Bible

Thanks a Million

Steve Ayres

Epilogue

So many things have changed... and so many things have stayed the same! We live in a perfect world of imperfect perfection, meaning that the universe is always making corrections in its eternal striving toward balance. The see-saw goes up, the see-saw goes down!

Historically, we ask, "Whatever happened to this or that?"

Well, there have been some changes! Today the former town of New Manchester, a.k.a. Manchester Mill and Town, remains a relic of the past as Sweetwater Creek State Park, boasting almost 2,400 acres as a wilderness state park right here in Lithia Springs, Georgia, formerly Salt Springs, formerly Bowden Lithia Springs, formerly Deer Lick. It is a beautiful place to visit and reminisce about what was once a bustling and thriving little town with one of the largest industrial buildings in the state, where Ginny and Anna Jett of *Fallow Are the Fields* worked during the Civil War. The park is, in my opinion, the crown jewel of Douglas County!

The renowned Sweetwater Park Hotel of *We Danced Until Dawn*, so glorious in its day, is now replaced with little plain houses, like where my grand-parents lived and I grew up cutting grass for a banana sandwich!

The Old Millhouse, where my family once lived, met a sad fate of being destroyed by fire in around 1985 or so. It started in the grand old fireplace and somehow caught up in the rafters around the old chimney. It was rented at the time and occurred during the middle of the night. I was there at 12:30 a.m., peering into the red coals. It was like looking into the depths of hell and just as scary! The cause was not clearly determined. Previously, we had sold the old mill, and the new buyers later vacated and deeded the property back to us partially because it was "haunted." Perhaps it still was! Many strange things happened, like unexplainable noises, little acts of broken flower stems, and cameras flashing out of control, not to mention the crunch-crunch-crunch of someone going up the old back staircase!

Four years of reenacting during the American Civil War centennial came to a close for me in April of 1965. I had been a member of the First Georgia Volunteers and the Twelfth Georgia Light Artillery, and I had traveled all over the southeastern United States reenacting battles. From Olustee, Florida, to Brice's Cross Roads, Mississippi, we went, and we sometimes fought the National Guard. Reenacting the Battle of Kennesaw Mountain was one of the more memorable times for me. Later, I would be part of the honor guard to dedicate the only Georgia monument in the National Military Park.

There were so many other things, like my trip to Europe, visiting seven countries, seeing Paris, Rome, London, and all the in-betweens. It was a marvelous trip for a nineteen-year-old, and my eyes were truly opened to the world!

Six Flags over Georgia came to Lithia Springs or almost, just barely down the road, and put this area on the map big time for folks from all over the world. What an attraction! I even worked there, like so many others had, but I worked as a caricature artist! It was fun and a great experience!

Today my family and I still live on the old family farm. My wonderful parents have passed on, but their memory lives on, in and around, and *Under the Wedding Tree*!

Tomorrow is forecast to be sunny and bright! I hope so!!!

It is bound to be another turn, in *"The Glory Road!"*

Epitaph of Life

Under the wedding tree,
Vast and gold,
I hear a story, ancient and old,
Of love, of war, of joy and pain;
Of days of living
Amongst the strain,
To struggle, to laugh,
To love, to gain,
To start all over and do it again.

(SDA)

Appendix

Miscellaneous and Additional
Sketches Just for Fun

The Wedding Tree

Too old the limbs to bear,
To nestle birds within my hair,

To weather the wind, the rain, and snow,
Not to mention the heat and rain so slow,

But so honored I once stood,
Above this lovely stand of wood;

Big and bold and full of hope,
I lent my strength upon this slope;

To young ones promising their love to share,
For evermore they promised, right there,

Three weddings in all and now even four,
Mom and Dad, and three children more;

Husbands and wives, sweethearts and friends,
Pledging their love 'till all time ends.

Yes, I have been a very blessed old tree, before they cut me down,
For 300 years or so I stood above this Holy, sacred ground;

And Great Granddaddy "Bill" loved this old tree,
Upon this hill so free;

As they stood together and witnessed the "Love,"
Before time cut both of them down, you see;

And now we see their example before us,
Their life force still amongst us.

Knowing that them and we,
And you and me;

Will forever remember,
The Wedding Tree

SDA
November 22, 2008
Ben & Amanda

R.B. Jett
& Major

Steve Ayres

1/31
(My GREAT GRAND FATHER)
of Steve Ayres + Gordon Ayres
Jenny Bond, Bo Seignious
& Jimmy Seignious
and Others

Transcribed from Charleston newspaper, Oct. 12, 1901
- - - -

MR. C. W. SEIGNIOUS
- - - -

Death of a Well-known and Highly-respected Charlestonian.

Mr. C. W. Seignious, a well-known and highly respected citizen of Charleston, died at his home, 317 East Bay, yesterday morning at 9 o'clock, after a lingering illness. While his friends knew that he was sick the announcement of his death was particularly sad, and his loss will be felt. Mr. Seignious was 53 years of age. He was born in Charleston, educated here and made it his home through life. He was the son of Mr. C. W. Seignious. He left a son by that name and a grandson, so that the name of C. W. Seignious will long be known in the community.

During the war Mr. Seignious volunteered in the Confederate army and fought gallantly for the cause he had espoused. When the war was ended he returned to Charleston and for the past twenty-three years has been engaged in planting rice. His three plantations -- Lewisfield, Salt Point and Exeter, located on the Cooper River four miles from Oakley -- were valuable paying properties and Mr. Seignious was successful in his ventures. He was married twice. By his first wife there was a family of four -- C. W. Seignious, Jr., Leroy Seignious and Misses Ethel and Rebe Seignious. He was married about two years ago and left one son by his second wife.

OLGA VIRGINIA SEIGNIOUS BOND

APPLICATION FOR MEMBERSHIP

UNITED DAUGHTERS OF THE CONFEDERACY

State: Florida
Chapter: Captain John Wesley Whidden
Town: Lake Placid
County of: Highlands

Confederate Patron: Great-grandfather
Name: Charles Washington Seignious, Charleston, S. C.

Reserves S. C. Militia, Company D, First Regiment, Charleston
Enlisted from the State of: South Carolina

Maiden Name: Olga Virginia Seignious
Married Name: Olga Seignious Bond
Husband: Samuel Joseph Bond, Jr.

FILL IN LINEAGE UP TO AND INCLUDING CONFEDERATE ANCESTOR OR RELATIVE ONLY

Olga Virginia Seignious Bond was born on the 21st day of May, 1931
Miami — Dade — Florida — USA

1. I am the daughter of

Luke Whitfield Brown Seignious — born May 8, 1906 — Atlanta, Ga.
and his wife — died Jan. 1975 — Lake Placid, Fla.
Olga Musin-Pushkin — born May 1, 1907 — Moscow, Russia
(maiden name) — died Jan. 1976 — Lake Placid, Fla.
married May 18, 1940 — Miami, Fla.

2. My father was the brother/daughter of

Charles Washington Seignious — born _____ — Charleston, S.C.
and his wife — died _____ — Chicago, Ill.
Virginia Ann Perry — born _____ — Charleston, S.C.
(maiden name) — died _____ — Miami, Fla.
married _____ — Charleston, S.C.

3. The said Grandfather was the brother/daughter of

Charles Washington Seignious — born 1848 — Charleston, S.C.
and his wife — died 1903 — "
Munin Butler — born _____ — "
(maiden name) — died _____ — "
married _____ — "

4. The said _____ was the brother/daughter of

_____ and his wife
born _____ where _____
died _____ where _____
_____ (maiden name)
born _____ where _____
died _____ where _____
married _____ where _____

5. The said _____ was the brother/daughter of

_____ and his wife
born _____ where _____
died _____ where _____
_____ (maiden name)
born _____ where _____
died _____ where _____
married _____ where _____

6. The said _____ was the brother/daughter of

_____ and his wife
born _____ where _____

Seignious	Charles Washington	Pvt.
SURNAME	GIVEN NAME	RANK

Co. D 1st Reg. Charleston Reserves S.C. Militia
SERVICE

6/5/1862   Charleston
DATE ENLISTED   PLACE OF ENLISTMENT

DATE	PLACE	KILLED	PAROLED	DISCHARGED
		N.A. 267/146		

CONFIRMATION OF RECORD:

Per Muster Roll 6/5/1862-8/21/1862

**OFFICIAL RECORD
ON FILE - UDC
REFERENCE DEPT.**

FORM 51-16M

Copy of Proof

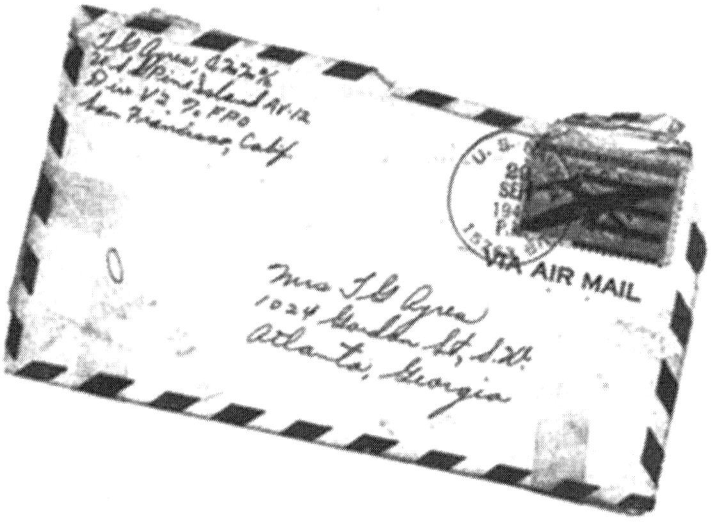
VIA AIR MAIL
Atlanta, Georgia

Aim High, aim high!

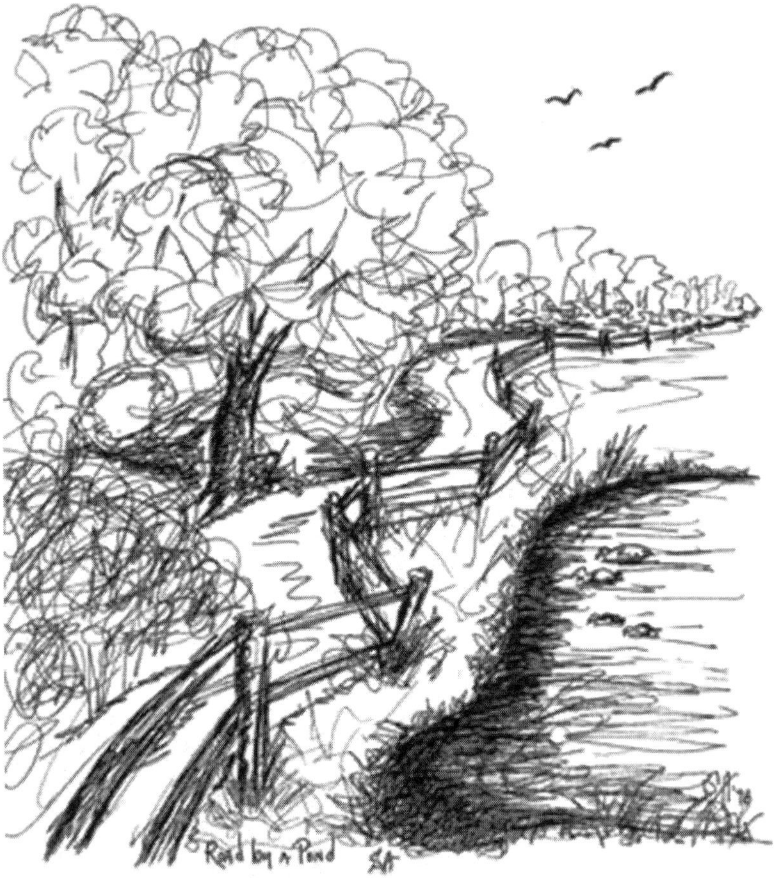
Road by a Pond

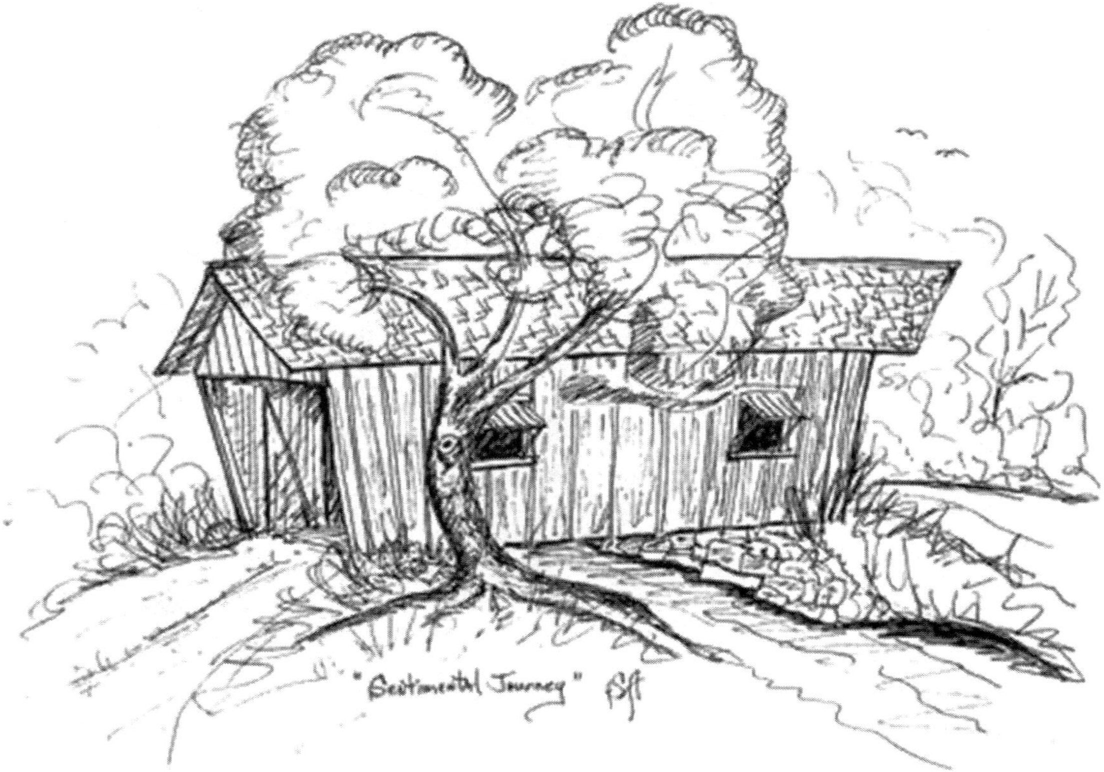
"Sentimental Journey"

The Old Swimming Hole

"Just Being Kids"

"Overland Stage" 1941

"Milling Time"
Benbrook Mill

Vacation in the Country — "Cleaning Fish"

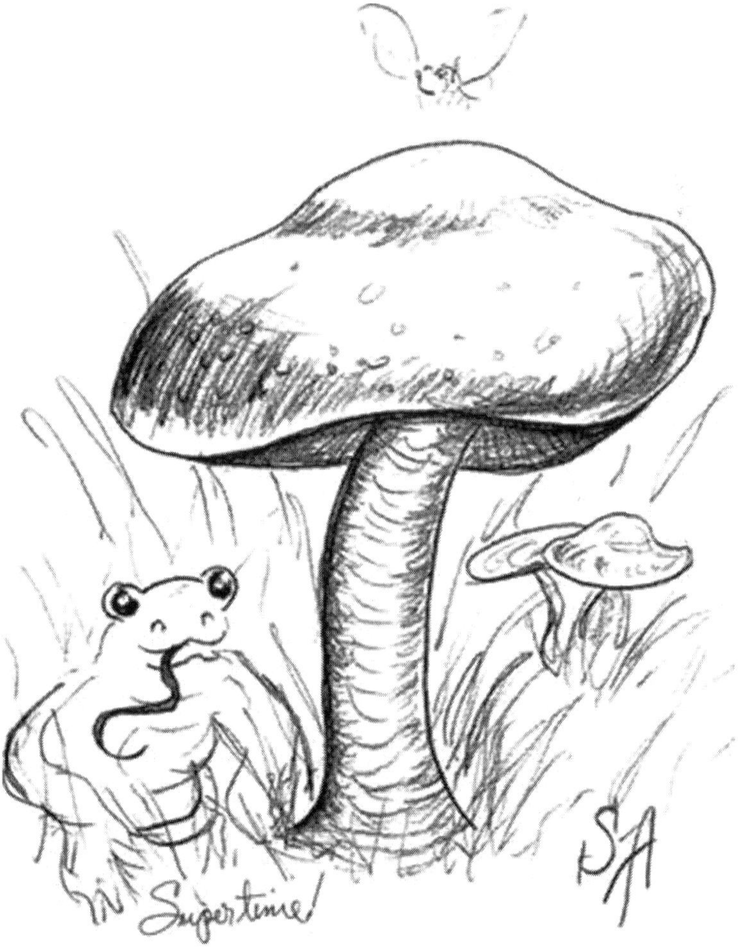

"Chicken in Paradise," "Panama City Beach" by PH '97

Wet Teeshirt Contest Tonight at La Vellas!
"Decisions, Decisions!"
Beach Bum!

"NFL Sunday"

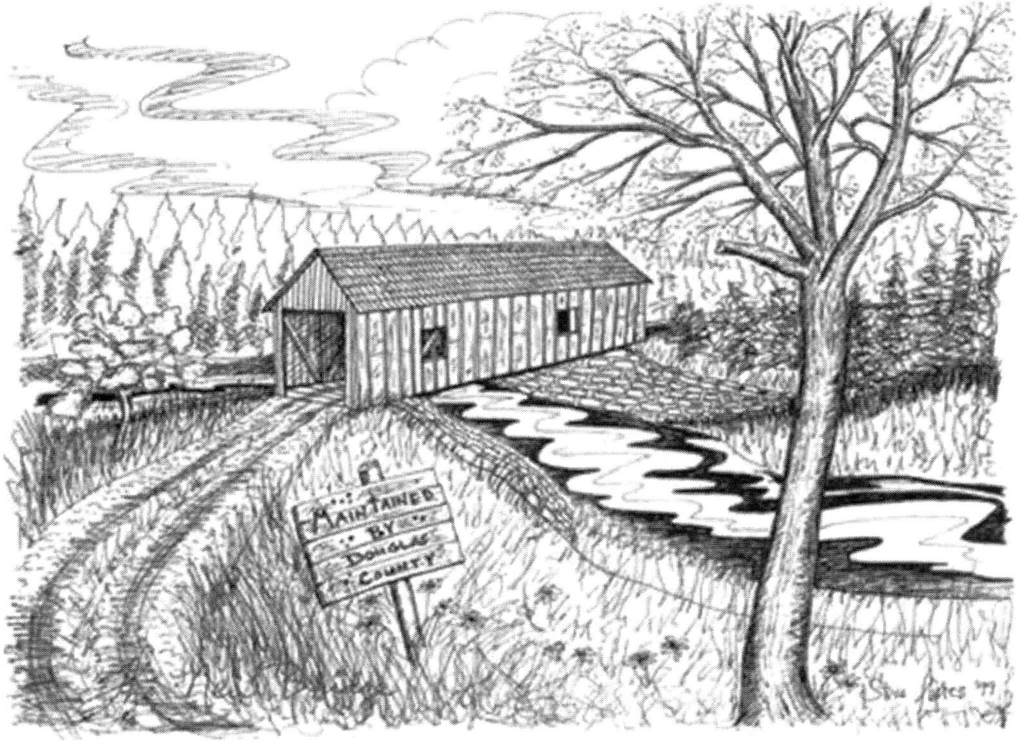
MAINTAINED
BY
DOUGLAS
COUNTY

J.A. Arguedas
1157 old Peachtree Rd
Lawrenceville, Ga. 30245

Ayres Realty Co
3600 Bankhead Highway
Lithia Springs, Ga. 30057

"Bridge Repair"

Amicolola Falls, Georgia

Grandpa's Old Mill

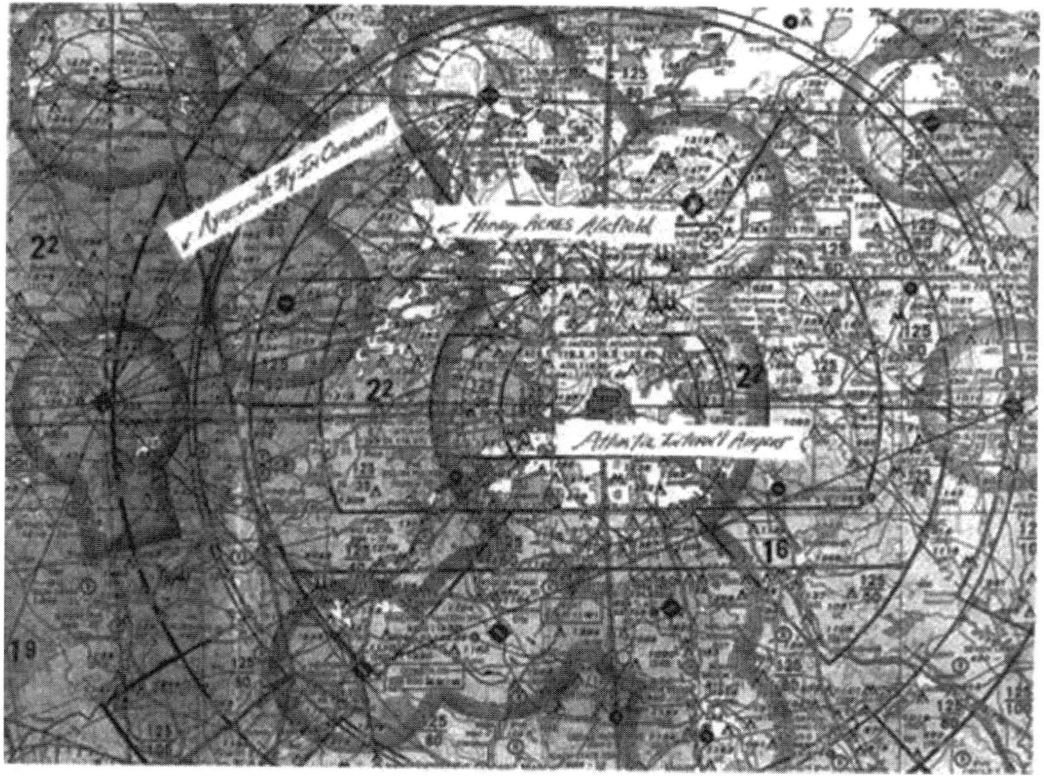

"Heading South"
SA '91

"Here Come Santa Clause"

Merry Christmas 1991

Merry Christmas
25/1/91

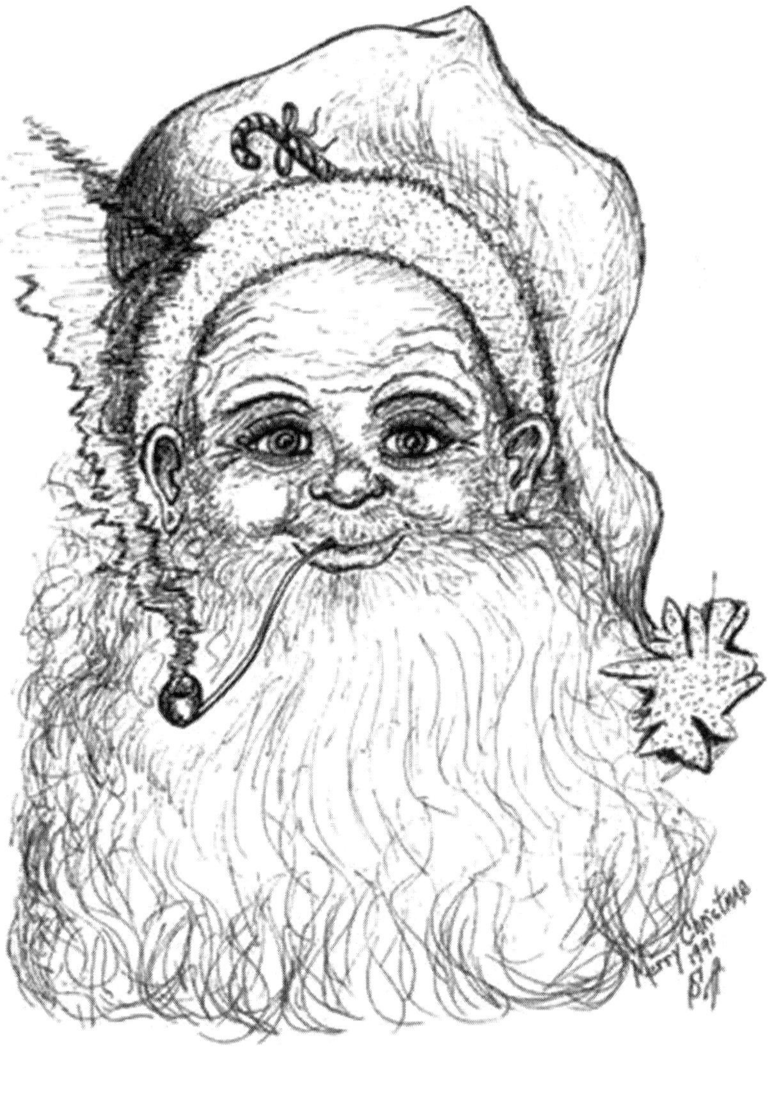
Merry Christmas

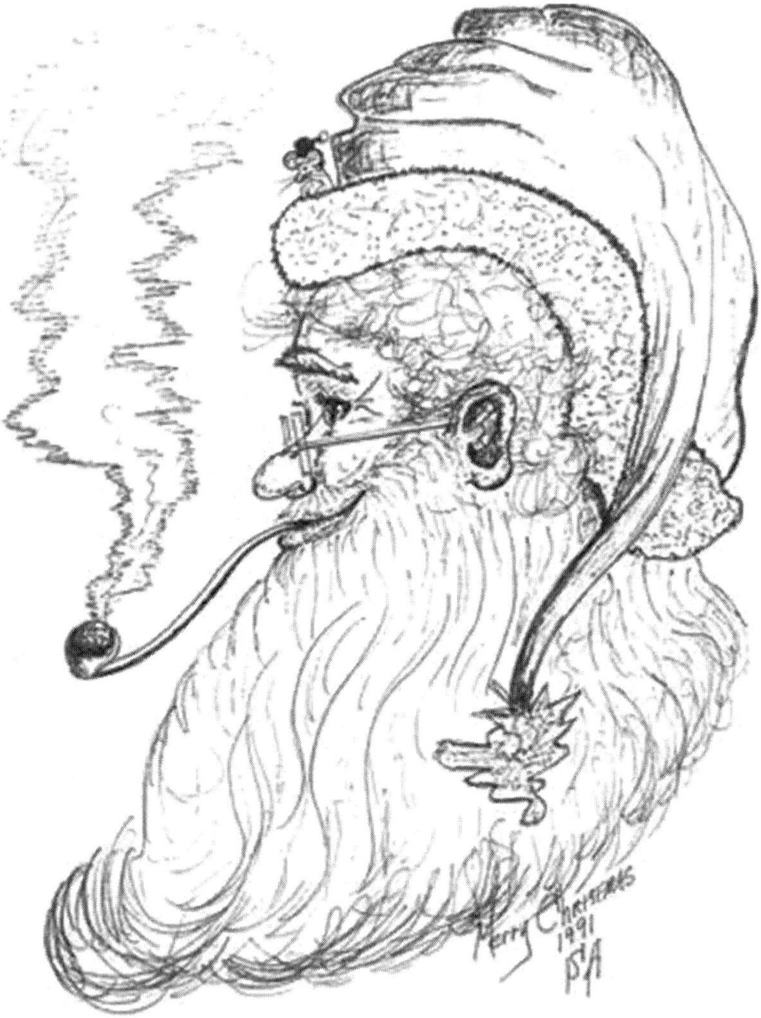
Merry Christmas
1991

Merry Christmas

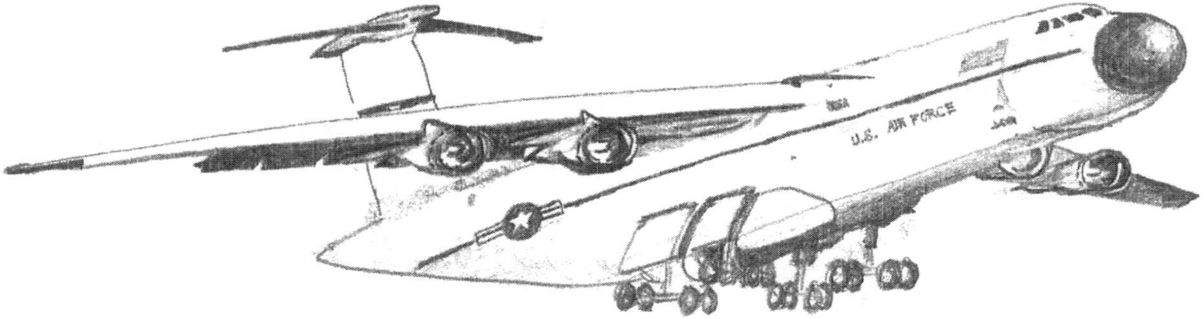

"Marietta, Georgia"
Lockheed C-5A Galaxy

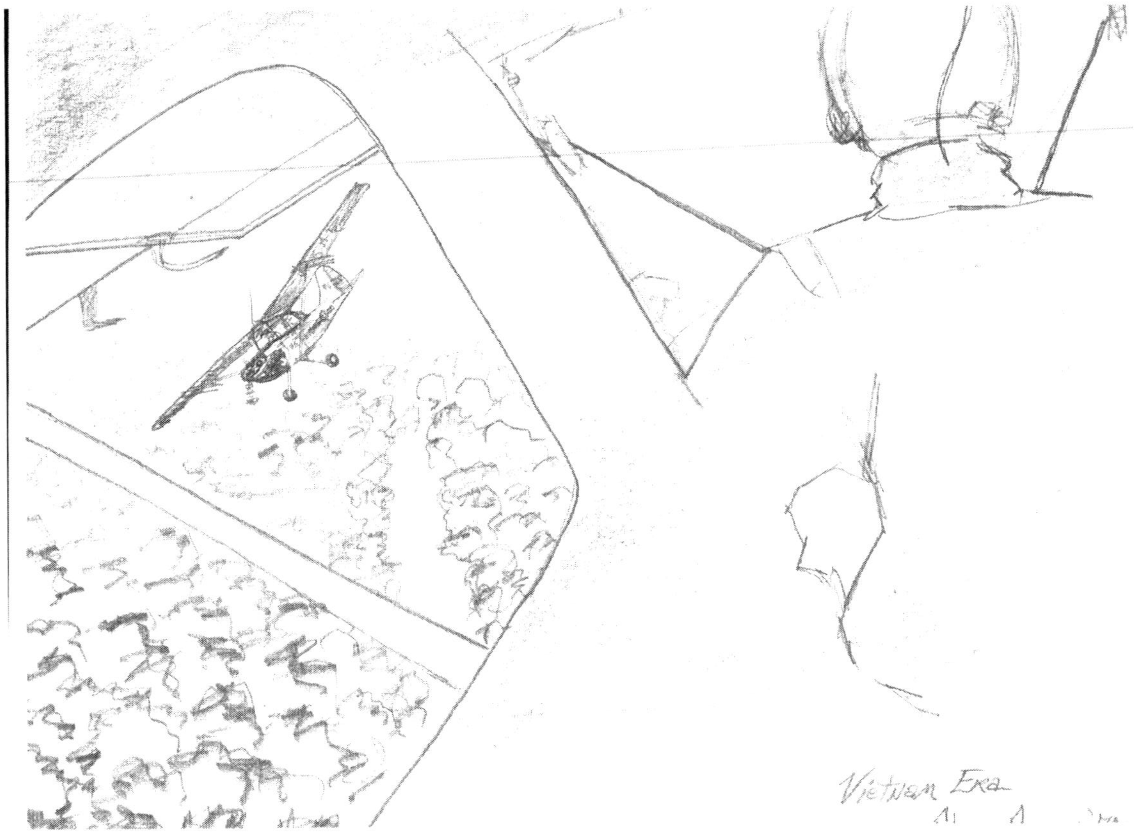

Vietnam Era

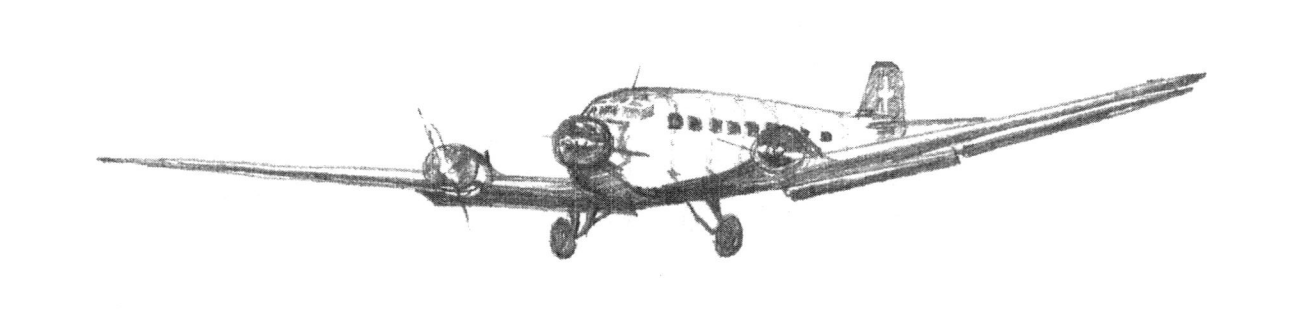

"On the Way Home"
German built Junker Ju 52
Swiss Air Force

"Closed on Sunday" Steve Ayres

1948 Stinson Voyager 108-3 & Kiba

You got the lunches?

67 Charlie Ready to Roll!

Let's go fly!

Just leave the doors open!

Making the most out of being laid up!

Who's More Busher?

Kiba in the pickup!

My Best Lifetime Friend and Flying Buddy Jerry + Frith Thanks Stu

Over Denver, Colorado
On the sim

Flying Long Island, New York on the rim

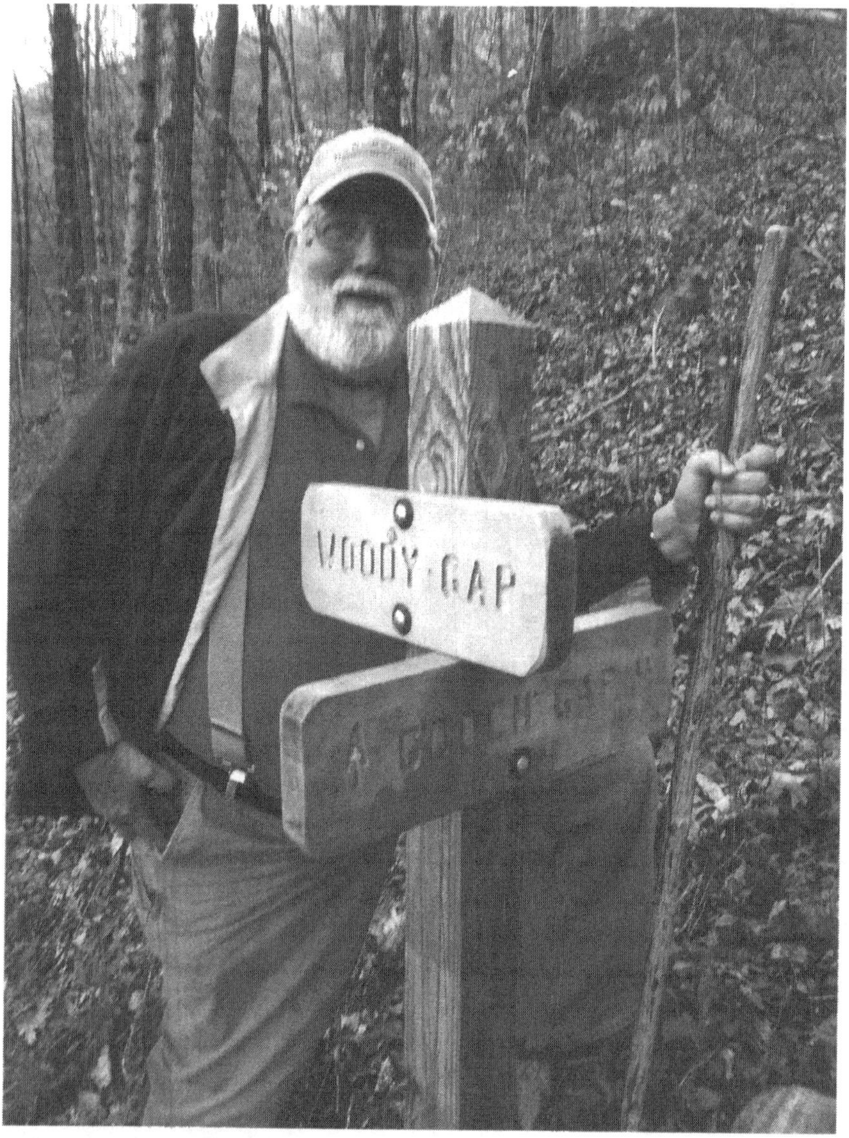
WOODY GAP

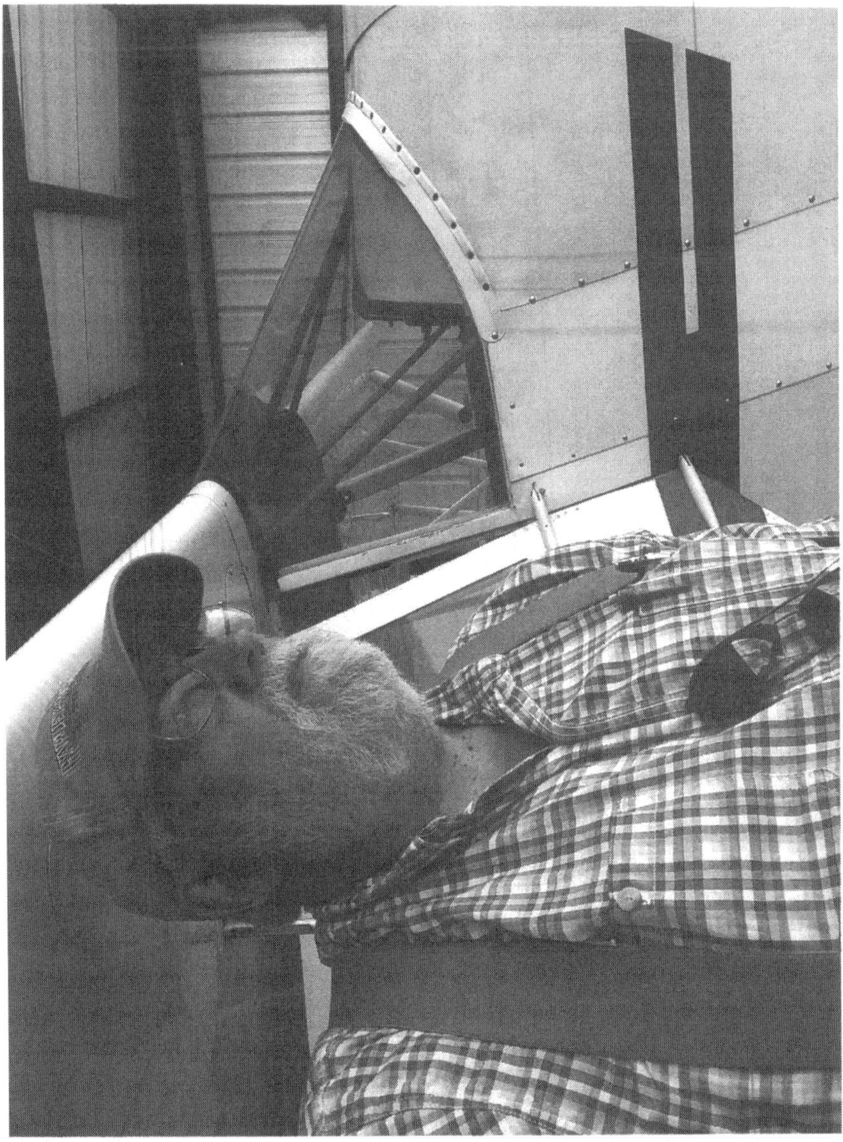

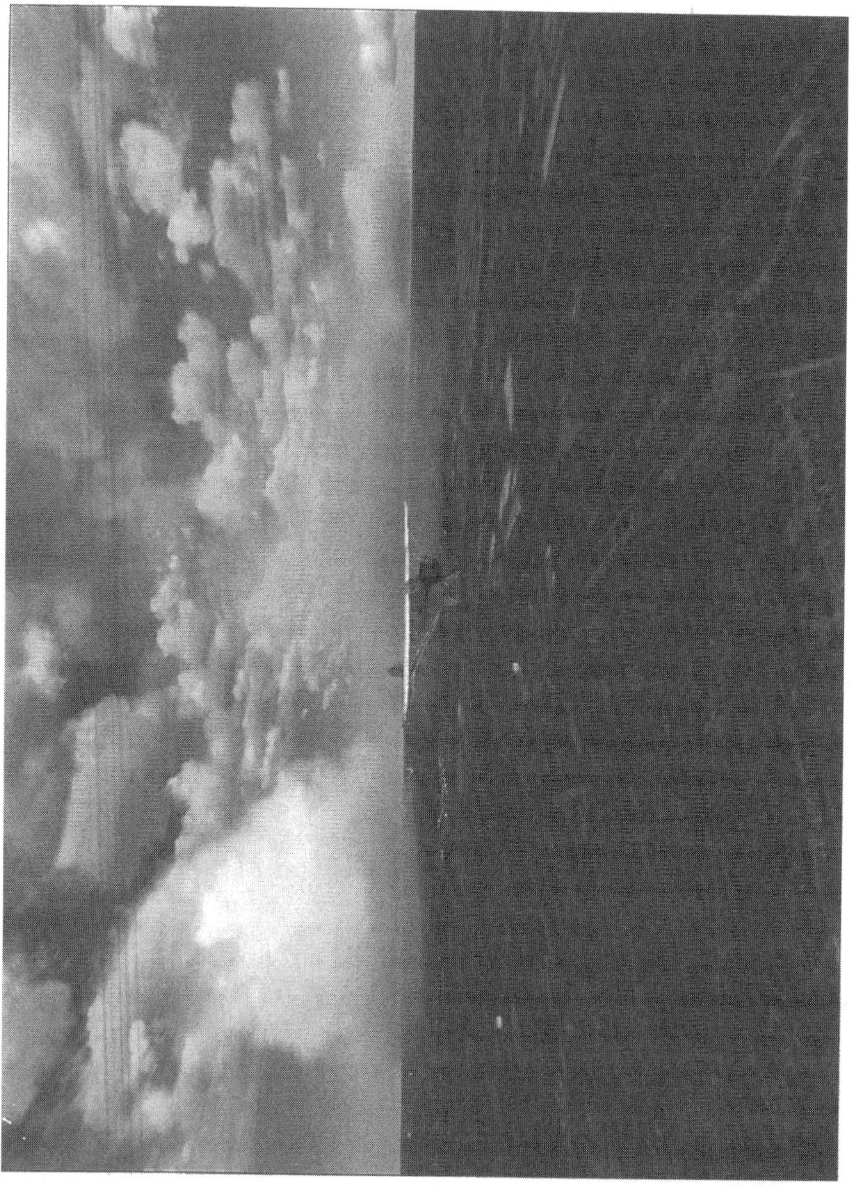

Final APP
FTY

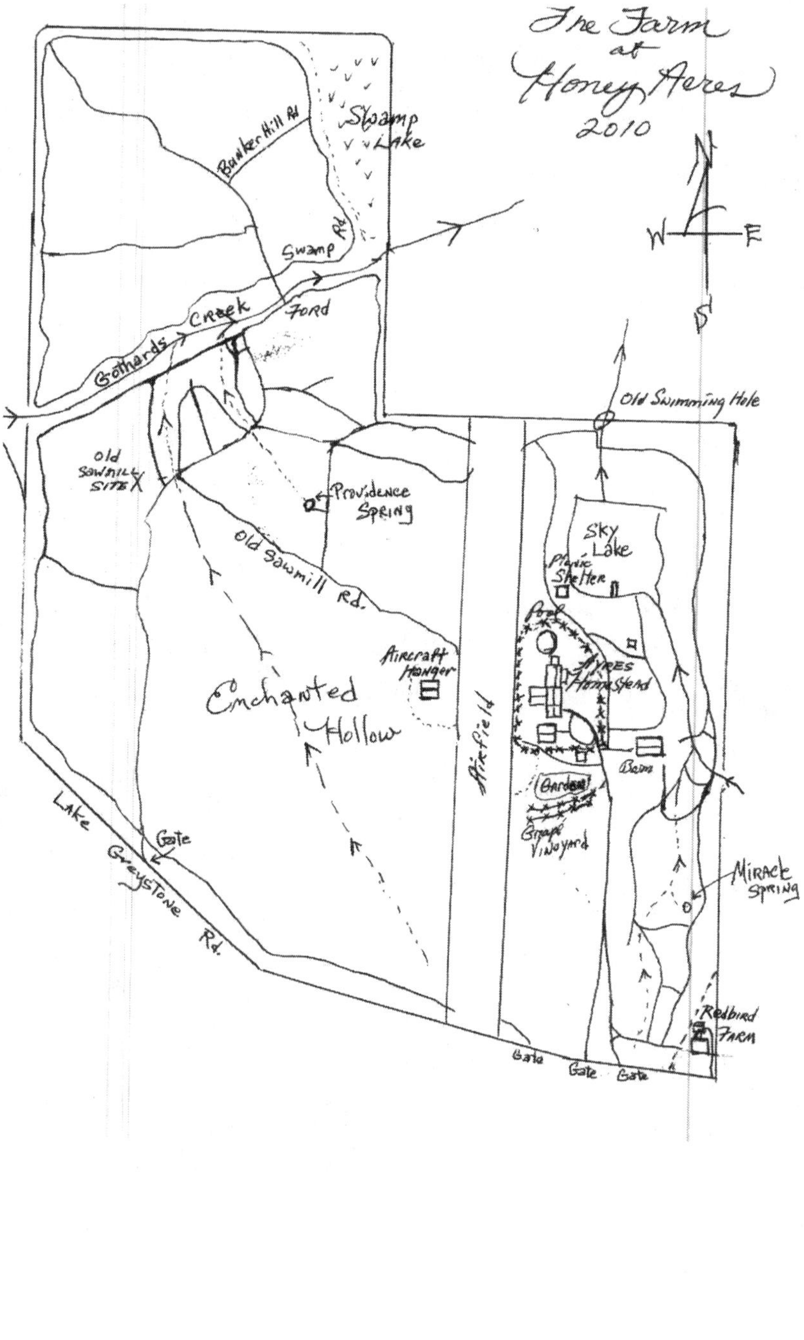

The Farm at Honey Acres 2010
N
W
E
S
Swamp Lake
Bunker Hill Rd
Swamp Rd.
Gothards Creek
Ford
Old Swimming Hole
Old Sawmill Site X
Providence Spring
Old Sawmill Rd.
Sky Lake
Picnic Shelter
Pool
Ayres Homestead
Aircraft Hanger
Enchanted Hollow
Airfield
Barn
Garden
Grape Vineyard
Miracle Spring
Redbird Farm
Gate
Lake Greystone Rd.
Gate
Gate
Gate

Arts + Crafts
Music
"The Bee Song"
by Steve Ayres
S. Beekeepers Assn.

Crafts
1st Place

1 Place

New Baby Chicks!

Amazing how fast they grow up!

The Author and his one string slide cigar box electric guitar!

Which he built himself! Playing to the kids!

Before this my mother opened
Blanche's Hobby & Gift Shop
just next door
50 years ahead of her time

← My Mother
← Same # Home Land Line

Our First Real Estate Office

"Flying the Board" BA '91

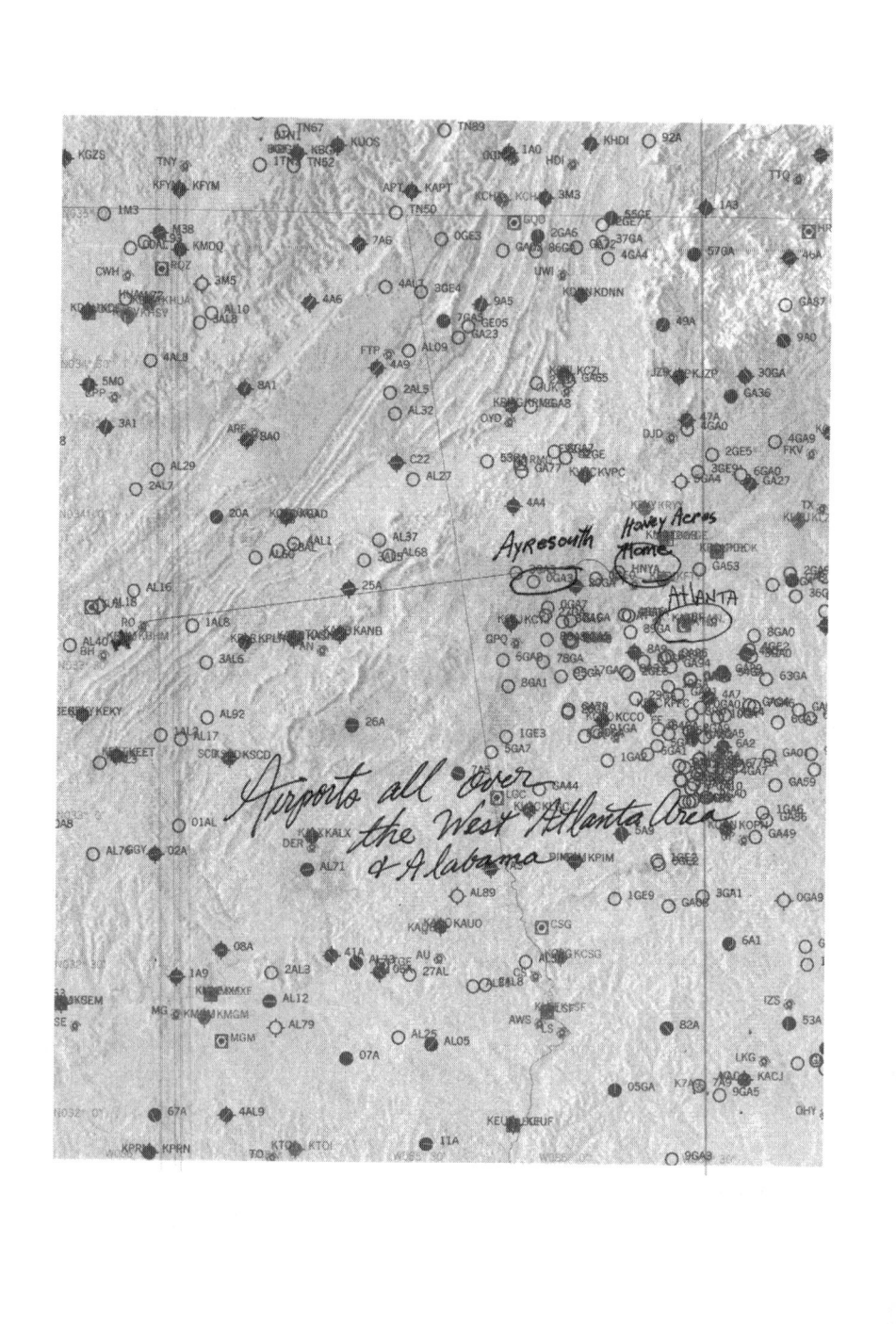

Airports all over the West Atlanta Area & Alabama

Ayresouth
Honey Acres
Home
ATLANTA

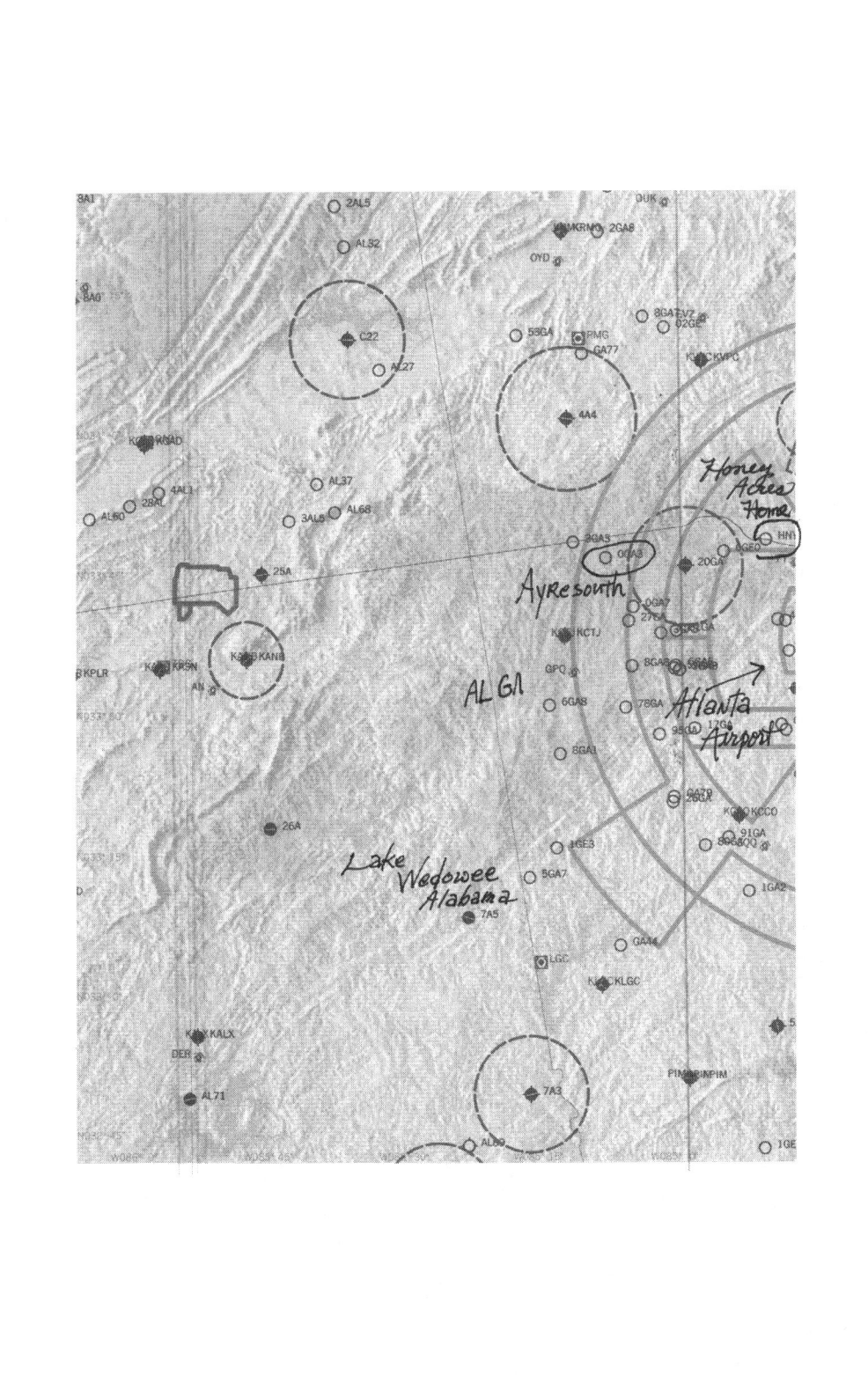

Ayresouth
Honey Acres Home
Atlanta Airport
AL GA
Lake Wedowee Alabama

FARM

It's where we gather